The PAPERLESS INDETECTIVE

TRISTAN DURIE

A *Harlan Valeri: Indetective* novel

ISBN: 978-0-9873-9881-9

www.paperlessindetective.com

ACKNOWLEDGMENTS

Thanks to Sarah, who must at times have thought I was going a little crazy writing this book (particularly when I suggested we spend the winter at an empty mountain resort). As always you were supportive and wonderful.

A big thanks to Nick Dent, who not only has a great name for an indetective but also dedicated countless hours to reading and commenting on an early manuscript. Thank you so much for your time and effort, I am forever grateful and so should be all my readers.

A special thanks to Harley, whose bizarre letter from the Tax Office back at Miller Street provided an even better name for an indetective.

An abundance of thanks to The Make Room for helping me get to the finish line with a fantastic website and some priceless enthusiasm when I needed it most, and particularly to the talented Lealah Dow for her brilliant cover design and illustration.

Finally, to those family and friends who read a draft because I somehow forced it on them, thanks for risking your time and a very awkward conversation, and if you enjoyed it thanks for your enthusiastic feedback. I was happy just to write this book, but to know you were happy to read it makes it all the more worthwhile. The Indetective genre is launched thanks to you.

CHAPTER 1

Harlan Valeri arrived at work with a sense of resignation he couldn't explain, and had been trying to suppress since breakfast. Or maybe it was breakfast, he thought as he stepped through the open gate and up a couple of steps to the front door. Bran flakes surely aren't what inspire people to greatness, especially after soaking up that pasty liquid they call skim milk. He doubted this diet was going to last the week. And it was only Tuesday.

The building he entered was set one long block back from the main street of Newtown. It was close enough to the station so Harlan could hear the trains coming and going all day, but just far enough so if he could hear one coming when he walked out the door, he knew it would be going before he got to the platform. Number 24 Whitehorse Street was a dull-looking former residence, a two-storey grey brick semi with three commercial tenants according to the signs mounted on the fence - a chiropractor, a tax agent, and an indetective.

Harlan passed the open doors to the chiropractor and tax agent, both with clients waiting inside watching televisions - morning talk-shows on an old-fashioned boxy TV in the chiropractor's, twenty-four-hour news on a wall-mounted LCD in the tax agent's. He counted seven people waiting in total. What were they doing that he wasn't? Apart from tax returns and spine adjustments, of course. He took a quick mental inventory of the two rooms - the TVs, a few chairs, some reading material on coffee tables. The chiropractor's had an urn of boiling water and a selection of tea bags. A mix of inspirational and propaganda posters hung on the wall - "Believe" under a picture of a rainbow, "Chiropractic Care Can Change Your World!" under a picture of the Earth. The tax agent had ads explaining how easy it is to claim tax back if you are British. Shouldn't they be saying how difficult it is, how only a qualified tax agent could possibly negotiate the red tape and cross-border bureaucratic bungling involved? He shook his head and started up the stairs leading to his office.

Harlan paused at the top of the stairs to admire the door in front of him. He was particularly proud of the lettering on the frosted glass that took up most of the top third of the otherwise mahogany veneer door.

HARLAN VALERI, Esq.
& Associates

*Sydney's first and oldest
Indetective Agency*

SINCE 2008

He remembered arguing with his then secretary, probably his first, about the wording when he had first peeled off the paper backing the letters had come on. "No point saying we're the oldest when we're the only one. Plus it looks stupid then saying we only just opened," she had said, fairly astutely.

"But, Miss Sowensoh, this door will be here long after you have gone, maybe even long after I have gone. It will become more impressive with time. Indetective agencies will be ten cents to the dozen one day, and we'll be able to point to this door and say 'We're no Johnnies-come-lately - we invented Indetection,'" he had replied rather grandly but somewhat less astutely, particularly given the rate at which the veneer was peeling off at the foot of the door. He was right on one point though. Miss Sowensoh had taken an early lunch that day and he never heard from her again, other than a series of progressively nastier emails requesting a half-day's wages.

Harlan shook off his reverie and unlocked the door, nimbly stepping back down to the top stair so he could pull it open. Entering his reception area, with no clients, no television, no posters suggesting you might not actually need an indetective, no reading material, not even any chairs for clients to sit on, he thought the place needed something. Maybe a fern.

He took off his jacket and glanced at the vacant desk. Two days in a row she hasn't turned up, he thought, before he remembered his office manager's cryptic response to his standard 'see you on Monday' Friday farewell. 'No, you won't' wasn't the traditional way of giving notice, but there wasn't much he could do about it now. It was time for another recruitment drive. He took his smartphone out of his jacket pocket and scrolled through his messages until he found his conversation with Signboy, then re-sent one of his previous messages.

Time for another sign run, usual deal.

Harlan guessed Signboy would take about half an hour to come into the office. He was probably in Kings Cross drumming up new business. Signboy had proven effective in identifying well-to-do men scoring drugs, sex, or both, and by following them around for a while spooking them into thinking they should take some precautions to keep their vices a secret. Meanwhile Harlan had arrangements with a few seedy characters around the Cross who were more than happy to put his business card into their clients' hands. Shrewd drug dealers, pimps, madams and game-runners knew the value of secrecy.

Signboy would, Harlan knew, drop the stalking work for a chance to post signs up. Being a university student, Signboy always needed cash and Harlan paid half up front for posting signs - the other half only if he noticed enough signs posted while walking around Newtown, a condition he applied earnestly.

Stalking, however, worked on trailing commissions ("Pun intended," he had told Signboy), and depended on bills being paid by clients who hired Harlan because Signboy had, by following them, convinced them they were being followed. In any case, stalking was best done in the evening, when potential clients were more likely after sex than drugs. Olympians and touring cyclists aside, people generally paid more to keep their sex habits private.

Reaching over the raised counter at the front of the desk, Harlan fished around in the recess beneath the counter for a few seconds before producing a manila folder. He opened the folder and flicked through the half dozen different coloured A4 pieces of paper within. He selected one after brief consideration and placed it on the counter, returning the manila folder to the desk below. He scanned the page again, reading the key passages aloud as he went, "Office manager wanted ... excitement a real possibility ... standard conditions ... apply in person ... " When he was finished, he left the page on top of the counter and turned away with a satisfied 'hmm', and a nod for effect.

Moving through to his private office, Harlan hung his jacket on a solitary hook behind the door, stepped smoothly around his desk and sat down in his ergonomic armchair to think hard what Signboy's real name was. He cursed himself for sometimes using only a description when creating a contact in his phone, then adopting that description as a nickname when his normally reliable name retention played up. He consoled himself by believing most people preferred their nickname, being less arbitrary than whatever their parents had come up with for them. Hopefully Signboy fell into that category. His meditation was disturbed by the familiar vibration of his phone, which displayed an unknown number as it began to ring.

He savoured exactly four bars of the bells and guitar riff from the Hall & Oates 1981 chart-topper, *I Can't Go For That*, before sliding his finger across the screen and putting the phone to his ear. "Harlan Valeri, Indetective, making your infidelities undetectable since 2008, how can I help you?"

"Hello, Mr Valeri," a woman's voice said nervously.

"Harlan, please. Who am I speaking to?"

"Harlan," said the voice, a little less nervously. "It's Marisa Foxe here. I'm not sure how this works, but I think I need your services."

Harlan recognised the name.

"The Marisa Foxe?" he asked.

"Well, I'm sure there is more than one, but I wouldn't be surprised if I'm the one you're thinking of."

The one Harlan was thinking of was the Marisa Foxe who was a burgeoning celebrity cook, the editor of a food and lifestyle magazine called *Zest for Life,* and the wife of Jonathan Foxe, the semi-celebrity CEO of the similarly burgeoning celebrity-focused charitable organisation, Celebrities Care. This was a phone call that could really turn his week around.

"Good," he said, trying and failing not to sound too excited. "Is it something you'd like to discuss over the phone, or would you rather come into my office?"

"Well, it would be good to meet you in person. It's a personal matter."

"All my matters are personal, Mrs Foxe."

"Then you should probably call me Marisa."

"Marisa, sorry."

"Are you free this afternoon? I can come to your office at two."

"Let me see." Harlan woke his computer up and opened the calendar, which he knew would show a vacant afternoon. "Yes, I can do two. Do you need the address?"

"No, it's on the back of your card."

"Ah, you have one of our cards, good." He always wondered what percentage of his business cards made it to prospective clients. Along with the signs he kept for recruiting office managers, they were the only paper he allowed in the office.

"I'll see you at two then."

"See you then, Marisa."

Harlan put his phone down on the desk and leaned back in his ergonomic armchair, letting it swivel naturally around. When he was facing the appropriate direction, he rose and stepped to the corner of his office where an old-fashioned-looking stainless steel espresso machine sat alongside a small coffee grinder on top of a solid marble plate, which seemed to simply be resting on a medium-sized bar fridge. He switched the machine on and set about making himself an espresso as he thought about his prospective client.

Marisa Foxe would be his first female customer, not counting his mother who had once hired him to smuggle in a big-screen TV without the neighbours seeing because, according to her, she lived in a street full of organised criminal gangs. Marisa certainly fit the demographic he had targeted recently. Ever since the drawn-out Tiger Woods scandal, where the star golfer's infidelities became public knowledge after his wife, Elin Nordegren, chased him out of the house with one of his golf clubs, Harlan was sure women in high profile couples would be just as eager as the men to keep the men's infidelities out of the public eye. Trying to deal with a personal crisis in the middle of a media circus was close to the most unpleasant experience he could imagine. People would pay good money to avoid it.

Harlan had also figured it wouldn't be difficult to illustrate to the betrayed wife of a prominent man the value of hiring an indetective to keep the confidentiality card up her sleeve in any divorce negotiations. Divorce lawyers everywhere must have relished the damage done to the world famous golfer's reputation and the financial impact from his loss of endorsements. No doubt there was already a formula to put a dollar value on post-settlement confidentiality. Multiply the level of fame by the value of sponsorship deals and the number of mistresses, and add a few zeros. If Elin Nordegren had had the sense to wield an indetective instead of a golf club, she could have gotten well over a billion dollar settlement based on Tiger's endorsements. As it was, she'd have to make do with barely a hundred million, and still live with a life-time confidentiality clause.

Harlan sat back down with a small cup of steaming coffee. He opened his desk drawer, where he kept a small, white sugar bowl and two piles of teaspoons (one clean, one dirty) along with his phone charger. He stirred a spoonful of sugar into his coffee, sucked the spoon visibly clean and added it to one of the piles. Only he knew which was which. Three short, extremely satisfying sips later, he placed the empty cup next to his laptop and woke it for the second time that day.

Just as he was about to set up Marisa's file in the template Signboy had created for him, he heard someone coming up the stairs. It seemed a little quick for Signboy to make it, so when he heard the front door open Harlan called out what he would to any unexpected visitor: "Is that you?"

If it was someone he should be expecting, it covered the fact he had forgotten the appointment. If it wasn't, it generally caused enough confusion to the visitor so Harlan could grab the upper hand in the ensuing encounter.

"It's just me," said Signboy, who was familiar with his boss's tricks and had learned how to counter most of them. Now Harlan wondered if he should be expecting someone else. The lanky young man leaned against the counter, straightening his T-shirt and pulling his short hair towards the ceiling as Harlan emerged from his office.

"Ah, excellent. That was quick. How's the stalking going?"

"Bit slow. But that's pretty normal since the credit crunch. So Loretta didn't last then?" asked Signboy, nodding at the empty chair behind the counter.

"Who? Oh, yes. No. Do they ever?"

"They might, if you paid 'em. Or remembered their names. Or kept that manila folder on your desk instead of theirs," said Signboy.

"True. But wouldn't that put you out of half a job?" Harlan, as usual, won the back and forth by playing his trump card.

"Yellow it is then," said Signboy, picking the page up from the counter. "How many?"

"Fifty should do," said Harlan, handing over a fresh fifty-dollar bill. "Twenty-five from the last job, good work. Remember to take the old ones down first, and bring the original back."

"Yeah, I know. So what else have you got going at the moment? Any work for a junior indetective?"

"Why, do you know one? Actually, there might be some interesting work coming up - I have a new client as of this morning. My first female client, in fact."

"A chick? That's weird. What's she want?"

"She didn't say. She's coming in this afternoon to meet me. My guess is it's the first of many after our new promotional angle."

"What angle's that?"

"I've been sending my mother to society events - dinners, fundraisers. She talks about how ever since that golfer was all over the news, women with high-profile husbands should be just as afraid of such a scandal as the husbands themselves. She's good at spotting the ones who look a bit nervous with the topic, and at some point discreetly gives them our business card."

"Great, so now we're frightening women who think their husbands are cheating on them into paying us to keep their husbands' habits out of the public eye?" Signboy had a great skill in putting complex concepts into a single sentence.

"I guess so. But we can actually provide a good service for them, so they can deal with the issue on their terms rather than when the tabloids appear on their doorstep. Or, they don't have to deal with it at all if they prefer."

"Right. Well, I'll take your word for it for now. I'd better get on with these signs. Oh, here you go." Signboy took a stick of chewing gum from his pocket and tossed it at Harlan.

"Gum?"

"When you messaged me I was following a guy pretty closely. I thought he might have heard my phone so I jumped in the nearest doorway, which happened to be a convenience store."

"Aptly named."

"I thought so. Anyway, for some reason I wanted to seem like a regular customer so I bought some gum. I know how you never like to be caught without it."

"Saves lives every day," said Harlan.

"Yeah, you always say that. But I know you actually use it for stuff." He pointed over Harlan's shoulder at the venetian blind covering the window, held in place at one corner with some chewed up gum. "Although I don't know why you don't just get it fixed."

"I like it closed. The clients appreciate the privacy. The gum just stops it rattling when the fan's on." He pointed behind Signboy where a large steel floor fan stood ominously, like a giant porcelain vase in a scene from a Jackie Chan movie. Having that in front of them probably did nothing for the office managers' morale either.

"Whatever," said Signboy, not really interested in the interior stylings of the office. "Okay, I'm outy. I want to do the signs before lunch, then I've got an afternoon lecture. Social Science and Policy." He clearly wasn't enthused by the subject.

"Sounds fascinating." Neither was Harlan. "I might have studied that when I dallied with academic pursuits. Majoring in Sociology and Anthropology, as if that was the best way to find my place in society."

"It's prob'ly not the best way to learn criminology either, but I have to do it."

"The old interdisciplinary trap. Anyway, I thought you were finished for the year?"

"Yeah, but they're offering it as a summer course 'cos so many students failed it this year, and it's a prerequisite for a few units next year. The uni needs the fees so they run a soft course over summer to get more students qualified."

"You failed a first-year social science unit?"

"Pfft, I'm not an idiot. I knew they'd be doing a soft one over summer, they have the last few years. So I just enrolled in that."

"Clever." It really was. "Actually, before you do the signs, can you do me a bit of a background check on Marisa Foxe - don't look at me like that, I know who she is. I'd like to know something I haven't already read in the papers, something I can use to impress her."

"I bet you would. Sure, I'll do what I can before lunch, then do the signs after the lecture. Or during, the notes are online anyway and they can't be interrupted by annoying questions from mature-age students. Are you using your computer?" Signboy knew the answer would be 'no', even if he was using it. Harlan was a natural procrastinator, any excuse would do to get him away from the task at hand. He walked past Harlan into the back office, calculating the money he'd make on the day. Harlan paid him by the hour for ad hoc work. If he researched till lunch and put the signs up in the afternoon, it was a pretty good day's work for a full-time student.

Harlan walked across to where Signboy had been standing, reached over the counter and grabbed the manila folder. Clever kid that one, he thought, taking the folder with him back into his office where Signboy was busy adjusting the ergonomic armchair. After locking the folder in his desk drawer, Harlan put on his jacket, checked his pockets, grabbed his phone and some loose coins from his desk, nodded goodbye to Signboy, and went out to buy a fern and a cooking and lifestyle magazine.

CHAPTER 2

When he returned to the office, Harlan didn't see the conspicuous black Mercedes-Benz saloon idling on the street directly in front of his building. At least, that could be the only explanation for how easy it was for the well-dressed minder who got out of the front passenger door to place one strong arm around Harlan's shoulders, relieve him of the fern that might, on a generous view, have been obscuring his vision with another strong arm, and usher him into the open rear door of the vehicle with nothing but a look of surprise offered in defence.

More curious than alarmed, Harlan looked around the interior as the door closed him in and the minder returned to his place in the front passenger seat, looking only slightly ridiculous holding the potted fern in his lap. A man in the driver's seat wore a smart charcoal suit, similar to the minder's. Behind the driver sat the man obviously in charge of the operation, dressed in an incredibly smooth grey suit with a very comfortable looking white shirt that looked perfect with the top two buttons undone.

"How about the leg room?" said Harlan to nobody in particular, stretching his legs in front of him. He was attempting to use diversion, another of his many tricks to get on the front foot in unexpected confrontations - but he was also truly amazed.

"Mr. Valeri?" The man seated across from Harlan in the rear seat seemed a little annoyed his guest's excitement over the generous-sized cabin had apparently overcome any fear after being abducted in broad daylight. The cool blue eyes went cold. The creaseless forehead dimpled in the centre. The firm clean-shaven jaw hardened until the thin lips all but disappeared. The short but tousled blond hair stood perfectly still.

"Is this thing modified?" asked Harlan, playing for more time to get his bearings. The man seemed familiar - Harlan had seen his face before, but not in three dimensions. "I mean, I'm a fairly tall man, and Biff there with the fern, he's pretty big. And we can both stretch out comfortably - even carry our favourite pot plants if we choose. It's truly amazing! I'm truly amazed." He really was impressed.

"It's the long-wheel-base model," said the man Harlan now recognised as Jonathan Foxe, as if every car in the world came in a long-wheel-base model.

"Jonathan Foxe!" Harlan turned to face the renowned philanthropist. "You should have called, my assistant would gladly have made you an appointment to see me." Harlan began calculating the odds of this being a coincidence. It didn't seem likely. He rolled his newly purchased copy of *Zest for Life* more tightly in his hand. Jonathan Foxe didn't need to know Harlan was reading up on his wife.

"You don't have an assistant. But despite such a clear indicator of mediocrity, I'm considering hiring you into my service."

"Well, I don't really know what the bit about hiring me into your service means, but I'm glad you're not holding my temporary staffing issue against me - I bet Biff didn't have an assistant when you hired *him* into your service, as you say."

"Quite." Jonathan Foxe gestured to the driver and the spacious vehicle moved away from the curb and up the street at a suitably dignified pace.

"So, what can I do for you? Apart from not press charges, of course. Or would you prefer I get a little Stockholmy?"

"Fair point. Sorry about that - I would have waited in your office, but ... Anyway, I understand you deal in discretion?"

Harlan thought for a second, then smiled. "I've never heard it put like that. Do you mind if I use it? Business cards, email signatures, that kind of thing?"

Jonathan Foxe didn't smile as he shook his head, then turned to look out the window. "I'm being followed," he said.

"Already?" Harlan marvelled at Signboy's initiative, even though he should have been researching his boss's abductor's wife. He then realised his slip. "I mean, I wouldn't have thought you'd be on their radar yet."

"Whose radar?"

"Blackmailers, people trying to take advantage. They follow famous people, people with reputations to uphold and money to spare, and hope they find something valuable. They generally work A-listers, I didn't think you were quite there. No offence."

"Right. None taken, I'm sure." Jonathan Foxe pressed a button on the rear centre console, as if every car had buttons on the rear centre console.

"Mine doesn't even have an armrest," Harlan muttered, but his attention was immediately drawn to the back of Biff's headrest, where an LCD screen had come to life. "Of course," he said, determined to not be impressed by anything else about the car.

The screen first flickered with a message bragging the following video was taken on Matt's iPhone. Harlan guessed Matt was Biff. Then a short video shot somewhere in the city centre showed Jonathan Foxe getting out of a slightly long-looking black Mercedes-Benz which, strangely, Harlan noticed immediately on the busy street. He bravely assumed it was the car he was now sitting in. The Jonathan Foxe on the LCD screen walked a short distance and entered the lobby of the Sydney Hilton. The camera panned back where he'd walked from, past the Mercedes-Benz to three cars back where a very ordinary, very blue model of the ever more ubiquitous Volkswagen Golf was parked, and a young woman (not Signboy, to Harlan's immense relief but also slight disappointment) in its driver's seat looked like she was making a big decision.

Harlan hated to accept a coincidence at face value, particularly one as unlikely as a woman and her husband independently approaching him on the same day. But it seemed for now he would have to accept this turn of events as being nothing more. It was extremely unlikely Marisa had hired a private detective to follow her husband, and then taken steps to hire an indetective as well. It was just as unlikely her husband had mentioned anything to her about being followed, because almost certainly his first instinct would be to suspect his wife of hiring a private detective to follow him, even if it was a young woman who didn't fit the stereotype. So Harlan ruled out the possibility both husband and wife were on the same page in relation to hiring an indetective but had just confused who was to do the hiring. Like both coming home with milk.

He abandoned trying to concoct a situation in which it wasn't a coincidence and returned his attention to the video, where the mysterious woman had apparently made her decision. She smacked the top of the steering wheel in frustration, made a quick note in a small notepad, then took out an old SLR camera with a telephoto lens attached and sat back with the lens resting on the top of the steering wheel.

The footage jumped - Harlan guessed by the natural light not much time had passed - and the woman sat up in her seat, pointing her camera down the street and taking photos. The footage followed her lead back past the

Mercedes-Benz to catch Jonathan Foxe approaching. Then the screen went blank.

"I want to know who she is and why she's following me. I want you to find out for me - I understand it shouldn't be a big stretch from your usual line of work. Take Matt's card - he'll provide you with my itinerary each night for the next day."

Harlan realised the minder was holding a business card over his shoulder, and took it.

"Mister Foxe, have you told anyone else about this? Your wife, for instance?"

"No. But I don't think she's involved, if that's what you're thinking. What I get up to isn't that high up on her list of interests." Another dramatic stare out the window.

Harlan wanted to press further but realised they had returned to his street and were pulling up in front of his building. Out of the corner of his eye he saw Jonathan Foxe press another button on the centre console, and his door opened for him. Harlan took the hint and stepped out, then turned around as he remembered something.

"Just a second - we need to discuss my rates ... "

"Accepted."

" ... incidentals ... "

"Of course."

" ... and you understand, this kind of thing can take ... "

"You have one week, then we'll reassess."

"Right then. Next time, please come up to the office."

"Next time I'll show you the big screen."

Harlan had to jump back as the door closed. The car pulled away just before Harlan remembered one more thing. "My fern!" he yelled. As he was about to run into the street to set chase, he realised he would have to jump over a small potted fern left carelessly in the gutter next to where the car had just been. He wondered which button had done that.

*

Signboy was gone when Harlan returned to his office, leaving him alone to wait for Marisa to arrive. He had a lot of things to do to pass the time. He wanted to find out a bit more about Jonathan Foxe and formulate some ideas as to who might be following him before he began the legwork. Signboy had left a document on the desktop for him to read with the title *Things you didn't know about MF*. He had the *Zest For Life* magazine to flick through so he'd know a bit more about what Marisa Foxe did. He also had a looming conflict of interest he should probably prepare himself for. So naturally Harlan spent the whole time browsing the Mercedes-Benz website.

Using a very impressive program that let him build and price a car with all available options, Harlan eventually discovered Jonathan Foxe drove around in a car worth more than half a million dollars. In fact, Harlan mused, he hired someone else to drive him around in a car worth more than half a million dollars. Or do they throw the driver in at that price point? They seemed to throw the long-wheel-base in, although Harlan had figured out on cheaper models it was almost twenty-thousand dollars to upgrade to a thirteen centimetre longer wheel-base. He was still marvelling at the vehicle when he heard a woman's voice from the front room.

"Hello? Mr Valeri?"

Harlan stood and took the few steps to his door in time to see Marisa Foxe pulling the front door closed behind her. She turned around and smiled cordially when she saw him. Harlan stopped for a second. He had seen her face so many times he felt that strange familiarity to her that people commonly feel towards celebrities, but she looked different in person. Her clothes were less glamorous - a professional looking skirt and shirt combo with a matching suit jacket - and while still incredibly beautiful she didn't have the flawless look he was accustomed to seeing on magazine covers. She noticed his surprise.

"I get my hair and make-up done for photo-shoots, and the odd public appearance for my husband. This is how I look when I have to do it myself." Obviously it wasn't the first time she'd had this reaction. It was also obvious she knew she was quite stunning whether done up professionally or not. She smiled again as Harlan stepped forward to shake her hand.

"Mrs. Foxe, very pleased to meet you. Sorry, I obviously expected a cardboard cut-out straight off the red carpet. Can I take your jacket?"

"Sure, and it's Marisa, remember?"

Marisa took off her jacket and handed it to Harlan, who suddenly realised he had no plan where to put it. Turning around he hesitated briefly in front of the fern he'd put on the counter-top, but none of the young fronds looked up to the task. Instead he lay the jacket neatly next to the fern, draped over the counter. Marisa watched with amusement. Harlan decided to get more hooks installed.

"Marisa, of course, come into my office. I'm between assistants at the moment, but at least that's given me the chance to greet you in person." Harlan hoped it didn't sound like he was flirting. It didn't. It sounded like he was an idiot, an impression it would take all of Marisa's generosity of spirit to resist at this rate.

"Not at all," said Marisa. Which didn't really make sense, but it was something she was accustomed to saying when people made fools of themselves in front of her, because they usually apologised for it. She looked over the counter at the empty receptionist's chair, then followed Harlan into his office.

"Can I make you a coffee? *Cappuccino, macchiato* ... " Harlan gestured vaguely towards his espresso machine.

"No, that's fine." Marisa sat opposite Harlan, sitting forward in the basic office chair, not quite leaning on the desk. "Actually, a cup of tea would be nice."

"Oh. I'm sorry, but ... " Now he gestured vaguely towards the open door. When he had an assistant, he could have a cup of tea brought up from the chiropractor's waiting room, once he or Signboy had trained them sufficiently in the art of surreptitious tea-making.

"I understand, it's fine." Harlan doubted she did.

"So, on the phone you said you needed my services?" Harlan pulled his laptop a little closer on the desk and made to look like he was pulling up her file. Instead he took one last look at the Mercedes-Benz S 65 AMG LWB before he closed the browser and opened Signboy's document, which he began to skim as they talked.

"Yes, that's right. I'm not sure what the usual way to approach this is, but my husband-"

"Jonathan Foxe," interrupted Harlan. He was reading about how they'd met. She was the chef in his first restaurant, opened in Sydney in 1995, and eventually head chef of a group of restaurants in Sydney they owned together.

"Yes, Jonathan." She said the name proudly. "My husband isn't perfect. But what he does is important to so many people."

Harlan read how they had sold the restaurants after their first child in 2002. Marisa had used the time away from restaurants to crystallise her plans for a cooking magazine, *Zest*, which she launched after having their second child in 2004. Jonathan had used the money from the restaurants to launch the Executive Club, a premium concierge service for the social elite of Sydney. He'd learned the value of celebrity in his years as a successful restaurateur. He sold the Executive Club in 2005 for a small-sized fortune and then created the Celebrities Care Foundation. As their profile grew, so did demand to hear more from Marisa than just recipes, and *Zest* became *Zest For Life*. It was rumoured she'd be releasing her first cookbook in time for Christmas, just a few weeks away.

"Of course," said Harlan. "Everyone knows the work Celebrities Care does - and everyone knows Jonathan Foxe *is* Celebrities Care."

"Exactly. So what happens if my husband's reputation is tarnished?"

"So is Celebrities Care. I see. You want me to protect your husband's reputation?"

"That's right."

"From what?"

Marisa sighed, looked Harlan in the eye. "The usual."

"I take it I can rule out drugs, gay sex scandals, gambling and alcohol then."

"Oh god, I hope so." Marisa smiled and looked away. "This *is* what you do, isn't it? I wasn't sure."

"It's within the ambit of what we offer. Your heart's in the right place, which is important. In the early days," Harlan hoped Marisa hadn't read the sign on the door too closely, "we took any guy who walked in the door, mostly serial adulterers who had no interest in changing their ways. These days, I like my clients to be using my services for the right reasons. Avoiding media attention, giving them a chance to change, to control their privacy, etcetera. Can I ask why you think my services are necessary?"

"Well, he's not being very careful. But also a friend suggested I contact you. That got me thinking about what we have to lose. What the Foundation has to lose. I guess I just want a bit of security." Harlan made a mental note to congratulate his mother on such a good job.

He paused as he read the last paragraph of Signboy's email. Apparently the Foxes lived well beyond their documented incomes. They had spent most of the money from selling the Executive Club on a Mosman mansion, and as an editor of just one of many titles in a large publishing house and a charity administrator, albeit a celebrity charity administrator, they shouldn't be living the high life they seemed to. Harlan wondered where the extra money was coming from. Considering Marisa's need for security, he guessed it wasn't from her.

"I'll be honest," Harlan said. "It's usually the subject who hires us. I expected to have more clients ... in your position. I'm sure you've seen the innocent party can suffer just as much when these things become public, particularly for the higher profile couples. But it's been a difficult demographic to reach."

"Yes, well it wasn't easy to come to you. It's a big step in a relationship to help your husband conceal his infidelity by hiring a private detective."

"*In*detective." Harlan had to admire her candour. "Probably up there with hiring a detective to uncover it," he said. "At least you know what I'm going to find." They shared a look that said neither of them believed that to be true.

"So, do I need to sign anything?"

"No, no. I wouldn't be much of an indetective if I kept records of all my clients."

"I suppose not. You don't seem to have any records of anything." Marisa looked around as if to prove her point. Unless Harlan was hiding files in his bar fridge or wardrobe, there was nothing in the room to indicate any business was occurring at all.

"Everything I need is in here," said Harlan, pointing to his laptop. "Or here," he said, producing his phone. "Or here," he added after a moment's thought, pointing to his head. "I don't even have a printer anyway. It's a paperless office."

"Trying to reduce your carbon footprint?"

"Something like that."

"I don't believe you." Marisa stared coolly into Harlan's eyes. His senses pricked.

"Why would you say that?" he asked. Most people accepted the environmental rationale for a paperless office. Only someone comfortable with deceit, or extremely paranoid about it, would suspect Harlan was lying.

"Because I recognise your name. Valeri." Or someone who knew the truth. Suddenly Harlan had trouble swallowing. "How is your father?"

"We don't really talk these days." Harlan's father had served time for failing to disclose material information to investors. He had invented a simple printer accessory that removed ink from paper as it fed into the printer, enabling people to reuse their paper rather than recycle it. Unfortunately a private investigator hired by the paper companies to discredit the invention found a discarded memo explaining the chemical used would slowly react with the fresh ink and it too would disappear over time. The resulting smear campaign, spitefully timed shortly after the successful floating of PaperWash, sent the share price plummeting and the company eventually liquidated. Fund managers who had used the float to boost investment in their sustainable investment options took the board to court, with the corporate watchdog not far behind. When Harlan's father was released after two years in prison, he didn't take well to the middle class grind having had a taste of the high life. He walked out on Harlan's mother after a few months and Harlan hadn't heard from him in the ten years since.

"It must be hard. Sorry, I'm not really prying. I just made the connection."

"Don't worry about it. It's been so long now anyway, I'm surprised you remember."

"It happened just after I'd put all my super into sustainable shares."

"Oh. You know the market overreacted - the ink should still have been visible after ten years according to Dad's product testing."

"I guess we'll never know."

"No. But I'll be glad when paperless offices are the norm. For the environment, of course."

"Of course."

*

Later that afternoon Harlan sat in his favourite restaurant waiting for Signboy and a bowl of pasta to arrive. In true Sydney fashion the popular rustic Italian *trattoria* didn't take bookings, so he'd arrived early and was now forced to summon up an appetite at the early bird hour of 6pm. Signboy had laughed when he'd invited him to eat so early, but said he would drop by and discuss the new client.

Harlan sipped at a glass of red wine, watching the busy pavement outside. Darlinghurst offered an interesting mix of young professionals heading home and absurdly dressed subcultural types heading to the bar or café most appropriate for their kind. There were still some glimpses of old Sydney too. The Italian-Australians drinking espresso and smoking cigarettes outside the café next door. The odd octogenarian couple dressed to impress for their nightly parade of the neighbourhood they must barely recognise as the one from their heyday. Harlan smiled as he pictured the Foxes right now, a world away across the harbour, where houses had front and back yards, double garages, harbour views and live-in nannies. And people had reputations to protect.

"Hey Harlan." Signboy, who was apparently in the middle of his heyday, arrived and sat opposite Harlan on the long communal table. He looked along at the empty seats. "Lucky no-one else eats this early, we wouldn't be able to say much in this place."

Harlan hadn't really thought about it. Another aspect of the case he had to be wary of - the Foxes were just about household names in Sydney.

He told Signboy about his meeting with Jonathan Foxe, limiting himself with some effort to just a couple of sentences about the car.

"So we're working for both of them?"

"It looks like it. I'll need you full-time for as long as it runs. Someone has to keep the rest of the business ticking along."

"You mean indetective work?"

"Only on a temporary basis. Certainly for one week, I'll need to be quite active working for Jonathan Foxe. Biff will be keeping his eye on me. Marisa's case might drag on a bit, but if he doesn't keep me on past a week, we'll be able to manage as usual."

Harlan's food arrived. He ordered another glass of wine as Signboy began salivating over the steaming bowl of *bucatini amatriciana.* "Have some," said Harlan, shovelling a portion onto his side plate and pushing it across the table.

"What is it?" Signboy didn't wait to find out before diving into it with his fork.

"*Amatriciana.* Tomato, chilli, *pancetta.* Garlic, of course."

"Pretty good. What are you drinking?" Harlan's wine had arrived, attracting Signboy's ravenous gaze.

"Chianti, have a sip." Signboy's enthusiasm as he tasted the Italian appellation made Harlan smile. "Let's call it a trial then. A week as Assistant Indetective."

Signboy stopped chewing his latest mouthful and looked up. "Bullshit!"

"No, it's not. It's just a trial though, don't get too excited."

"Assistant Indetective. Sounds good. Does this mean I'm an associate?"

"No, it means you're an assistant indetective, that's all."

They were both happy to leave it at that as they raced to finish their plates of pasta, Signboy with the advantage of not having to break regularly for a sip of wine.

"That was great," said Signboy when he finished. "Thanks. So what time does an assistant indetective clock in on his first day?"

"First thing in the morning. I'll show you what you need to do and then get on Jonathan Foxe's tail as soon as possible."

"And what time's 'first thing'?"

Harlan stood and put two twenties on the table, paused, then added a five. "Why don't you make that your first case? See you at the office," he said, and left Signboy sitting there alone for maximum comedic effect.

"Very funny," Signboy said as Harlan left the table.

At the door, Harlan looked back to see Signboy checking the blackboard menu. Next he counted the money Harlan had left and pocketed the five dollar tip just as the waitress got to the table. Harlan could only smile. He'd have to take it into account when setting the new assistant indetective's hourly rate. Enterprise like that had to be rewarded.

CHAPTER 3

It was eleven o'clock the next morning when Harlan caught up with Jonathan Foxe and his entourage. Harlan had turned up at his office a little later than usual after walking all the way to the train station before remembering he needed his car. He hadn't been in the mood for Signboy's lecture on what 'first thing in the morning' meant when he finally arrived at work, and because of the state of the filing in the absence of a secretary, it had taken longer than he expected to get Signboy up to speed on the other live cases he needed to cover. The gambling wealth creation executive, the gay principal of a Catholic school, the ice-addicted junior barrister. He'd also had to give Signboy the combination to the safe under his desk (1-9-3-9) and talk him through its contents (a key Harlan didn't know anything about other than it wasn't the missing key to petty cash; a key for a safety deposit box where he moved clients' items for storage of longer than a week; a rack of Star City Casino chips the gambler had given him to hold onto a month ago; and a mobile phone he was holding for disposal once the ice addict decided he had given up for good).

Then it was a twenty minute drive from Newtown to Double Bay, in the eastern suburbs, where Jonathan was scheduled to be. He knew Biff would notice his late start, but he hoped he could at least get onto their tail before the mysterious woman in the Golf. Surely having a detailed itinerary sent to you the night before was worth a couple of hours' head-start?

Harlan groaned as he arrived outside the café where he knew Jonathan Foxe was meeting the Celebrities Care Foundation's PR rep. The blue Golf was parked across the street from the café, and as Harlan drove on looking for a park a few cars along he saw Biff leaning against the side of the Mercedes-Benz, checking his watch as Harlan went past. Harlan parked on the next block and made himself comfortable. They were scheduled to meet until midday.

Harlan used the time to ponder how he was going to juggle working for both Marisa and Jonathan Foxe. He hadn't told either about the other - technically they were both after different things so he was comfortable treating them as completely separate clients, with separate bills.

Again he wondered what had brought the husband and wife to approach him on the same day. Jonathan Foxe hadn't even considered his wife would be interested enough in his affairs to hire a private detective, let alone hire an indetective to make sure nobody else was. And Marisa hadn't seemed that concerned about his behaviour, only his reputation. She'd mentioned a friend had given her the card. Maybe it wasn't Harlan's mother? That would save him a commission at least.

Marisa's was his first case where he wasn't hired by the subject. She had told him she believed her husband was having an affair - she had never caught him out and he had never told her he had cheated on her, but she seemed certain he had a mistress. They had agreed Harlan would just report back to her whether Jonathan Foxe was likely to be caught cheating on his wife by anyone else, based on Harlan's observations over a couple of weeks. He would focus on evenings and weekends as much as possible - she doubted Jonathan would try to squeeze in any weekday rendezvous with the busy schedule he had with Celebrities Care. Marisa had hoped Harlan could be more active, but she didn't want her husband to know she had hired him. The usual course of observing and then coaching in the art of discretion, with full knowledge of the current precautions being taken, wasn't available.

Jonathan Foxe's case was a bit more complicated - Harlan was used to having clients who were being followed, but until now it had always been by a private detective hired by the wife. Harlan was pretty sure he could rule that out since he was working for Marisa himself. He was also confident he could rule out a member of the paparazzi. Subtlety wasn't exactly their strong point, and although this woman had been a bit clumsy, she was obviously trying to follow Jonathan Foxe around without being detected. For now Harlan limited his list of possibilities to a serious journalist or some kind of government investigator.

There were a number of reasons a journalist would be interested in Jonathan Foxe. There's nothing like success and popularity to attract a muckraker. And the mysterious discrepancy between the Foxes' lifestyle and income would attract not only a journalist with a good eye for a story, but also the attention of the Tax Office, the Securities and Investments Commission, or even the police. The low-budget investigation this woman was carrying out meant she could be any of those.

At midday Jonathan Foxe left the café as scheduled, getting into the back seat of the Mercedes-Benz which then headed toward his lunch meeting on the other side of the city in Darling Harbour. Harlan made sure the blue Golf followed, noting its registration as it passed, then backtracked a couple of blocks to avoid arousing the woman's suspicions before also heading towards Darling Harbour.

Jonathan was meeting the celebrity agent Mick Dawson at a popular steakhouse that looked across Cockle Bay back towards the city. (The water in Darling Harbour had its own name for some reason Harlan had often sought but never discovered.) It was clearly Mick Dawson's choice - Harlan doubted Jonathan would choose to eat at a restaurant with such broad appeal. Harlan liked the venue - it was crowded enough that the woman following Jonathan around would be able to follow him into the restaurant to see who he was meeting. Harlan would have a better chance of finding out more about her than just watching her sit in her car. It also made a passable steak and chips, one of Harlan's simpler culinary pleasures, and he was starving after missing breakfast.

After a short drive through the cross-city tunnel he pulled into the multi-storey car-park nearby and nearly choked when he checked the prices. One hour would cost him twenty-five dollars to park. Swearing, he took the ticket from the machine and drove under the rising boom gate. Even though he would charge incidentals to clients, he was well accustomed to arguing over each item, particularly items with ridiculous price-tags. Doing some sums he quickly figured it wouldn't be anywhere near cheaper to have a driver who could drop him off and find some free parking, but he did see the sense in it once you factored in your own time. At some value of time and parking, it would be stupid not to have your own driver.

Harlan saw Mick Dawson as soon as he rounded the corner from the car-park onto the Darling Harbour promenade. He was hard to miss - a huge man in a white suit with a red cravat and aviator sunglasses. Harlan couldn't believe he still had the ponytail that was his trademark when he first came to prominence in Australian show business, promoting the first large-scale music festivals to attract international acts back in the eighties. The once striking blond hair was now a humbling grey, but it still came across as ostentatious. He was sitting with Jonathan Foxe at an outside table, drinking a stubby of beer as he listened to whatever it was his companion was saying.

He noticed the woman following Jonathan at a table about ten metres back, just inside the restaurant proper. She was ordering from the menu but clearly keeping an eye on Jonathan and his companion. Harlan spotted a table behind her and made straight for it, ignoring the waitress whose job it was to keep the front section full. "I'll just get you a menu sir," she said, annoyed despite the place being just about full anyway. Harlan figured if anything he'd done her a favour by seating himself.

Harlan played it cool, ignoring the woman who sat at the next table. He looked around for Biff, but he must have stayed with the car, or be taking his own lunch somewhere. Then he watched the conversation between Jonathan and Mick Dawson. It was clear Jonathan was pitching something to the agent, most likely trying to get another big name on the Celebrities Care ticket. There couldn't be that many left, although it was probably a constant struggle to keep them involved.

The waitress returned with the menu and Harlan just managed to order a Coke in the split second she wasn't looking anywhere but at him. After the drive and quick walk in the hot sun, he needed refreshing. As she left he took note that the woman at the next table was drinking tap water, and had been given a steak knife. Not much, but it was information nonetheless. As were the facts she had a basic backpack under the table where Harlan guessed she kept her camera and notebook, among other things; she wore fairly plain jeans and a black singlet top, and a pair of black and white Chuck Taylor sneakers. There was also a dark green knitted cardigan over the back of her chair which Harlan cleverly assumed to be hers. It was probably the most telling object given the scorching start to summer they were having. It seemed overly cautious to carry an extra layer around. Maybe she was visiting a progressive mosque later? That would explain the lack of a scarf that could be used as a hijab. Although not having a scarf didn't really need an explanation given the scorching ... Harlan gave up running mental laps trying to explain the cardigan and instead casually took out his phone, switched it into camera mode and after just in time remembering to switch the flash-mode to off, took a photo of her for the file.

After putting his phone away, Harlan turned to the menu. He had been there a couple of times with international clients who valued the view more than the food, but he wanted to check he could still order his standard steak meal - sirloin, rare, chips, beef and peppercorn *jus*. No salad. It was as close to a *steak frites* as Harlan could construct from the menu, but it never reached *Parisienne* standards. He had fallen in love with the simple dish on the one family holiday his father had made time for before the PaperWash crash. He briefly considered a glass of red wine to at least give the meal a chance of withstanding the international comparison, but decided it wasn't the best idea within view of his client. The waitress returned to the table and took a small computer from her belt.

"Ready to order?"

"Sirloin, please, rare. Chips, beef and peppercorn *jus*. No salad. Thank you."

"Do you want a side salad?"

"No, thanks."

"It usually comes with salad."

"I know. That's why I said 'no salad'."

"So just the steak and chips."

"Yes, please. And the beef and peppercorn *jus*."

"Okay. I'll be back with your Coke in a second. Still or sparkling?"

"Still Coke?"

"No, water - still or sparkling?"

"Just the Coke thanks."

"Certainly, enjoy your meal."

The waitress left. Harlan looked around for someone to roll his eyes at and caught the woman in front of him looking over her shoulder. She smiled to indicate she had heard and was on his side, then turned back to face towards where Jonathan and Mick Dawson sat devouring a couple of steaks.

Harlan wondered why he'd felt the need for someone else's assurance he wasn't crazy, then he wondered whether he'd regret being noticed by the woman he was supposed to be investigating. The waitress returned with his Coke just in time to stop him wondering anything else, like why the woman's smile made him feel the way it did. She placed a small glass bottle of Coke in front of him, and a glass of ice alongside it. Then she pulled a steak knife from her apron to replace the regular knife already set, and left him again before he could ask why a steakhouse didn't set steak knives as the default, and replace them only when some freak ordered a chicken Caesar salad at a steakhouse. He guessed it was another question he would never know the answer to.

Pouring ice-cold Coke out of an ice-cold glass bottle into an ice-cold glass filled with ice-cold cubes of solid water was one of Harlan's most favourite things to do. It took him back a lot further than a good *steak frites* to the days before PaperWash when Coke was something his mother considered an indulgence. He was savouring the moment so much he nearly missed when the woman he was supposed to be watching pulled her camera out of her backpack and, under the pretence of photographing the cityscape in the background, took a few photos of Jonathan Foxe and Mick Dawson. This distraction caused Harlan to miss the few seconds long window of opportunity where he could take the first sip of his glass of Coke and feel the effervescence on his nose. That was also one of Harlan's most favourite things to do, and he was quite disappointed to miss it, despite a desperate attempt to catch the end of the window when he realised it was too late.

Harlan assumed the woman knew who Mick Dawson was, so he thought she must have been taking photos as evidence. This was consistent with his theory she was either a journalist or government agent of some kind. But what was so interesting about Jonathan Foxe meeting with Mick Dawson?

Harlan wasn't one for wild speculation, and he had no information that would allow him to pursue the question with any other technique he was familiar with. Which was lucky, because just then the waitress returned to put a plate of food in front of him that pushed the question to the very back of his mind with such velocity it was forgotten. He wouldn't even remember he had asked himself the question when he had the exact same thought again later that day while replaying the scene in his head. He would of course remember the plate of food.

The steak was big. Char-grilled to perfection and dripping in a thick marinade the bistros of Paris would do well to experiment with. The chips were thick, golden and wonderfully crisp. Harlan poured the tub of *jus* over everything and set to work, keeping an eye in front of him so he wouldn't miss the others leaving.

Within minutes he was mopping up the last of the *jus* with the last chip when he heard the woman in front of him ask for the bill. Harlan sensed an opportunity to take a big step in the case. As the woman's bill arrived, Harlan made sure she wasn't paying in cash, then finished the last of his Coke and left the table. He approached the register by the entrance and asked if he could pay his bill. As the cashier handed it to him, the waitress dropped off a small tray with another bill and a credit card. Harlan read the name on the card, committing it to memory. Jennifer L. Randall. The cashier snatched the tray from the counter and gave Harlan a strange look.

Pretending nothing had happened, Harlan took the correct change from his wallet and left it on the counter - he'd had little success expensing tips in the past and although he suspected Jonathan would be more accommodating as a former restaurateur, with the parking about to tick into a second hour he decided not to chance it. He left the restaurant rather awkwardly at the same time as Jonathan Foxe and Mick Dawson. Harlan and Jonathan pretended they didn't know each other as Harlan held the door for them. Following them out onto the promenade, Harlan was within earshot long enough to hear Mick Dawson tell Jonathan almost threateningly to "sort something out with this benefit bullshit" before they headed in the opposite direction to the car park. As he headed back to his car Harlan wondered what benefit Mick Dawson was talking about. Jonathan might be having trouble getting exposure for some Celebrities Care event, he thought.

Getting back to the task at hand he dialled up Signboy's number on his phone. Signboy answered almost immediately.

"Harlan Valeri & Associates, you've reached Assistant Indetective ... " Harlan cut him off.

"I've got a name."

CHAPTER 4

Harlan abandoned the Jonathan Foxe convoy for the afternoon in favour of researching Jennifer L. Randall from his office. Signboy had a few routine checks to do on other cases and would join him at four. Meanwhile, Harlan had accomplished the following:

He had created a document headed *Things we know about Jennifer L. Randall*. In it he listed her name (Jennifer L. Randall, which hyperlinked to the photo he had taken of her at the steakhouse); her approximate age (late twenties to early thirties, hyperlinked to the same photo); her car (blue Volkswagen Golf, early 2000s, NSW plate AKO 19N, all of which formed one hyperlink to the photo he had taken of her car outside the café); her fashion tendency (casual, again hyperlinked to the steakhouse photo) and her possible profession (journalist or government agent, not hyperlinked to anything because it was mere speculation). It was more than he knew about most people, but it wasn't much to go on and for some neurotic reason he hated having multiple hyperlinks to the same photo. It needed work.

He had searched the social networking triumvirate of Facebook, MySpace and Twitter. He was a little surprised to find none of the sites had fashion tendency or car registration as search criteria. In fact Facebook and Twitter had no search criteria other than name. Searching for Jennifer Randall returned hundreds of results on each, and there was no way to reduce the number of hits. He trawled through profile photos for a while before giving up. Myspace was easier - he could limit the search by age and location, but didn't find anything.

He had searched the White Pages online. Initially he thought it too had a strange restriction to its search engine when it had nowhere to enter someone's first name. Then he realised 'initial' probably meant first initial, not the initial that appeared on someone's credit card. J. Randall, Sydney, returned a few results, but hopefully it wouldn't come to breaking into her home to find out what she was up to, so he left it at that.

He had googled her. This had been the only fruitful effort of his digital detective work. Sure it was closer in magnitude to the utricle of a rootless duckweed than a giant squash, but it was fruit nonetheless. A few articles by a Jenny Randall had been published online. The articles related to charity work in South Africa and were published on Australian-based websites ranging from travel magazines to charity organisations. Harlan couldn't dismiss the charity link as coincidence, so he bookmarked the articles. There was no further information about the writer so he considered that trail of enquiry, as fruitful as it was, to be a dead-end for now.

The net result of his effort since lunch was Harlan returning to the *Things we know about Jennifer L. Randall* document, adding '(Jenny?)' after her name, underlining 'journalist', putting a question mark after 'government agent' and adding the words 'or disgruntled charity worker' followed by another question mark. When Signboy arrived it was no wonder he was unimpressed by Harlan's progress.

"I thought you were a crack Indetective? You have someone's name and registration and you can't find out anything about them?"

"There's a reason it doesn't say detective agency on the door. I never thought about how poorly indetection skills would transfer to detection. I guess they are more like polar opposites than the prefix suggests. An old adage once again proved wrong."

"What old adage?" asked Signboy.

"There's a prefix in misdirection, but no misdirection in a prefix."

"That's not an adage. I don't really know what makes an adage, but that's not one or I'll eat my hat."

"If you bring me a definitive list of adages and it's not on there, I'll eat mine," said Harlan, not a hundred per cent sure such a list didn't exist. Not that it really mattered. Neither of them ever wore a hat.

"Deal," said Signboy. Apparently being promoted to Assistant Indetective meant it was now up to him to cut the childish arguments short. "So what's the next step with Jennifer Randall then?"

"I thought you'd never ask," said Harlan, a phrase which whenever spoken made the asker of the question wish they hadn't asked it in the first place, either out of fear of what might be the answer, annoyance at how smug the person they asked had just become, or both. In this case it was both, and Signboy was quite justified in wishing he hadn't asked.

"I'm going to get back on the trail of Jonathan Foxe and see if I can't find out some more about this Randall woman, and you're going to use that photo I took of her and imported to my desktop to go through the Jennifer, Jenny and Jen Randalls on Twitter and Facebook and see what you can find."

"That should be easy. Oh, you might wanna change shirts before you go out - you've got a coffee stain there. You should really stop using those small cups if you're gonna make such a mess."

"No, that's Coke from that steakhouse in Darling Harbour, I tipped the glass too much trying to catch the effervescence on my nose." Harlan entered a brief episode of concentration.

"Are you okay?" asked Signboy, unaccustomed to seeing Harlan go quiet like that, and a little concerned at his boss's desperation to get Coke on his nose.

"Yes, yes," said Harlan, coming out of his trance with a gleam in his eye. "Also, can you do a bit of a search on Jonathan and any history or connection he might have with Mick Dawson?" He had asked himself that question again, thinking it was for the first time.

"What am I looking for?"

"Something that makes their having lunch together interesting to Jennifer L. Randall." Harlan left Signboy shaking his head and questioning whether this was really the career path for him. He had two unappealing tasks ahead of him, and it was already after 4pm. It was small consolation Harlan had just left the office with a large Coke stain on the front of his shirt.

*

Harlan remembered the stain en route to Jonathan's pre-dinner meeting at the Celebrities Care head office. Fortunately the stain was fairly centred and he kept a tie in the glove box for just such an occasion. Unfortunately, and unknown to Harlan, the tie in the glove box wasn't his back-up tie for concealing stains. It was a tie he had stained on another occasion and then replaced with his back-up tie because he had been wearing a shirt that didn't look good with either one, two or three buttons undone. Any more than that was only appropriate in a cocktail bar on Mykonos.

Harlan pulled out what he thought was his back-up tie after pulling up across from a three-storey office building in the industrial zone of Alexandria, which sat south of the city centre on the way to the airport. "Fifteen minutes to anywhere ... " was the famous claim on the billboard advertising the many thousands of apartments popping up in the rezoned residential areas of Alexandria and neighbouring suburbs. Famous because of the asterisk the development company was forced to add when threatened with a misleading and deceptive conduct charge by the Australian Competition and Consumer Commission. The ACCC was looking for an easy victory after years spent challenging the cola duopoly only to have the High Court refuse to consider the cola market as being separate to the soft drink market, which included juice and milk. This drastically diluted the respective market shares of Pepsi and Coke who set about acquiring juice and milk companies so fast the ACCC had no time to prosecute their temporarily false claims they each had fifty per cent of the soft drink market. Harlan pondered all of this deliberately to allow his subconscious mind to tie his tie for him in a perfect double Windsor knot, the only way he knew how to do so. This unconventional approach had an unfortunate side-effect because his subconscious mind had no way of communicating to his conscious mind the much more obvious and somewhat ironic orange juice stain on the tie he had just used to cover up the Coke stain on his shirt.

As Harlan was adjusting the rear-view mirror to see how his subconscious mind had done, he noticed the car between him and the blue Golf had left. Then for the second time that day he made eye contact with Jennifer Randall. To Harlan's alarm the flash of recognition on his face made the journey to replicate itself on her face at a speed his client the high-frequency/low-latency trader (with a burlesque drag queen as an alter-ego) would pay a lot of money to achieve when sending his (or sometimes her) orders to market. While his response was to adjust the mirror again and generally pretend as though nothing had happened, hers was just about conceptually opposite. She got out of her car, walked quickly up to Harlan's passenger window and knocked excitedly.

"Quick, let me in," she said.

She's good, Harlan thought. Having no real option, he reached across and unlocked the passenger door. As she got in and closed the door behind her, Harlan tried desperately to think how he could control this particular confrontation.

"What do you think of the legroom?" he asked, his voice breaking slightly as he saw just how green her eyes were up close. It was a pathetic attempt, but she wouldn't know the full story so might just think he was being weird. Which he was.

"What? It's fine." She didn't skip a beat. "So, you first, or me?"

Harlan, afraid of losing all coherence if he continued to look into her eyes, was now busy studying his tie, which he'd just discovered had a huge orange juice stain on it, so she decided she should go first.

"Jennifer Randall, investigative journalist. I'm trying to link him to some dodgy practices at Celebrities Care-sponsored education centres in South Africa." She looked at Harlan for a response. He was now pretending to be distracted by his tie, but really picturing how that statement would change his document about her. "That's not coming out you know."

"What? Oh, the tie. No, I don't think so. I forgot it was there. Never try to drink orange juice in the car as a replacement for a full breakfast at home." Harlan took the tie off and threw it into the back seat.

"Neither is that."

"What? Oh, the shirt." He had forgotten the reason he had the tie on in the first place. "That's just Coke, from lunch."

"Even worse. As a meal replacement and a stain."

"It doesn't matter, I can just cover it up with a tie. Another tie."

"Right. So what about you?"

"Well, I'm covered up with the shirt. Not that I'm stained, or anything."

"I'll take your word for it." Jennifer giggled at Harlan's confused state, which didn't help him out at all. Her lilting laugh only added to the allure of her eyes. "No, I mean why are you following Jonathan Foxe around?"

"I'm not, exactly." Harlan immediately regretted his answer. He hoped he would get another chance to confirm her assumption he was following Jonathan, and not her. He doubted she would be so forthcoming, in both the friendly and informational senses of the word, if she knew he was being paid by Jonathan Foxe to find out about her.

"Yes you are. You were at the café in Double Bay this morning - I always notice these cars because of the little spoiler on the back, my Dad used to have one." Harlan wondered whether it was her Dad who had sold him his car needing a new radiator and four new tyres. "Then we practically had lunch together, and now here you are outside the head office. You must be following him." Bingo.

"Yes, that's all true." And finally Harlan's mental agility returned from its brief holiday. "I am following him."

"I know." Another lilting laugh.

"I'm following Jonathan Foxe, that's right." Harlan wasn't great at first impressions, unless his aim was to appear quite strange and more than a little stupid. Fortunately, she seemed to be amused by just about everything he said.

"Because ... " she tried to lead him on, her accompanying smile only making Harlan stay silent longer.

"His wife hired me." It had the merit of truth, at least. And it did explain why he appeared to be following Jonathan. Which he was. Harlan was just beginning to appreciate the complexities of the overlapping cases he had gotten himself involved in.

"His wife? So you're a private detective then?"

Harlan grimaced. "Yes. I'm a private ... detective." He found the idea abhorrent after what had happened to his father, but was also aware that if he had learned anything that afternoon, and he had learned only a very small amount, then one thing he had learned was he wasn't much of a detective, so it couldn't challenge his identity too much to pretend he was.

"You don't look like a private detective."

"What do you mean?"

"Well, aren't they either immaculately dressed, overconfident and irresistible or smutty, disgusting slobs?"

Harlan didn't know what to say. He was disappointed she found him resistible, but pleased to hear she didn't see him as a smutty, disgusting slob despite the stains on his clothes.

"And I'm neither?"

"No, you're something else entirely. I'll let you know when I figure it out." Jennifer looked thoughtfully at Harlan, again winning the staring contest as he shied away. "So, she thinks he's cheating on her?" She sounded dubious.

"Yes. Well, she seems to be very sure of it."

"Hmm. It's possible. But he's very busy. I can't keep up with him all the time, but I haven't seen anything to suggest he's not faithful."

"How long have you been following him?" Harlan had remembered he was supposed to be finding out about her. It sounded like something a detective would ask in the situation. At least, it had a question mark at the end of it and wasn't about the legroom.

"Just a couple of weeks. Although I have a part-time job too at a café - these long-term freelance investigative pieces aren't the best-paying gigs around. Too speculative for most editors to even bother with."

"But you found an editor who bothered with this piece?" Even the great Hercule Poirot would be proud of that one.

Jennifer checked her watch - it was close to 6pm. "Look, I better go, he usually has early dinner plans. A man that busy can't afford to wait an hour for a table. Here." She took her notepad out, turned to a blank page and wrote a phone number on it. "Call me later and we can exchange notes. Maybe we can help each other out."

"Sure, um. Thanks." Harlan almost had everything he needed for Jonathan, and it was only day one of the investigation. Jennifer smiled goodbye at Harlan, pressing the piece of paper with her number on it into Harlan's hand before she got out, then dashed quickly back to her car. Harlan watched her in the mirror. He could think of nothing he could give her that would help her out - other than Jonathan's daily itinerary, which he thought would be a bit difficult to explain if he was, as he had told Jenny, solely in the employ of Marisa Foxe. In fact, he was quite sure when he told Jonathan what he had so far, his job would become stopping Jenny from finding out anything at all. That, or Biff would be called in. Harlan hoped it wouldn't come to that. Something told him calling her later on wouldn't make it any easier for him to complete his assignment for Jonathan. He already had mixed emotions, and they'd only spoken for a few minutes. Still, what was the worst that could happen?

CHAPTER 5

Harlan drove back to his office. He knew from the itinerary that Jonathan was meeting Marisa for dinner, so there was no point in going along to watch. Plus he needed to steer Signboy down the Mick Dawson line of research. What Jennifer had said about Celebrities Care had piqued his interest in that regard. Dodgy practices were certainly the celebrity agent's area of expertise. And now he was in contact with Jennifer there was no point searching for her on a social networking website. He might be friends with her on Facebook before the end of the night in any case.

He thought he should give Marisa some confidence he was working the case since he hadn't spoken to her all day. He took a risk and sent her a text message asking if Jonathan was going out tonight. A risk because she might already be with Jonathan, in which case she might have to explain the text message somehow, and a risk because he was driving and should have been giving that his full attention. She replied almost immediately that she was meeting Jonathan for dinner (which Harlan of course knew) so he should take the rest of the night off. He wrote back that he would call her the next day to brief her on the case so far.

This gave Harlan a legitimate reason he could give to Jennifer to explain why he wasn't on the stakeout for that part of the evening. He would call her when Jonathan's schedule for the day was complete, when Harlan assumed he would go home with his wife after dinner.

Harlan arrived back at the office to find Signboy in his chair falling asleep at the computer. It hadn't been a fun couple of hours by the look of it.

"How's it going?" asked Harlan.

"Yeah, good. I mean, I have ruled out hundreds of Jen, Jenny and Jennifer Randalls on Facebook, but I haven't found her yet and I've only been able to rule out about half of them. There's too many people with stupid avatars or pictures of their pets or babies to be too systematic about it. I haven't got to Twitter yet, but I reckon it'll be the same thing." Signboy stood up and stretched as he talked. He clearly wanted to be doing something else.

"What about the Mick Dawson stuff?" Harlan casually circled the desk towards his chair, hoping Signboy would take the hint and circle the desk away from his chair, so it wouldn't feel like he was the guest in Signboy's office.

"I thought I'd focus on the paying job first, not just satisfying whatever curious whim you might have had as you walked out the door." Signboy pulled out Harlan's chair for him then circled the desk as well. He sensed Harlan's discomfort and was enjoying it. Normally it was Harlan making people uncomfortable.

"I'd rather you didn't try to decide which tasks are related to the job at hand and which are curious whims. What might seem like a curious whim to you could well be the thing that cracks a case wide open." Harlan pushed the seat back in as Signboy circled around to the other side of the desk. Signboy gestured for Harlan to sit down in the ergonomic armchair. Harlan leaned on it instead and gestured for Signboy to sit down in the guest chair across from him.

"I thought an indetective's job was to keep cases wrapped in enigmatic shrouds? That's what you said to me when I first started." Signboy now stood behind the guest chair, with two hands on its back, mirroring Harlan's stance.

"Good, good recall. Very impressive. And quite correct." Harlan balanced his weight between his feet and engaged his core. He was ready for a long stand-off. "But as we've already learned in this case, we are trying to do the opposite. That is, see through the enigmatic shrouds. And I'm beginning to think we'll accomplish more with curious whims than systematic detective work."

"Because we're rubbish at systematic detective work?" Signboy was quite comfortable leaning on the guest chair. Neither of them was going to sit first.

"Well, let's say we're beginners. Anyway, that curious whim I had was spot on. I think. At least, Jennifer seems to find it quite interesting."

"It's Jennifer now?"

Harlan filled him on what had happened, leaving out the bit about the stains. And the lilting laugh.

"Excellent detective work. Or was that a curious whim, getting spotted and having her jump into your car and peel back the shrouds for you?"

"Somewhere in between, I guess." Harlan had to admit, it wasn't his finest effort. He didn't have to admit it out loud though. "Anyway, I think it would be advantageous if we knew exactly what she was after. If we had something to offer her when we trade notes tonight ... "

"Yes?" Signboy guessed Harlan was, again, just out to make a good impression.

"Well, that's it I guess. That's what we're after."

"Good, the kind of vague assignment an assistant indetective can really sink his teeth into. Well, let's get some food first, I'm starving."

"It's not too early for you? I thought it was cool to eat at 9pm these days?"

"No, it's cool to eat at eight-thirty. It's acceptable to eat at nine because it's cool to be late and have to wait for a table. But when I'm hungry I prefer your approach. Get in early. Just don't be seen, that's all."

*

After some cheap and cheerful Thai food from the bustling avenue of Thai restaurants that is King Street, Newtown, Harlan and Signboy were back in the office. Harlan had spun his computer around so Signboy could work on it from the guest chair, while Harlan then drifted into the front room to call Jennifer.

Calling young, attractive women had never been Harlan's *forte*, or in any list that could be made of what someone might call his strengths, or even in any list of what *he* might call his strengths. It just wasn't a thing he was good at. So like any rational person (which some people would argue was very unlike Harlan), he was procrastinating. He had set up an entry for Jennifer in the contacts book on his phone. He had added the photo he took of her at the steakhouse, cropped to make it look more like a profile picture of a friend than a picture a stalker would have of his object of obsession. But now he had run out of things to do. So he pressed call.

It rang a few times. Harlan imagined her enjoying the first few bars of *I Can't Go For That*, which was extremely unlikely, but not as unlikely as Harlan thought. Hall & Oates had recently been discovered and made popular again by gen Y (which included Jennifer) and those of gen X that missed them the first time around (which included Harlan). Although, there was still a lot of music out there much more likely to be a young woman's ringtone.

"This is Jenny."

Harlan waited a second to make sure it wasn't the start of a hilarious voice mail prompt that tricked the caller into thinking it was the actual person speaking.

"Hello, anyone there?" she said. If it was a voice mail prompt, it had gone past funny, if in fact it was ever funny, and was now just very, very annoying.

"Hi, Jennifer?" said Harlan.

"It's you! Jenny, please." Harlan grinned, leaning against the reception counter. He knew she wouldn't have an annoying voice mail prompt. And she seemed excited to hear from him.

"Jenny, hi."

"Hi. Sorry, I never caught your name. You were too busy being awkward and evasive in the car."

"It's Harlan."

"Harlem?"

"Harlan. As in ... with an N." Sometimes he wished he was called John, but then he would remember how similar it sounded to Shaun so wouldn't necessarily remove all name-related confusion from his life. Also it was often a nickname for the toilet. He was much better off with a name that to most people didn't sound like anything other than a fake basketball team, once people got over the whole 'I've never heard that name before where does it come from?' ridiculousness.

"Harlan. Unusual. Anyway, what are you up to? I'm dying to hear what you know about Jonathan Foxe. And his wife for that matter."

"Of course." Harlan hadn't expected her to initiate a meeting, even though that was basically the pattern of their relationship so far, and it was why she had given him her number and asked him to call her. "I can meet you in about half an hour. Where were you thinking?"

"I wasn't. Where are you?"

"Newtown."

"That's not where I was thinking. How about you come to Darlinghurst. I'll find somewhere and let you know the address."

"Sure, okay. I'll see you around nine." He should have stopped talking then. "I could get the train, but that might take longer than half an hour by the time I walk up from Central. A taxi is probably best, but you can never count on them having change, and I only have fifties after just going to the ATM. Of course, I could use a credit card, but I've heard about people's details being recorded by fake card readers in taxis and the next thing you know you've financed a terrorist act somewhere."

"Harlan?"

"Yes?"

"Take a taxi. Try a fifty first. Then use a card, but make sure you get a receipt."

"You think that's safe?"

"I think a drink with me is worth the infinitesimally small risk involved." Harlan was no expert, but if pressed he'd describe that sentence as flirtatious.

"Of course, sorry Jennifer. See you soon."

"Bye Harlan."

He put his phone in his pocket and walked back into the office.

"Wipe that grin off your face. There's no way she's interested."

"I wasn't grinning, I was just laughing about something."

"Sure. So where are you meeting her?"

"Darlinghurst. She'll let me know where exactly."

"Cool, you can give me a lift. I'll come back first thing and get started on this properly."

"Get started? What have you been doing?"

"Listening to you of course. So are you going to change shirts now? You can't let her see you like that twice in one day."

Harlan went to the wardrobe in the corner behind his desk. He was relieved to find his back-up shirt hanging there, still with the dry-cleaning plastic on it. He took the Coke-stained shirt off and threw it over the back of his chair. He picked up the roll-on deodorant sitting on the shelf at the bottom of the wardrobe and applied it, then he removed the dry-cleaning plastic from his back-up shirt and put it on. Reaching back into the wardrobe he pulled out a bottle of mouthwash, took a swig and pushed it around in his mouth while he buttoned up his shirt. Looking around, he remembered the new office flora in the front room. Pushing past an amused Signboy he walked to the fern and spat the mouthwash into the soil. He ran his hands through his thick hair, not sure whether he should be patting it down or messing it up and in the end doing a bit of both.

"All right, let's go," he said, and walked out the front door. Signboy switched off the lights and followed him.

"What did you do before you got the fern?" he asked as they went down the stairs.

"Swallowed," said Harlan. "But it was a little disgusting."

"Unlike spitting it in a pot plant."

They squeezed past a shocked looking woman with an incredibly straight back leaving the chiropractor's, and made their way out onto the street.

"Come on," said Harlan as he saw Signboy heading towards his car. "Let's get a taxi. I'll probably have a couple of drinks and see if I can't peel back some more shrouds."

"Just focus on the enigmatic ones first."

*

After dropping Signboy somewhere clearly out of his way, Harlan asked the taxi driver to drop him in the middle of Darlinghurst. He would then check his phone for Jennifer's directions and walk to meet her.

"All right mate, just direct me. It's easier."

"I don't know exactly where I'm going, can you just drop me in the middle of Darlinghurst."

"What do you think this is?" The taxi driver raised his voice in the traditional way they do when asked something out of the ordinary. "I need an address mate."

"I don't have an address."

"You want to look at the map? Here." He handed Harlan a ring binder that struggled to contain an ageing Sydney street directory, unbound and hole-punched.

"No, I just want to go to the centre of Darlinghurst, you must know where that is."

"Mate, I'm a taxi driver. I'm not a bloody cartographer. You show me on that map where is the centre of Darlinghurst. I'll take you there."

Harlan couldn't argue with the logic, so he looked for the page with Darlinghurst on it but he found it difficult to turn the pages in the ill-fitting ring binder. "You know, this is a lot harder to flick through than a book."

"You got your own map mate?"

Harlan did. He pulled out his phone and opened up the *Maps* app. He typed in 'Darlinghurst' and pressed search. A map of the surrounding area came up, with a pin dropped at what looked like the centre of Darlinghurst. A couple of double-taps later and Harlan had zoomed in to where Darlinghurst Road crossed Burton Street.

"Darlinghurst Road please, corner of Burton."

"See mate? Told you so."

"No you didn't."

"I did, I said give me address, I'll take you there. You gave me address, now I can take you there."

"It's that simple is it?" Harlan handed the ring binder back to the driver, who jammed it down the gap between the passenger seat and the centre console.

"You know mate," said the driver, "I think *Victoria* and Burton is more the centre of Darlinghurst." All of a sudden he was a cartographer.

CHAPTER 6

Jennifer's text message directed Harlan to a cocktail bar at the back of a French restaurant he'd never heard of on Victoria Street, a few doors up from Kings Cross. It was only a short walk from the corner of Burton Street, where Harlan had eventually persuaded the taxi driver to drop him off, even though it wasn't, according to the taxi driver, the centre of Darlinghurst. Harlan had never seen someone hold an opinion so strongly within five minutes of first having it. At least he had change for a fifty.

He found the entrance to the restaurant, which was essentially a flight of stairs leading up from the footpath, and went in. At the top of the stairs he found himself in a busy French restaurant that seemed very 'in', and decided to lie to Jennifer and tell her he'd been here before. He didn't want to seem out of touch.

A waitress approached him and he told her he was there to meet someone for a drink. She ushered him down a walkway that separated the kitchen from the bathrooms and led to a dark, cosy cocktail bar with some light jazz coming from well hidden speakers.

Harlan looked around the couple of small groups seated in Louis XV style lounges and armchairs but didn't see Jennifer. The waitress pointed him to a couple of armchairs in the corner. "In the corner there, it's just the two of you?"

Harlan nodded and sat in the chair facing out from the corner so he could catch Jennifer's eye when she arrived. "There's the cocktail list, I'll bring you the wine list as well." The waitress went to the bar, grabbed a clipboard from the top of a pile of them, then returned and handed it to Harlan. "There's snacks on the cocktail list as well. Back in a minute to take your order."

"Thank you," he called after her, but she was already halfway back to the restaurant. He was about to turn his attention to the cocktail list when he noticed a a dark green knitted cardigan over the arm of the chair in front of him, and a familiar looking backpack on the floor. Either she was here already, or Harlan's general scepticism of coincidences was being tested to its limits. He decided the waitress must have known he was here to meet Jennifer and shown him to where she was sitting. He assumed she was in the bathroom, and had told the waitress she was waiting for someone. Someone handsome. That's probably what she said.

He looked around. The waitress hadn't returned. The other groups were quite occupied with themselves and weren't paying him any attention. He thought he might be able to check the backpack for her notebook, flick through it, peel away a few shrouds and put it back before she returned. He went through it in his mind, timing it. Ten seconds, that's all I need, he thought. It's what a detective would do. This last thought made up his mind for him. An indetective had more integrity than that. He turned his attention to the cocktail list, scanning the page unsuccessfully for a drink he recognised. He made a mental note to further develop his proposal to the city council that all bars had to serve at least seven prescribed, traditional cocktails made to an official recipe. Wouldn't it be great if you could walk into any bar in Sydney and order a Hemingway Daiquiri? Of course it would.

"Harlan, you found it. Have you been here before?" Jennifer sat down across from him as he looked up. He half-stood and waved his arm towards her chair to be polite, but realised that didn't work when she was already sitting, so awkwardly sat back down.

"Hi Jennifer." Now he was torn between pretending he wasn't out of touch and showing off his ability to follow simple directions. "Ah, no. But your directions were quite easy to follow." Perfect. It almost sounded like a compliment.

"Jenny, please. I won't tell you again," she said, smiling. "Cocktail?"

"Sure, sounds good. Unless you wanted to get some wine." He hoped she would. He didn't want to get the waitress to explain the cocktails to him in front of Jenny, and he was afraid to order anything if he didn't know exactly what went into it. A few years back he'd found pickled ginger and a wasabi floater in a Kyoto Mule at an overly experimental cocktail bar.

"Ooh, tough one. Yes, let's get wine. You choose."

Harlan was amazed at the speed with which she could make decisions. And now she was asking him to make one. He picked up the list and flicked through it. He needed to narrow the field.

"What do you feel like?"

"Red. Nothing fancy."

"Okay." He picked a low to mid-range price point and settled on a couple of Burgundies. He chose the one with *Chateau* in the name and looked for the waitress.

"Oh, something Australian of course," said Jenny. "Carbon footprint and all that."

"That's a thing with wine?"

"I wouldn't call it a thing - it's just something that's easy to do. Wouldn't it actually make your life easier if you only ever had to look at the Australian wines on a list? Probably save you money too."

"Yes, it probably would." Harlan had always chosen wines to match the cuisine, Italian at an Italian restaurant,

French at a French restaurant. He thought he was immersing himself in the culture, not destroying the environment.

"There you go, so you can do yourself and the environment a favour at the same time."

"Perfect. I run a paperless office for the same reason."

"Really?" Her eyes lit up. "I'd love to see it sometime." That wasn't a good idea until he'd come clean about being an indetective.

"It's not that interesting, really. Just a bunch of empty shelves."

"Ha, funny and green," said Jenny, smiling appreciatively. "Let's hope the environmentally-friendly wine is more impressive than the paperless office then."

"Sure thing." He looked at the list again, chose the most French sounding Australian wine he could find and got the waitress's attention, who had just come back into the room. "We'll have the *Chapoutier* shiraz, please."

"Excellent choice, sir." It definitely wasn't saving him money.

"South Australian," he said to Jenny as the waitress took the list away.

"I'll check the label you know," she said, smiling again. He believed her.

"So, how was dinner?" he asked.

"Boring. He met his wife, they had dinner at some posh place in the city, then they went home. Where were you?"

"Oh, I had another case to work on. Marisa told me she was meeting Jonathan so I doubted he'd be doing much adulterating."

"Thanks for telling me! I ate some takeaway Japanese in my car waiting to see them leave."

"I didn't think, sorry."

"It's the worst cuisine you can have takeaway. Sushi in a plastic box. We could have come here for dinner, the food's amazing." Now he really was sorry.

"I'll make sure I tell you in the future."

"Good. I was thinking we can make each other's lives a lot easier. There's no point in us both following him around in two cars all day."

"We could carpool? Carbon footprint." Harlan impressed himself, at least.

"No, I mean we can take turns. Then catch up every day and tell each other what happened."

Harlan thought about it. It obviously made sense. And there was the bonus of catching up with Jenny every day. But surely Biff would notice if he was only there half the time.

"Look, Jenny. I'd love to help you out. But I need to account to my client for my time."

"Come on, Harlan. She doesn't need to know you aren't following him all the time. I'll take photos and make notes of any funny business his wife might be interested in, and give it all to you. You'd really be helping me out - I need to pull some more shifts at the café or I'll be on the street soon."

"Look, let me think about it. I've never worked with anyone else on a case before." He couldn't help thinking how he was getting paid twice for the work he was doing, while Jenny didn't seem to be getting paid at all. He knew he would agree to her proposal before the end of the evening.

The waitress arrived with the wine. "Sorry, I had to get it from the cellar. Well, the wine fridge out the back." She showed Harlan the label. He nodded. It was definitely the wine he'd ordered. Jenny leaned forward to see the label as well, and also nodded. It was definitely from South Australia.

The waitress deftly uncorked it and poured some into an oversized wine glass for Harlan to taste. Harlan put his nose to the glass and inhaled. Then he waved the glass in a horizontal circle, causing the wine to whirl impressively around inside the vessel. He waited for it to settle down and smelled it again, then took a sip. "Excellent," he said to the waitress.

"Do you want me to decant it?"

"Yes, please," said Harlan. The waitress took the wine away.

"That was quite the production," said Jenny, looking a little impressed. "But now she'll take another five minutes with it, and I'm dying for a drink."

"It needs it. It's been in that bottle for twelve years."

"So it's got some sediment in it?"

"Probably. But also it needs to stretch its legs, get a bit of air."

Jenny was dubious for the second time that day. "I don't mean to be rude, but I'm going to check that." Harlan looked on astonished as she pulled out her own smartphone and began prodding the screen.

"What are you doing?"

"I'm googling 'decanting'. People can't just go around touting conventional wisdom like gospel these days. I mean, look what happened to gospel." She was now reading something on the screen. "I like to be sure of something before I take it on as knowledge."

"So you're a sceptic?"

"I try to be. Here." She held the phone across the table for Harlan to read. She had highlighted a sentence, which Harlan read aloud.

However the effectiveness of decanting is a topic of debate, with some wine experts like oenologist Emile Peynaud claiming that the prolonged exposure to oxygen actually diffuses and dissipates more aroma compounds than it stimulates, in contrast to the effects of the smaller scale exposure and immediate release that swirling the wine in a drinker's glass has.

Jenny took her phone back with just a faint suggestion in her eyes of having told him so.

"So I have to rely on you now Harlan, because you're the only one who's tasted the wine pre-decanting. You'll have to tell me whether it improved it or not. Did the swirling improve it?"

"Definitely - it releases all the wonderful aromas, which enhances the whole drinking experience." He saw her prodding the screen of her phone again. "Look, why don't you just see for yourself? It will still work after it's decanted. Actual experience is how knowledge comes about in the first place. And please don't google that."

She stopped prodding for a second. "Sounds more like a philosophy than a fact anyway," she said. "Okay, fine, I'll put it away. This 'experience' better be good though." She winked at him. He couldn't imagine ever saying no to her after that.

The waitress returned again, this time with a crystal decanter that was essentially a long, curved pipe shaped like the frame of a lyre, open at both ends with a wide midsection. The displaced wine sat in the belly of the decanter. She held it at one end and tilted it over Jenny's glass, so that the wine ran out the other end into the glass. She did the same for Harlan, wiping the rim of the decanter with a white napkin after each pour, then took the decanter, still with more than half the bottle left in it, back to the bar.

"Gee, it's like a little piece of theatre, isn't it?" said Jenny, picking up her glass. "That's probably why people really get wine decanted, for a free show."

"Ha, maybe. So, take a good smell and a small taste first, then give it a good swirl and see what happens."

"That's what she said."

"Sorry?" Harlan wasn't familiar with the popular joke.

"That's what she said - you don't know the joke?"

"No, I, sorry?"

"I guess you don't work in a big corporate office. A great way to avoid popular culture I've found, but I have enough friends who do so I don't miss out. Basically whenever anyone says something that, in more of a bedroom context, could be sexy, you say 'that's what she said'."

"Or 'he said', in my case."

Jenny laughed so hard she forgot the lilt.

"No, that means something else," she said when she'd stifled the laugh sufficiently. "Don't worry, you're clever. I'm sure you'll catch on. Now, let me see how this tastes."

"That's what she said," said Harlan, more tentatively than he would have liked.

"Ha, perfect, first time. Just don't overdo it." She gave Harlan a warning look as he was about to do just that. When he stopped himself, the look became a smile and she returned her attention to her glass of wine.

She did as Harlan advised, smell-sip-swirl-smell-sip, closing her eyes at the end as she concentrated on the taste. "Yep, it's good. I will definitely do that with every glass of wine from now on. I'm not convinced about the decanting though. Are you going to give me a full tasting course now, how to identify blackberry undertones?"

"No, not at all. I wouldn't know how. That's all you need to know. Then it's just about finding wine you like. I've never understood the endeavour to describe complex flavours by comparing them to other complex flavours. I imagine a group of blackberry connoisseurs somewhere, trying to describe to each other the difference in flavour between blackberries. 'First I get cabernet, then a hint of merlot. Definite traces of shiraz in the aftertaste.'"

Jenny laughed again. She really had a nice laugh. He wanted to hear it often.

"I'd always want to taste for myself anyway. With wine and blackberries," she said. "So was the decanting worth the effort?"

Harlan tasted the wine.

"I'd have to say, there is no discernible difference."

"But it was a good show, and I think we just about managed to have an enjoyable conversation either side of it. So, now you're more relaxed, and we've got a nice bottle of wine to get through, let's talk Jonathan Foxe."

*

By the time they had finished the nice bottle of wine, Harlan knew a lot more about Jenny and Celebrities Care.

In 2009, Jenny had been a volunteer in South Africa. She worked at a drop-in centre for street kids in Johannesburg, teaching English and drug and sex education and helping those who were interested to try to find a home or get back into school. There were also regular visits by doctors to test for diseases and hand out medicine. The centre got by on donations raised around the world by former volunteers, some local donations, regular fundraisers and a small bit of government funding. She had been working there for close to six months when the Celebrities Care Foundation started supporting the centre.

A Celebrities Care outreach manager began working at the centre and others like it across Johannesburg. He ran a campaign amongst the volunteers to focus on forging partnerships with local businesses that could eventually give the kids jobs and get them off the street. At that point Jenny had to leave the country to get a new ninety-day visitor's permit.

When she returned a few weeks later, she wasn't welcome at the centre. A woman wearing a Celebrities Care badge told her to leave or she would call the police. Jenny tracked down a couple of the kids she knew and asked them what was going on. They had also been told they weren't welcome at the centre anymore. One of them was told it was because he was too young to work. The other had been told his English wasn't good enough to complete further training. Both kids had started hanging out with local gangs again.

One boy she knew stayed on at the centre and kept in contact with her over a Gmail account she'd helped some of the kids set up for when they were using the centre's computers. He now worked twelve-hour shifts in a call centre and lived in a dorm arranged by Celebrities Care for graduates of the centre who worked with Celebrities Care partners. He hadn't heard from the other kids since they'd been turned away.

Horrified at what she'd found, Jenny went back to the centre for answers. The woman there was true to her word and called the police. The immigration police. Jenny had a visitor's permit with eighty-five days left on it, but it was her third consecutive permit. Unable to satisfy the immigration police she was a genuine tourist given her stated occupation as journalist, and unsure what her rights were as a volunteer, Jenny was deported and on a plane back to Sydney by the end of the day.

After she got home she emailed a doctor she had met volunteering at the centre to see if she knew anything. The doctor was now back home in Chicago but told Jenny about the changes she'd seen before she left. She explained to Jenny that only Celebrities Care employees were kept on, and the centres were now just providing free vocational training for working in call centres or in data entry, but only to kids aged sixteen or above who spoke good English. She guessed the businesses who sponsored the centres were providing the training and then hiring the kids. Before she left Johannesburg she had complained to a local politician about the kids being turned away and the medical services being stopped. He told her that for the first time these centres were getting tangible results and no-one (apart from her) was complaining, so she had, regretfully, left it at that.

Jenny's theory was that these businesses had done similar things in other parts of the world, also with Celebrities Care as a partner. She found former volunteers with similar stories from their time in India. They'd had similar problems trying to challenge Celebrities Care because they were actually getting some kids trained and off the street.

Now Jenny was trying to bring the practices to light, but she had learned not everyone saw a story in it. To get someone to pay her any money upfront, she'd had to promise Jonathan Foxe was involved. Following him around for a couple of weeks hadn't yielded much evidence, but it had confirmed her suspicions something funny was going on at Celebrities Care. Jonathan Foxe lived more like the CEO of a merchant bank than a charitable foundation.

Jenny then shared with Harlan her unfounded hypothesis that this was where Mick Dawson came into the picture. Jenny had suspected the companies taking advantage of the Celebrities Care training centres were all related, and Jonathan Foxe was somehow benefitting personally by offering exclusive access to his global network of cheap, trained labour. Unable to identify the companies involved from Sydney, she hadn't been able to give much credence to her theory. But after seeing the dynamic between Jonathan and Mick Dawson, she had a hunch the celebrity agent was the key, which would enable her hopefully to trace the corporate connections from the top down.

In the same time Jenny had learned from Harlan only that Marisa Foxe seemed to Harlan to be a nice, down-to-earth person who simply wanted to know more about her husband's infidelities. Harlan hadn't said any more than that - he knew he'd have to come clean about being an indetective at some point, but he was having such a great time he didn't want to spoil it with a discussion about the morals of what he did. He was worried she wouldn't approve.

This was a big mistake on Harlan's part. Not because she would approve - she definitely wouldn't - but because it would have been much easier to tell her before they slept together. And although they didn't sleep together that night, despite their ordering a second bottle of shiraz and Harlan making her laugh at least three more times (including only one 'that's what she said'), they left each other both quite sure they would before too long.

CHAPTER 7

"Well, you've got two choices," said Signboy. "You can go to Jonathan Foxe and tell him what you know, and just carry on working for his wife. There's no way Jenny will know you ever worked for him. Or, you can tell Jonathan Foxe you can't do the job and make an enemy of one of the most powerful men in Sydney on the off chance this young woman, who's clearly out of your league, will lose all her senses and sleep with you at some point."

It was the next morning, and Harlan had caught the train into the office to fill Signboy in on what had happened the night before. He had, of course, agreed to Jenny's suggestion of splitting the workload, and she was working at the café all day. They sat in Harlan's office, Harlan in his armchair and Signboy in the guest chair across from him, with the laptop facing Signboy so he could fill in the *Jennifer Randall* document as they talked. Signboy had, with a wisdom beyond his years, distilled the complicated situation down to one decision point for Harlan. It was clear which option Signboy preferred.

"Or," countered Harlan, "I can carry on as is, and hopefully Jenny will have enough for her story before I have to report to Jonathan next week." Harlan, as usual, was trying to defer making any decision.

"How long has she been following him around?"

"Two weeks."

"And how much has she found out?"

"Nothing."

"Right."

"But I can't report back to Jonathan now - if he knows what she's after, he'll be able to make sure she has no chance of finding out anything. Or worse, he could get Biff to make sure she stops looking."

"You think he'd do that?"

"I don't know - people do rash things when they have something to hide."

"Like hire an indetective?"

"Exactly. They don't stop what they're doing, they take steps so they can keep doing it."

Signboy thought for a moment.

"What was the agreement you had with Jonathan?"

"That I would find out who was following him and why," said Harlan, with a very slow dawn of realisation crawling across his face. "Just a second, I'm having a thought." Signboy suspected Harlan was having the thought he'd had a few seconds earlier.

"So," Harlan continued. "Theoretically it wouldn't be contrary to my agreement with Jonathan Foxe to help Jenny out."

"And ... "

"And helping Jenny out is the best way I can make sure she doesn't make an issue of his philandering, to the extent there is any, which means it's also consistent with my agreement with Marisa."

"But what if Jenny succeeds?"

"If Jenny succeeds - well then she'd be very grateful for any help we provide. Of course, Celebrities Care will be scandalised, Jonathan Foxe will be ruined, and Marisa will be lucky to avoid ruin herself."

"If that happens - are we gonna get paid?"

"Not likely, although if I can keep my contract with Marisa secret from Jonathan, and my contract with Jonathan secret from Marisa, and my relationship with Jenny secret from them both ... "

"And your contract with Jonathan secret from Jenny," added Signboy.

"Yes, of course. If I can do all of that, then we just might get paid by both Jonathan and Marisa and not blow our, I mean my, chances with Jenny."

"Sounds like you've come to a decision then."

"Yes," said Harlan. He leaned forward, pulled the laptop across the desk towards him and opened up a new document.

"Do you really have to write this down?"

"I'm doing a flowchart."

"God. I'm going to get a Coke then, you'll be a while. Want one?"

"Yes, thanks," Harlan said without looking up. He was working away at the keyboard quite determinedly.

"My shout again is it?"

"Take it from petty cash."

Signboy ignored this last ridiculous suggestion from Harlan and went out the door. They hadn't seen the key to petty cash since four secretaries ago, and because Harlan didn't know how much money was in there he had never bothered to break into it or get the lock changed. "Can't be too much in there," Harlan said whenever it came up, and he was right.

*

After he finished his flowchart, had a Coke with Signboy, gave him some tips for carrying on with the rest of their caseload and got bored when their research on Mick Dawson didn't immediately yield results, Harlan remembered he was going to call Marisa.

"I'm going to call Marisa," he told Signboy, and went into the front room. He knew Signboy would be listening in, but that would just save him from recounting the conversation later. He found Marisa's number in his phone and pressed call. He was wondering what ringtone a celebrity chef might have when she answered a few seconds later.

"Harlan, hi." Caller ID.

"Hi, Marisa. How are you?"

"Well, thank you for asking. How's it going?" Marisa was being overly professional. Harlan guessed she was with someone.

"So far so good, I would say. Your husband's a busy man, meeting people all day long, in a professional capacity I mean. And he seems like he's well protected, he has his driver and bodyguard with him whenever he's on the move, always in the Mercedes-Benz. Doing well for a charity man." Harlan thought he might get her insight into how the entourage was funded, but after a second's silence he realised she wouldn't bite. Luckily he had another thought. "Can I ask you something?" Harlan was acting on a curious whim again - although this one wasn't completely unlike systematic detective work.

"Of course."

"Well, how can you be so sure your husband is having an affair?"

"You don't think he is?"

"Oh, I have no idea. I was just wondering why you're so sure, when you said you'd never caught him."

"Just a second." Harlan heard what sounded like Marisa covering the phone with her hand and then ask someone if she could be excused for a moment. A few muffled footsteps and a closed door later, "It's a lot of small things, really." Harlan noticed her natural voice had returned. "He seems quite distracted when he's at home. He often leaves the room when taking calls."

"That could be things going wrong at work," said Harlan. "He probably wouldn't want you to think he's not on top of everything."

"Maybe. But this has been going on for years, since the last few months of the Executive Club. Look, I'll give you a better example. Earlier this week he ordered some flowers at our local florist, but I never received any flowers. Why would he need to send someone flowers for work?"

"Hmm, you're right. That's more suspicious. Let me look into it - what's the name of the florist?"

"You're going to cringe."

"What is it, Florist Gump?"

"Oh my God, that's pretty bad. No, it's not far off though. It's Floral 'n' Hardy."

"Wow. I can't wait to see it. And what day did you say this was?"

"I found out the day I called you actually, so it must have been Monday that he ordered the flowers."

"Okay, I better get back to it. Good talking to you."

"Thanks Harlan, speak soon."

Harlan put his phone away and called ahead to Signboy as he went back into his office, "Signboy, can you get me the address of Floral 'n' Hardy, a florist on the North Shore, I'm off on another curious whim."

"I knew you said Florist Gump, I thought my ears were playing tricks on me. Maybe we should come up with a name like that."

"I don't think so Signboy. People expect a certain amount of dignity when they entrust someone with their personal affairs," said Harlan, checking his pockets and scanning the surface of the desk for money. "Now, it's high time we broke into that petty cash box. I might need some cash to loosen the florist's lips."

*

The florist was in Mosman, on Military Road. It was one of the few streets north of the harbour Harlan could find without looking it up first. To get there from his office he had to drive across the Bridge, which he hated. It was much better to look at than drive across. He was always frightened the lights indicating the direction of each of the eight lanes of traffic would change, sending him hurtling into oncoming traffic without any warning. So when he came onto the bridge from the Western Distributor, he crossed two lanes of traffic to be in the far left lane, which he figured was the least likely to become southbound instantaneously, being four lanes of traffic away from the other southbound lanes. After crossing the Bridge safely, he then had to cross six lanes of traffic, because two lanes appear out of nowhere at some point, to be in the far right lane to turn right onto Falcon Street, which became Military Road.

After following Military Road further than he ever had before, to within about fifty metres of where a roundabout splits it unceremoniously into three different streets, Harlan spotted Floral 'n' Hardy in the middle of a row of neighbourhood shops. He'd never been to Mosman. Even at the height of the PaperWash success, his father had refused to move to the North Shore, preferring to join the ranks of the new elite overlooking a beach in the eastern suburbs. Still, Harlan assumed society operated here in a similar way to the parts of Sydney he was familiar with, so he didn't think twice about holding up traffic to perform a parallel park a couple of car spaces past the florist. By the time he had parked there were about four cars backed up, waiting for him to finish.

Hopping quickly out of his car, Harlan was able to take a good look at each of them, as they drove past deliberately slowly, taking a good look at him and his car as they did. He checked the parking signs to see if he had done something illegal, but it was a thirty minute parking spot at all times. Looking at the row of cars parked there to see if maybe he had got the angle wrong, Harlan realised what was going on. He had just parked a fifteen-year-old Mitsubishi outside the local shops in one of the richest suburbs in Australia. It didn't quite fit with the standard issue German luxury cars it was surrounded by. Harlan hoped he was dressed suitably to enter the florist.

The florist had a wide entrance, with flowers carefully arranged spreading out onto the footpath. Harlan was slightly disappointed they hadn't extended the theme beyond the quirky name. Not even a pair of bowler hats worked into the signage on the front window.

There was no other customer in the store, and Harlan spotted the solitary worker behind the counter at the back. She looked like she was probably the owner, maybe in her fifties, wearing a plain black apron and glasses that hung around her neck when she wasn't wearing them. She was wearing them at that moment, studying a sheet of paper Harlan guessed was the list of orders for delivery that day. He hoped he wouldn't be reduced to looking through the garbage for Tuesday's list, but he wasn't confident of getting information from the woman. She looked like a local.

"Can I help you dear?" she said, looking up and taking her glasses off, letting them hang down. She spoke like a local too.

"Hi, I hope so. I work for one of your clients, Jonathan Foxe?" he said, approaching the counter.

"Mister Foxe," she corrected him, as if he wasn't bred well enough to be familiar with the great man. "Really?" She put the piece of paper down and looked Harlan up and down.

"Yes, and ... " as he was about to ask for the information he was after, Harlan realised he wasn't going to get it from her. Luckily a much better idea appeared right at the front of his mind, where he had no chance of missing it. "He sent me here to arrange another flower order, same as last time."

"That's very generous of him. And what was the order?"

Harlan thought for a second. He felt he had to give the right answer or she would send him away.

"Well, he didn't tell me. He's a very private man, you know." He held his breath.

The woman slipped her glasses back on, pulled some loose sheets of A4 paper from beneath the register and leafed through the top couple of pages. She apparently found what she was looking for and looked over the top of the page and her glasses at Harlan.

"And when does he want this?"

"Oh, right away, he said it was very important."

"Well, it probably is. *He* is a very important man," she said, looking Harlan squarely in the eyes. The implication by omission was clear. "Our deliveries have all gone out for the day, but for Mister Foxe I can arrange a courier especially. Please tell him they will be delivered this afternoon."

"Great, thank you. I will," said a relieved Harlan. "Oh, can you give me the invoice?" He still didn't have any information.

"I'll send it directly to Mister Foxe, and put the flowers on his account." She took her glasses off again, and gave Harlan a very final looking stare. "He's a very private man, you know."

"Indeed." Harlan took a look around the store and made his way out. It looked to him like all the arranging and dispatching took place in a room through a door behind the counter. He doubted she would want her regular customers running into the likes of delivery men in her store.

He returned to his car, dodging a couple of condescending looks from locals as he unlocked it using a key and got in. He pulled the car out from the curb and took the next left, heading around to the back of the shopping strip. Sure enough, where he approximated was the back of the florist he saw a sign which said 'Floral 'n' Hardy Courier Entrance'. He parked about twenty metres further up the street and watched the back entrance in his rear view mirror. He hoped the woman wasn't bluffing about the courier. He couldn't wait to get back to familiar surroundings.

*

About an hour later, Harlan pulled up in a loading zone across from where the courier had parked in the city outside a large office building on one of the many one-way streets that criss-crossed the city. He hadn't been able to see the courier put the flowers in the van outside the florist, so he was relieved to see him open the back of the van and pull out a large wreath of white flowers. An odd choice for a mistress, Harlan thought. He got out of his car, decided he had to chance the parking ticket and timed his walk across the road perfectly to enter the building through its sliding doors just after the courier.

He followed the courier to the bank of elevators and waited with him. He tried to read the label on the flowers but it was impossible without being too obvious. A crowd of people had gathered by the time a lift opened, and Harlan had to sacrifice chivalry for a moment to make sure he got into the same lift as the flowers. Raising his eyes apologetically to the woman he had rudely not let into the lift in front of him despite the fact she was the last to arrive and he one of the first, he missed which button the courier pressed. He'd have to follow the courier out of the lift without being too obvious.

Because the lift was so crowded, Harlan had to step halfway out at each of the first few floors to let people out, almost getting caught between the doors each time he stepped back in. Finally Harlan noticed the courier pushing his way to the front of the elevator, and when the doors opened he confidently strode onto the floor and to his right. After a few steps he realised nobody was following him, so he did a graceful about-turn to see the flowers disappear around the corner at the far end of the floor. Harlan ran after them, slowing to a fast walk as he rounded the corner. He had entered the reception area of the Hope

Foundation, a well-known charity devoted to ending unnecessary deaths from preventable diseases, starvation and poverty in the developing world. Its logo was a wreath of white flowers, to emphasise the cost of not giving all you could. It had been a powerful motivator over the years and one of the few symbols of charity to endure in the face of the rising dominance of the Celebrities Care publicity machine.

Harlan was just in time to hear the courier announce to the receptionist, "Flowers for a Stephanie Clarkson". Harlan didn't immediately recognise the name, but it seemed familiar.

He continued to the waiting area and sat down, lifting a copy of the *Australian Financial Review* absurdly high in front of his face just in case the courier had noticed him downstairs or in the lift. He waited until he was sure the courier had long gone, then put the newspaper down. On the wall in front of him was a picture of a woman laying a Hope wreath on a symbolic grave at a fundraiser. The plaque underneath read 'Stephanie Clarkson, CEO, at the 2008 Hope Benefit at the Sydney Opera House'.

Harlan stood up and walked back past the quizzical-looking receptionist. "Wrong floor," he told her, theatrically shaking his head at his own stupidity, and rounded the corner into an empty elevator bank. Rubbish at detective work my foot, he thought, as he congratulated himself on breaking the case wide open.

CHAPTER 8

Harlan couldn't wait to share his discovery with Jenny. It didn't appear to have much of a connection to her investigation, but he couldn't wait to see her again. He easily convinced himself he should go directly to the café she worked at in Surry Hills and tell her what he'd found.

On the way, he called Signboy. He was using a handsfree kit that plugged into his phone, so according to the rule-makers this time he was giving the road sufficient attention while communicating with someone over the mobile network. He told Signboy about Jonathan sending the wreath to the CEO of the Hope Foundation.

"So she's his mistress? Makes sense I guess, same industry, they've got an excuse to be seen together."

"Quite the opposite, they're fierce rivals. And who would send a wreath to their mistress? No, that was a professional gesture. I want you to dig around, see why two rival charities might want to get into bed together, so to speak."

"Sure, I'll add it to the list."

"Put it at the top of the list, send me a message with something in the next half hour, I'm going to meet Jenny now."

"But isn't she working?"

"Yes, I'm going to her café."

"But as far as she knows, you're following Jonathan around all day."

"Ah." Harlan had forgotten in his excitement. "I'm sure I can explain it easily. I'll just tell her I saw him go into a movie marathon or something, so thought I'd use the time productively."

"No," said Signboy. "You're not going to tell her that."

"No, I'm not." Harlan was stuck for an idea. He was getting close to Jenny's café. In fact, he noticed her Golf parked on the side of the street. In between two other Golfs. "Golf, Golf, Golf ... Golf ... Golf," Harlan counted five Golfs on that block alone.

"Yep, that's better, go with that," Signboy thought Harlan was just thinking out loud. "I'll get you something on the Hope Foundation."

"What?" said Harlan, but Signboy had hung up. He wondered what he meant, but was interrupted when he had to slam his brakes on to avoid running into the back of yet another Golf. "Golf!" he yelled, coming up with the much better cover story Signboy had thought Harlan had already come up with when he hung up on him moments before.

Harlan found a park around the corner from the café. He went to the parking meter and put in the few coins he'd found in the aptly named petty cash box, which before it was broken into was worth a lot more than the loose change it yielded. Returning to put the parking voucher on display in his car, he noticed he already had a parking fine. He spun around in a full circle to see where the inspector was, but couldn't see one. Harlan would have left the scene in a hurry too if he'd pulled such a swifty on a perfect stranger.

He wondered what the law was - technically he had parked without paying, but there was no way to pay without parking first. He took the infringement notice out from under the windscreen wiper, disappointed with himself for getting caught on such a technicality. Maybe he should have double-parked, paid, then parked legally. Of course he didn't yet notice the fine was from outside the Hope Foundation half an hour earlier, where Harlan had committed a deliberate breach of the council by-laws and therefore was quite justifiably penalised.

He reclaimed the excitement that had caused him to miss the ticket in the first place and walked around the corner to see Jenny serving an outside table. She looked up at him. There was a smile in her eyes, but there was also a big question. Harlan sat at an empty table and perused the menu while he waited for her to arrive and ask the question, then hopefully smile the smile. He noticed out of the corner of his eye that she disappeared inside for a few seconds, then came out without her apron on. He focused on the menu. He didn't want her to think he had been watching her too closely.

"Hi Harlan, what's going on?" She was standing at his table with her hands on her hips. He looked up at her. It was clear the question had put the smile on the back burner for the moment.

"I have a minor break for you." The smile returned briefly, but was again pushed off her face by the question.

"Great - but why aren't you following Jonathan? We were going to catch up tonight, you could have told me then."

"He's at a corporate golf day - it was at a private course so I couldn't follow him in. I watched from my car to make sure he teed off and then thought I'd do something productive."

"A golf day - do they still do that? Wasn't that supposed to go out with the glass ceiling?"

"Yes, well, when they get rid of the glass ceiling, I'm sure it won't be too far behind. Although, women's golf is one of the fastest growing sports around at the moment."

"Don't they call it ladies' golf?"

"Maybe they do. It's definitely women's tennis though, isn't it?"

"Except at Wimbledon - that's ladies."

"Really? So they're women everywhere else and when they go to Wimbledon they're ladies? Maybe they have an irrational fear of alliteration at the All England Lawn Tennis and Croquet Club."

"Apparently not. Maybe they have an irrational fear of women. Anyway, I've only got five minutes, is your car here? We should go somewhere a bit more private to discuss this break of yours." Jenny leaned a bit closer. "We're talking about household names here, remember?" Now her face was a picture of very serious excitement, with no room for a smile to squeeze in. Harlan gave up on the smile for now and decided to work with the excitement.

"Yes, around the corner, follow me."

She did, and a few moments later they were once more sitting in Harlan's car.

"So, what's the big break?"

"It's actually thanks to you Jenny." Apparently he couldn't resist one more crack at a smile, and this time her face did indeed crack into one. Who would have thought some sincere flattery would do the trick? He enjoyed it for a full second. "Your doubts about Jonathan cheating on Marisa made me ask myself why I assumed he was. And the answer was I had just taken Marisa's word for it. So I called her and asked her why she was so sure. She said a friend had told her he had bought some flowers at their local florist, but Marisa never received them."

Harlan explained how he had gone to the florist and ended up at the Hope Foundation head office.

"So why is Jonathan cosying up to a rival charity?" asked Jenny.

As if on cue, Harlan's phone announced he had received a message with four exciting keyboard chords.

"Is that *Your Kiss Is On My List*?" asked Jenny.

"Wow, I'm impressed. I mean, it's just *Kiss On My List*, but the song recognition was the impressive part. You're a fan?"

"I love Hall & Oates. Well, I only know a few songs, but they're pretty big at the moment."

"What are you talking about? They were an eighties duo."

"It's true. Don't make me google it Harlan - I'll have to take you out sometime, I guarantee you'll hear them played." Harlan liked the suggestion, and the abundant smiles accompanying it. He resisted the temptation to ask why the current generation couldn't create enough good music of their own.

"Okay, well." He was a little lost for words as he pictured the two of them dancing to *Maneater*. "Anyway, I think that message will be from my assistant about the Hope Foundation." He opened the message which, as Harlan paradoxically had predicted after it arrived, was from Signboy and was indeed about the Hope Foundation.

"The Hope Foundation are having their 2010 Hope Benefit this Saturday night," Harlan paraphrased to Jenny.

"So what's that got to go with Jonathan Foxe?"

"I think I know. At that steakhouse yesterday I heard Mick Dawson threaten him about a benefit."

"So he wants his celebrities to get a piece of the exposure at the Hope Benefit. He wants Jonathan to get Celebrities Care included somehow. And Jonathan needs to keep Mick Dawson happy. Mick Dawson is his link to most of the celebrities that endorse Celebrities Care," said Jenny, an intensity building in her as she reasoned it through.

"Endorse?"

"Well, whatever you call it. Anyway Jonathan and Mick need each other because of Celebrities Care, but if another charity is getting big exposure, then Mick could just send his stable members there."

"Except no other charity is providing his business interests with free training and recruitment for call centres and the like in developing countries." Harlan was catching the bug now.

"Right," said Jenny. "So what gives Mick the upper hand in the relationship? You don't threaten an equal, do you?"

"I'm not sure that's a rule. But I agree, Mick Dawson has some kind of hold over Jonathan, beyond what we already know. I mean, there must be a lot of celebrities who aren't signed to Mick Dawson and would be happy to support Celebrities Care."

"Money?"

"It's usually money. I doubt Jonathan owes him any money though, the man's loaded."

"Well, we don't know much about that," countered Jenny. "I mean, I know his story, roughly, and he certainly lives a luxurious life. But he wasn't rich to begin with, and he's never been on any of the money lists."

"Sounds like a job for an investigative reporter to me," said Harlan.

"Or a detective?"

"I don't think so - detectives aren't much use if something isn't happening right at that moment. No, you need to do some backgrounding."

"Well, I'm sure I could use your help," smiled Jenny. Did she know that's all it would take? "Anyway, for now let's assume Mick has this hold over Jonathan, but we don't know what it is. We just know Jonathan has to get Celebrities Care involved in Saturday night's Hope Benefit. And Jonathan is sending Stephanie Clarkson the wreath, well wreaths, thanks to you, to what, bring her to the table? Sounds pretty desperate."

"It does," agreed Harlan. "But that's just because we don't know the full story. Maybe they've already met a few times and come to an arrangement - you said you hadn't been able to follow him the whole time. Maybe the wreath is a thank you, or just a sweetener."

"Well, if they have agreed anything, they'd want to announce it pretty soon. The Benefit is on in two days, and Jonathan's out playing golf? It doesn't quite add up."

"No, you're right." Harlan squirmed a little in his seat. Now he had a few lies going with Jenny, not the ideal basis for a romance. Traditional, but not ideal.

"Look, I've got a couple of hours left here - why don't you get your assistant to ring up the Hope Foundation, say she's a journalist ... "

"He."

"Oh, very progressive. I'm impressed."

"He's not a PA, he's an assistant in ... detection." Harlan caught himself just in time.

"Like an assistant detective? Not so progressive then. I wouldn't let him hear you calling him your assistant, he won't like it. Anyway, get him to call and tell them he's a journalist, and he's heard Celebrities Care might be involved in the Benefit somehow - they'll want to give him information if there is any because that would mean a story about the Benefit."

"Not a bad idea. Why shouldn't I just call?"

"Because you have to get back out to the golf course. If anything's happening it has to happen today, you can't rebrand an annual benefit in just one day. You need to be on Foxe's tail as soon as he signs his scorecard. I'll call you when I finish up here." Jenny opened the passenger door and slid out of the car - her adrenalin was pumping and Harlan found it inspiring.

"Excellent - I will speak to you then, then."

"Oh, and Harlan," said Jenny, leaning her head back into the car through the open door. "Thanks for coming to tell me. It shows you care. About the case." She was a little flustered. Harlan wasn't used to being on this side of awkwardness. "We might make a moral crusader of you after all."

"Absolutely," said Harlan, but it wasn't clear to either of them what he was referring to. Jenny smiled again and closed the door, heading back towards the café. Harlan let himself watch her go for just a few seconds, then pulled up that day's itinerary on his phone to see what Jonathan Foxe was actually up to. He sensed his loyalties were about to be tested - and that meant he would have to lie to Jonathan Foxe to protect Jenny. Then he would have some serious lies going with everyone involved in the case.

CHAPTER 9

The drive from Jenny's café in Surry Hills to the Celebrities Care head office in Alexandria took Harlan through fourteen sets of traffic lights over eleven kilometres. At one set of lights he had to stop twice because only a couple of cars went through before the green turned to orange again. It made for an interesting audio track at least. Harlan always adjusted the volume of both the stereo and his own singing in line with the speed he was driving. He loved travelling at high speed because the road and engine noise gave him the freedom to crank the stereo up and sing along at the top of his voice. At the other end of the speedometer he put the stereo close to mute and sang in barely a whisper because he didn't want to draw attention to himself when the car was crawling in traffic. With the volume low, though, he felt self-conscious about his mouth moving. He made sure to tap the steering wheel and nod his head so anyone who saw him would know he was singing along to music, which is socially acceptable, and not think he was talking to himself, which isn't. Of course he could just be disguising talking to himself by nodding his head and tapping the steering wheel, but he doubted many people would think that critically when they saw him.

When he finally pulled up outside the office, he wondered not for the first time if there was a stereo that linked somehow to the car's speedometer so he wouldn't have to drive with one hand on the volume knob so often - particularly if traffic was only going to get worse with time, which was the general consensus.

Harlan's next and infinitely more pertinent thought was about where the black Mercedes-Benz was. More specifically, he wondered why the black Mercedes Benz wasn't there. According to the itinerary, Jonathan would be in the office from two till three, which meant the Mercedes-Benz should be parked in one of the vacant car parks outside the entrance to the building. Harlan smelled a figurative rat. The itinerary had been spot on every other time he had relied on it. It was possible the driver and/or Biff could have taken the car out for a while, but so far they had only done that when Jonathan was at lunch, so they too could grab lunch. Still, there was twenty minutes before Jonathan was due to leave, so Harlan decided to walk around the block to see if the car was lurking nearby.

On the opposite side of the block to where the Celebrities Care office was Harlan came across a gadget store. What caught his eye was the claim that came third on the list of gadget categories painted on the glass door. *PI/Detective/Spy Equipment*. Checking his watch, Harlan decided he could spare five minutes to see what kind of equipment a real detective might have in their arsenal.

Pushing the door open, Harlan stepped into a bizarre cross between a toy store, a camera store and a place where pimps came to outfit their cars and bedrooms. The room was small, about the size of the inside of a shipping container, with a glass counter along the back wall, facing the door Harlan had just come through. The other sides were all floor to ceiling glass cabinets, breaking only for the front door, filled with an impressive array of items for sale. What he'd say were toys dominated the left hand side of the shop - figurines of cult television and movie characters that spoke at the push of a button, a retro-styled lolly machine, hand-held computer games and a variety of other electronics aimed at grown men with a nostalgic nerve connected to their wallet. The pimp section dominated the right - disco lights, strobe balls, lava lamps and laser displays. Just about anything that could set the mood in the backseat of your Holden Commodore or the corner of your parents' basement.

The glass counter housed the items Harlan assumed were indicated by the 'PI/Detective/Spy Equipment' description on the door, containing dozens of items from pen and tie cameras to hi-tech listening equipment and bug detectors. As Harlan stepped forward to the counter to see what he might be able to use, a man appeared through a door in the corner of the shop. Harlan guessed the guy was the owner, but if he wasn't, he would definitely use his staff discount on items from the left-hand side of the store. He looked normal enough, but the nervous energy he emitted when he saw Harlan would have been enough to power an XBox and a Playstation for a week, which would have suited him perfectly if a machine existed that could harness nervous energy. Plus he was wearing a *Star Trek* T-shirt.

"Hello?" he asked.

"Hi, just saw your shop and came in to look at the detective equipment. I think listening devices are what I'm after."

"They're all here under the counter. Are you looking for bugs or high-powered listening devices?"

"What's the difference?"

"A bug you put somewhere, and it can either record or transmit what it hears. A listening device you operate to hear something up to a few hundred yards away. It's like a satellite dish for conversation." The man pointed at what looked like a hand-held satellite dish with some chunky headphones attached to it by a cord.

"Looks a bit serious. Let's see the bugs."

The man stepped sideways and cleared a couple of comic books off the glass counter to reveal a series of innocuous looking black plastic boxes, ranging in size from a matchbox to a smartphone, arranged beneath the glass.

"Two types - one is like a one-way mobile phone. You put a SIM card in it, charge it up, leave it somewhere. You can dial in from anywhere in the world and hear what comes through its microphone. The more you pay, the better the microphone and battery life. The other type is like a reverse radio. You charge it up, it soaks in the sound around it and broadcasts it over a radio frequency. You need to be in the vicinity, or have a receiver in the vicinity, to hear it. Both kinds you can also put a recorder inside, but that adds to cost and size."

"Wow. So how much will one set me back?"

"Anything from fifty to four-hundred bucks. If you actually want to rely on it at some point, it's worth making the investment. You don't want the battery to run out when you need it, and you don't want to miss a conversation because you skimped on the microphone."

"Of course. Well, I don't need the recording function - if I get one with a SIM card I can record it at my end. So what's the best SIM card based bug without a recorder?"

"That would be this one." He opened the cabinet from behind and reached under the glass counter to grab a black box roughly half the size of Harlan's smartphone. "The Bugboy 300. You'll get three-hundred minutes of talk-time, and an amazing one-hundred-and-twenty hours standby. That's because it is virtually turned off until you call it. It's got the best microphone out of any of them, and is completely silent."

Harlan was impressed at the man's ability to reel off so many features without the slightest hint of enthusiasm, although somehow he felt he was still being challenged to pick a better one. He was tempted to try, but the clock was ticking. In fact, every sufficiently powered mechanical clock in the world was ticking.

"What's the absolute best price you can do on that?"

"My best price? Hmm ... Retail's two-hundred-and-fifty dollars. I couldn't do it for any less than two-twenty, that's more than ten per cent off."

"I'll give you two-hundred."

"Done," the man said so quickly Harlan strongly suspected he'd paid over the odds. He reluctantly handed over his credit card for payment. The deal was done, there was no honour in reopening the negotiation. He managed to put his buyer's remorse behind him during the payment process so when he took the packaged Bugboy 300 he thanked the man profusely and promised he'd be back as he walked out of the store.

Checking his watch again he saw it was two-fifty-five. He rushed back around the block to find two things lingering. First, the palpable absence of Jonathan's vehicle. Second, the figurative stench of rodent. Jonathan had to be somewhere else. It was the only fact capable of explaining both phenomena.

He got into his car, putting his new purchase in the glovebox. He thought about calling Biff. He had his number, and he was sure Biff would love to hear from him. Biff would certainly know where Jonathan was. But then Harlan would have to have some explanation handy as to why he didn't know where Jonathan was already. That wasn't necessarily difficult since Jenny hadn't been following him around all day, but he didn't want to arouse Biff's suspicions, and he figured it didn't take much to do so.

The impressively rich melody of his smartphone's ringtone filled the car. Given the situation, Harlan only allowed himself two bars of the deep studio sound that was apparently so popular right now before he answered.

"Harlan, quick, are you near a TV?" It was Signboy.

"I'm trying to find Jonathan Foxe right now, can this wait?"

"Well, I'm looking at Jonathan Foxe right now. Are you near a TV?"

Harlan looked around in his car unnecessarily, then looked at the buildings around him and noticed a Harvey Norman megastore on the next block. Thanks to the Celebrities Care Foundation taking the cheap rent option out of the CBD and in the middle of central Sydney's warehouse and homewares shopping district, he was near about a thousand TVs.

"I can be, what is it?"

"Put it on the news channel if you can - you've gotta see this press conference."

"Right, I'll do my best. I'll call you afterwards. Actually, Signboy?"

"Yes?"

"Jenny suggested you call up the Hope Foundation and tell them you heard Celebrities Care might be involved in their Benefit. Tell them you're a journalist."

"They'd think I was the worst journalist in the world."

"Why?"

"Just get to a TV!"

"Okay, okay. And you call the Hope Foundation."

"Sure, whatever," said Signboy, who then ended the call.

Harlan got out of his car and sprinted along the street towards the Harvey Norman. Running through the double sliding doors, he headed to the back of the store where an impressive bank of televisions showed the latest Disney animation to hit DVD.

"Excuse me," he said to a staff member walking purposefully past him.

"Hi, do you need a hand?" He was a teenager, obviously an expert in his field.

"Yes, I was wondering if you could switch a TV onto Sky News for me?"

"Ha. Are you going to buy one?"

"Well, if I had the time I would have pretended to want to buy one and then somehow got you to show me how Sky News looked on it, but I'm in a bit of a hurry. So I have to just ask you for a favour."

The boy looked around. There was nobody else in the TV section.

"Sure, why not. Beats rearranging the small appliances." He walked up to the bank of TVs and reached behind one of them, pulling out a remote control. He pressed a couple of buttons and the TV in front of him now displayed a game of cricket, surrounded by animated monsters. "What number is it?"

"Um, six hundred and one, I think," said Harlan. He knew with absolute certainty, but people are rarely proud of recalling three digit channel numbers, particularly for the news channels.

"Okayyy," the boy said, giving him a strange look that meant if Harlan was ever in this situation again, which wasn't very likely, he would pretend to have no idea what number channel he was after.

The screen went from the cricket match to a press conference, as Harlan had hoped. Jonathan Foxe sat behind a table covered in microphones, and alongside him was Stephanie Clarkson. Behind them was a large banner that read "The Hope Celebrities Care Benefit 2010". Hanging on the front of the table were two wreaths of white flowers either side of the Celebrities Care logo of "Celebrities Care" written out like an autograph, the two words on top of each other, with two Xs after "Care". Harlan thought the two wreaths looked good - much better than one.

"Can we get some volume please?" Jonathan Foxe was speaking and Harlan couldn't lipread. He needed to hear it to know what was being said.

The boy turned the volume up on the monitor, so Harlan had to get close to distinguish the sound of the press conference from the sound of the intergalactic war happening on every other screen.

" ... and we think combining the profile of Celebrities Care with the great tradition of the annual Hope Benefit will really benefit the Hope Foundation and, I hope, Celebrities Care."

"And, of course," said Stephanie Clarkson, "the millions of unfortunate, disadvantaged and often forgotten people of the third world, who are the reason and the inspiration for everything we do at the Hope Foundation, and, I'm sure, Celebrities Care."

"And to demonstrate just a small part of what Celebrities Care is bringing to this partnership, one of our celebrities has come along today to announce something very exciting about the inaugural Hope Celebrities Care Benefit. Would you please welcome Andrea Stacy."

The room burst with camera flashes as the Australian soap star and fledgling Hollywood actress joined the table. The boy next to Harlan suddenly seemed more interested in the press conference and less interested in the battle for the universe taking place around it.

"Thank you," she said, but Harlan couldn't figure out why. Maybe she thought that's what applause sounded like. He doubted she'd done her time in theatre. She began reading from a piece of paper on the table in front of her.

"First I'd like to say how excited I am that the Hope Foundation has asked us to be part of their annual benefit, which raises vital funds for the most desperate people on our planet. And when I told my good friend Christian Dieter," she paused long enough for Harlan to place the name as the young Hollywood heartthrob *du jour*, "that I had to fly home from the set of our new film, *Camp Vamp*, to take part in the first annual Hope Celebrities Care Benefit, he was excited too. So excited that he's going to join us at the State Theatre on Saturday night. Along with all of your favourite celebrities who care. It's going to be the most amazing gala event ever. And that's why, also for the first time, the Hope Celebrities Care Benefit will be broadcast live on TV here in Australia, and replayed the same day in the United States."

The starlet handed back to Jonathan, who reeled off a very impressive list of celebrities who would appear and/or perform at the Benefit. When they began to field questions, it was soon very clear most questions were directed at Andrea Stacy about her new film. "Okay, you can turn it back to the kid's movie now," Harlan said to the boy.

"That's cool, I could watch her all day."

"Excellent. Well, that's what she's there for." Harlan took one last look at the screen to see Mick Dawson appear behind Andrea Stacy to declare there'd be one last question for her, then he headed toward the door. As he stepped onto the footpath he looked up and down the street dramatically, as though he expected reporters to appear and ask him what he thought of the big news. When none did, he returned to his car. It was still over an hour before Jenny finished her shift. He wondered how he would explain Jonathan getting from the golf course to the press conference so quickly. Nine holes, too easy. He got out his phone to call Signboy. Hopefully he would know where the press conference was held.

"Hope Foundation," was the unusual choice of words Signboy used to answer the phone.

"What?"

"It was at the Hope Foundation's head office - you're calling about where the press conference was right?"

"Yes, thanks. What are you up to? You didn't call the Hope Foundation, did you? I see what you meant on that one, you would have seemed quite foolish."

"No Harlan, I'm not an idiot. I've just been digging into the financial world of Mick Dawson all day. It's pretty interesting."

"Excellent. Can you put that on hold and meet me at the Hope Foundation as soon as possible? I think we need more than one of us this afternoon. We've just been given a new deadline."

"This would be for the unpaid work of helping Jenny bring down potentially our most lucrative clients ever?"

"Precisely."

"Excellent. I'll be there soon - I can't hear a train so I haven't missed it." Harlan heard Signboy already running down the stairs as he ended the call. He should have made him Assistant Indetective years ago.

CHAPTER 10

Traffic was much lighter heading back into the city, and it took Harlan just twenty minutes to arrive outside the building that housed the Hope Foundation office. He slowed as he passed, noticing a few photographers waiting outside the entrance. He hadn't missed anyone leaving then, it was unlikely Jonathan or Mick Dawson would leave before Andrea Stacy.

After an unsuccessful loop of the block looking for a park, Harlan settled for the same illegal park he had used that morning. As he pulled into the loading zone he finally made the connection that this was most likely where he'd received the parking fine. Confirming the time and place on the infringement notice, he was relieved he hadn't been as harshly prosecuted as he'd thought at Jenny's café, but was still convinced he had identified a dangerous trap for the unwary. "Double-park, pay, park," he said to himself a couple of times, a mantra he hoped he'd remember the next time he parked legally.

As he was checking the photographers were still there, his passenger door opened and Signboy jumped in.

"How long have you been here?" asked Harlan.

"Just a few minutes. You haven't missed anything, I asked one of the photographers who they were waiting for, and they said they'd been told Andrea Stacy would be leaving at about three-forty-five."

"Good thinking. Okay, so we've got Jonathan Foxe and Mick Dawson in the building. Now the deal's been done, Jonathan can let the Celebrities Care staffers take care of the details. I think he and Mick Dawson will go to some kind of celebratory drink or late lunch or early dinner, together. It might be our best opportunity to learn more about the extent of their interlaced business interests."

Across the road there was some excitement building among the photographers. A limousine pulled up at the curb, and a few seconds later Andrea Stacy came out of the sliding doors marking the entrance to the building, flanked by Mick Dawson on one side and Biff on the other. "Just who do you work for Biff?" Harlan wondered aloud.

Andrea Stacy posed for a few photos before Biff opened the rear door of the limousine. The actress got in, followed by her agent. Biff closed the door then let himself into the front passenger seat of the vehicle, which seemed to pose for a few photos itself before it pulled away from the snapping photographers. There was no sign of Jonathan Foxe.

"What do we do?" asked Signboy.

Harlan made a snap decision as he thought Jenny would in that situation.

"We follow them."

*

There are few vehicles easier or more annoying to follow than a limousine. It's bigger than any other car, it moves slowly so the occupants don't spill their *Champagne*, and the people inside it are so self-absorbed they would never notice the same car behind them no matter how long or convoluted the journey. While they leisurely trailed the limousine through the city streets, Harlan had an idea.

"Signboy," he said ominously.

"Harlan," Signboy mimicked.

"Do you remember how we met?"

"Of course. You caught me picking your pocket, I told you a heartbreaking story of neglect and you offered me a job."

"Right. Well, I'm sure there's a better name for it, but do you think you could reverse pickpocket someone?"

"You mean drop something in someone's pocket without them noticing? It's called a Schapelle Corby. I could probably do it, but I don't know if I'd get away with it. With pickpocketing, you only need a few seconds to get away - the person usually notices before too long, but not before a good street kid has time to take the cash out of the wallet and drop it in the nearest bin."

"Ah, so you think if you slipped something into someone's pocket they would discover it sooner."

"Depends what it is. I reckon I could drop some lint in someone's pocket and they'd never know. Or with you, some biscuit crumbs or something like that, you'd never know. With Schapelle Corby, it was a few kilos of marijuana in her boogie board bag. I guess it helps if it's something the person would normally be carrying anyway."

"No doubt. What about an innocuous-looking black plastic box about half the size of an iPhone?"

"What are you talking about?"

"Open the glovebox."

Signboy opened the glovebox and pulled out the Bugboy 300 still in its packaging

"Bugboy 300? Where'd you get this?"

"I chanced upon a detective supply store near the Celebrities Care office. Open it up, let's see what we've got."

Signboy opened the box and pulled out a plastic tray containing the Bugboy 300, a battery, and a charger.

"We probably need to charge it first," said Signboy.

"There's a car power cord for my Discman in the centre console, see if that fits it."

"Discman. That is so nineties." Harlan refrained from pointing out the first Discman was released in 1984. It seemed irrelevant in the digital age, and would only serve to reinforce Signboy's point, unless he just had a particular grievance with the last decade of the twentieth century.

As Signboy pulled the car charger out of the console, Harlan swore.

"What is it?" Signboy asked, noticing they had pulled over.

"They pulled into that hotel entrance."

They watched as the limousine came to a stop and a man dressed ridiculously in an old-fashioned porter's costume stepped up to the vehicle and opened the passenger door. Andrea Stacy stepped out on her own, and the porter escorted her through the revolving door and into the hotel. The limousine pulled slowly away and back out onto the street in front of Harlan's car.

"Perfect, he must be going to meet Jonathan now," said Harlan. "Quick, plug it in, we don't have much time to charge it."

Fortunately the cord fit the Bugboy 300 battery charger. Signboy unwrapped the battery from a delicate foam bag and slid it into the charger. The charge light came on.

"Okay, what else do we need?" asked Harlan.

Signboy read the back of the box. "A SIM card. Do you have a spare SIM card lying around?"

"No. Do you?"

"Of course not."

"This is important Signboy - you've got your phone on you don't you?"

"So do you!"

"I'll get you a new one."

"That hardly makes up for the inconvenience of a new phone number. You should get me a new phone, at least that way I'd be getting something out of it. One of those smartphones you're always banging on about."

Harlan thought about it. If Signboy was going to be a full-time assistant indetective, he would need a smartphone anyway.

"All right. I'll get you a smartphone."

"Sweet. All right, let's get this thing working." Signboy took his phone out, turned it over, removed the back panel, removed the battery and slid out his SIM card as though he'd done it a thousand times before.

"I've never even seen my SIM card," said Harlan.

Signboy ignored him as he took the Bugboy 300 out of its delicate foam bag and turned it around in his hand. He then removed a sliding panel to reveal a compartment for the battery and a SIM card slot. He inserted the SIM card, then lay the Bugboy 300 and its panel in his lap, next to the charging battery. Then, as if remembering something important, he took a pack of chewing gum out of his pocket and squeezed two pellets into his mouth.

"Ready to roll."

"Good," said Harlan. "Normally, I'd like to test it, but I think we should devote all the available time to charging it."

"Normally? So most times you're about to slip a brand new bug into someone's pocket, you give it a test call to see it's working do you?"

"No, I meant in normal circumstances. That's why I said 'normally' instead of 'usually'."

"So I should have just mocked the possibility of us ever preparing a new bug for use in 'normal circumstances'. Well, just pretend I did that instead."

"Fine. Point taken."

Harlan had followed the limousine down Macquarie Street towards Circular Quay, only briefly wondering what was even slightly round about it as they took the last turnoff to the left before the street ran down the remarkably straight Eastern side of the quay towards the Opera House.

"Okay, I think we'll be there shortly, not many places left in this direction," said Harlan, following the limousine around a right turn onto Phillip Street and downhill in the direction of the harbour, stopping directly behind their quarry at a red light.

"Let's hope it had some charge in it to start with then," said Signboy as he deftly took the battery out of the charger, pushed it into its compartment, slid the panel back into place and held up the Bugboy 300 for them both to marvel at.

Looking around, Harlan realised where Mick Dawson was headed.

"Quick, cut across this forecourt, they'll pull over around the other side and Mick Dawson will get out, cross the street and head into Customs House. That's your chance."

Signboy undid his seatbelt and jumped out of the car just as the light turned green. Harlan followed the limousine slowly around the forecourt, watching Signboy out of the corner of his eye as he kept pace, striding past the flowerbeds seemingly designed to convey important navigational information to passing helicopters. The limousine completed the circuit of the forecourt and pulled into a parking bay as Harlan had predicted, this time in the traditional way before it had happened. He drove past and parked at the front of the parking bay, about three cars up from the limousine.

Harlan watched in his mirror as Biff let Mick Dawson out of the back of the limousine. Mick Dawson carried a black leather satchel bulging with pockets on either side. Signboy reached the pair and was able to place himself on the same side of Mick Dawson as the satchel as they crossed the road. Sloppy work, Biff.

The three disappeared around the corner of Customs House. A nervous minute passed, during which the limousine departed, before Harlan saw Signboy running around from the back of Customs House, having continued around the magnificent sandstone building. He had a bloody nose and a torn shirt but was grinning like a maniac as he ran across the street and got back into Harlan's car.

"What the hell happened?"

"That was awesome," said Signboy, catching his breath.

"What happened to you? Did you plant the bug?"

"Hell yes! I Corby'd 'em like no-one's ever been Corby'd before. Except maybe Corby."

"So what happened to your face? And your shirt?"

"Well, it could have gone smoother."

"So they saw you."

"You could say that. I stole his bag, and the bodyguard chased me down, threw me to the ground, and took it back."

"So how did you plant the bug?"

"In the bag! Keep up. I couldn't get to his pockets because of the bag, and all the bag's pockets were zipped up, so I just grabbed it and started sprinting. As I ran I slipped the bug into the zipped compartment on the flap."

"So as soon as they check the flap, they'll find the bug?"

"Why would they check the flap? When Frankenstein caught me, I'd closed the zip, the flap was open, the main bag was unzipped and I had his laptop half out."

"Biff - let's call him Biff, one insulting nickname is enough for that idiot."

"Whatever, Biff. Anyway, it's in the flap, and I put some chewing gum on it to stop it jiggling around. It was the best I could do and I think it was pretty good. What kind of man uses the outside zip on the flap anyway?"

"Yes, good point. And good use of chewing gum. Saves lives every day. We'll see if it does the trick here. Worst case scenario is we've wasted two-hundred dollars, a SIM card, and you've blown your cover for nothing. Now, any sign of Jonathan Foxe?"

"Wait, that thing cost two-hundred dollars? You got taken. I bet I could find one for less than a hundred online."

"Well it was a spur of the moment thing. Besides, if I had bought it online we wouldn't have had it yet, would we?"

"Depends when you bought it. Still, you could have bargained."

"I did, he wanted two-fifty for it. Anyway, I don't want to get into a thing about it," said Harlan a little belatedly. "Did you see Jonathan Foxe?"

"No, no sign of him."

"We'll just have to assume he's there for now. Who else would Mick Dawson be meeting at Cafe Sydney at four in the afternoon after cracking such a big deal?"

They were interrupted by a tap on the passenger window. A man in a fluorescent yellow vest and a utility belt that would give Batman pouch envy stood by the car, pointing at the parking sign at the end of the bay. "Drop-off only mate," the complete stranger called through the closed window.

"What a fuckwit, we've only been here a couple of minutes," said Signboy. Harlan started the engine and flicked his indicator on.

"Come on, I've already got one fine today."

"You on a commission or something you prick?" yelled Signboy as Harlan pulled out of the parking bay. The parking inspector had already turned away, revealing the odd phrase emblazoned across the back of the vest, "CITY RANGER".

"So that's what redheads do."

"What?"

"City ranger," said Signboy, making 'ranger' sound like the derogatory colloquial epithet for red-haired people.

"It's ranger, soft 'g'. Like bushranger."

"I know, it's just a joke."

"A racist joke."

"Racist? It's not racist, there's no such thing as a redheaded race."

"Well, what is it? Making fun of someone based on their genetic make-up. Genetic discrimination I guess. It's essentially the same thing."

Signboy went quiet for a few seconds.

"I never thought of it like that."

"What does 'ranger' even mean?"

"It's really 'ranga', with an 'a'. I think it's short for orangutang, cos they have red hair too."

"Well, I think you should stick to insulting them because of their job choice, not for the colour of their hair."

"He didn't even have red hair. Besides, it can't be that big of an issue, the Prime Minister's one, isn't she?"

"You're right. That means there's no discrimination against them in the whole country. Just look at the USA."

"Well, *that's* racist."

Harlan shook his head, letting Signboy have the final word for once as he pulled into a legal parking space a couple of blocks away. He pulled out his phone and brought up Signboy's number.

"Okay, let's see how you did."

"What do you mean? I did great. If that overpriced Bugboy thing doesn't work, it's not my fault."

"Fine, let's see how this Bugboy thing does."

He pressed call, then speaker, and placed the phone on the console between them where they could both hear the ringing sound clearly. For a second Harlan paranoically imagined Mick Dawson searching his bag for the source of a mysterious outburst of Hall & Oates music. Then the ringing sound stopped.

" ... was great. They bloody loved her. It's practically a CC benefit now." It was Mick Dawson's Aussie drawl, muffled somewhat but clear enough to convey he'd had his fair share of *Champagne* in the limousine and was probably adding to it already in the restaurant.

"Don't talk like that Mick - Stephanie was hard enough to get across the line in the first place, if she feels we're taking over I'm sure it will be a one-off." That was Jonathan Foxe.

"If it's a one-off she's after, I'd gladly give it to her," said the vulgar businessman. "Whaddaya reckon Jonno, you think she'd mind if I slipped her the old Micky?"

"Watch it Mick, here she comes."

Harlan hung up.

"What's wrong?"

"We have to conserve the battery, remember? They're not going to say anything we want to hear while Stephanie Clarkson's there. She must be joining them for a late lunch to toast the deal. I doubt she'd want to spend much more time with them than she has to, especially if they're getting more drunk than they already are. Let's give it an hour or so and try again."

"So we've got a spare hour do we?" said Signboy, holding up his SIM card-less mobile phone.

"Look in the mirror, no-one's going to sell you a phone looking like that."

"Oh, yeah, forgot about that." Signboy rubbed his nose. "It's fine, I'll wash up at a pub or something, and we can duck into Lowes and grab a cheap shirt to replace this one."

"Alright then, we have to be quick though."

"Harlan, please. How long could it possibly take to wash my face, buy a new shirt and get a new phone?"

CHAPTER 11

"I'd like to get an iPhone, please."

They were in a mobile phone shop on George Street, a few blocks west from where they'd parked. Signboy had been incredibly quick cleaning up, using the bathroom in a McDonald's to wash his face and then purchasing the first flannelette shirt he tried on in Lowes. Then he had led Harlan into the mobile phone shop, walked up to the first available salesperson, and told him he'd like to get an iPhone, please. This was the guy criticising Harlan's bargaining technique.

As if reading his mind, Signboy turned around and almost whispered to Harlan, "All the pricing's set, these people can't do deals or anything. I might get them to throw in a couple of 'accessories' at best."

"An iPhone, good choice," said the salesman, as if it was only the most astute customers who would pick out the iPhone. They followed the salesman to the back wall, where the full range of exactly one model of iPhone was displayed. The salesman took the iPhone off the wall and handed it to Signboy, who had to step closer so the antitheft leash could reach his hand. Signboy made a few gestures with his fingers on the screen.

"The iPhone 4, the newest iPhone. Up to 32gig memory, five megapixel camera, HD video camera and a built in e-reader."

"It doesn't work," said Signboy, prodding at the screen. The salesman laughed.

"That's just the display model mate. So you can feel it in your hand."

"Okay. Well it feels great. But I'd like to have a play with one that works."

"Have you used one before?"

"Yeah, I know a few people who love showing them off," he said, nodding over his shoulder at Harlan.

"Excellent, you will too once you've got one. I'll get one out for you. What model are you after?"

"This one," said Signboy, after pointlessly scanning the wall for alternatives.

"16gig or 32gig?"

"Ah. Well what's the price difference?"

"Depends on the plan. You pay a different monthly handset cost depending on the model, and the plan." The salesman pulled a leaflet from a dispenser on the wall, unfolding it for Signboy to see.

The leaflet displayed all the plans for each model of iPhone. There were seven different plans laid out, with the monthly plan cost and monthly phone cost set out for each model under each plan. The salesman folded the leaflet closed after about three seconds and made to put it back, but Harlan reached around Signboy and took the leaflet, opening it again to try to make sense of the matrix within.

"How much do you use your phone?" the salesman asked Signboy.

"Um, average I guess."

"And what are you paying now?"

"I've got a prepaid."

"Excellent. What do you reckon you spend on that every month?"

"About fifty bucks, give or take."

"Then I'd recommend the $59 cap plan. It's got over five-hundred bucks of calls per month, unlimited text and 2gig of downloads."

"Of course you would. But I only spend fifty bucks now."

The salesman smiled at Signboy like he was about to do him a monumental favour.

"Mate," he said. "If you get a prepaid iPhone, let's say the 32gig model, it'd cost you a thousand bucks." He opened a draw at the bottom of the display and pulled out a brand new 32 gigabyte iPhone 4, still in its box, giving it to Signboy to hold. Then he pulled a calculator with an oversized display out of his pocket and faced it towards Signboy, pressing its buttons as he continued to talk.

"If you pay that off over two years it comes out to forty-one-sixty-six a month. And that's before you've even made a call." The calculator agreed, with a few additional sixes on the end that might have been useful if they were pricing up the phone in Zimbabwean dollars, but they weren't even using those in Zimbabwe anymore.

"On the $59 cap plan you pay an extra ten bucks a month for the 32gig model, that's only two-forty, saving you seven-sixty on the handset alone." This time the calculator agreed exactly.

"And you get five-fifty bucks of calls a month, saving you an amazing eleven-thousand, seven-hundred and eighty-four bucks in calls, with the handset savings of seven-sixty, that's a total of twelve-thousand, five-hundred and forty-three bucks you save in two years and that's before you look at the unlimited text and 2gig a month of downloads."

"Wow," said Signboy, reading the calculator's display. "How often do you practice using a calculator upside down?"

"Sorry?"

"Oh, nothing. Well, that's all pretty impressive. Harlan, what do you think?"

"Hmm? Oh, right," said Harlan, looking up from the leaflet. "Now, all you have is cap plans, is that right?"

"Yep."

"And you set the call rates, right? I mean, there's no industry standard or anything?"

"Sorry?"

"Not your fault. You see, you're just telling us it's five-hundred and fifty dollars worth of calls. If you halved your call rates, it would be two-hundred and seventy-five, and so on."

"I guess so, but those are our standard rates."

"Yes, but if all your customers are on a cap, and you can afford to sell five-hundred and fifty dollars worth of calls for only fifty-nine dollars, not to mention the thousand-dollar phone for two-hundred and forty dollars, then aren't the call rates complete bullshit?"

The salesman stood still, staring at Harlan.

"Alright Harlan, you've made your point," Signboy jumped in. "Are we getting the phone or not? We don't have all day remember."

"Yes, yes, we're getting the phone. You know that's better than mine don't you? Yours is a 4, mine's just a 3."

"Is it? Excellent."

The salesman, still recovering from a serious shock to his belief system, realised he'd made a sale.

"Excellent stuff. Is that in your name?" he said to Harlan. He had repressed a memory in record time.

"Yes, unfortunately." Harlan looked at Signboy, sizing up the risk he'd just taken on.

"Okay, I just need a few deets from you, then a quick credit check over the phone and we can sign you up."

"You need to check my credit to give me over twelve and a half thousand dollars?" Harlan followed the man to a desk in the corner of the store with a computer somehow built into it. The salesman ignored his comment and sat excitedly at the keyboard. A few minutes later, Harlan had given the salesman just about all the personal details he could think of, spoken to a complete stranger (maybe a graduate of a Celebrities Care training centre) about his personal finances, and signed a twenty-four month contract without reading a single word of it.

"Thanks very much, enjoy your new phone," the salesman said as he led them to the entrance, with Signboy already signed into Facebook on his new smartphone. "Your first bill should arrive in the mail in the next week or so."

"I'm sure it will," said Harlan, convinced he had signed up to something more than a sixty-nine dollar per month commitment for two years.

They hurried back to the car. The city was now teeming with people leaving work for the day, and Harlan figured that Stephanie Clarkson would be on a similar timetable. There was no point calling the Bugboy 300 with all the people around, he wouldn't hear a thing. Also he was expecting Jenny to call when she finished her shift at five o'clock and didn't want to take her call walking on the street. The car was the appropriate place for personal calls.

"You didn't get him to throw in any extras," he said to Signboy as they approached the car.

"You're the one who bought the phone." Signboy having the last word was becoming routine.

*

Jenny called on the stroke of five o'clock, just a few seconds after Harlan and Signboy had gotten back in the car. Harlan was surprised to see Signboy nodding his head to his ringtone, but hurried to answer the call without raising the point.

"Jenny," he answered, a hint of urgency in his voice.

"Harlan, what's happening?" More than a hint.

"Jonathan's at Cafe Sydney with Mick Dawson. We tailed Mick there and managed to plant a bug on him before he went into the restaurant. Now we're sitting in my car on Young Street, getting ready to listen in on the action."

"A bug - wow Harlan, great stuff. I've got to hear this. I'll be there in five minutes. Wait, who's 'we'?"

"My assistant and I."

"Oh, okay, I look forward to meeting him. See you shortly."

After making sure she'd hung up, Harlan smugly told Signboy she sounded impressed about the bug.

"Great, she'll be looking forward to meeting me then, seeing as how I was the one who planted it."

"That's what she said."

"What? That doesn't make sense. And since when did you start making 'that's what she said' jokes?"

"That wasn't a joke. That's what she said, she was looking forward to meeting you."

"Oh, right. You should warn me next time, it's not a phrase you can just throw around."

Harlan wondered what he'd done wrong, just as Signboy realised he'd done something else wrong.

"Hey, what do you mean 'my assistant and I'?"

Harlan remembered Jenny warning him about this, but following in the strict traditions of any warning-giver she hadn't given him any tips on what to do if he didn't heed the warning.

"What do you think I mean?"

"I'm not your assistant, I'm an assistant indetective."

"What's the difference?"

"There's a big difference."

"I mean, what's the nature of the difference?"

"One means I just help you out, the other means I'm an indetective in my own right, just an assistant one."

"What do you think makes you an assistant indetective then, as opposed to an indetective?"

"Well it's just a progression isn't it? A career path."

"Then I think we've given you an inappropriate title. I mean, you wouldn't say a dental assistant is on the way to becoming a dentist, would you?"

"Hmm, so what should it be then?"

"You come up with something, you're the one who doesn't want to be called 'assistant'."

"What about 'Junior Indetective'? I am pretty young after all."

"Fine, you're a junior indetective, congratulations. Second promotion in as many days," said Harlan, glad to be done with the conversation.

Signboy pulled out his new phone and started playing with it.

"What are you doing?" asked Harlan.

"Changing my email signature, my Facebook status, tweeting and messaging my Mum."

"Right. So does this mean I can tell people that you're my junior?"

"No."

Harlan noticed Stephanie Clarkson walking up the footpath towards them.

"Oh shit, the bug." They had forgotten to check in with the bug because of all the enterprise bargaining going on. Harlan picked up his phone and dialled Signboy's old number, which of course was now the Bugboy 300. Again he put it on speaker and placed it on the centre console. After a few seconds, an engaged signal filled the cabin. Harlan and Signboy looked at each other in befuddlement. They were distracted from their mutual discombobulation by the rear door opening behind Signboy, and Jenny jumping into the backseat.

"What's going on?" she said to the two confused faces peering over their shoulders at her.

"It's engaged," said Harlan.

"What's engaged?"

"The bug."

"Oh. Oh, sorry, hi," Jenny said to Signboy. "You must be ... "

"Sorry Jenny, no time for introductions," Harlan cut in. "Signboy, who else would be calling your number?"

"What day is it?"

"Thursday," said Jenny, noticing that Harlan was checking his watch which didn't have the day of the week on it.

"That'll be my Mum then. She always calls on Thursday, just as I'm getting ready to go out. She reckons it's the only time she knows I'll be home. I try to tell her it doesn't matter with a mobile, but she just doesn't get it, you know what mums are like. What?"

Harlan and Jenny were looking quite sternly at Signboy.

"Call your Mother!" they cried in unison.

"All right, okay. Geez, you sound just like her."

He pressed the screen on his phone a few times and held it to his ear.

"It's ringing."

"Great, maybe she's hung up then." Harlan tried the bug again but it was still engaged.

"She's got call-waiting. I bet she's trying to remember what to press now to pick up the new call."

The three of them were frozen with anticipation, Harlan and Jenny staring at Signboy who held his phone to his head with one hand and was pointing at it dramatically with the other. Suddenly his eyebrows rose excitedly and his free hand started pointing frantically back and forth at the phone, indicating his mother had answered.

"Mum!"

Harlan and Jenny could just make out the beginnings of an inane conversation coming from Signboy's ear. Harlan tried the bug again in case Signboy's Mum had hung up on the other call when taking Signboy's. She hadn't.

"Tell her to hang up," Harlan whispered as violently as he could.

"Mum, look I'll call you later and we can chat, okay. I need you to hang up the other call." Signboy shook his head at the others, again indicating his phone from which came more conversational sounds.

"Mum, please! I need you to hang up the other call ... Yes, I know it's my number ... Yes, I know it's not me ... We're using it for work ... It's a long story, I'll tell you later ... It's kind of important, please just hang it up Mum! ... Thank you ... Mum?" He put his phone down into his lap.

"What happened?" asked Jenny.

"She hung up on us."

"Oh. Well does that mean she hung up on the bug?"

Harlan was already calling it. "Engaged," he announced unnecessarily as the repetitive tone reached all of their ears at roughly the same time.

"Give her a couple of seconds," said Signboy.

Harlan waited exactly two seconds then hit call again. A few nervous moments passed before the ringing tone came down the line. A few awkward high-fives ensued before they concentrated on Harlan's phone. The ringing tone stopped and the unmistakeable clink of glasses let them know once again they had a direct line to the outer zip-pocket on the flap of Mick Dawson's satchel.

CHAPTER 12

"Jonno, mate." Mick Dawson had obviously maintained his drinking pace during the meal.

"Mick." It didn't sound like Jonathan Foxe liked being given a bricklayer's nickname.

"Come on. This is a celebration. What's the matter?"

"Nothing, I am celebrating. We just toasted to a great Benefit on Saturday. There's a lot to do between now and then, that's all." He sounded tired more than anything else.

Jenny caught Harlan's eye and mouthed 'benefit?'. Harlan did his best to indicate he'd fill her in later with some odd hand gestures. Then he remembered the Bugboy 300 was a one-way listening device.

"I'll fill you in later," he said out loud, only to be shushed by Signboy. Mick Dawson was talking again.

"Yeah, well just make sure you've got your best people on it. This goes smoothly, and you'll be raking in more donations than you know what do with." Harlan, Signboy and Jenny exchanged glances. It was sickening to hear someone talk about people's donations like a windfall.

"Luckily for you," he continued, "the Balmoral Brawler knows exactly what to do with it."

"Ooh, shit," said Jenny, remembering something important. She reached into her backpack and pulled out a slightly old-fashioned dictaphone - old-fashioned in the sense it still used mini cassette tapes. Holding it up to Harlan's phone, she pressed the record button, and the tape nostalgically started turning. Meanwhile Signboy had used his new phone and a certain omnipotent search engine to discover 'Balmoral Brawler' was a self-styled nickname for Mick Dawson that had never really caught on outside of when the self-styled 'Balmoral Brawler' referred to himself in the third-person or was referred to correctly in the third person as *the self-styled 'Balmoral Brawler'*. As he began to relay all this, Jenny and Harlan shushed him. Jonathan was speaking again.

"Look, Mick, don't you think we should be a bit careful about letting this get too big? I mean, what if it all comes out?"

"You'd be fucked mate."

"I know."

"Good. Then you'll bloody well keep it to yourself, won't you?"

"Of course," Jonathan sounded a little snivelling, he was obviously more than a little scared of Mick Dawson. "But what about you, what would your investors think if they knew what we were doing?"

"What they already think - that I'm a bloody genius who'll do anything to make them all rich. Why do you think they call me the Balmoral Brawler anyway?"

"Yes, right."

"Look, here's the next move. You divert all your resources to bloody India and South Africa. I've got no use for your bloody gobbledygook speaking Cambodians, Laots, and wherever the fuck else you're operating. I need English speakers. I've got companies crawling over each other's dicks to use my call centres - you can't *give* me a big enough workforce."

"Laotians."

"What?"

"They're called Laotians, not Laots. They're not your drinking buddies."

"Too bloody right they're not. Anyway, that's what you need to do on the ground, keep growing the call centres."

"Those people need our help."

"Aw, boo-fucking-hoo. We are helping people mate, we're giving them jobs. Give a man a fish and he eats for a day, but teach a kid to answer phones and navigate through scripted conversations, and he's worth his weight in gold."

"Bastard!" Jenny yelled at the phone. "I bet that's what he sees when he looks at people too, just bars of gold walking around waiting to make him rich."

Mick Dawson wasn't finished. After an audible scull of what Harlan hoped was beer and not expensive wine, he continued.

"Listen, Jonno. I'm at the top of the ladder. Sure, I had to push a few people off to get here. But now I'm here, I can't reach the people at the bottom of the ladder. I can't help them. I can only pull the next person down the ladder up a rung. Then he can help the person below him, and so on. Eventually ... "

"Eventually another Mick Dawson comes along and pushes his way to the top." Jonathan said, surprising the three listening through Mick's satchel.

"Ha, not in this bloody life mate. Look, I'm offering you a hand here mate, let me pull you up a rung."

"Or what?"

"Or I'll kick you off the fuckin' ladder, that's what. Now shut up and listen. You take your existing operations and focus them in India, South Africa, anywhere else you've got poor kids who speak English. The loot we get from this Benefit, you throw it at new centres so you don't have to wait till you shut down the centres in Cambodia and what have you. Now when we launch this Kisses initiative, you'll have a new income stream, you'll have more corporate partners than you can poke an orphan at, and we'll be taking our cut at both ends. Jonno, are you with me?"

"What about this person who's following me?"

"What?" It was more of a 'please repeat what you just said, I didn't hear it because I was too busy sculling my beer and wasn't raised to say 'pardon" 'what?' than a 'you better not have just said what I think you did' 'what?'.

"The person following me."

"You're not still worried about that are you? I've got Biff here looking after you."

Harlan smiled at the thought of Biff sitting there quietly this whole time, and the fact he actually had to put up with that nickname from his boss. Signboy caught his eye with a nervous eyebrow raise, giving Harlan a slight sense of alarm. Shit. What if Jonathan Foxe mentioned him? He looked at Jenny who looked alarmed herself. He remembered she wouldn't have known that Jonathan Foxe was aware of her.

"I've hired that guy," Jonathan continued. "But what if ... " Their old friend the engaged tone returned. Jenny looked from Harlan to Signboy, and back again.

"What happened?"

"Battery must be dead," explained Signboy. "We didn't have time to charge it fully."

"And who knows how long your Mum was listening for, Signboy. She probably thought she was in the conversation." Harlan picked up his phone and cut off the tone.

"Hey," Signboy made as if to defend his Mum somehow, but realised it was probably true.

Jenny looked deflated. "He spotted me. He knows I've been following him."

"Or me," said Harlan. "He could have been talking about me, I've been following him just as much as you this week. And you spotted me, remember."

"Well that's even worse, now we don't know who he knows about and who he doesn't, so he might as well know about both of us."

"I see your point, yes." Harlan was relieved she didn't seem to have heard Jonathan say he'd hired someone.

"And what was that bit about him hiring someone?" It was a short-lived relief. "What does that mean?"

"Prob'ly another bodyguard," said Signboy, not making eye contact with her. Harlan didn't like the idea of getting Signboy involved in the lie and decided to tell her the truth, but Jenny continued her train of thought before he could say anything.

"No, he's had the same guy the whole time. Maybe it's more of a security consultant or something. I don't know, who would you hire if you thought someone was following you and you had something to hide?"

"Look, Jenny," said Harlan, trying to convey he had something important to tell her. She didn't pick up on his seriousness and carried on with her autopsy of the conversation they'd just heard.

"Anyway, look at what we got out of it - Mick Dawson practically laying out the Celebrities Care scam and revealing himself as the puppet master of the whole thing, all on tape. Brilliant! And a new lead on this 'Kisses' thing - that's got to be dodgy too. So," she said, smiling again and filling the car with adrenalin. "Who's going to take me out to dinner and fill me in on this whole Benefit thing?"

"Wait, you said it's Thursday night right? Harlan cooks on Thursdays."

"I've done it twice. I wouldn't say 'I cook on Thursdays'."

"Harlan, I didn't pick you for a chef."

"He's a great chef. Come on Harlan, you always cook too much anyway."

"Yeah, come on Harlan," Jenny added playfully.

"I haven't said anything yet, there's no need to badger me. Sure, let's do it. Signboy, you can tell us what you found on Mick Dawson as well."

"Where's the term 'badger' come from anyway?" asked Signboy as Harlan pulled the car out from the parking spot and began to navigate his way out of the city.

"The animal. It's like a weasel. I imagine it's pretty tenacious and attacks in packs, so when someone is being harassed, they say they're being badgered." Harlan saw Jenny getting her phone out in the backseat. "I'm just guessing though," he added, expecting to be proved wrong shortly. You can't make anything up these days.

Jenny found what she was looking for. "To badger someone - comes from badger baiting, an old British 'sport'. A badger was placed in an artificial sett and dogs were let through a small tunnel to attack the badger. The owner would pull his dog out and if the two animals were attached, separate them and start again. The aim was to see how many times you could pull your dog out attached to the badger within one minute, and people would bet on it. Harlan, that's horrible!"

"I've never even heard of it, don't blame me."

"Apparently it still goes on at underground venues in the UK. How can people be so cruel? It's disgusting."

"Whatever cruelty you can imagine, you can be sure people have thought of it before you and probably tried it out too. Some people are capable of anything."

"I bet Mick Dawson would enjoy a bit of badger baiting if there was any money in it," said Signboy.

The mention of Mick Dawson brought an end to the conversation. The three sat with their own thoughts for the rest of the journey to Harlan's apartment in Redfern. Signboy and Jenny plotted ways to bring down Mick Dawson, while Harlan planned every detail of a three course meal he hoped would impress greatly. He had decided to save coming clean to Jenny about being an indetective hired by Jonathan Foxe to investigate what she was up to for another day. It wouldn't make great dinner party conversation.

CHAPTER 13

By the time they arrived at Harlan's single-storey terrace on a quiet, tree-lined street in the fashionable Eastend of Redfern, Jenny and Signboy were glad of the distraction. The idea of exposing a man as powerful as Mick Dawson was daunting enough on its own. Added to that was the collateral impact to Jonathan Foxe's reputation, Celebrities Care's *bona fide* charity work and now the innocent bystander in the Hope Foundation. And all they really had were moral objections against the commercial exploitation of disadvantaged youths and charitable donations being diverted from where they were most needed to where they best suited Mick Dawson's business interests. It wouldn't even make the five o'clock, six o'clock, six-thirty or seven o'clock news. "Famously aggressive businessman puts shareholders first" was the headline Signboy kept coming back to in his mind. They really needed something more.

"Here we are, my Redfern mansion," Harlan announced as he cut the engine. He'd parked in his usual spot on the street just outside the front of his house.

"That says no parking," said Jenny as she got out of the car, pointing to a hand-painted message on a sloped part of the gutter that looked like the entrance to a driveway, but didn't have a driveway backing it up.

"Yes, I know. I wrote it. The previous owner tore up the driveway for some reason but left this little ramp, probably to make it easier for whoever inevitably reinstates the driveway some day. On its own, the ramp's pretty effective already in keeping people from parking here. With the sign, it's an almost impeccable system of car deterrence. Shall we?" He gestured across the footpath for the others to follow him as he stepped through the ageing but functional wooden gate to his purely ornamental front yard, counting through the dozen or so keys on his keyring as he went.

"Isn't this East Redfern?" asked Jenny, looking up and down the street.

"Don't get him started," said Signboy, holding the gate open for her.

"East Redfern?" Harlan had turned to face them, holding his chosen key out in front of him.

"Great," said Signboy, who knew what was coming and had no interest in it.

"Um, yeah." Jenny didn't know what was coming, but it was actually the kind of thing that did interest her. "I have a friend who lives near here, and she always calls it East Redfern."

"She should look at a map sometime," said Harlan, turning away and stepping up to his front door. "There's no such place. Unless the National Association of Real Estate Agents publish their own map these days. They'd have to put one out pretty regularly though to keep up with the encroachment of the 'fashionable' suburbs into the less desirable ones."

"Why would they do that?" Jenny stepped through the gate behind Signboy who was shaking his head as though he could dodge each word of the conversation through cranial agility alone.

"It's a twenty-year plan. They start calling this end of Redfern 'East Redfern' in all their real estate ads and brochures. After a few years it becomes common parlance because everyone who has rented or bought since the plan started prefers to call it 'East Redfern' as well. You'll even find people arguing over where the boundary is between 'East Redfern' and Redfern." Harlan had opened the security door, and now it rested against his back as he worked his way back around his keyring to find the front door key.

"A plan, hey? So what's the purpose of the plan?"

"To keep the bubble going," he called over his shoulder as he placed a key in the deadlock. He turned to face them for the home stretch. "After a few more years 'East Redfern' is just as real as Redfern, and then they start to do the same thing again, only this time they start shifting the boundary between Surry Hills and East Redfern, until eventually you're left with just a few blocks around Redfern station that are still Redfern, and everything between there and South Dowling Street is now Surry Hills.

"And of course every house in what used to be Redfern gains in value as it goes from being in Redfern to being in 'East Redfern', to being in Surry Hills, so the commissions for the real estate agents get bigger and bigger. That's why they're so hung up on this 'Location, Location, Location' slogan. Changing the location through nomenclature alone is the cheapest way to increase a property's value."

"There you go Jenny," said Signboy. "Now you can put your friend back in her place, Redfern, and her rent should go down."

"But aren't they all made-up names anyway? I mean, what does it matter?"

"Exactly! It doesn't matter." It was a strange way for Harlan to conclude his argument. But everyone was happy to leave it behind in the ornamental front yard and move inside as Harlan clicked the deadlock open, pushed the door inwards and followed it into the house.

By the time they reached the living area at the back of the house, Harlan had conducted a brief tour of his home for the first-time guest. This consisted of reaching each doorway off the hall that ran most of the length of the house, announcing the primary function of the room within and leaning inside to flick a light switch on and off to give Jenny a quick impression of each chamber in both the fading light of day and the steady glare of electrified tungsten.

"Master bedroom (click, click) ... spare room (click, click) ... bathroom (click, click) ... laundry (click, click)," said Harlan as they moved down the hallway, before leading Jenny into the open plan kitchen/dining/living area that spilled out through bi-folding doors onto a small paved backyard. Signboy came last, having let Jenny ahead of him at the front door so she could get the full benefit of the tour he knew Harlan gave every first-time visitor.

"Okay, so you two make yourself comfortable, and I'll start preparing a magnificent feast for us. Signboy, will you get a drink for the new guest?"

"Aren't I a guest too?"

"Yes, of course. I was forgetting myself."

"You mean you were forgetting me."

"Trying to, maybe, sorry. Jenny, would you like a drink? Some wine perhaps?"

"Sure, I can work on my swirling technique."

"Perfect. Please, please take a seat," Harlan said. "Why don't you both sit here at the breakfast bar so we can all talk while I cook."

Jenny took Harlan's advice, and perched on a white plastic and chrome stool she found under the outside rim of the kitchen bench. Signboy preferred to stand, leaning against the wall next to Jenny. Harlan already had his head in the fridge filling his arms with all the fresh vegetables and herbs he could carry.

"I like your place Harlan, it suits you," said Jenny. "Kind of understated in appearance, in between suburbs, good for entertaining. Some kind of a quiet sophistication about the place."

"Thanks, I guess," he said, frozen for a second as he enjoyed the compliment. He wiped the grin off his face and turned around to face them, dumping the food on the bench. "I've been here for years now, I guess I've made it my own." He opened a cupboard beneath the bench on his side, pulled out a small frying pan, a chopping board and a pile of small stainless steel bowls, and put them on the bench. He turned around to put the frying pan on the gas stovetop behind him, switching the stove on before turning back.

"Let me just get an entree on and then I'll see to the drinks," he said, taking some fresh figs and cutting them into slices. He took the chopping board with the sliced figs with him back to the stovetop.

"So, Signboy," Jenny said, seeking some kind of assurance she should call him that. He nodded, which would have to be enough for the moment. "What happened today - one minute Jonathan Foxe is playing golf, and the next he's celebrating with Mick Dawson?"

"Oh, yeah. Well I think he must have cut his golf short because when I got back to the office from lunch I saw him on the TV in the tax agent's waiting room." Jenny didn't quite follow and looked at Harlan to see if she'd heard correctly, but he seemed to have his mouth full tasting something and struggled to provide a meaningful gesture while laying slices of cured meat on a white rectangular platter, so she accepted it on faith and let Signboy carry on.

"Anyway, I watched through the open door as the news guy introduced a joint press conference between the Hope Foundation and Celebrities Care to make a big announcement. That's when I called Harlan to see if he was watching."

They both turned to Harlan, expecting him to continue the story, but instead he finished crumbling some hard cheese over the top of the same platter, and pushed it across the bench. "*Buon appetito*." he said, handing a fork to each of his guests.

"Wow, Harlan. It looks amazing. What have we got?" Jenny's fork hovered over the plate as Harlan described the starter.

"We've got some thin slices of *bresaola* covering the plate. On top of that slices of lightly caramelised figs. There's some *pecorino* cheese, almonds, rocket, and a healthy drizzle of olive oil. Now, about that wine."

Harlan walked around the bench and opened a cupboard against the wall behind where Signboy now leaned forward over the bench taking turns with Jenny to try to put the perfect mouthful together. Harlan had revealed a well-stocked wine cabinet of about three dozen bottles stored horizontally, close to his eye level. Below that was a large selection of spirits and liqueurs standing on a shelf, alongside two crystal wine decanters. He took a few seconds to choose a bottle, a few more to choose a decanter, then closed the cupboard with his elbows and returned to his side of the bench. Jenny and Signboy hadn't noticed, they were too busy devouring the starter. Harlan helped himself to a quick mouthful while there was still some left before decanting the wine.

"I thought we agreed there was no need to decant wine?" said Jenny.

"Really? I remember you suggested it was all about the theatre involved, that was all."

"I also introduced you to the raging debate among oenologists about whether it was in fact harmful to the wine, remember?"

"Well, let's just say I like the theatre of it then." Harlan didn't mind admitting it. In any case he had invested almost a thousand dollars in his small collection of crystal decanters (technically the equal smallest collection in the world, since you could never call one decanter a collection), and he wasn't going to stop using them just because there was no practicality to them. It would have to be a much better reason than that.

He poured the wine through a filter into the decanter, which was more of a traditional shape than the one in the French bistro, with a wide, round belly curving up into a narrow neck, angled at the top for pouring. Again opening a cupboard on his side of the bench, he retrieved three stemless wine glasses and poured a generous portion into each.

"A toast," he said, holding his glass up. "To the Hope Celebrities Care Benefit."

"To the what?" asked Jenny, her glass frozen inches short of Harlan's.

"The Hope Celebrities Care Benefit - that's what they were announcing."

"You mean, Jonathan managed to gatecrash the Benefit?" She put her glass down on the bench. "How did he do that?"

"It seems they made the Hope Foundation an offer they couldn't refuse. Live television coverage in Australia, replayed at primetime in the USA, major star-pulling power. Andrea Stacy was at the press conference, and apparently Christian Dieter is flying out for the Benefit as well."

"What are they going to do, just stand on stage with their cherubic good looks?"

"I reckon they'll be singing mainly." Signboy was pleased to be able to offer his expertise here. "He's been in a couple of those *High School Musical* movies, and she was the little girl in the red dress in the Australian production of the *Schindler's List* big-top musical. Remember?"

"Oh my god, that's right." Jenny picked up her backpack from the ground and pulled out a small laptop. She made some space on the bench in front of her and set the laptop down, flipping it open to turn it on as she did so. "Okay, so Mick Dawson rolls out the stars, the TV networks come on board, and Stephanie Clarkson takes her annual Benefit from being a thousand-dollar-a-table charity ball to a multimillion-dollar charity concert. We need to warn her just who she's getting into bed with. Let's put our case together and see what we've got."

She opened up a blank document and headed it *Mick Dawson, Jonathan Foxe and Celebrities Care - What We Know.* Signboy, reading over her shoulder, smiled at the similarity between her methodology and Harlan's.

"That's just what he does," he said, drawing a subtle blush from both of them.

Jenny then set out a few headings, and quickly documented what they had learned from the transition at ground level from providing drop-in and education services to corporate training and job placement, up to the relationship between Mick Dawson and Jonathan Foxe, which was basically a mutual distrust where one had more to lose and the other had more to gain.

"Okay Signboy, why don't you take over and set out the other side of the circle, from Mick Dawson down through his companies to their arrangement with the Celebrities Care centres." Jenny stood up to let Signboy sit on the stool and get to work.

"Need a hand Harlan?" Jenny walked around into the kitchen where Harlan was stirring a boiling pot of pasta with one hand and sautéing *pancetta* and sage in a frying pan with the other.

"Just about done actually," he said as he stopped with both hands and took a sip of his wine. "How'd the swirl go?"

"I can't stop actually," she said, swirling the wine in her glass as she spoke. "That smells great, by the way. What are we having?"

"It's a new favourite of mine, quite easy to make but so good to eat. *Orecchiette* pasta, with *pancetta*, sage and peas. Want to taste?" He took a teaspoon and dipped it into another frying pan where some peas were simmering in a shallow broth with more *pancetta* and some garlic. He held it up for Jenny to taste. She blew on it lightly, then put her hand on Harlan's to help guide the spoon to her mouth. Signboy watched them over the laptop screen. He wondered when was the appropriate time to make his excuses and leave, but it certainly wasn't before he got a bowl of pasta.

"Mmm, delicious." Jenny left her hand on Harlan's as she savoured the mouthful. Harlan was concentrating on keeping his hand at a comfortable height to encourage Jenny to maintain the contact, but after a gratuitous second and some fleeting self-conscious eye contact she removed her hand from his and turned back to Signboy.

"So, how's it looking?"

"I reckon we've got something that if we showed it to that Clarkson lady would put her off doing any more deals with Celebrities Care, but it doesn't quite get us there in terms of shock value that might scupper the Benefit at this point."

"Is that what the aim is, to scupper the Benefit?" asked Harlan as he strained the pasta over the sink.

"Well, isn't it? Wouldn't that be the best way to get at Mick Dawson, and get the biggest exposure for Jenny's article?"

"I don't think so." Harlan had returned the pasta to the pot and was now stirring through the pea and *pancetta* mixture. "The Benefit would just go back to being the Hope Benefit, and Jonathan Foxe would have to give more ground to Mick Dawson to make up for missing out on the Benefit's exposure. So the only real outcome would be condemning Celebrities Care to being nothing more than a third-party provider of training centres to Mick Dawson's outsourcing empire."

"So what are you suggesting we do?" asked Jenny.

"I don't know," said Harlan.

Jenny walked back around the bench to inspect Signboy's handiwork on the laptop, which amounted to a few sentences establishing that Mick Dawson owned companies that were supporters of Celebrities Care and were also involved in joint-ventures with call centre operators in South Africa and India.

"So we're basically back to where we were this afternoon," she said. "We still don't know why Mick Dawson has such a hold over Jonathan Foxe - but we hope it's something pretty bad, otherwise we don't really have that much."

"Famously aggressive businessman puts shareholders first," muttered Signboy.

"Exactly," said Jenny. "Doesn't pack too much of a punch, does it?"

"All right, let's see if we can't think better on full stomachs - dinner is ready."

CHAPTER 14

Harlan carried the pot of steaming pasta, along with a bowl of rocket, grated parmesan and sliced pear salad, around the bench and placed them on the dining table.

"Maybe we should clear this up a bit first," said Jenny, indicating the clutter all over the table. Harlan grabbed a few books that were lying around and placed them on the bench. Signboy grabbed a pile of stuff that consisted of a copy of *Zest For Life*, a few receipts, and a business card. He carried the pile down to the coffee table between the sofa and the TV, examining it as he went.

"Who's Matthew Loman?" Signboy came back to the table, holding the business card up.

"I don't know, why?"

"Because he works for one of Mick Dawson's companies. In fact, apparently he works for a few of them."

"Biff!" Harlan recognised the card as the one he'd been given in Jonathan's car. "Wow, his last name's Loman! Perfect."

"Wait, Biff?" asked Jenny. "Jonathan Foxe's bodyguard?"

For an indetective, Harlan was doing a good job of leading Jenny to his secret.

"Yes, he kind of spotted me in the car park out at the golf course." The indetective skills kicked in automatically, denying Harlan his chance to come clean. "I pretended I was a detective following another one of the golfers. He asked me for a card in case his boss ever needed my services, but I told him I didn't have one. So he gave me his and asked me to email him my details."

"Harlan, you're a liar!"

"Wait, Jenny, I can explain."

Signboy wanted to hear Harlan try to explain everything, but it wasn't necessary due to Jenny making the most palatable logical conclusion available to her. For a sceptic, she was doing a good job of taking Harlan's word for things.

"So it *is* you Jonathan's seen following him. And you had me thinking it might be me."

"Well, you know. A professional's pride, maybe. I didn't want you to think you were better than me at my own job. Plus, I thought Biff went for my cover story anyway. It was a pretty good one."

"You still should have said something Harlan. We're supposed to be a team, remember?" It really wasn't going to go well when Harlan eventually came clean.

"Anyway," Signboy figured the moment was gone, and brought their attention back to the card. "Biff's card has three logos on it. One is Mick Dawson's celebrity security detail service, Dawson Security. One is his celebrity agency, Mick Dawson Represents. And the other is something called the Executive Lounge."

"The Executive Lounge? Isn't that Jonathan Foxe's old business?" asked Jenny.

"No, that was the Executive Club. It is a bit of a coincidence though. Let's talk while we eat." Harlan was keen to redeem himself with Jenny, and figured her taste buds were his best chance at the moment. He went back into the kitchen and opened yet another cupboard, produced three large pasta bowls and returned to the table with them. As Jenny and Signboy sat down across from each other, Harlan dished out three full bowls of pasta.

"Can I use your laptop, Jenny?" asked Signboy. "I think I've seen that name before, the Executive Lounge."

Jenny grabbed her laptop from the bench behind her and passed it to Signboy. Harlan had grabbed a plate from the bench and from it sprinkled the sautéed sage and pancetta over the top of the served pasta. Then he grated some *parmigiano reggiano* onto each bowl for the finishing touch.

"Okay, that looks seriously good Harlan, pass one of those bowls over here." Harlan obliged and Jenny dived straight in. "Wow, it's delicious. You were right Signboy, he can cook."

"That's not all I was right about, listen to this. Executive Lounge is fully owned by Jonathan Foxe Holdings," said Signboy, reading from the laptop screen as his first mouthful hovered in the air above his bowl.

"That doesn't make sense - so Biff does work for Jonathan Foxe?" Harlan was intrigued enough to put his eating on hold too, but left his fork resting in the pasta.

"No - because Jonathan Foxe Holdings is fully owned by Dawson Concierge Pty Ltd."

"How do you know all of this?"

"I spent all morning tracing Mick Dawson's businesses to tie him to the Celebrities Care call centre training scam. He's got companies all over the place, it's a complete mess, so I followed a few false leads, and this was one of them. I made a note because of the Jonathan Foxe connection, but because the Executive Lounge had nothing to do with Celebrities Care, I kind of forgot about it."

"And how are you doing all this research?"

"Company searches, mostly. It's not cheap."

"What do you mean by 'not cheap'?"

"Well, about five-hundred bucks or so I've spent. Don't worry, I kept all the receipts on your computer."

"Oh, good, you've kept the receipts. I'll just bill them to Marisa Foxe, I'm sure she'll be happy to pay for them."

"All right, I get the point. I'll be more careful in future. But so should you, your credit card details are on auto-complete on your computer, anyone could use that computer to buy something with your card."

"Oh, good, you used my card. I'd hate for you to be out of pocket from all of this."

"That's what I figured." Signboy paused to see if Harlan had any other objection, taking the opportunity to have his first mouthful of pasta. "Mmm, one of your best, Harlan."

"Thank you. Well go on, tell us what you did next."

"It wasn't that difficult really. There are websites where you can put in someone's name, and you'll get a list of all the companies they are a director or shareholder of. That's only around fifty bucks. And luckily Mick Dawson doesn't have much of an imagination, as you've already seen. He pretty much calls a company by what it does, so it's just a matter of looking down the list and following the ones that make sense. Eg., Mick Dawson is a shareholder and director of a company called Dawson's Offshore Outsourcing, of which he is also the CEO by the way, which owns two companies. Subcontinental Outsourcing and Sub-Saharan Outsourcing."

"And these are Australian companies?"

"Yep. Anyway, it's pretty boring, but basically those companies have joint ventures with companies in India and South Africa that run the actual call centres and data entry centres."

"And Celebrities Care?" Harlan noticed with a little glee Jenny had motored through half of her pasta while he and Signboy were talking.

"Subcontinental Outsourcing and Sub-Saharan Outsourcing both carry the Celebrities Care logo on their websites, and brag about putting back into the communities they do business in through their support of the Celebrities Care centres."

"So," said Jenny, putting her fork down for the first time since being served, "They exploit the kids on one hand to make running the call centres cheaper, turn the kids they have no use for back out onto the street, and then they use their 'support' of Celebrities Care to create goodwill to attract customers. Talk about nerve."

"Indeed," said Harlan. "And what about the Executive Lounge? What can we find out about that?"

"I'm just looking now, but not much. I can see by the company search it used to be called the Executive Club, but it doesn't have a website, so there's no way of knowing exactly what it does. Although it does come up on a few adult dating websites."

"Wait, now you're doing searches on my laptop?"

"No, I'm logged into Harlan's computer remotely. How did you think I remembered all of this stuff?"

"I guess I just thought you were clever."

Now Signboy blushed a little. "Anyway," he said, trying to get back on track. "That's all we know."

"But that's something, Signboy," said Harlan. "So it was Mick Dawson who purchased the Executive Club from Jonathan Foxe. For some reason Jonathan Foxe Holdings came across with it. And then Mick Dawson turned it from a high profile celebrity concierge service for which everybody wanted to get hold of the number, to nothing more than a logo on Biff's business card and apparently some mentions on various adult dating websites."

"So we have to look into this Executive Club/Lounge thingy now?" Signboy was a bit annoyed at himself for not having followed it up earlier.

"That and this Kisses thing Mick Dawson was talking about. That's another thing we don't know anything about," said Jenny.

"Why don't you eat first Signboy, it's getting cold. Who wants some more wine?"

"Yes, please," Jenny said, passing her glass to Harlan. Signboy had his mouth full, so simply pushed his glass across the table towards Harlan. "I love these glasses by the way. Much easier to swirl."

Once he had refreshed all three of their glasses, he reached across the table and pulled the laptop in front of him. "Now, let's see what we can find out about the sale of the Executive Club."

*

After an hour of googling, title searching, passing the laptop around, and a brief unresolved argument about why Harlan didn't have a home computer and a printer (in which Harlan was able to rely untested on his standard carbon footprint justification), Harlan, Jenny and Signboy cheered each other as Signboy typed the last few words of a new section in Jenny's document, which was beginning to read like the damning exposé Jenny was hoping for. Under the heading *Why Mick owns Jonathan*, they had written the following:

In 2005 MD purchased the Executive Club, a well-known celebrity and executive concierge business, from JF. At the time the sale was rumoured to be worth around $5m. Soon after it was reported JF purchased his current family home in Mosman, for $4.5m. However, property title searches show the owner is Jonathan Foxe Holdings, the holding company for the Executive Club which was now MD's. So, MD owns JF's family home and his former business which now appears to be nothing more than a high class escort agency. Best guess is JF somehow got into debt with MD, settled the debt with the Executive Club, and launched Celebrities Care under MD's direction as part of an ongoing agreement under which he got to live in the Mosman house. To the outsider, it looked simply like JF had sold his business and the money had gone into the new home and launching Celebrities Care, and if anyone ever looked into it they would see the owner of the property as Jonathan Foxe Holdings and look no further. If JF stops cooperating with MD, he loses the family home and has to explain everything to his wife, *including how he got so far into debt back when he owned the Executive Club.*

"Good work," Jenny said, patting Signboy on the shoulder. "The only people who can answer the remaining question of how Jonathan got into debt in the first place are he and Mick Dawson, but our case is strong enough to warrant an answer - this document, along with the tape of Mick Dawson and Jonathan Foxe, demands the explanation. The only question for us is, what do we do with it?"

"Well, we definitely want to take it to Stephanie Clarkson at some point, so she can avoid the Hope Foundation getting caught up in the fallout," said Harlan.

"And Jonathan Foxe?" asked Signboy. "Shouldn't we give him a chance to explain first? Seems to me he's a bit of a victim, if we can show him a way out, he'd probably tell us whatever we want."

"True," said Jenny. "Although I don't see how we can approach him without Mick Dawson finding out. What about Marisa Foxe?"

"Marisa Foxe?" Harlan bounced the idea around in his head a few times. He liked it. It may have had something to do with his wanting to avoid Jenny confronting Jonathan Foxe, which would be a real blot on his record as an indetective. "She hired me to look into Jonathan Foxe because she suspected he was having an affair. I could go back to her with all of this explaining why he has behaved a bit secretively over the years. In fact ethically I should, she is my client after all. If I explain to her about the Hope Celebrities Care Benefit, about the kind of guy Mick Dawson is and what he's doing to her husband and countless street kids in developing countries, she'll want to get to the bottom of it as much as us. And she'd have a better chance of confronting Jonathan without having Biff around as Mick Dawson's eyes and ears."

Jenny looked at Harlan, weighing up the options. "How quickly do you think she'll act?"

"I don't think she'd do anything rash, but she seems a confident, forthright person. I'm sure she'll speak to Jonathan pretty quickly and go into damage control, helping him turn the spotlight onto Mick Dawson. Of course, if she's not going for it I could scare her a little by telling her a journalist is on to the whole thing. And if I tell her it's Mick Dawson you're going to nail in your story and not her husband, I'm sure they'll want to help you with your article, just to make sure."

"What about the family home? Wouldn't that be just as much a ransom to her as it is to Jonathan?"

"She must have some money somewhere, she does pretty well out of her magazine, surely. Plus she's getting into cookbooks now."

"Hmm, you'd be surprised. I mean, I know it's slightly different, but in my experience there's not much money floating around in the publishing world."

"Well, let's go to Marisa first. If she won't help us get Jonathan to fill in the gaps for your article, then we'll hope she keeps quiet in time for us to go to Stephanie Clarkson and she can expose the whole thing at the Benefit."

"And I'll have to make the most of that to make up for the holes in my article. All right Harlan, I'll trust your instincts on this. So first thing tomorrow you go to Marisa, okay?"

"Agreed. First thing."

"I think you better agree a time with him Jenny, Harlan doesn't mind using loosely defined terms to his advantage."

"Nine o'clock then," offered Harlan, to which Jenny nodded and smiled. With that settled, a comfortable wave of tranquility flowed through the room, taking all thoughts of Mick Dawson with it as Harlan, Jenny and Signboy let themselves sink down its back. It had been an intense evening, and now they felt they could relax a bit before it all kicked off again tomorrow.

"Now, Harlan," said Jenny. "Why don't you crack open another bottle of wine and I'll help you with the dishes?"

"Right," said Signboy. "Um, Harlan, I've left my thumb drive in Jenny's laptop, it's got the document and an mp3 of the tape recording on it. And I'll be off then," said Signboy, who knew enough about the world to know Jenny wasn't really interested in just helping Harlan with the dishes.

"Oh, come on Signboy, you don't have to rush off," said Harlan, regretting it immediately as he caught Jenny's eye communicating better than most fully developed vocal cords could that yes, he did have to rush off.

"Shut up Harlan, I'm going. You think I don't have somewhere better to be on a Thursday night? Plus, I've already clocked up enough overtime for one day. See you Jenny, good luck with the dishes," he said cheekily as he let himself out.

Harlan grabbed another bottle of wine but skipped the decanter this time, filling their glasses cavalierly straight from the bottle. Without a word he and Jenny took their glasses into the kitchen and set about tidying up as though they'd done it together a thousand times before.

An hour later they were drifting off to sleep in Harlan's bed, having removed each other's clothes and negotiated a complicated series of sexual positions with the same familiarity that had made washing up together seem so natural, all achieved using no other words than each other's names, although Harlan had switched dramatically from Jenny to Jennifer towards the end of the naked part of the evening.

CHAPTER 15

Harlan woke alone the next morning. It was eight o'clock if his alarm clock was to be believed. He rose quicker than usual and had a shower. He was dressed by the time he came out into the kitchen and found Jenny's note explaining she'd left to track Jonathan Foxe from his home when he left for work. Harlan considered the logistics and shook his head. She would have had to leave well before six to pick up her car and get to Mosman early enough to be sure not to miss him. He was grateful she didn't wake him.

Remembering his promise to contact Marisa, he decided to call her straight away, expecting to have to head into the city to meet her. He went back to his bedroom and dug out his phone from the trail of his clothes stretching from the door to the bed, picturing the previous night's exuberances as he went. He shook his head again. He was banking a great deal on his general good fortune to avoid anyone getting hurt from all of this.

He returned to the kitchen, picked up Signboy's thumb drive Jenny had left for him, and called Marisa. He played with the thumb drive as he waited for her to answer, as though it would guide him through the exchange.

"Harlan, hi. How are you?" Marisa answered, her voice achieving the sense of incredible distance possible only through a car speaker-phone.

"Hi Marisa. I'm well, how are you?"

"I'm well too." An expectant silence waited for Harlan to break it. After a couple of seconds he realised it was his responsibility to lead the conversation, having called. He had been staring at the thumb drive, framing his next sentence.

"Right, yes." Not that one. "Marisa, I need to see you urgently to discuss some important information I've discovered about your husband." That was it.

"Oh. Of course. Look, I'm just getting into work now, can I call you back from my desk? I just need to check my schedule."

"Sure, I'll speak to you then."

"Okay, I'll call you in a minute."

Harlan busied himself putting away the dishes Jenny had left to dry once he'd finished the washing part and was left with idle hands and a specific sin in mind to occupy them with. He smiled as he congratulated himself on never getting a dishwasher. It would have been a little sordid cooking a meal for someone then taking them to bed without first having made a genuine attempt at doing the dishes together. The balance of favours might have left a sour taste in his mouth. He was just putting away the last pieces of cutlery when Marisa called back.

"Hi Marisa."

"Harlan, hi. Look, I know it's important but I have a very full morning, so can we meet at eleven? Can you come to my office? You know the ACPBL building?"

"Sure thing, I'll see you then."

"Thanks Harlan." She sounded busy enough to hang up without saying goodbye, and she was.

His morning suddenly wide open, Harlan decided to head into the office and see what Signboy was up to and maybe check on the other cases they had. It had only been a few days, but these things could blow up from time to time if you weren't on top of them. The last time he'd left the drive thru-addicted school teacher alone this long he'd had to fabricate a last-minute school excursion to the Bradman museum in Bowral to explain the number of brown paper bags and white paper cups on the floor of his client's people-mover's backseat.

He went back to his room and found his trousers from the day before, transferring his wallet and keys from them to the ones he was wearing. Patting his pockets and running a verbal checklist of 'wallet, smartphone, keys' Harlan walked back out of his bedroom feeling he'd forgotten something. He wandered around the kitchen and living area, scanning surfaces vaguely until the odds reached a point where he figured he was statistically unlikely to have missed anything too important.

It was only as he turned to leave that he spotted the thumb drive sitting behind the sink where he'd left it. He might have to add a few seconds to the random visual sweep. Although if it's always in the last place you look, shouldn't reducing search time lead to finding things more quickly? He was halfway to work before he dismissed both the logical and illogical thoughts he'd had and decided not to change a system that had worked for him up to and including then.

*

It was nine o'clock when Harlan parked near his office, the earliest he'd arrived all week. He again failed to notice the slightly elongated Mercedes-Benz parked across the street, this time with no newly-purchased foliage for an excuse. He entered the building, helped himself to a plastic cup of water from the tax agent's water cooler, and watched some footage of teenage girls screaming as Christian Dieter arrived at Sydney Airport before he made his way upstairs. He did notice, only at the last second, the office door hanging wide open and some cigarette smoke wafting from within.

"Signboy," he called ahead in a reprimanding tone as he reached the doorway.

"Expecting someone else?" It was Biff. "You shouldn't leave your door unlocked like that." He was leaning with his back against the counter, his elbows holding him up and one foot folded across the other, facing the stairwell. It wasn't a flattering look for a man starting to spread around the middle who persisted with slim-fit shirts tightly tucked into his trousers. Harlan could see two clear windows of belly before the shirt regained itself and held fast up to Biff's chest.

"If you're here about the job, you're wasting your time. It said clearly on the poster I'm after someone who presents well." Harlan took a couple of steps into the room, leaving the door open behind him, hoping Biff would take it as an invitation.

"Hilarious." Biff straightened up, took one last lungful of toxins from his cigarette, then stubbed it out at the base of the fern sitting next to him on the counter, leaving the bent butt in the soil. "I'm just here to check up on you. You know, see just how much a waste of money you are for my boss."

"Of course. I can appreciate your concern. Mine is a very subtle art, I wouldn't expect you to see the immediate value in it." Harlan watched Biff as he spoke, trying to measure how loose a cannon he was dealing with. Biff seemed completely in control though. "So, what can I show you to set your mind at ease? Case notes? Surveillance photos?"

"Where were you yesterday? I didn't see you or the girl."

"Really? We were around. You had a big day Biff, meeting celebrities, eating at fancy restaurants. And you never sent me a revised itinerary."

"It all just kind of came up. I'll try to get you an invite next time." Conveying sarcasm obviously wasn't one of Biff's strengths, but Harlan figured it was safe to assume that's what he was going for.

"A pretty big night too, I bet. After a coup like that, Jonathan was probably out all night celebrating, especially with a party animal like Mick Dawson for company. And yourself, of course."

"I don't drink on duty."

"Well, that wasn't really the point, but it's good to know. Anyway, if that's all ... "

"Shut up, *In*detective." Biff stepped forward to within a foot of Harlan, looming as threateningly as possible without having to lean on him for support. "Just remember who your boss is."

"Who my boss is?"

"Who is your boss."

"Your boss is my boss."

"Exactly, and he asked me to give you your orders."

"Funny, after yesterday I thought your boss was my boss's boss."

"He is. I mean, they are. No. Just, find out who the girl is and call me. The new deadline's tomorrow."

"Tomorrow? Did my boss say that, or yours?"

"I said it."

"But that's not enough time. I need a full week to profile somebody."

"So improvise. I've done you a favour by leading her here, surely you can do the rest."

"What?" Harlan felt like he'd just dropped a few storeys in an elevator. Once his proverbial stomach returned to its anatomical home, he remembered he couldn't let Biff see his alarm. "She's here? I didn't see her car outside, that's funny."

"Didn't seem like you saw mine either, which is funnier. What kind of a detective are you?"

"*In*detective, two different things," replied Harlan reflexively. "Okay Biff, well, good work then. Where are you heading next? Probably better if I don't just follow you straight out the door, she'll realise something is up," he said, hoping Biff wouldn't realise anything was up.

"Back to pick up Mister Foxe from the CC Office." Biff finally stepped away from Harlan and towards the door.

"In Alexandria? Perfect, I'll follow you in a few minutes, and pick up the trail of the blue Golf there."

"I don't care how you go about it. Just get it done by tomorrow, *In*detective. Three p.m." Biff threw one last menacing stare in Harlan's direction and left, swinging the door shut behind him.

Harlan took the opportunity to panic.

"Fuck, fuck, fuck." He walked over to the counter and looked around desperately for anything that might help him.

"Fuck, fuck, fuck." He walked into his back office and looked out the rear window, gauging the drop to the ground below. It was quite high.

"Fuck, fuck, fuck." He sat down in his ergonomic armchair. It was time to face reality.

"What's up?" said Signboy, climbing out of the cupboard in the corner of the room. It wasn't exactly the reality Harlan was expecting.

"Signboy, what are you doing here?"

"I was here when that thug got here. I recognised a clear intention to do violence in his voice when he called your name, so I hid in the cupboard. Lucky I did cos he would've recognised me from planting the bug. We'd be screwed if he saw me," said Signboy, walking around the desk and sitting in his usual chair.

"Good thinking, or instinct, whatever it was. Well, at least that's one artificial reality we've constructed that remains intact. Unfortunately another is about to come under serious threat."

"What do you mean?"

"Jenny followed Biff here. She would have seen me enter sometime after him, and then him leave a couple of minutes later. I expect she'll knock on the door any second."

"Fuck."

"That was pretty much my reaction."

"No chance she'd believe he was seeing the chiropractor? Or getting his tax done?"

Harlan was surprised to find himself considering the brazen suggestion - just play dumb and hope Jenny accepted the most unlikely coincidence since the Foxes had independently turned up on Harlan's doorstep on the same day as just that.

"Want me to hang around?"

"No, I don't think so. This may get personal."

"So last night?"

Harlan nodded. Signboy stood, shrugged his shoulders as some form of encouragement, and headed out of the office.

"Oh Signboy?"

"Yep?" His head came leaning back through the doorway.

"Don't go too far. Still a big day ahead."

"That's the spirit. Call me when you need me."

Harlan leant back in his chair, which didn't give an inch. He fumbled with the levers on the chair's side, cursing Signboy. Finding the correct lever, he finished what he'd started and leant back in his chair, this time to a comfortable recline, bouncing slightly either side of forty-five degrees. He subconsciously began spinning slowly around, walking his feet over each other to pick up speed, then letting them drag lightly on the carpet to slow down. He was just slowing down for the third time when Jenny walked in.

"Harlan - are you all right?"

"Jenny." He sat up, which caused him to spin faster again until he jammed his feet on the floor, his back to Jenny. "Please, sit down," he called over his shoulder, then slowly worked his way back around to face her.

"Harlan, what's going on?" She looked genuinely confused, and a little afraid. Harlan stopped himself from making up a ridiculous story and took a deep breath.

"Jenny, I want to explain. Everything."

"Well, of course you do now. I didn't hear you wanting to explain anything last night."

"Jenny, please." Harlan leaned forward, as if they were separated by physical distance alone and he was laying the first bridgework that would bring them together again. "I wanted to tell you, as soon as I started having feelings for you, that first night. I even started to at some point, but it was just, I don't know. Difficult. Please, let me explain now."

"All right, go on then." She was sitting bolt upright in her chair, her whole body tensed up in an echo of some primal self-preservation instinct.

"Okay, I'm just going to come out with all of it at once," he said, then waited for her to tell him it was a good idea. In the absence of her approval, he leant further forward in his chair, his elbows leaning on the desk. For some reason he noticed she was carrying a black leather handbag instead of her backpack. He wondered if she'd made the change to try to impress him, which made him feel even worse about what he was about to say. Seeing no defendable alternative, he went ahead and said it anyway.

"On Tuesday morning Marisa Foxe called me and arranged to meet with the aim of her hiring me. Before she arrived, I was briefly abducted by Jonathan Foxe, with the help of Biff, during which abduction Jonathan Foxe purported to hire me into his service to find out about a woman following him in a blue Golf. Shortly after my release, Marisa arrived and hired me to observe her husband and let her know if any of his affairs were likely to become public.

"The next day, I began both jobs concurrently, and in the afternoon you jumped in my car and told me exactly what you were doing, and proposed we meet. I was, shall we say, smitten, and also intrigued by your story, and I decided not to let Jonathan know of my breakthrough in his case. I met you later that night and the rest you know."

Jenny didn't move. Her face gave away no emotion. Her silence prompted Harlan to offer more.

"Look, I haven't told Jonathan or Biff, or Marisa, anything about you, or us. I've been working on your side ever since we met, the only thing I kept from you that would have been any use to you is the nightly itinerary Biff emails me so I know where Jonathan will be the next day." Jenny raised her eyebrows at that. She was getting up at 5:30am every day to get to Mosman and follow Jonathan Foxe when he left his home, while Harlan had his daily itinerary sent to him the night before.

Harlan continued, "I was just having such a good time getting to know you I didn't want you to, um ... "

"Get to know *you*?" Her voice was quite restrained, given the circumstances.

"Well, kind of. What I do, anyway."

"What do you do, Harlan? What's an *In*detective?"

"So you saw the sign? I was going to say it sounds worse than it is, but it actually sounds pretty innocuous. It's better to say it could be worse than it sounds, but it's not as bad as all that and is actually not that bad at all, the way I try to do it." Harlan saw Jenny's confusion grow so went back over what he'd just said in his head. It made perfect sense to him.

"Okay," he continued, "so the word, indetective, is obviously related to the word detective. I coined it myself actually. I toyed with a few prefixes, and I was close to going with 'private vestigator' at one point, but it just doesn't have the same ring to it."

"Harlan?"

"Jenny."

"What are you talking about?" Her voice had gone from restrained to strained, which was a step backwards, having wasted a lot of energy trying to follow Harlan's rambling. He picked up on this, and tried to be more direct.

"A couple of years ago I started an indetective agency. Protecting people's privacy, pulling the wool over prying eyes. For personal reasons, I was particularly determined to prevent the damage by private detectives uncovering secrets whose only offensive characteristic was their being secret in the first place."

"Personal reasons?"

Harlan considered how the justification held up without telling her the full story. It wasn't exactly the Great Wall. With an ominous sigh, he began telling her about his father, PaperWash, and the harmless secret that ruined his family's lives and cost many others a significant portion of their retirement savings.

"That sounds terrible. He's never tried to contact you or your mother?"

"No. But let's not get right into that now, it won't get us anywhere, believe me." This earned another raised eyebrow. "Please, let me go on - I want to tell you everything about the business. That was just a preamble, trying to explain how I came to be doing what it is I do."

"Okay."

"It started with just covering people's tracks. Giving them alibis and tips on how to be more discreet, general advice on how to minimise the chances of getting caught doing something they didn't want out in the open. We worked for adulterers, alcoholics, people with drug habits, gambling habits. People who had something to hide, and needed help hiding it."

"That's horrible." Jenny added a scowl to emphasise her point.

"You're right. It was disillusioning, to say the least. I had what I thought was a great idea for a business, but it turned out to be one moral tragedy after another. And distinctly unrewarding, in every sense of the word. But I only really appreciated it when Signboy came on board. Having him help me out here and there got me thinking whether each job was something I wanted him to get involved in. And most of them weren't. That's why we offer a fuller service now. We refer clients to counsellors. We manage them going into rehab without the press finding out."

"Doesn't that make you redundant at some point?"

"That was the risk. But we've found clients who turn their lives around are more likely to not only pay their bills, but also refer us to friends, people they know in the same situation. Let's face it, people don't usually talk about these sorts of things, but when they've made a breakthrough they suddenly become the authority on the matter and won't shut up about it."

"But you're still essentially helping people keep secrets."

"Jenny, people make mistakes, it doesn't make them bad people. And not all secrets are bad either - people are entitled to their privacy. The advantage of being a one man agency is I have total control over who my clients are. I don't take on scum. I take on clients who want to deal with their secrets, but want to do it secretly. Some people would suffer dire consequences if their secrets came to light, for them, their families, their companies. We help them control how they deal with these things, so it doesn't blow up in their faces at a time and in a way they wouldn't choose."

"Give me an example."

"Well, my father for one. But take Marisa. She suspects her husband of cheating. She doesn't want it all over the news, so she hires me. If I found evidence of him cheating, I would analyse the likelihood of it coming out, and advise her accordingly. I'd also offer to refer her to a counsellor who can help her think things through, and of course I'm there to listen myself.

"Or consider a gay man who's been living a double life. He doesn't want his wife to find out through some sleazy detective, or worse, the newspapers if he's a public figure. If he's lucky enough to get his hands on my card, I can help him keep it a secret while he gets counselling or what have you, to the point where he's able to see a positive future if he comes out, and can do so in a private, compassionate way."

"Okay, I guess there's nothing wrong with those examples. Based on that, you could almost say you're doing a public service. So how many scorned women or temporarily closeted gay family men have you got on your books?"

"Well, these are recent innovations in the indetective industry."

"How many?"

"We have eight current clients, of which one is a woman and one is gay. But I've only been promoting to women since the Tiger Woods scandal, and I just thought of the gay opportunity the other week because of that politician filmed leaving a gay sex club."

Harlan was leaning well over the desk now, but Jenny hadn't moved a millimetre in his direction.

"I just don't know how to take this. And I don't need the distraction right now."

"I know. I promise, Jenny, there's nothing else. You now know more about me than, well, anyone. And I won't lie to you again. But, let's put the personal stuff to the side for now. Work with us until you've got your article, we'll keep it professional and keep helping as much as we can. If along the way you realise I am the same funny, interesting bloke you thought you'd met ... Well, you won't need to ask me twice to let you give me a second chance."

"I don't have much choice really, there's no way I can do it alone." Jenny looked unsure, which was a big improvement on when she first sat down.

Harlan remembered his appointment with Marisa and checked the time on his phone.

"Shit," he said. "Sorry, I've got an appointment with Marisa at eleven, it's already ten-thirty."

Jenny checked her watch and found the same thing. When she looked back at Harlan her eyes had hardened, the steely resolve had returned. Again he saw Jenny the investigative reporter, not Jenny the confused and disillusioned lover. A real professional.

"Do you want me to come with you?" she asked.

"No, I think it's better if I leave you out of it. She's my client and I wouldn't want her to think I had been helping a reporter investigate her husband unless it's absolutely necessary, even though it's got nothing to do with adultery."

"So you've been juggling this thing all week? I couldn't do it. It's exhausting just hearing about it."

"It's self-preservation as much as anything. You should have seen the look in Biff's eyes this morning."

"You should have seen mine when I saw you walk in here after him."

"Yes. Look, Jenny, I'm really sorry. Really. I don't want this to come between us, but I understand it's not the dream job you'd choose for a prospective partner."

"It could be worse," she said, a hollow smile on her face. "Merchant banker. Corporate lawyer. Property developer. At least you've got a reason for what you do."

"Sounds like my client list," said Harlan. "Your parents would be happy though, all solid jobs. Anyway, you're welcome to hang around, I've really got to go - I promised a beautiful woman I'd do something for her." Harlan stood, looked Jenny in the eyes, smiling reassuringly. It was his best 'I'm a good guy let me prove it to you' look. When she half-smiled back, he turned and left the room.

"Okay, I'll let myself out," Jenny called after him. "Might grab a cup of tea first or something." She looked around for anything tea-related and after confirming there were no teabags near the espresso machine was about to try the front room when she heard Harlan call back from the top of the stairs.

"Try the chiropractor's."

Jenny checked her posture, then realised he was talking about getting a cup of tea.

CHAPTER 16

The *Zest for Life* headquarters were in the corporate centre of Australia's largest publishing house, ACPBL. After the many mergers, spin-offs and joint ventures endemic to the publishing and media industry as it weathered the digital age, nobody knew what the initials stood for anymore. But apparently it still boasted enough brand power to be given naming rights to one of the tallest skyscrapers in the CBD. Fortunately, it was nice and close to Town Hall station which made catching the train quicker and getting a parking fine very unlikely.

Although it had been in Signboy's brief, Harlan hadn't really appreciated Marisa's magazine being just one of dozens of glossy publications in the ACPBL stable until he entered the lobby. It reminded him of standing in line at one of the major supermarkets, except the magazine covers had been blown up to ridiculous proportions, framed, and hung tastelessly on every square centimetre of wall space. With a few minutes to burn having hit the train running, he took a look around.

He remembered Jenny's comment about there not being much money in publishing. He assumed she meant for the employees, which was the same as most industries.

It was hard to imagine someone wasn't making a lot of money as he scanned the familiar names on the wall. He spotted *Zest for Life* on one side, not exactly prominent but at least it was in good company. *Eat, Drink, Travel* on one side, and the financial spin-off from Marisa's title, *Invest for Life* on the other. When he thought of Marisa as just one of what must be close to fifty magazine editors churning out stand-filler for a listed company, he doubted his previous assumption that she could be independently wealthy.

"Can I help you, sir?" The young woman sitting at reception had singled Harlan out as more of a loiterer than a legitimate visitor. He had been browsing the magazine titles for a couple of minutes.

"Yes, please. I have a meeting with Marisa Foxe."

"She'll have to sign you in. Is she expecting you?"

"Yes. I have a meeting with her."

"Yes, you said. I'll let her know you're here, Mister ... "

"Valeri. Harlan Valeri."

Harlan rolled his eyes as she used her computer to link her headset to the phone in Marisa's office.

"Mrs. Foxe?" Her voice had a friendly note Harlan noticed had been absent when speaking to him. "I have a Harlan Valeri here to see you ... that's fine, thank you." He was impressed she got his name right first time. It was a rare thing.

"She's sending someone down to collect you. You can take a seat."

"That's okay, I'll continue browsing if you don't mind."

"They're not for sale."

"I know that. I'm just browsing." She was really getting on his nerves. He moved away to browse in the furthest corner of the lobby. He was admiring the courage of a young woman to pose as a cheap burlesque dancer on the cover of *XY Monthly* when a much friendlier voice called his name. He turned around to see an incredibly thin-waisted young man he assumed to be Marisa's gay assistant (two assumptions really), wearing a pinstripe shirt and dark trousers astonishingly almost too small for him.

"Hello?" said Harlan.

"Hi, I'm Darren, Marisa's personal assistant, she asked me to come down and sign you in," he said as though it was a personal favour to Marisa and not part of his job.

Harlan followed him over to the desk, where he and Harlan both signed a page in an oversized book and the receptionist handed Harlan a visitor's pass.

"You must display that at all times. It's a two-hour pass," she said as Darren led Harlan towards the elevators.

"Don't worry about her, she's a complete bitch," said Darren quietly as he pressed the up button to call an elevator.

"I gathered."

An electronic chime sounded as the elevator in front of them opened.

"I can always pick which one will open," Darren confided as he showed Harlan into the lift. He pressed number 42 and then the 'close doors' button repeatedly without checking to see if anyone was coming. Harlan liked his moxie. It paid dividends immediately as the empty lift rose straight to the 42nd floor without either of them feeling they needed to make small talk.

The lift doors opened onto a wide corridor with ageing blue carpet on the floor and wallpaper that could once have been white on the wall opposite. An improvised printed sign indicating left for *Your Money* and right for *Zest for Life* was stapled on the wall.

"We move around a lot in this building," Darren explained as they followed the arrow to the right. "Makes it less obvious when they cancel a title. Morale can be a little ... fragile around here."

"Even at *Zest for Life*?" Harlan hoped the title wasn't just a clever name for a magazine.

"Oh no. Working for Marisa is inspirational. We're not your average ACPBL title, trust me."

They came to a double door with an electronic card scanner next to it. Darren turned sideways and gyrated briefly in front of the scanner, eliciting a beep and a flash of the scanner's small red light, followed by the click of the doors unlocking. He blushed slightly at Harlan before pushing through the doors and leading him into the *Zest for Life* office space. It wasn't what Harlan had expected.

The area took up half of the floor, about the size of a European Handball court. It was a completely open space, with windows spanning the three exterior sides. To Harlan's extreme left there was what looked like a commercial kitchen with a photography studio at one end, which was exactly what it was. The opposite end of the floor looked more like a traditional news room, a tight network of desks where the pages of the magazine were produced. In between there and the kitchen was a series of themed pockets aligned with the other sections of the magazine. Fashion, cosmetics, early childhood, film, books, travel, gadgets. It was like a walkthrough exhibition of the issue in production. Harlan estimated there was about thirty people spread throughout the floor. Five of them were gathered around a table by the kitchen, Harlan guessed shooting a plate of food for the recipes pages. One of them was Marisa.

"Please, Mr Valeri, wait here. I'll grab Marisa for you."

"Thanks Darren."

Darren nodded in appreciation. Not many people remembered a personal assistant's name. Harlan watched as he approached the group and got Marisa's attention. She said something to the rest of the group and headed in Harlan's direction. He noticed the people she left behind spread out a bit, taking seats and checking their mobile phones. Obviously Marisa didn't want them to continue without her, and was expecting a short meeting with Harlan.

"Harlan, hi. Let's go into my office."

Harlan nodded a little solemnly, and followed her to the other end of the floor where a couple of offices were built into the interior wall. She led him into the last office, and asked him to close the door behind him.

"So, what have you got to tell me?" She was sitting behind her desk quite naturally. Harlan figured she was expecting him to tell her something she already knew. He decided to play it straight.

"First, I haven't found anything to suggest your husband is having an affair."

"Really?" She sat forward a little, raising her eyebrows.

"Yes. The flowers were for professional reasons - you might even have seen them at his press conference yesterday, a white wreath. It's the Hope Foundation's symbol."

"Okay, so that explains the flowers." Now she narrowed her eyes. Harlan shifted in his chair, adjusting to the new mood of his audience.

"Well, I didn't really want to focus on whether he's having an affair or not. There's something else going on I think you should know about."

Marisa's face changed slightly, a little colour disappearing.

"What are you talking about?"

"I think you're husband's in trouble." He regretted saying it immediately as her expression graduated to alarm.

"What trouble?"

"Not physical, nothing like that. At least, I don't think so. But he's gotten involved in some shady activities, and I think he's being blackmailed to keep it up."

"Shady activities? Blackmail? Harlan, what are you talking about?"

"How well do you know Mick Dawson?"

"Mick Dawson?" He might just as well have said Evonne Goolagong based on how high Marisa's eyebrows jumped. "Well, we've known him for years, ever since our restaurant days when he was bringing in a different client of his every week. Then he helped Jonathan with the Executive Club, and after that with Celebrities Care. I guess he's as much a friend as a business associate could ever be. Why? What about him?"

"I think he's blackmailing Jonathan to allow him to misappropriate Celebrities Care's network of outreach centres, and use them to support his own business interests."

"What? That's ridiculous. Do you know what you're saying? Mick Dawson is probably the biggest supporter of Celebrities Care. Without him, there are no celebrities, and without celebrities, there's no Celebrities Care." Harlan thought about it. The reality wasn't too far from the syntax of what she was suggesting.

"I wouldn't come to you with this if I wasn't sure. I know you'll need a bit of time to come to grips with it, but Jonathan needs your help here. If this Benefit goes ahead tomorrow night with Celebrities Care onboard, the stakes will get a lot higher and Jonathan will find it much harder to turn things around. Mick Dawson is tightening the screws already. And Marisa - I'm sorry to say but this involves you too."

She glared at him defiantly. "I've done nothing wrong!"

"I know, I meant your house."

"Our house?"

"It's actually owned by Mick Dawson. This goes back to the Executive Club, Jonathan barely saw a cent from the sale, but Mick Dawson set him up with the house and Celebrities Care and that's what he's blackmailing him with."

"What you're saying is crazy. That was years ago." Marisa looked sideways out of the office window. Harlan wondered which part of the skyline with distant harbour glimpses she was seeking guidance from. She seemed to get what she was after and turned back to face him.

"What proof do you have?"

Harlan produced the thumb drive from his pocket and placed it on the desk.

"It's all on there. The theory, documentary evidence of the corporate connections, the land title search on your home, a recording of Mick Dawson discussing the whole thing with Jonathan."

Marisa looked at the thumb drive, but Harlan could tell she had no interest in picking it up.

"And what do you want me to do with all this?"

"That's up to you. I just thought I'd show you what I'd found. But if you want to help your husband, you need to talk to him. Find out what happened at the Executive Club that led to Mick Dawson owning your home."

"I need some time to think."

Harlan decided not to mention Jenny's article. Marisa seemed upset enough to confront Jonathan already, and if he needed to use it later it would look better if he suddenly became aware a journalist was investigating the whole thing and he got in touch with Marisa straight away. In any case he figured it was safer to keep Jenny, and his relationship with her, well hidden for as long as possible.

"Of course, I understand. Just remember, after tomorrow night it's going to be more than just Celebrities Care caught up in all this, and Celebrities Care itself will be a much bigger albatross around Jonathan's neck."

"Albatross?"

"I think so. Anyway, you know what I mean."

"Most of the time."

"Then you're doing better than me." The joke landed as well as he could expect in the circumstances. Marisa let him off lightly by starting to wrap up the meeting.

"Thanks, Harlan, for coming to me. I know it would have been easier to ignore and just stick to the brief."

"Oh, well, it's all part of the service, of course. We aim to exceed expectations. We ... " Seeing Marisa turn and look out the window again, Harlan realised his bluster was as welcome as his humour was at the moment, so cut short his promotional speech. "Anyway, so do you want me to carry on with the case, considering?"

Marisa turned back towards him. "Are you going to guarantee my husband isn't cheating on me, after watching him for three days?"

"Guarantee? No, I couldn't do that."

"Then carry on. What more damage could you do?" She turned back to the window. Harlan figured the meeting was over, and let himself out. Darren was hovering outside the office, waiting for them to finish. Harlan simply nodded at him and headed towards the elevators.

"Mr Valeri," Darren called, falling in behind Harlan.

"Yes?"

"Marisa asked me to give you this when you left."

Harlan stopped and turned to see Darren holding out a cheque for him.

"She never makes people ask for money, Mr. Valeri," he said proudly.

Harlan took the cheque and pocketed it without looking at the amount. It was important never to seem like you needed it.

"Thanks Darren." He turned away and continued to the elevator.

"A pleasure, Mr. Valeri." He meant it. Even fewer people retained a personal assistant's name for more than thirty seconds.

As he rode down in the elevator, Harlan received a message, causing him to wonder how he had reception inside a falling metal box in the middle of a concrete and metal building, but not in his own backyard. Checking his phone as he walked out of the elevator and straight through the lobby, he saw it was Signboy telling him to get back to the office as soon as possible. It looked slightly odd to see 'as soon as possible' in full in a text message, but Signboy knew how much Harlan hated acronyms, even ones everyone knew the meaning of.

He used the short walk to the station to debate with himself whether to call Signboy and ask him what was so urgent, or just savour fifteen minutes of blissful ignorance and find out when he got back to the office. By the time he reached the stairs heading below street-level and down into the station, he had settled for ignorance after his imaginary decision coin landed on its edge and rolled into the street in front of an oncoming bus. Some coins were better left untossed.

As he approached the turnstile he realised he was still wearing the ACPBL visitor's pass. He was surprised the receptionist hadn't caught him on his way through the lobby. He hoped it would set off alarm bells when his two hours was up. Maybe it was just one of a series of mistakes she made every day in her job, and this would be the straw that broke the back of the camel that was her supervisor's patience, causing her to lose her job. Harlan smiled as he reached the platform for the inner west line. Just one minute of ignorance had given him this much satisfaction. He was looking forward to another fourteen.

CHAPTER 17

As he arrived at Whitehorse Street for the second time that day, Harlan wished it was the first and hoped it was the last. After about six minutes of imagining the ACPBL receptionist's drawn out descent until ultimately she went back to school, finished her high school certificate and enrolled in a law degree, all he could think about for the rest of the trip was the damage he had done to his relationship with Jenny. He desperately wanted to undo it, but wondered if he was putting the cart before the horse. Wasn't focussing on the relationship what got him tangled up in his own web of lies in the first place? He decided to forget about the relationship for now and focus on the Jonathan Foxe case. Maybe if he got to the bottom of it for her she'd be so grateful she'd give him another chance.

Before he went in, he scanned the street for cars he might recognise, or shouldn't be there. He could be a slow learner sometimes, but he was a learner nonetheless. He spotted a blue Golf halfway down the block. He couldn't say it was definitely Jenny's from this distance, but Harlan knew enough about statistics to confidently, and correctly, assume it was. He walked up the stairs to his office expecting a lukewarm reception. What he found was an empty one.

"Signboy? Jenny?" He walked through to his office, not knowing what to expect. It was empty. He looked for a note or something similar on his desk, but there was none. He walked around and shook the mouse to exit the screensaver, hoping for a clue where they might be. All he revealed was a well organised desktop.

He went back out to the reception area, again looking for some kind of indication as to their whereabouts. Again there was nothing. He wondered if Biff had had a change of heart and came back to take matters into his own hands. He decided finally to call Signboy just as he heard steps coming up the stairs, and then laughter as Signboy and Jenny walked in the open door.

"Where have you two been?" The remnants of panic in his voice were enough to cut the laughter short.

"Settle down Harlan, we just went to grab an early lunch," said Signboy.

"Signboy's just been telling me some of the hilarious stories from your past cases." Harlan searched Jenny's face for any of the hurt and disappointment so prominent just ninety minutes earlier. He found only a trace or two. "How'd it go with Marisa?"

"Well enough. She seemed upset, but I think she'll take it up with Jonathan in time. The trick then will be getting them to talk to you."

"That shouldn't be too difficult. As you said, if I'm going after Mick Dawson, they'll be happy to give me their side of the story."

"That was clever of me, wasn't it." Harlan had again misjudged his audience, as Jenny offered only the slightest nod and smile at his comment.

"Here, we figured you wouldn't have eaten." Signboy handed Harlan a foil-wrapped package the shape of a large burrito. "It's from that place you like, *Guthman Y Gometh*. Spicy Chicken *Guerrero* burrito." He lisped the name of the Mexican fast food chain-in-waiting.

"Excellent, thank you. No need to lisp though, it's Mexican." Harlan began peeling the foil from one end of the burrito.

"Yeah, but it sounds funny."

"And only at the risk of offending anyone who speaks Spanish with the lisp sound. Or anyone who, random chance forbid, has a lisp."

"Come on, Harlan, he knows it's Mexican. That's why it's funny." At Jenny's interjection he decided to drop it. He still had a lot of ground to make up with her. And it was funny.

"Fair enough. I am starving actually, I haven't had breakfast." Mexican wasn't Harlan's favourite cuisine, being mostly derived from street food in an impoverished country. But done properly the flavours were sharp and enticing, and, if wrapped well, a burrito was easily the most satisfying meal you could eat on the move without staining a tie. Particularly if the tie is folded safely in the glovebox.

"They actually had a breakfast burrito special, bacon and eggs inside," said Signboy. "I told them they should call it an Aussie. Like the pizzas."

"I think 'breakfast' makes more sense," said Harlan, unwrapping his lunch burrito. "What's particularly Australian about bacon and eggs? I never understood the connection. Anyway, what's going on?"

Jenny and Signboy looked at each other, then at Harlan, reminding him of an ABBA film clip. Jenny had apparently been designated speaker through some non-verbal agreement, because it was she who spoke.

"We thought we'd look into Jonathan's Executive Club days - you know, just in case Marisa doesn't come through, maybe we could put enough dots together that joining them will give us a pretty clear picture of why he owed Mick Dawson millions of dollars."

"What did you find?"

"Not too much. But the Executive Club wasn't without its critics. We think we've found someone who can help us, a journalist who was leading a campaign against the Executive Club before it was sold to Mick Dawson."

"A campaign against the Executive Club? You mean he had a problem with celebrities and wealthy people having exclusive access to the best restaurants and nightclubs?"

"She. Diane Adams."

"Diane Adams? She still writes for the *Herald*, she does those opinion pieces."

"That's the one. She wrote articles implying the exclusive access side of the club was just its legitimate front, if you believe establishing a cultural elite is legitimate. She practically accused the Executive Club of also providing prostitutes and drugs to its members."

"Which would explain why it's an escort service these days, it's a remnant of what it used to be," said Harlan. "Sydney has become so obsessed with fame and fortune there's no need for the 'legitimate' services of the Executive Club as it was back then. What kind of an A-lister needs to be a member of some club to get in the back room of a nightclub?"

"True," said Jenny. "But don't underestimate the role the Executive Club played in influencing Sydney's bar and club scene. Operators learned how valuable it was to have celebrities walking in and out of their venues. Of course they have a lot of money themselves, but when the social pages talk about them hanging out in a private room at some trendy bar, it brings in the real money who want the same treatment and will pay a ridiculous amount for it. Plus the front room will always be full of people who get a thrill from the rumours of who's there that night, and from telling their friends about it the next day.

"Anyway, back when that was still a couple of years away from becoming the social norm, Diane Adams regularly wrote these articles criticising the Executive Club. Then one day she just stopped. The same week the sale to Mick Dawson was announced."

"That is interesting. We should go and talk to her about it."

"I told you Jenny," said Signboy. "Harlan doesn't believe in coincidences."

"No, I do believe in them. I'd be irrational not to. I just ascribe to them the appropriate statistical probability when I'm factoring them into my decision-making."

"So what's the appropriate statistical probability to ascribe to this one?" asked Jenny, enjoying stringing the syllables together, and slightly making fun of Harlan.

"Let's just say it warrants further investigation. So how do we get in touch with Ms Adams?"

"We call her. I have her number."

"You know her?"

"No - but I know a couple of cadets at the *Herald*, I told them I was after a quote from her for a story I'm working on. Which is kind of true."

"Do you think she'll talk to us? Aren't you a competitor, as a freelancer?"

"Actually it's a *Herald* publication, their *Weekend* magazine, that picked up my article. So if it comes to it, I'm sure I can drop a couple of names and get her talking. I'd rather not, it's better if a freelancer can put their story together without any help from the publisher. That's why I went through my friend who's a cadet there instead."

"Newspaper cadets," said Harlan. "They can be worth their weight in gold."

"How so?"

"I've got an arrangement with a couple of them around the place, they tip me off on what's going to be in the social pages each day. If one of my clients is in there I can alert them beforehand. Usually a robust threat to sue will get the mention pulled - it's only the social pages after all, there's always plenty of other crap going on. If that fails, at least they get some notice before the paper comes out."

"Well, I doubt my friend would be involved in tipping off people about the social pages," said Jenny, provoking an awkward moment.

Harlan couldn't tell if her disdain was based on journalistic snobbery, journalistic integrity, or if she just wasn't sold on the indetective profession yet. Considering the day he'd had, he favoured the latter, so didn't challenge her on it.

"Okay, so let's give this Diane Adams a call then," he said, trying to dispel the tension by diverting her attention to the task that had brought them together in the first place. "The clocks are ticking."

"I think it would be better if it's just me," said Jenny. "She might like the idea of helping a young female journalist writing her first big story."

"Sure, makes sense. Then why did you wait for me?"

"Well, you know. We are a team, Harlan." She looked into his eyes, and he sensed for the first time since he'd told her the full story there might still be a chance with her.

"Thanks," was all he could muster as a response.

"Come on, let's do it in your office," said Jenny, leading the way.

"So I should leave then?" joked Signboy.

"Very funny," said Jenny. Harlan was confused, it was a line of humour he usually didn't get, and as usual he didn't get it in this instance.

"We will need another chair actually Signboy - do you want to rustle one up?"

"Sure thing."

Signboy left out the front door as Harlan followed Jenny into his office to find her sitting in his ergonomic armchair. Apparently she was going to milk this for a fair while. He sat in the guest chair across from her and concentrated on eating his burrito.

"Why doesn't he just grab the receptionist's chair?" asked Jenny.

Harlan held up a hand while he finished a mouthful before answering.

"It's stuck behind the desk. You have to move the desk to get the chair out, and it doesn't move far enough before you need to move the fan. It's a whole process." It was an elaborate but harmless lie he'd used before to cover the fact his office wasn't big enough for two ergonomic chairs - not just in the same way corrupt towns in the Old West were never quite big enough for two headstrong gunslingers not afraid to operate outside the law, but also aesthetically.

"Oh."

They didn't say anything more while Jenny pulled her phone and notebook out of her handbag, flipping through the notebook to find Diane Adams' number. Just as she folded the book open on the right page, Signboy returned with a boxy, carpeted chair that would have looked more at home sitting in a waiting room somewhere, and had only recently been doing so.

"You guys have a storeroom downstairs or something?" asked Jenny.

"Yeah, something like that," said Signboy, putting the chair next to Harlan and sitting down.

"Okay, here goes," said Jenny, dialling the number. Harlan and Signboy looked on, both realising they hadn't done much planning for the call. Harlan thought it was a good opportunity to show he had faith in Jenny and said nothing, despite his strong instinct to offer some advice on how to proceed. Signboy actually did have faith in Jenny, so was confident she would get the right outcome without his help.

Jenny was holding the phone to her ear but the others could still hear a muffled ringing tone that was cut off by a similarly muffled woman's voice after a few seconds.

"Hi, Ms Adams. My name's Jenny Randall, I hope you don't mind me calling you but I was hoping you could help me out with an article I'm writing on Jonathan Foxe." Harlan and Signboy strained to hear the response but neither could make out the words. Half a conversation would have to do for now.

"Sure," Jenny continued. "I'm a freelancer, and I've been working on a piece about Celebrities Care and the work it does. As you'd expect, it's become a piece about Jonathan Foxe as much as Celebrities Care. Doing a bit of backgrounding I found a couple of articles you wrote in 2004 and 2005 about the Executive Club. I really think my article would benefit from your insight into that period of his life, particularly about how he went from being Sydney's Hugh Hefner to Sydney's Bono."

Harlan studied Jenny's face for her reaction to what Diane Adams was saying, but found himself just admiring the way her brow creased slightly as she concentrated on listening. Jenny gave him a quick look he decided was either to say 'stop staring at me' or 'you've got salsa all over your face'. To be safe, he stopped staring and used the serviette that came with the burrito to wipe around his mouth. He missed Jenny's eyes lighting up.

"Really? That would be great. What time suits you? ... Yes, I can make three ... Yes, I know the street." As she took down the address in her notebook, Jenny noticed Harlan tapping his chest, eyebrows raised. She made a quick decision to include him in the meeting. "Oh, Ms Adams ... Diane, of course. Do you mind if I bring my co-author? ... Great. Okay, we'll see you at three."

Jenny beamed at Harlan and Signboy as she took her phone away from her ear.

"She wants to talk in person, this afternoon, at her home in Darling Point."

"Perfect, great work," said Harlan. A knock came on the outside door, which they then heard open.

"Mr. Valeri? It's Shannon, from downstairs."

"Come through," Harlan called out. A man with straight shoulder-length hair and a thick, apparently regularly conditioned moustache appeared at the door.

"Mr. Valeri, sorry to bother you, you haven't seen ... " he stopped mid-sentence when he saw the chair Signboy was sitting on. "Mr. Valeri, I've asked you not to take our chairs - they're for my patients."

"Are you the chiropractor?" asked Jenny.

"Yes, Shannon. Pleased to meet you."

"I love your tea selection."

"Oh, thanks. Well, again, that's just for patients as well."

"I think the urn's a bit low. I like my tea really hot."

"If the water's too hot, you can scald the tea, and lose many of its medicinal and spiritual benefits, not to mention ruin the flavour. I stock only delicate herbal teas. For my patients."

"Oh, okay. Fair enough." Jenny was already using her phone to google the ideal brewing temperature for tea.

"Shannon, we're just about finished here anyway," said Harlan. "Signboy will bring the chair back down shortly."

"Please don't forget this time, last time you had the chair up here over the weekend, and Saturday's my busy day. I don't have many patients who can tolerate standing up for too long, or sitting on the floor for that matter."

"Don't worry, I'll bring it right down," said Signboy. "Although I don't think the chair's doing them any favours either, it's not exactly an ergonomic dream."

"Well, I have a suggestion box for a reason, so if my patients aren't happy with the chairs, I'm sure I'll hear about it. Good afternoon then." He turned and walked back through to the outside door.

"Oh, wait, Shannon," called Jenny. He reappeared at the door. "I've still got your mug, sorry," she said, pointing to a plain white mug sitting on the corner of the desk. The chiropractor stepped forward and took the mug, then left without speaking.

"What a riot," said Jenny.

"You should meet the tax guy," said Signboy.

"Well, we've got a couple of hours," said Harlan. "Who fancies putting on a bit of a masquerade for Biff?"

They decided it was too risky for Biff to see Signboy again, so he was to prepare a 'round the grounds' update on the other cases on their books while Harlan and Jenny put in some time on Jonathan's tail for Biff's benefit. According to the latest itinerary, Jonathan had a full day at the Celebrities Care office overseeing preparations for Saturday night, so Harlan followed Jenny there. They made sure they drove past Jonathan's car, which was parked out the front in its usual spot, in case Biff was hanging around, and then they parked in clear view of the offices to have the best chance of Biff seeing them and thinking Harlan was still on the case.

After about half of an hour of doing nothing, Jenny called Harlan and suggested she leave the car to grab a coffee or something, and he take the opportunity to pretend to break into her car and rummage around. Jenny left the passenger door unlocked and walked to the next block to find a café. Harlan used a coat-hanger he'd removed from his dry-cleaning in the back seat to pretend to unlock her door like he'd seen in so many movies. Unfortunately in his effort to make it look realistic, he managed somehow to lock the door. He was still trying to unlock it again when he saw Jenny come out of the café she'd gone into on the next block, so he gave up and ran back to his car. If Biff was watching, he'd think two things: Harlan was still following Jenny around; and he was still a learner in the detective game. If he decided to go for a personal best and went on to think a third thing, it would be that Harlan hadn't made much progress with either.

When they eventually left for their meeting with Diane Adams, Harlan was a little surprised not to have seen any movement from Jonathan or Biff. Sure, they had the biggest night in Celebrities Care history to plan for, but Jonathan hadn't stayed in the same place for more than an hour up to then, so it was strange to see him, or not see him, in lockdown like this. Harlan dismissed as paranoia the notion maybe they weren't the only ones putting on a performance, but he couldn't help feeling he was missing something.

CHAPTER 18

Diane Adams lived in Darling Point, an ageing eastern suburb nestled on the southern side of Sydney Harbour between Rushcutters and Double Bays. As Harlan followed Jenny along Darling Point Road, he found it hard to believe it was only a stone's throw from the hectic Cross. He had always dismissed the harbourside eastern suburbs as culturally sterile and over-privileged, and nothing he saw along the tree-lined ramble Jenny led him on suggested to him he should give them further consideration. It was one of the places Harlan thought would be far better off succumbing to rising sea levels.

They drove most of the way along the point before turning into a quiet, residential street, finding a park each without much hassle. Harlan caught up to Jenny as she checked the numbers of the nearby houses.

"This way," she said, and started walking down towards the end of the street.

"These places are so quiet," said Harlan. "I haven't seen a single person since we turned onto Darling Point Road."

"That's why people love it here. Not everyone needs to feel they're living in a vibrant city whenever they step outside."

"I guess. There must be something better than an open-air nursing home to step out in though."

"It's not that bad. Diane Adams lives here, it must have something going for it."

"Something other than Diane Adams living here I should hope."

They reached what Harlan thought was the end of the street but was actually a hard left hand turn. Harlan had the feeling they must be close to the water, but all he could see were apartment buildings.

"This is the one," said Jenny, pointing to an apartment building Harlan assumed backed onto the water. From the street level it was only one storey high, but as they walked down the driveway they realised the building went down about ten storeys before hitting the shore of the harbour. The driveway veered right into a parking area where Harlan noticed, but kept to himself, the ample visitor parking. He followed Jenny left through a sliding door into a small corridor with banks of mailboxes on either side, and a large intercom on the wall next to the sliding door at the other end.

"Number 410," Jenny read from her notebook as she approached the intercom. "Four-one-zero-Bell," she said to herself, pressing those buttons.

"Hello?" A woman's voice answered.

"Diane - it's Jenny Randall, we spoke on the phone earlier."

"Hello? You have to push the T button to talk."

Jenny held down the T button.

"Diane - it's Jenny Randall, we spoke on the phone earlier."

"Okay Jenny, one second."

They heard a buzz.

"Did you get it?"

"We heard it," said Jenny.

"You have to push the door when you hear the buzz."

"Sorry, I thought it was a sliding door."

"It is, but it's a little off kilter, so you need to give it a shove when you hear the buzz, and the buzz will do the rest."

"Okay."

"Ready?"

"Yes."

"I'm pressing buzz ... now."

They heard the buzz again. Harlan pushed the sliding door in a little, and sure enough the buzz did the rest as the doors slid open. Harlan and Jenny walked through and located a stairwell to their right when they heard the voice from the intercom again.

"Did you get it?"

Jenny thought about going back to answer the question.

"She'll figure it out," Harlan said to Jenny. "Four-ten, this way." A sign on the wall next to the stairs told them apartments 1 to 710 were downstairs. They took the stairs down four flights, where a sign on the wall opposite the stairwell told them apartments 406 to 410 were to their right. They followed the sign and found apartment 410 at the end of the corridor. Jenny knocked lightly on the door.

"We come down four flights of stairs, she doesn't have time to open the door for us?" Harlan whispered to Jenny.

"Shh." Jenny didn't want to get off on the wrong foot with Diane Adams. The romantic corner of her mind told her this meeting could lead to a career-defining mentor-protégé relationship.

The front door opened, revealing the familiar-looking Diane Adams, whose portrait accompanied all of her *Herald* opinion pieces online and in the newspaper. Harlan had also seen her on more than her fair share of panel shows over the years, offering her insight into whatever political issue captivated the intelligentsia at the time.

Her shoulder-length auburn hair was tied back in a pony tail, and she was wearing the fashionably rectangular glasses reserved for her more serious television appearances. She dressed casually in a T-shirt and jeans, and Harlan was surprised to see her with bare feet. He wasn't an expert in social etiquette by any stretch of the most flexible imagination, but he would have put shoes on if expecting complete strangers at his house.

"Jenny, please come in. Good to meet you," she said, standing aside to let Jenny walk in. Harlan followed. "And you must be ... "

"I am. I'm Harlan Valeri. How did you know?" He shook her hand as he went past, pleased to get the pressure and pace of the handshake just right.

"I didn't. I, um." She had experienced probably the most common reaction to meeting Harlan for the first time. There was no appropriate response.

Jenny had walked through the short entrance hall into a small open-plan kitchen and living area, which opened out onto a balcony overlooking Double Bay to the east. This distracted her from giving Harlan the look she intended as he joined her, which was designed to tell him to try to not be too weird because this was a very important meeting. She'd been practising it in the car for most of the trip there.

Diane Adams had regained her composure and followed them through to the living area. She let them admire the view for a few seconds, which was enough to let Harlan get on the front foot again.

"Ms. Adams, what an amazing apartment," he said, walking through the open folding doors and right up to the balcony railing to scan the panorama. "You must be close to the *Masterchef* house. That's in Darling Point isn't it?"

"I think so, yes."

"Stunning view. It makes more sense now."

"What does?"

"People living here. There's something about looking out over water, isn't there?"

"I certainly think so. My landlord values it pretty highly too."

"I bet. Are any of these boats yours?" Harlan waved his arm at the hundred or so small sailing vessels bobbing contentedly on the glistening waters below.

"No, no. They're just there to remind me I'm an interloper, even though I've been here a few years now."

"I know how you feel," said Harlan. "We used to look over Tamarama. They've got a whole squad of surfers working round the clocks to remind people who just live there that they're not making the most of it. Most days they're just bobbing up and down too."

"Used to? Where are you now?"

"Redfern."

"Oh. Anyway, can I get you a cup of tea or coffee?"

"No, thanks," said Jenny. She wanted to get on with it.

"Umm," Harlan was considering whether he felt more like a glass of coke with ice or a double espresso, but Jenny caught his eye and managed to give him the look she'd been working on. "Could I just get a glass of water, please Ms. Adams?"

"Sure. Please, call me Diane."

"Of course. Is it your day off?"

"Not really, I try to work from home as much as possible. I hate going into the office, and I don't really have to since I became a columnist. Please, take a seat," she said over her shoulder as she poured Harlan a glass of water.

Harlan and Jenny contemplated the two sofas that were the only seating options in the room, set facing each other over a coffee table, side on to the view. They sat on the sofa against the wall of the living room, the balcony to their right and the kitchen to their left. Diane brought the glass of water over and placed it on the coffee table in front of Harlan, then she sat in the sofa facing them.

"Do you mind if I make a tape?" asked Jenny. "I don't think I'm going to want to miss anything you've got to say."

"Don't they teach shorthand anymore? Harlan, you must have learnt it?"

"I'm not really classically trained."

"No, I didn't think so." She let the statement sit on the table for a few seconds, the silence a tacit understanding between them that Harlan wasn't exactly what he said he was. "Sure, tape it, but we're going to have to make some rules about what you use it for."

"Don't worry," said Jenny. "I'll just make notes off it and then reuse the tape."

"That's fine then, go ahead."

Jenny pulled her dictaphone out of her handbag, checked the tape was at the beginning and pressed record, placing it on the table so she could also take notes.

"So, Jenny. Harlan. How can I help you?"

Jenny talked Diane through the article she was writing, but didn't mention how Mick Dawson was the puppeteer of the Celebrities Care call centre work, or that no money ever passed hands when Jonathan Foxe sold the Executive Club. She wanted to get a feeling for Diane's attitude before she brought out the big guns. When Jenny was finished, Diane looked from Jenny to Harlan, and back.

"Well, it sounds like a good story. It's not what I was expecting after you called, but I'm not all that surprised."

"Oh, thanks," said Jenny, a little slighted by the lukewarm response. "Well, as I said on the phone, we were hoping you could help us with your experience writing about the Executive Club. I just can't get my head around why Jonathan Foxe sold the Executive Club and turned around and started up a charitable foundation. I mean, I can see the connection in terms of using the contacts he had made over the years to harness the power of celebrity to work for charity, but something must have made him change direction so drastically."

Harlan finished his glass of water and watched Diane for a response. Like Jenny, he wasn't sure yet whether they could count Diane as an ally. She seemed to be taking a long time thinking about the question.

"Diane, sorry to butt in," said Harlan. "What were you expecting after we called?"

"I don't really know. When you described him as Sydney's Bono I wasn't sure whether you were taking a positive slant or not."

"Narcissistic, tax-dodging, annoying-music-making marketing genius who wears sunglasses at night, or third world crusader with a back-catalogue that can open any door in the world for a tête-à-tête and makes unisex rubber bracelets socially acceptable. I see how you could get confused," said Harlan.

"Exactly. And I'm still not sure. Maybe because you haven't made up your mind yet. Jenny, you said you were a freelancer. Who are you writing this article for?"

"I pitched it all over the place, but actually it's the *Herald* who have given me an advance, to run it in the *Weekend* magazine as a profile piece."

"Really?" said Diane, looking at Jenny with some newfound respect. "So why did you call me out of the blue? You could have gotten Vincent to set up a meeting with me."

"Vincent?" asked Harlan.

"The *Herald* editor, Vincent Argyle," said Jenny.

"Harlan, if you want to make it as a journalist you should really know the players in the industry." Diane seemed to smirk as she played along with Harlan's act.

"Of course, I was just ... it's a common name, that's all."

"Anyway Jenny, I'm glad you didn't. How much have you told Vincent about your article?"

"I haven't spoken to him. It's being organised through the features editor of *Weekend*."

"Good. The less Vincent knows the better."

"Why's that?" asked Harlan.

Diane looked them up and down, and even looked out at the balcony apparently but quite unnecessarily to make sure they were alone. She looked suspiciously at the dictaphone on the table, as if she could warn it not to let the tape fall into the wrong hands. Then she sat back in her sofa and held her head high as if she was about to make a statement so grand it would make Winston Churchill cringe.

"Because it was Vincent who bumped my last article about the Executive Club, and then manoeuvred me into a new role as a political commentator to make sure I wouldn't bring it up again."

Luckily for Diane, like Churchill during the war years, she had a partisan audience. Harlan and Jenny leaned forward synchronously.

"So what was your last article about?" asked Jenny.

"A party. The Executive Club hosted an ARIAs after-party and things got completely out of control. I wasn't able to get anyone to talk about it in detail at the time, and haven't since for that matter. All anyone would say is it was the absolute pinnacle of the Executive Club era. 'Sybaritic' is the word I used in the article. Apparently no guest went without anything they desired. Unfortunately some got more than that though."

"What do you mean?" asked Harlan. Next to him Jenny was taking notes furiously. It was hard to imagine she'd need the tape as well.

"Two girls overdosed on heroin. They were both models, paid to be there by the Executive Club. I'm sure they were paid to do more than just walk around and look pretty though."

"Prostitutes?" Harlan inferred.

"Yes, prostitutes was what I wanted to imply at the time. Anyway, Jonathan Foxe was questioned by police about it but never charged. I wrote an article soft on facts because I couldn't find a source, and Vincent was able to convince the rest of editorial we shouldn't run it."

"What about the two girls?" asked Jenny. "Surely they had friends, family who knew what they were doing?"

"Almost certainly. But who comes out and says 'yes, my friend or daughter was a prostitute'?"

"And the police? Surely they knew what was going on?"

"I spoke to the investigating officers after they'd questioned Jonathan. They said it was a vanilla OD, and that's all they were interested in."

"So not having a source explains why Vincent was against the article, but why did he give you a promotion?"

"That's the question, Jenny. And I didn't know the answer until I heard about Mick Dawson buying the Executive Club. It didn't make any sense. The two girls ended up as one paragraph on page four, although they got a bit of coverage in other papers. Enough so anyone would have been thinking twice before going to another Executive Club party. Plus the A-list scene had exploded. Club and restaurant owners were catering to the in crowd on their own, they didn't need the middle man anymore."

"So why would Mick Dawson pay top dollar for something in such decline?" A leading question from Jenny.

"Exactly. And the amount, what was it, four or five million?" Jenny nodded. "Even if it wasn't in decline, it sounds like a lot of money for a business with no assets other than a few limousine leases. I'd be surprised if anywhere near that amount of money passed hands.

"So I asked Vincent about it. That's when he got angry. He told me I should pull my head in and mind my own business. He even told me Mick Dawson had a lot of friends, which I thought wasn't really relevant to the story. Anyway, I had my hands full with my new job, which is exactly what Vincent wanted. Eventually I guess I just decided it wasn't worth it, so I never brought it up again."

"The classic power-play of the market economy - keep people busy enough, you can get away with anything," said Harlan, who had been silent for longer than he was used to.

"Well, something like that, I suppose," said Diane. "I don't think Vincent had anything to do with the Executive Club though, I think we were just doing Mick Dawson a favour. Or someone else who was looking out for Mick Dawson."

"So," said Harlan, standing up and walking towards the balcony. Suddenly he turned back towards Jenny and Diane, holding up a finger to indicate he was about to join some dots in front of them.

"Jonathan Foxe throws a party. Two girls he hired as prostitutes die from drugs he supplied. He is questioned by police, but no charges laid. The journalist who has been hounding him writes an article about it, but can't find a source. The newspaper not only cans the article, but promotes the journalist to keep her from ever looking into the Executive Club again. Jonathan Foxe appears to get off scot free."

Jenny and Diane nodded, both on the edge of their sofas.

"Not so," he continued. "The very same week, he sells his business to Mick Dawson. They put out a press release, saying it sold for four and a half million dollars. Sounds like a lot of money, but we know the truth."

"What's the truth?" asked Diane. She'd been watching Harlan's performance with utter fascination.

"Mick Dawson didn't pay a cent for the Executive Club. Not a brass razoo."

"How do you know that?"

"Because Mick Dawson paid three and a half million dollars for a house instead, in which Jonathan Foxe and his family have been residing ever since. And I'd be willing to bet all the brass razoos in the world Mick Dawson also bankrolled Celebrities Care until it was up and running. He still provides Jonathan with a car, a driver and a bodyguard."

"That's not much of a bet," said Jenny. "A brass razoo's worthless. It's not even real. That's the point."

"Really?" Harlan was stunned. "Then why would people complain about not having one?"

"They're not lamenting the fact they don't have one, they're illustrating how broke they are."

"Oh. I see. Well, the brass must be worth something."

"They don't exist Harlan, there is no brass."

"Okay. I'd be willing to bet all the gold in the world, how's that?"

"It makes more sense."

"It's a rhetorical bet anyway, Jenny, it doesn't have to make sense."

Diane cleared her throat. She was amazed her guests could get sidetracked by such a trivial argument at such a critical point in Harlan's postulations. Luckily Jenny had kept her racist accusations over Harlan's earlier use of the phrase 'scot free' to herself. The inevitable googling and backtracking when she found it had nothing to do with the Scottish wouldn't have made the best impression.

"Sorry, Diane," said Harlan. "Where was I?"

"Mick Dawson owns Jonathan Foxe's house, bankrolled Celebrities Care ... " said Jenny, helping things get back on track to make up for her part in the digression.

"Right," said Harlan.

"And?" Diane was desperately hoping there was more.

"That's what we know. What I was getting to, though, is shortly after Jonathan narrowly avoids serious criminal charges and slanderous newspaper articles, he seems to hand over his company for nothing more than rent-free accommodation and a brand new career in philanthropy."

"So," said Diane. "You're saying Mick Dawson pulled strings, with the police and with the *Herald*, to get Jonathan off scot free, as you said, in return for the Executive Club, but then bought Jonathan Foxe a house and has been supporting him ever since? What's the point of that?"

"That's where Celebrities Care comes into it," said Jenny. It was her turn to stand and make a point, heading in the opposite direction to Harlan and reaching the kitchen before she turned around. "It wasn't just Jonathan feeling guilty about the two girls who paid the ultimate price for Sydney's A-listers' predilection for hedonism. It was part of the deal. Well, two deals when you break it down. First, I bail you out of trouble with the police and keep the press off your back if you give me your company, which would be nothing without me anyway. Second, I'll get you back on your feet and set you up with a charitable foundation to keep you out of trouble, but you have to use the foundation for my nefarious purposes."

"I see," said Diane.

"No, that's not quite right," said Harlan. "This is where my expertise comes into it. Jonathan had to come out of it looking like he'd just made millions. Otherwise he would have to explain to his wife how he sold his company but didn't even have a brass razoo to show for it."

Harlan paused to get a nod he felt he deserved from Jenny for using the colloquial term properly. When Jenny realised why he'd paused, she smiled and gave him a thumbs up instead, which was good enough.

"And trust me, I wouldn't have come as far in my profession as I have if I didn't understand the lengths men will go to to keep things like that from their wives. Wife. Wives or wife?"

"You said men, so it should be wives," said Jenny, hoping to move things along to prevent Diane becoming too curious about Harlan's profession.

"But if you say wives, it sounds like they have more than one wife," said Diane, getting caught up in the pointless digression this time, to Jenny's relief.

"If you say wife," said Jenny, "it sounds like they share the same wife. Wife should go with his, not their. So it would be 'the lengths men will go to keep things from his wife', which is obviously wrong."

"You're right," said Diane, impressed again by Jenny. "So it is 'their wives', but that's still ambiguous because one of the men could have many wives."

"Not in this country though, so I think we can live with it," said Harlan. "Anyway, so the first deal, as you put it Jenny, would have been unacceptable to Jonathan because he had his wife to think of, even though it got him out of trouble with the police and the press. Then Mick Dawson thinks of a way to solve Jonathan's problem with his wife, and at the same time get a successful entrepreneur beholden to him, without actually risking anything because he still owns the house. To Mick Dawson it's just another investment."

"Maybe he even cooked up the Celebrities Care scam at the same time," said Jenny. "He definitely would have had a say in what Jonathan did next."

"Maybe they cooked it up together?" said Diane.

"Maybe. We have enough for now though. Jenny, I think we'd better go, there's a lot to do before the Benefit."

"Oh, you're going tomorrow night?"

Harlan and Jenny exchanged glances. They weren't sure Diane would be so impressed with their plans to disrupt the benefit.

"We're hoping to go," said Jenny, as she picked her things up off the coffee table. "It would be a good setting for the article I think. You know, Jonathan Foxe on top of the world, but what exactly is going on behind the scenes, that kind of thing."

"Sounds good. Look, I have a spare ticket, they always send me two to these things for some reason, it's just a headache finding someone to go with usually. It's not ideal, but at least one of you will have a VIP ticket. Fancy being my plus-one, Jenny?"

"Sure, I'd love to. Thanks a lot." Jenny was chuffed.

"You don't mind, Harlan?" asked Diane.

"Mind? No. Why should I mind? I'll get a ticket somehow."

"I meant because I'm taking your girlfriend."

Jenny and Harlan went crimson.

"It's very obvious, the way you bicker. Don't worry, your secret's safe with me."

"Thanks, but-" said Jenny, starting to protest.

"Yes, thanks," said Harlan, cutting her off. So long as it wasn't a Foxe or a Dawson, the more people who thought she was his girlfriend the better. "Anyway, we should go, we're still a few sources short for the article. You've been a great help though Diane, we're that much closer to the full story." Harlan held up his hand indicating a very small distance with his thumb and index finger, which was the opposite of what he meant.

"Don't mention it." Diane stood up and followed Harlan and Jenny to the front door. "So Jenny, the tickets will be at the door tomorrow night. Meet me there at six thirty, we can grab a drink beforehand. You know the State Theatre of course?"

"Sure, I won't be late. Thanks again."

"Oh, and Jenny?"

"Yes?"

"Be careful who you talk to about this article. Just because it's seven years on, doesn't mean people don't still want things kept secret. In fact, it sounds like for some people there's more reason now to keep it secret than there ever was. Good luck."

With that and a sympathetic smile, Diane closed the door on them. They walked back towards their cars, a little additional tension between them after Diane's 'girlfriend' comment.

"So what now?" asked Jenny.

"Let's pick up Signboy, then head back to the Celebrities Care office to keep up appearances; but I'm also curious to see what Jonathan and Biff are up to. Meanwhile we get Signboy to find out what he can about these two dead girls, although it sounds like there won't be much to find. Also Marisa hasn't called yet, it's probably worth me calling her. We can't afford to sit around waiting too long."

"And if she's no help?"

"Then we lead the horse to Mohammed."

CHAPTER 19

Harlan called ahead while driving and asked Signboy to do a quick internet search for any story about the dead models. Then he decided to call Marisa. He didn't want her to think he was hassling her and thought it would sound more casual if he was driving. She answered on the first ring.

"Harlan, hi."

"Hi Marisa. I just thought I'd give you a quick call to see how you're going. I know I dropped a bit of a bomb on you this morning."

"A bombshell, yes. Look, sorry Harlan but I've been flat out all day, I haven't had a chance to even think about it, let alone look at the thumb drive you left me." So she was choosing denial. It was a common phenomenon that made his job a lot easier than it should be. Often people faced with the most distressing revelations seemed more than anything to want to just get on with their lives. It was like they could ignore the use-by date on a carton of milk if they'd already made their cappuccino.

"That's fine, I just wanted to see how you were going. If you do want to talk about it you can always call me."

"Okay, thanks Harlan. I've got to go."

Harlan didn't quite know what to make of the call. Even if it was denial, she seemed to be fairly casual about it. He guessed you didn't get to be the editor of a high profile publication without being able to put your personal life to the side. Still, he would have felt better if she'd shown some anger towards him for telling her in the first place, but she seemed to have no reaction at all. It troubled him for the rest of the drive to Whitehorse St.

They were about twenty minutes early for the Friday night traffic, so were able to get in and out of Newtown fairly quickly. With Signboy in Harlan's car they headed to the Celebrities Care office in Alexandria.

"How'd you go with the dead models?"

"Not much," said Signboy, pulling out his phone and bringing up a note he'd made. "It was a story for a couple of days, then it wasn't. Jonathan Foxe was a person of interest, questioned once but released without charge."

"Just as I thought. We might need to dig a bit deeper. Maybe rustle up my contact in the police department."

"You have a contact in the police department?"

"Of course."

"I've never heard you mention that."

"It's a professional courtesy, keeping a source to yourself."

"What, are you a journalist now?"

"No, it's just ... it's only natural to be a bit protective of a source in the police force."

"A police force source."

"Sure. Look, it just never came up. Now you're more involved, there's plenty more to the business you'll learn about."

"Now that I'm an equal."

"Now that you're officially the lowest ranked worker at the agency, for a short trial period."

"Thanks." Signboy sounded hurt.

"Too far? You know I'm joking." Harlan's voice carried as much concern as the vibrating air particles that carried it allowed. "We couldn't have done any of this without you."

"Tell me about it," said Signboy again, now sounding his usual cocky self. Having landed an accidental blow, Harlan decided to quit the verbal sparring for the rest of the drive. Signboy wanted to get the learning underway.

"So who is this police force source anyway?"

Harlan groaned. He never enjoyed talking about his past, especially when it involved someone else's past as well.

"What's wrong?" said Signboy.

"We started out together," said Harlan, accepting Signboy wasn't going to let it drop easily.

"As indetectives?"

"As cops."

"Wait, you were a cop?"

"No, but I enrolled at the academy. We were roommates, I got kicked out, we stayed in touch. End of story."

"What did you get kicked out for?"

"I said end of story."

"'End of story' as in you'll tell me one day, or 'end of story' as in none of my business?" Signboy knew Harlan was stubborn about these kinds of things, so didn't want to press him. Harlan, though, still felt a little guilty over his previous barb, so decided to treat Signboy like an equal by opening up to him.

"The short version is he wanted to be a cop and I didn't. He got busted taking part in some kind of initiation prank. When it looked like he might get kicked out over it, I stepped forward and took the blame, knowing how important becoming a cop was to him."

"So he pretty much owes you his career?"

"Well, I never saw it that way. But I think he does."

"What was the prank?" asked Signboy, with a mischievous glint forming in the corner of his eye.

"That's not my part of the story. You'll have to ask him when you meet him."

"Oh." Signboy had gotten more than he'd expected, so left that line of questioning for another, more personal one.

"Why were you training to be something you didn't want to be?"

"That, Signboy," said Harlan, turning the car into the Celebrities Care street, "is a very good question. But one for another time. *This* time is for that 'round the grounds' you promised me."

Signboy filled Harlan in briefly on how the rest of his practice was travelling without him. The cocaine-loving barrister in a custody battle needed a reason he was photographed letting a man into his apartment for only couple of minutes at two a.m. on a school night. The high-stakes gambler with the at-times puritanical wife had a poker game next Tuesday night he'd need a solid alibi with documentary evidence for. The local councillor who was working up the courage to become a whistle-blower over a particularly corrupt property development had found his incriminating evidence almost solely incriminated him so was having second thoughts about the whole thing. And the drive thru-addicted school teacher had started taking the bus. Harlan thought briefly before giving Signboy some pointers.

"Tell the barrister to hire his drug dealer retrospectively as a clerk who delivered him a thumb drive pertaining to the most honourable and non-drugs related case he's currently working on, and being a dedicated father he made sure it was after the kids were fast asleep so as not to disturb them in what is already a very stressful period in their young lives. Make a booking for me at Rockpool Bar & Grill for Tuesday night and tell the gambler he's taking a client to dinner. Tell the councillor to stop pretending he's capable of turning over a new leaf and if he wastes our time any further it won't be him threatening to blow the whistle. And tell the teacher to watch out for vending machines. Wait, don't mention vending machines, I think there's a high transference risk there. Just tell him we'll check in again next week."

Signboy finished making a note on his phone. "Yeah, that councillor did sound like a bit of a prick," he said when finished.

"Indeed," said Harlan. "We're here, you'd better sit low."

Harlan was pleased to see the Mercedes-Benz was in the same spot when they arrived. He parked a couple of spots behind Jenny, across the road about twenty metres down from the office and the Benz so as to keep Signboy well out of sight. Despite the big weekend ahead for the organisation there was a regular trickle of people leaving the Celebrities Care office. Harlan wasn't surprised. Leaving work early on a Friday was a basic human right these days.

He was surprised though when Jonathan came out of the front door so early, with Biff in tow. They walked to their waiting car, Biff opening Jonathan's door for him when they reached it. Harlan saw Jonathan looking around before he got in. He looked distressed, as though he was searching for someone to rescue him. After a second Biff placed a hand on Jonathan's shoulder and helped him into the car. It looked very much like Jonathan Foxe was a prisoner in Biff's custody.

Harlan's phone rang. It was Jenny.

"Hi," he answered.

"Did you see that?"

"Interesting, wasn't it."

"What should we do?"

"Follow them. It's time I spoke to Jonathan I think, but we need to get Biff out of the way first."

"Okay," said Jenny, then hung up. Jonathan's car was already moving away. Jenny followed it first, then Harlan.

"We've got a regular convoy going," said Signboy, enjoying his first taste of action for the day that didn't involve cowering in a wardrobe.

"Anything but, I'm afraid. This could be a tricky car chase at this time of the evening. We need to be right on top of Jonathan's car when he gets out."

"What for?"

"I'm going to do to Jonathan what he did to me when we first met."

"Abduct him?"

"Well, offer him a ride. I'm confident he'll come along voluntarily."

"What about Biff?"

"That's where you come in. You need to get Biff to chase you again, then I'll pick Jonathan up."

"Are you crazy? He'll kill me if he catches me again."

"So don't let him catch you. He won't chase you too far, he's got to stay close to Jonathan. That's why we have to be close when they stop. This needs to be our smoothest operation yet."

"Okay," said Signboy, not completely convinced. "So if you drive off with Jonathan, what am I supposed to do, catch a train home?"

"Call Jenny, she'll pick you up."

"Well, let's call her now then, I want her to be ready when this shit goes down." If Signboy was going to be acting like a street hood, he was going to talk like one too apparently. Harlan put it down to adrenaline.

"Okay, use my smartphone. Put it on speaker."

Harlan passed his phone to Signboy, who woke it up with a swipe of his finger. He entered a four-digit code to unlock it, and began searching for Jenny's entry in the phonebook.

"You know my code?"

"It's pretty obvious Harlan, your birth year. As an indetective, you should work harder on your codes. And change them every now and then."

"My birth year? How old do you think I am? It's the year my favourite book was published."

"Ahh, so that's it. I was only joking about the birth year. It's the same as the safe, that's all." Harlan had forgotten he'd had to give Signboy the combination to the safe for his increased duties.

As Signboy found Jenny's number and pressed call, Harlan wondered why Signboy hadn't asked what the book was. Was his generation so uninterested in what had gone before they were happy to leave any curiosity dating back past their lifetime unexplored?

"Harlan - looks like we're headed towards the city." Jenny's voice sounded like it was a lot further away than the ten metres between their cars. Not for the first time Harlan cursed the phone manufacturers for not putting a walkie talkie function in every handset.

"Sure does," he said. "Now, when they stop, can you drive around the block and wait for Signboy. He's going to need you to pick him up."

"Why, what are you doing?"

"Signboy's going to get Biff out of the way, and I'm going to get Jonathan to jump in my car."

"Wait, what? Signboy, that sounds dangerous. He carries a gun you know."

"Don't worry, I can outrun him on a crowded street. He's not going to pull a gun on me."

"What if he does? Harlan, can't you give him your gun?" Jenny sounded a little panicked, so Harlan ignored the reckless character of the suggestion and focused on the practical problem with it.

"I don't have a gun."

"What? Surely you need to carry a gun in your line of work."

"Possibly. But *I* don't carry one."

"You should, for protection."

"That's why I don't."

"What?"

"I don't carry a gun for protection."

"Well, you should."

"Should what?"

"Carry a gun for protection!"

"What did I just say? I don't carry a gun for protection."

"Signboy, what the hell is he talking about?"

"He read a study that said people who carry guns are ten times more likely to get shot or something like that, so he stopped carrying a gun. For protection."

"That's what I said," said Harlan. "I don't carry a gun for protection."

"I think you should find some other way of saying that," said Jenny. "I still think it's a stupid idea. Make sure you're careful Signboy, don't take any chances. Harlan, how do you know Jonathan's going to go for it?"

"He has to. Marisa gave us nothing when I called. Anyway, he needs a friend right now. I look like I can be a good friend, when I want to. Look like one, that is. I always am one, I think. And right now I want to look like I can be one, so we should be fine."

"So long as you don't talk too much," said Jenny, amazed she was able to follow Harlan's convoluted stream of verbosity, but unsure how a desperate Jonathan Foxe might react to it. "I hope you're right, otherwise this whole thing could unravel."

"Don't worry. Just don't let Biff see Signboy getting into your car."

"Okay. Good luck Signboy, I won't be far."

They were approaching the city centre when they ended the call. Signboy had made a valid point, the streets were as crowded at 5:30pm on a Friday as they were at any other time of the week. It was hard to picture a professional like Biff pulling out a gun with so many witnesses.

Harlan and Signboy were nervously quiet as they felt the guerilla-like operation approaching. Harlan was composing his lines for Jonathan. He figured he'd only get to try one or two to persuade him to jump in the car before Biff gave up on Signboy. He'd decided to let his facial expression cover the friend approach, while his speech would focus on the desperate situation Jonathan was in. A veritable one-man good-cop/bad-cop routine.

Signboy was visualising his encounter with Biff. He figured Biff just seeing him wouldn't be enough to draw him into a chase. He'd need to pick his pocket or something, or hopefully he or Jonathan were carrying something, like with Mick Dawson. He knew in the crowd Biff couldn't catch him, even carrying a bag. His plan was to get a few corners in early and lose him entirely before calling Jenny.

"Here we go," said Harlan as he saw the black Mercedes-Benz pull over to the left hand side of the one way street they were on. They were outside a low-key office block Harlan didn't recognise on Clarence Street, a couple of blocks west of Wynyard Station. He guessed it was where Mick Dawson conducted his business from.

Jenny's Golf drove straight past Jonathan's car, indicator on so it looked like she was looking for a park. Harlan pulled over immediately, double-parking beside a four-wheel-drive two cars back from the Mercedes-Benz, which gave Signboy enough cover to get out. He held the door open and looked back at Harlan.

"Don't be so dramatic Signboy, you'll be fine. We'll meet up later and laugh about it."

Signboy smiled uncertainly. "Later then Harlan," he said, before closing the door and walking around the back of the four wheel drive. Harlan edged his car forward so he could see what was going on at the Mercedes-Benz. Down the street he saw Jenny making the next left, preparing for Signboy to make his way around the block when the time came.

Biff had already exited the Mercedes-Benz and was opening Jonathan's door on the footpath side of the car. Harlan wasn't sure whether it was because he was still Jonathan's bodyguard, or because they had put the safety lock on his door so he couldn't jump out at a red light. Biff clearly reached in and helped Jonathan out, so it seemed more likely to be the latter. Harlan could only see their heads and shoulders over the car's roof, but it looked like Jonathan had brought something out of the car and Biff was now confiscating it.

Signboy appeared from behind the four wheel drive, and Harlan saw him accelerate past the next car so by the time he reached Biff and Jonathan, he was sprinting. There was a brief flurry as he burst in between them and kept going. Judging by their reaction, he had intervened in the confiscation by stealing whatever it was Biff was confiscating. As planned, Biff set off in pursuit, yelling the famously ineffective "Come back!" as he went. It didn't look like he had recognised Signboy.

Harlan watched Signboy put some distance between him and Biff and then edged his car further forward. He started to call to Jonathan but realised his passenger window was up. He leant across and began to roll it down, straining against the seatbelt. He stopped when it was halfway down, and called out.

"Mister Foxe, over here!"

Jonathan Foxe had been watching Biff crash his way down the street pursuing Signboy, but turned to face where the voice was coming from. He saw Harlan's car and turned back to watch the chase, apparently assuming nobody with a car that old could have any business with him.

"Mister Foxe, it's me, Harlan Valeri!"

Jonathan turned back again, ducking this time to see all of Harlan's face.

"Mr. Valeri, what are you doing?"

"I'm here to help you, trust me. I know you're in real trouble with Mick Dawson, come with me and we'll find a way out of it."

It seemed to be working as Jonathan rounded his car and approached Harlan's.

"What are you talking about?"

"I know everything. The Executive Club, the call centres, the house. Let me help you."

Harlan leant across to open the door, shoving it open a little too forcefully, causing it to smash against the Mercedes-Benz and bounce back.

"Shit," he said. "Sorry about that." They could both see the door had dented the side panel on the Mercedes-Benz, and taken a bit of paint with it as well. The line of cars building up behind Harlan's helpfully pointed it out with a series of beeping horns.

"Quick, jump in. We don't have long." They both looked down the street and saw the disruption to the flow of the crowd had stopped. They had either made the corner and gone around it or the chase was over. Jonathan looked at Harlan, then looked at the dent on the Mercedes, and then looked up the street where still neither of them could see Biff. Finally, he jumped in the car and pulled the door closed.

"Let's go then," he said. "I know a place."

CHAPTER 20

Harlan pulled out straight into traffic, changing lanes immediately to put a line of traffic between them and Biff, hoping the horns beeping as he cut a couple of cars off wouldn't attract too much attention. Jonathan slumped back in his seat to be as out of view as possible, giving Harlan a good look at the other side of the street. The driver had gotten out of the Mercedes to inspect the damage where Harlan had hit the car with his door. He didn't seem to be concerned about what had caused it, using a handkerchief to scrub away the remnants of paint from Harlan's car before returning to his seat.

Harlan scanned along the street, and was relieved to see Biff heading back to the Mercedes-Benz with no sign of Signboy. Harlan too then sat back in his seat, not wanting to be spotted. It seemed the operation had gone perfectly.

"Was that your bag?" Harlan asked. The traffic started moving, and Harlan turned right at the next intersection into more traffic, as he swung around the corner catching a glance of Biff in his rear view mirror standing by the Mercedes looking up and down the street for Jonathan.

"Sorry?" Jonathan was understandably distracted.

"That kid stole something, was it your bag?"

"Oh, yes. It had a few things in it for the Benefit. I guess I won't be playing much part in it now anyway."

"Yes you will, you have to. We won't be too long, just say you needed to get away for a bit. They need you, remember."

"We'll see. It's Harlan, isn't it?"

"Yes, that's right. Don't worry, we'll get the bag back, he works for me."

"Really? How will I explain getting the bag back?"

"Good question." Harlan thought for a second.

"Turn right here," said Jonathan.

"Okay." He turned right, they were now heading south along York Street. As they joined the flow of buses through the York Street interchange Harlan felt like he imagined a gazelle would, caught among the wildebeests in the Great Migration. It was ridiculous to speculate what a specific antelope might feel in a specifically antelopic situation, but it distracted him from the brooding figure in the passenger seat for a good minute.

The familiar string opening of Canon No. 5 came from Jonathan's jacket pocket. He ignored it, letting his phone ring out. No doubt Biff was on the other end of the call.

"You could just tell them you went around the block in the other direction, maybe the kid ran straight into you," said Harlan, breaking the silence with what he thought was a good suggestion.

"Sure," said Jonathan, although Harlan suspected he wasn't really listening. He looked deep in thought. "Left here," he said, as they approached King Street. "Then right onto George."

"Where are we going?" asked Harlan. He'd stopped at a red light at King Street.

"Darlinghurst Road, the Kirketon Hotel. I want to get out of the city for a bit, they won't look for me there."

"I know where it is. Why don't you take it easy while I drive?" he said unnecessarily. Jonathan was staring into space. He showed no signs of exerting himself anytime soon.

*

Daylight was just suggesting the possibility of fading into a balmy summer evening as Harlan parked near the Kirketon and roused Jonathan from his thoughts. There was an awkward moment as Jonathan habitually waited for someone to open his door for him, but at least it lightened his mood a little when he realised his mistake. He didn't have a bounce in his step, but Harlan no longer worried he'd have to carry Jonathan inside.

Darlinghurst Road was filled with the exciting bustle of Sydneysiders who had clocked off work for the week and had a perfect forecast for the summer weekend ahead of them. Harlan wondered how many of them would overdo it tonight and miss one or both days of the weekend with a hangover. With his own weekend shaping up the way it was, he wondered if any of them would trade.

He and Jonathan walked up the few stairs at the hotel entrance, Harlan holding open the door strangely located on the second of five stairs. Jonathan walked through with a quick "Thanks", then led Harlan straight through the small hotel reception area, past a long bar deserted apart from the bartender, and to an unmarked door at the back of the room. He pushed through, holding it behind him so Harlan had time to step through, then led Harlan down a short passageway to where a dimly lit, opulently furnished and surprisingly crowded cocktail bar opened up before them. A man in a black waistcoat and white shirt met them at the entrance.

"Mister Foxe, how are you this evening?" asked the host. He must be a regular. There's something impressive about going somewhere with a regular, unless it's a methadone clinic. Harlan was suitably impressed.

"Fine, thanks," said Jonathan, who didn't seem to know the man who knew him.

"Are you here for dinner or just a drink?"

"Just a drink, thanks."

"Okay, follow me through to the den, please." They did as he asked, struggling through the Friday night revelry that pervaded the room. A few heads turned as people recognised the famed philanthropist. The movement of heads turning to see Jonathan and then snapping back to avoid being seen staring created a buzz with a momentum of its own. After just a few seconds Harlan was sure everybody in the bar knew Jonathan Foxe was present. He just hoped none of them were too well-acquainted with Mick Dawson.

They came eventually to the back wall, where two suspicious vertical lines in the luxurious gold threaded wallpaper ran from floor to ceiling roughly a door-width apart. The host inserted an old-fashioned key into a surreptitious key hole close to one of the lines, turned it once, and pushed on the wall. It swung open arrogantly into a room more opulently furnished and dimly lit than the main bar, but surprisingly, and infinitely, less crowded. As they entered the den Harlan counted only half a dozen dark leather armchairs and lounges spaced generously around the room. From the absence of other guests he guessed it was a very exclusive room he had been brought into, as if the hidden door entry wasn't enough to go on.

The walls either side had glass-cased liquor cabinets built into them from waist height, with intricate woodwork framing collections of presumably rare and valuable alcoholic indulgences. The front and back walls had the same wallpaper as the main bar, with a shelf built along the back wall at a dangerous height for shins but a convenient height for the adjacent lounges.

The host showed them to the back of the den as if there were degrees of privacy in an empty room. They sat in armchairs facing each other across a small, dark wooden table, their backs slightly turned to the rest of the room. Jonathan still looked exhausted and a little dazed, while Harlan looked as if he was about to explode, so impressed was he with the situation he was in.

"So, what can I get you?" asked the host.

Jonathan reached into his jacket pocket and pulled out a key that looked at a glance more ornamental than anything else. A tiny, old-fashioned key on an elegant silver keyring with the number 29 carved into it using just the right amount of calligraphic flair. He handed it to the host who apparently needed no other communication. The host headed to the cabinet on the side of the room by the secret door. Looking over his shoulder, Harlan realised the cabinet on that side was divided into a few dozen locked and numbered compartments, most of them with a bottle of Scotch, brandy or liqueur in them. He watched as the vested man located compartment 29, unlocked and opened it, and withdrew from it a tall bottle. He carefully carried the bottle back to them and placed it on the table, shining a small torch on the label he had positioned so they could all see.

Harlan read the label out loud, giving each vowel and consonant its standard contextual English pronunciation: "Laphroaig Islay Single Malt Scotch Whiskey Cairdeas. Aged thirty years."

"A present from Mick Dawson," said Jonathan.

"It's pronounced La-Froyg and Eye-la, actually," said the host, now holding two delicate looking glasses, thistle-shaped with an out-turned rim, sitting on a flat, round base. He placed them on the table either side of the bottle. "Laphroaig is the distillery, and Islay is the island. Gaelic words actually, the island was under an Irish king before it became part of Scotland."

"Eye-la?" asked Harlan.

"Not Islay."

"Oh. Sorry."

"Not at all, it's just that a lot of people enjoy learning the native pronunciation of the various Scotches, as well as the stories behind them."

"Thank you," said Jonathan, dismissing the vest. He wasn't in the mood for alcohol university. He turned to face Harlan. "Do you like Scotch?"

"Sure. I mean, it's not my favourite. I do like stories though."

"Me either," said Jonathan, missing Harlan's second remark. "But it's the most dramatic drink I could think of."

"I did like the story though," repeated Harlan. "Gaelic Scotch."

Jonathan again ignored Harlan's enthusiasm for distilling trivia and opened the bottle of Scotch. He poured a generous shot, almost a double, in each glass, what a connoisseur would call a wee dram (but a pedant would point out was more like two fluid ounces). He leaned to his left where Harlan saw a water dispenser of some elaboration sitting on the shelf that ran along the wall. A crystal bowl with a decoratively crafted silver lid, housed on a matching silver stand with three silver taps spaced equally running out from the bowl. Jonathan used the nearest tap to dispense a couple of drops of water in each glass, then sat back with his glass held in front of him.

Seeing Jonathan was still a bit wired and not very talkative, Harlan didn't push the confessional. Instead, he picked up his glass and settled into the expansive leather armchair like a crouton sinking slowly to equilibrium in a comforting bowl of thick, velvety soup. He took a sip of the Scotch. The smooth liquid searched around his mouth, grabbed a few sinews in the back of his cheeks and pulled them taut, causing Harlan to wince embarrassingly. When released though, they set a wave of warming numbness flowing through his mouth, following the Scotch down his throat and into his belly, where it was duly dispatched to all his extremities. Harlan had never been so aware of the efficiency and reach of his circulatory system. The additional weight of contentedness caused him to settle deeper in the armchair. A crouton would have absorbed too much soup and sunk.

"What do I do now?" asked Jonathan.

Harlan shook his head clear of the alcoholic daze he had succumbed too. With great effort he pulled himself out of the soft leathery embrace of the armchair to perch attentively on its edge.

"We'll think of something, don't worry. But if I'm going to help you, you need to tell me everything."

"You said you know everything. That's why I came with you."

"I may have exaggerated. But I know a lot. If you start at the beginning, I'll let you know the bits you can skip."

"The beginning?"

"The Executive Club. Isn't that where it all started?"

"You could say that. I'm more inclined to say that's where it all fell apart."

Harlan hoped he was inclined to say a lot more about it, but didn't want to push him. He took another sip of Scotch, hoping Jonathan would do likewise and it would loosen his lips. The whiskey went down a lot easier the second sip, and Harlan sighed his content. Jonathan followed Harlan's lead and, after letting out a sigh of his own, sat forward in his chair.

"Before I start, just how can you help me, exactly?"

"By exposing Mick Dawson. Painting you as the victim. Extricating Celebrities Care from Mick Dawson's grip and preventing him from tainting the Hope Foundation with his dirty brand of cut-throat capitalism."

"Right," said Jonathan, not sounding convinced.

"Look, Jonathan, you started Celebrities Care for a reason, I'm sure it was something along the lines of wanting to do some good." Harlan waited for Jonathan to nod in acknowledgement before he continued. Jonathan nodded.

"What I'm saying is, it's not too late. We can hit Mick Dawson where it hurts."

"His wallet?"

"No, I was thinking of reputation, but you're right. All he cares about is money." Harlan thought for a second. "Let's start with reputation. Then Celebrities Care can get its house in order, stop being treated like Mick Dawson's sweatshop."

"So you know all about that?"

"Yes. But I can help you turn Celebrities Care into the charity you always dreamed of running."

"That's possible. It is a charitable foundation, Mick Dawson has no formal role with it. If it came to light we were dealing with parasitic companies taking advantage of our outreach centres, we'd have to put a stop to it. So how do we expose him without it looking like I'm involved?"

"In the press. I know a journalist who's already working on a feature article about this whole thing. If you give me your side of the story, the article can focus on Mick Dawson as the bad guy. If you don't, I guess there'll be questions about your role as well."

"A journalist?"

"Don't worry, she knows Mick Dawson is at the centre of it all, that he's got a hold over you and you can't say no to him. She wants to write the full story, but you need to cooperate."

"She? Who is she?"

Harlan wondered how much he could trust Jonathan. His relationship with Jenny was known only to Signboy and Diane Adams at this point. Jonathan picked up on Harlan's reluctance to answer the question.

"So I'm supposed to give you my life story, but you won't even tell me who you're going to share it with? I insist Harlan. As a show of faith."

"Okay," said Harlan. He was sure it would come out eventually anyway. "Her name is Jenny Randall. She's the one who's been following you around."

"What?" Jonathan looked, quite understandably, incredulous. "The one I'm paying you to investigate? Now you're working with her to investigate me?"

"That's what it looks like, doesn't it. And I suppose it's true. If there was an indetective code of conduct I'd be in breach of it." Harlan studied Jonathan's face for something, but whatever he was looking for wasn't there. "Look, it didn't take long for us to figure out that Mick Dawson is the one she should be investigating. That's why

I had to see you tonight, so we can help each other by getting him out of the picture."

"How would that help you?"

Harlan thought one show of faith was sufficient, so kept his true motivation of helping Jenny to himself.

"Because it's the right thing to do."

He realised what he had been looking for in Jonathan's face, because he saw it now. Complicity.

CHAPTER 21

"Okay, the Executive Club," said Jonathan, in a voice portending the story to follow. "It was actually Mick's idea from the start, but he was happy for me to run with it. He was too busy promoting concerts and representing celebrities. It sounded more fun than running restaurants, so I convinced Marisa we should sell up and get into something new. She was sick of the restaurant business anyway, and wanted to start a cooking magazine, which would be easier to run with the children we always planned to have.

"The Club took off. It was before the super clubs with private rooms started opening up in the city, and the growing Sydney A-list scene needed help finding places to party on the occasions they didn't want to be seen - which was more often than you'd think.

"Mick introduced me to all the bar and club owners, arranged a partnership with a limousine company. He convinced the venues they should pay the Executive Club for getting celebrities through the door. My job was basically to know who was in town and where they wanted to party, then make sure they would be looked after. Of course, I'd let the paparazzi know as well, that's where the value was for the venues.

"After the first year we were pretty established, and the business seemed to take care of itself. It wasn't just Mick who was using the Club. We'd get calls from other agents whenever a celebrity came to town. By then I was partying as much as the clients, and Marisa was busy with our first child and closer to launching her magazine so didn't even notice what I was up to. That's when the drug dealers arrived."

"They weren't there already?" asked Harlan.

"Of course, they were. I meant that's when they wanted to be part of the Club. There wasn't much of a negotiation process, but it was a good arrangement so I didn't see much point in fighting it. As you say, the drugs were going to be there anyway."

"What was the arrangement?"

"They paid the Club to get on the list. The dealers became A-listers themselves, hanging out at the private parties and making more money than the rest of us. Everyone got their cut though. They paid us to get invited and they paid the clubs to turn a blind eye. Not only drugs, they also brought in escorts - a real hit with the A-list."

"So essentially you were getting a commission on drugs and prostitution?" Harlan put it bluntly.

"I guess so. I was having too much fun to really think about it."

"So what changed? Why did you sell it?"

"First, Mick came up with the idea of expanding the business. Not just celebrities, basically anyone with money. We didn't think people would pay us just to get invited to our events, so we came up with exclusive memberships which we ran for the venues. We charged a ridiculous amount on an annual basis, equivalent to paying a hundred dollar cover charge or more if you went once a week. They were snapped up."

Harlan noticed they'd both finished their Scotch. He refilled the delicate glasses, took some pleasure from using the water dispenser as Jonathan had, and made himself comfortable again. Jonathan didn't seem to notice any of it as he continued his story.

"So now things are getting out of control. We've got private functions, secret rooms, packed full of people competing to see who can spend the most money. Cocaine is laid out on tables, beautiful women are available by the hour. Of course the A-list moves on to more tasteful, more private parties, arranged by us, so we start getting B-listers to make appearances. Footy players, soap stars, reality TV stars. They're looking for the exposure and love thinking they're the richest people in the room, blissfully unaware that the no-names in there make multiples of what they do.

"It all came to a head one night. Our biggest party ever. The A-listers were back because it was an after-party for one of their biggest nights of the year, the ARIA awards. Mick had locked in the international stars, some rapper and a couple of actors, to come to our after-party, and everyone else followed.

"It was insane. Impossible to imagine. It cost fifty-thousand dollars just to decorate the function room in a jungle theme, for no particular reason. There was fake smoke everywhere, world-class DJs, and the room was packed. There were models all dressed in Tarzan-like outfits, practically naked, serving drinks and whatever else you wanted. The only thing that mattered to everyone that night was having as much fun as possible. And they did.

"And then it all stopped. There was some screaming from one corner of the room where people were running out of the unisex toilets. I went in just as a couple of guys bashed in the door to a cubicle where two girls were passed out on the floor, faces pure white, not breathing, vomit running down their faces. Within five minutes the place was empty except for me, a couple of barmen who had tried CPR, the two dead girls and a thick carpet of dry ice fog which had made its way under the door."

Harlan struggled to imagine the scene. He wondered if the fleeing DJ had bothered to stop the music, or if the needle was just jumping at the end of the track dramatically. Or would there even have been a needle? He couldn't remember when nostalgia had brought them back.

"So what happened next?"

"The police arrived. None of us had seen what happened, but I went with them to make a statement anyway. I felt responsible, even though I didn't know the girls."

"They were escorts?"

"I don't know. They were dressed in the jungle outfits, so they were paid to be there, at my party."

"But you'd never met them?"

"Not that I remembered. I told the police I didn't know who they were, gave them a guest list, which only included the celebrities anyway. Members got in by flashing their key-rings. And that was about it. Mick picked me up from the station. He was worried about me. He told me I introduced those girls to the guys supplying drugs."

"But you hadn't."

"I don't know, everyone there was completely wasted, including me."

"So how did Mick Dawson know?"

"I don't know. He usually keeps a cool head, no matter what he's on."

"Okay, so Mick Dawson picks you up and scares you into blaming yourself even more." Harlan began to see just how manipulative Mick Dawson could be.

"I guess so. The next few days are a bit of a blur. I remember seeing the news online the next day, Mick telling me it wasn't good that people knew I'd given a statement. He said he'd look after it, but because I'd spoken to the police and given them a guest list, he couldn't have me running the Club anymore. I didn't care. I was more worried about the drug dealers thinking I might turn them in."

"Did you think about turning them in?"

"I don't know if you've dealt with any high-end drug dealers, but they're not the kind of people you want to get on the wrong side of. You can't be fooled by the expensive suits and the glamorous company they keep. They're hard criminals."

"So you didn't think about it?"

"All I could think about was *not* turning them in."

It was Jonathan's turn to play bartender. Getting this off his chest seemed to have loosened him up a little, and distracted him from his current predicament.

Harlan took his third glass of Scotch and held it to his nose. Now he was accustomed to the taste he could even enjoy the strong alcohol-rich aroma. Jonathan watched him with what looked like amusement.

"I think you would have enjoyed the Executive Club back in the day. New experiences all the time, new drinks, new drugs. New women."

"I don't think I would have fared too well. I'm somewhat prone to overindulgence."

The reference to overdoing it reminded Jonathan of the dead girls, making him slide back into his serious monologue.

"At some point Mick told me I didn't have to worry about the drug dealers either, and said he'd look after me when I was ready to get back to work. I never heard from the police again, and the papers dropped the story completely. I spent a couple of days around the house, spending more time with the kids than I ever had. It put things in perspective, and I knew I wanted to do something positive with my life. In a broader sense than just helping rich and famous people have great parties."

"So you thought of Celebrities Care."

"Kind of. All I knew was what celebrities wanted to do. I don't think I could have even run a restaurant I'd been away so long, so I needed something new. I noticed all the charities using celebrities more and more, so I figured if there was a charity associated with lots of celebrities, it would be able to do a lot of good. Look at LiveAid and that type of thing. I told Mick what I was thinking. Then he got that look in his eye, and said he could help me."

"What look?"

"If life was a cartoon, it would be a dollar sign."

"Ah. So you think he was setting up Celebrities Care to be a business from the outset?"

"It was obvious at the time he only cared about the positive publicity he would have on tap for his celebrities. The call-centre side of it came later, I doubt even Mick could have planned that from the start. Anyway, I guess I was just too excited to let his one-way mind deter me. Plus I couldn't do it without him. He offered to get me started with cash and a ten year MOU to give my charity access to his celebrities, and vice versa."

"MOU?"

"Memorandum of Understanding."

"Like a contract?"

"No, it's less than a contract."

"So either of you can walk away at any time?"

"Not exactly. Legally, it could be a contract."

"So why not call it a contract?"

"People don't like signing contracts."

"But they like signing MOUs?"

"Yes."

"I see." He didn't.

"I don't think you do. It's not important anyway." It really wasn't.

"No, let's get back to your story. So Celebrities Care is born, but why the trumped-up sale of the Executive Club? Why the house?"

Jonathan sighed regretfully, took a sip of Scotch, sighed contentedly, then sighed regretfully again as he prepared to finish his oral history.

"Mick's idea, again. He wanted to keep it going, said it had a lot of goodwill. He said it would look better in the papers with a big price attached to it. There was nothing to it though, it was all PR. I just signed the company over to him for next to nothing."

"And the house? The start up money for Celebrities Care?"

"The start-up money was a favour to begin with, a donation in the end - fully tax-deductible for Mick. I reckon he's gotten good value out of it over the years. I'm indebted to him and he knows it. The house was also a favour, another way of obligating me so he could do what he wanted with Celebrities Care. I had almost nothing to show for three years of the Executive Club, but I couldn't tell Marisa I'd spent everything on booze, drugs and crazy parties. So we decided to tell her the same story we told the press, that I was getting millions for the Club. Mick said he was always happy to invest in real estate anyway. It all went in the MOU."

"You're not worried if things don't work out with Mick he'll kick you, Marisa and the kids out? You said yourself, the MOU's not a contract."

"He'd never kick Marisa out - they're old friends. It was Marisa who brought Mick's business into the restaurants, that's how it all started. Anyway, that part of the MOU's pretty tight. It's also written into my employment contract with the Foundation somehow. I think he writes off a year's worth of rent every year as a donation as well. And if it does all go to shit, I have been better with money this time around. I live an expense-free life on an executive salary. We wouldn't be out on the street."

"So why do you let him control Celebrities Care?"

"I don't know. I do feel indebted to him, he gave me a second chance. Plus the celebrities are his. We need them to raise all our money. And everyone knows it's Mick's charity - no-one would go behind his back to appear for us when there are other charities around."

"It all sounds pretty messy," said Harlan. Finances and contracts weren't strong points of his, and indebtedness he avoided like a plague.

"Luckily I have people who worry about most of that stuff for me. Actually they're Mick's people. I guess I've pretty much let him run my life the last few years." Jonathan stared distantly with the realisation.

"Don't worry, we're going to sort it out," said Harlan, wondering what they could possibly do about it.

"How?" Jonathan looked desperate. Harlan knew to keep him on side he needed to leave him with hope. The thought triggered the beginnings of a plan in Harlan's mind.

"I think I've got it. We can make Mick Dawson obsolete without tarnishing the Celebrities Care reputation, and maybe even keep you in the house."

"I don't understand."

"Good, it's better you know nothing about it anyway. What do they call it, plausible deniability? For now, you'd better get back to work. The longer you're off the radar, the harder it will be to explain." Harlan was buzzing, the adrenalin taking the depressive effects of the Scotch and pointing them all up. He couldn't wait to put his plan into action.

"And how do I explain being away this long?"

"Like I said, tell them you saw an opportunity to clear your head for a minute, and you took it. Have another quick Scotch, they'll think you just went to drown your sorrows. No, not for me, I need to sharpen my senses, not dull them."

Jonathan poured himself a full thistle of Scotch, without water, and drank it in one go. Harlan guessed it was at least a fifty-dollar shot.

"Now get a taxi back to wherever it is you're supposed to be. Give me your direct number and I'll let you know the battle plan later tonight."

Jonathan started to recite his number but changed his mind.

"No, I'll call you. Who knows when I'll be able to take your call without arousing suspicions. Give me your card." Card was right, Harlan was down to the last he kept in his wallet. Jonathan took the understated brown rectangle and stood up to leave, wavering slightly before gaining his balance. "Now, can you spare me some cash for the taxi?"

"You don't have cash?"

"I never use it."

"Of course. Here." Harlan stood as well, again produced his wallet from his pocket and this time handed Jonathan an increasingly overstated twenty-dollar note. "What about here, do we need to pay them anything?"

"No, that's my own bottle."

"So what's in it for them?"

"Harlan, what have we been talking about? Just because we came in here, everyone out there will tell their friends about the back room at Eau De Vie. And if they recognised me ... "

"They did."

"So much the better. They're less likely to care they just paid twenty dollars for a cocktail. In fact, they expect to pay top dollar in a place where celebrities use the secret room. They want to."

"I see," said Harlan, unconvincingly.

"No you don't. But you're not one of them," Jonathan gestured towards the front bar, "so it doesn't matter."

"I'll take your word for it then."

"Good. Now, I'll get back to the Benefit war room, and you go off and hatch your master plan," said Jonathan as they headed back to the secret door, with a generous dollop of bravado that had Harlan believing they could actually pull it off.

CHAPTER 22

Once he'd put Jonathan in a taxi, Harlan called Jenny to see where she and Signboy were. She answered almost immediately.

"Harlan, how'd it go?"

"Swimmingly. He's just gone back into the fold now, but we've definitely got him on side. Where are you?"

"Grabbing a burger in Darlinghurst, we were starving."

"Perfect, I think I need a bite to sober up. Whereabouts?"

"You mean where exactly? Or do you want to know approximately where we are?"

"Exactly," sighed Harlan. He'd deliberately added the word 'whereabouts' to his vocabulary-in-use when he became an indetective, and wasn't thrilled to find Jenny patronising it.

"Burgerman, just off Victoria Street, around the corner from where we had a drink the other night."

"I know the one," he said, relishing the anticipation of a tasty burger and chips. "See you in a minute."

As he crossed the road and started to cut through the carwash that spanned the block between Darlinghurst Road and Victoria Street, Harlan realised he was a lot closer to Burgerman than he thought. He slowed his pace slightly, wanting to be as near to a minute in arriving as he could in case Jenny was impressed by that kind of thing.

About forty-eight seconds later Harlan arrived to find Jenny and Signboy sitting out the front of the fashionable burger joint on bright red pods that passed for chairs. The pods set off satisfyingly against the black of the tables and asphalt underfoot, and picked up the red in the quirky tomato-shaped sauce bottles on each table, all accentuated by the large illuminated signage overhead casting a clean white glow about the small frontage. Just as satisfyingly, there was no one else sitting at the outside tables, affording them enough privacy for the conversation they were about to have.

Jenny and Signboy were finishing off their burgers, with an empty bowl between them Harlan assumed had been full of chips not long before. If Jenny was impressed by accurate, off-the-cuff approximations of travel time over short distances by foot, she didn't show it.

"Hi," said Harlan, enthusiastically.

Both with mouths full, a nod with raised eyebrows was apparently all the greeting Harlan was going to get from either of them. Mistaking their focus on the burgers for iciness towards him, he erred on the side of spinelessness and decided to wait to be invited to sit down. Jenny took a sip from a glass of red wine before finally offering Harlan a seat by pushing a spare red pod from under the table towards him with her foot.

"You came here to meet us Harlan, you don't need an invitation to sit down," said Signboy. Maybe he wasn't so mistaken about the iciness.

He sat at the side of the table for two, catching the waitress's attention through the large open sliding glass door that led inside. She brought out a menu and took Harlan's order for a double espresso before heading back inside.

"A double espresso?" Given the hour, Jenny obviously assumed he'd be joining them in having a drink.

"I told you I needed to sober up."

"Oh, that's what you said? It wasn't the best reception."

"Strange, I was only a hundred metres away," said Harlan, again wondering whether the right people were in charge of optimising mobile phone traffic.

"So what have you been up to then?" asked Signboy, as he finished off a longneck of Coopers Red.

"Is that the high alcohol one?" asked Harlan.

"Sparkling ale, five-point-eight per cent," said Signboy, nodding.

"Is that high?" asked Jenny.

"This is three and a half standard drinks, if you believe the label," said Signboy.

"What *is* a standard drink?" asked Jenny.

"A standardised unit of alcohol so we can measure different types of alcoholic drinks against each other to ascertain their relative alcoholic strength," said Harlan, belying his own level of intoxication.

"No, I know that," said Jenny. "I meant, how much alcohol is in a standard drink?"

"No idea. I'm surprised you're not googling it already though."

"Good call," said Jenny, now busy with her phone.

The waitress returned with Harlan's double espresso.

"Thanks. And I'll get the chilli relish burger. With a side of chips."

"Chilli Relish with *fries*, sure thing." She gathered the empty plates and bowl from the table and headed back to the kitchen. Harlan threw a confused look around the table, but apparently the others weren't so strict in their classification of deep fried pieces of sliced potato to notice. He contented himself stirring some sugar into his coffee.

"Ten grams of alcohol," said Jenny, reading from her phone.

"Grams?" said Harlan. "Geniuses. Why wouldn't they make it mils? Okay, Signboy, how big's that bottle?"

"Seven fifty mils."

"Seven fifty, five-point-eight per cent, that's forty-three and a half mils of alcohol." He paused to sip his coffee and allow Jenny to be impressed by his mental arithmetic, then continued. "So if that's three and a half standard drinks, then one standard drink is a bit less than thirteen mils, about twelve and a half."

"Great, what do we do with that?" asked Signboy. "Anytime we know the percentage, we're going to know the number of standard drinks anyway because it will be right next to it on the label."

"Lay off, Signboy," said Jenny, defending Harlan much to his gratification. "Now, Rain Man," she said to Harlan. "How many standard drinks have you had? And you can flesh out the story by telling us everything that happened with Jonathan Foxe."

"Six," he said, after doing a few calculations in his head. He finished the rest of his coffee in one gulp and looked around to confirm they were still the only ones sitting outside. "Now here's the flesh."

*

"So what's your idea?" asked Jenny.

Harlan had managed, through a combination of skilful paraphrasing, increased rate of speech and an almost dangerous under-reliance on oxygen, to relay all of Jonathan's story and allude to his master plan before his burger and fries arrived. And then they did.

"Just a second," he said, scoffing a few fries at once by feeding them lengthways into his mouth. "Mmm, good," he said after just about swallowing them all. "Clearly chips though." With hindsight, he was now quite annoyed at the waitress for purporting to correct him when he had called them, quite correctly, chips.

"Told you so," said Signboy to Jenny. And then to Harlan, "She didn't believe me, had to look it up on her phone earlier."

"Surely they're whatever they want to call them?" said Jenny. "It's not like they're branded or anything."

"And what did the internet have to say about it?" asked Harlan.

"Inconclusive."

"Bullshit," said Signboy. "It said the yanks call everything 'fries', but the rest of the world calls French fries 'fries', and these things," he picked up one of Harlan's chips to demonstrate the thickness, "are 'chips'."

"Like I said, inconclusive."

"Well, call me crazy," said Harlan, invitingly, "but I like to think we live in a world where you can put a word on a menu, and most of your customers will know what to expect when they order it. And I'm confident most people who come here would call this," Harlan mimicked what Signboy had done earlier, "a 'chip'."

"Well, to stop you doing a vox pop on it, I'll concede the point," said Jenny, feigning magnanimity as best she could. "It's good to see you're not just an expert on enjoying wine and making amazing Italian feasts in your own kitchen. You can still enjoy a burrito for lunch and a burger and chips for dinner."

"I wouldn't want to meet someone who didn't enjoy a burrito for lunch and a burger and chips for dinner. Or a home-made Italian feast for that matter. Anything done well is worth enjoying in my book."

"Except your steak - you had that rare the other day I noticed."

"Ha, nice." Harlan smiled at Jenny who was wearing the cheeky grin he thought he might never see again. As he made eye contact the grin faded slightly. Harlan got the impression she wanted to have one more conversation on the topic before things could go back to the way they were before. He did his best to nod his understanding in her direction.

Harlan shifted his attention to the burger sitting in front of him. He folded back the top of it with his thumb to check the contents before using both hands to compress it as he lifted it to his mouth. By the time he'd taken a bite, chewed and swallowed and wiped his hands and mouth, they all realised he wouldn't be able to lead the conversation and enjoy his burger at the same time.

"Why don't I just get you started, then you two can figure the rest out and it will feel like your idea as well?"

"Sure," said Jenny, laughing a little. Watching someone eat and waiting for them to talk was strangely amusing to her, especially something as potentially disastrous as a burger.

"We wouldn't want your patty to go cold or anything," said Signboy, again with a little attitude Harlan was finding harder to dismiss.

"Okay," he said, doing a little double-take at Signboy over the petty patty comment. "Why did Celebrities Care want to be involved in the Benefit?"

"Exposure," said Signboy.

"Plus legitimacy," added Jenny. "Hope has an untarnished reputation, Celebrities Care can't shake the cynical view that celebrities are only involved to promote themselves. If the Hope Foundation accepts Celebrities Care, the cynics are more likely to as well."

"Exactly. And why did the Hope Foundation want Celebrities Care involved?"

"Exposure," repeated Signboy.

"Plus legitimacy," added Jenny, again, this time surprising herself. "To younger people, Celebrities Care might be the only charity they relate to. If Celebrities Care thinks the Hope Foundation is 'cool' enough to hang out with, so will Celebrities Care fans. I mean donors."

"Exactly. And how can we keep everyone happy but cut Mick Dawson out of the picture, permanently?" Harlan left the question hanging and returned to his burger, confident when he emerged Jenny and Signboy would have concocted the same plan he had, maybe even improved on it.

Signboy was the first to speak.

"They only need Mick Dawson for the celebrities," he said.

"So we need to get the celebrities to dump Mick Dawson?" said Jenny. "That should be pretty easy. We just need to approach all the celebrities in his stable, tell them what a rotter he is, and they'll immediately dump the guy who's helped get them where they are today. So how do we get in touch with them in the first place? Call their agent. Oh, it's Mick Dawson."

"Settle down," said Signboy. "I would have said the same thing a week ago. But think about it - you're about to publish an article that tells the world what a crook the Balmoral Brawler really is. If you gave a celebrity a heads up, I'm sure they'd be keen to distance themselves from him. And tomorrow night, most of his celebrities will be in one place."

"Yes, but he'll be there too. And it's practically his event now."

"It's only his event as long as he controls the celebrities."

"So we get the celebrities to turn on him?"

Signboy nodded. Jenny looked at Harlan, who wiped his mouth after a particularly messy bite and nodded too.

"We get the celebrities to turn on him," repeated Jenny, her eyes brightening as the plan unfolded in her mind. "They dump him, make their appearance at the Benefit anyway, Celebrities Care and Hope get what they want. In fact it's even better, there'll be more exposure because of the Mick Dawson fallout, more legitimacy for Celebrities Care because the celebrities will have done something for the right reasons, and even the Hope Foundation is better off if the fact of the celebrities denouncing Mick Dawson inspires their fans on the night."

"We just need to get to the celebrities, away from Mick Dawson," said Signboy, realising that would probably be a lot harder than mere speculation over burgers and beer.

"So we need full access at the Benefit. Which means Stephanie Clarkson."

"Right," said Signboy. "We go to her with the story, get her on side. She could even help get Mick Dawson out of the way for a while."

"She won't want Hope to be tarnished by association," said Jenny. "She'll have to help us."

"But, she'll want to know Jonathan Foxe is on our side too - probably more than just our word as well," said Signboy.

"Okaaay," said Jenny, drawing out the word as she thought. "He's calling Harlan at some point. Harlan can tell him to give Stephanie Clarkson a signal, or a code word or something, to let her know he's in on it. You know, in case he doesn't get a chance to speak to her without Mick Dawson hanging around. We tell her what the signal is, so when she sees it she knows we're telling the truth about Jonathan Foxe."

"Bravo," said Harlan, wiping his mouth for the last time. "Pretty much what I came up with. But I like the signal for Jonathan, great idea. I was just relying on him getting some time alone with her. And I wasn't counting on the celebrities to do the right thing, but I don't see how it would work without them now. It wouldn't be much of a Benefit without the entertainment."

"So, much better than what you came up with then," said Signboy.

"Yes, I guess so."

"That's the plan then," said Signboy, as if it were the last word on the matter. "How do we get an audience with Stephanie Clarkson on her busiest day of the year though?"

"Tough one," said Harlan. "I was hoping Biff would send me through the new itinerary, surely she'll be meeting with Jonathan at least once during the day. We could tail her after that and get her alone."

"But he hasn't?" asked Jenny.

"No, not yet. Might come through a bit late tonight, Biff's had a busy evening."

"Or Jonathan has had a change of heart, and we're screwed."

"No, trust me. He was resolute by the time I left him. Let's give Biff till morning. If nothing comes through, I'll hassle him for it. I am, after all, supposed to be watching Jonathan's back."

"Hmm." Jenny took her phone out and started jabbing at the screen. "In the meantime, I'll follow her on Twitter, if she's on the ball she'll be tweeting regularly leading up to the Benefit."

"Good idea," said Harlan. "Failing all that I think we stake out the venue first thing. She'd have to be in and out of there a few times through the day."

"Good idea." said Jenny. "Just a thought, though. Shouldn't we check Jonathan's story somehow, before we put ourselves at risk to help him out."

"You don't believe him?" asked Harlan.

"Well, I don't know, I wasn't there. But even if he was as convincing as Meryl Streep, I'd like so see some evidence. Or at least have someone corroborate it."

"Meryl Streep?"

"She's a very good actor," said Jenny, defensively. "Sixteen Oscar nominations don't lie."

"Okay, I know. I saw *Adaptation*. So who do you have in mind?"

"Signboy mentioned you might have a police contact. There'd have to be a file on what happened."

"I guess so. But it's Friday night. You don't hold onto contacts very long if you hassle them on Friday nights."

"So leave it till the morning, it shouldn't take too long to check out."

Harlan wondered what was different about Saturday morning, but didn't have the energy to argue.

"Okay, I'll call him in the morning, see if he can dig up the file for us."

"Perfect," said Jenny.

"All right," said Signboy. "Now that's sorted out, I'm heading off, meeting some friends for a drink. Good luck tomorrow."

"Good luck?" Harlan couldn't believe his ears.

"For the Benefit. I hope it all works out."

"You're going to be there Signboy - we need your help."

"Harlan, I know you don't have a formal work-life balance policy written down anywhere, but tomorrow's a Saturday. You don't hold onto junior indetectives very long if you assume they'll work on Saturdays without any notice."

Harlan realised he had been taking Signboy for granted. Maybe that explained his newfound hostility.

"Please, Signboy. You know we can't do it without you. I'm sorry I assumed you'd be working without asking you. Whatever it takes, I can do. Days off, overtime, whatever."

"Nah, it'll take more than that. I'll think of something." The friendly smile showed signs of returning to Signboy's face as he pondered how he would make Harlan pay. "So when and where are we meeting?"

"Why don't you just check in with me when you're up and about. We should be able to take care of Stephanie Clarkson and my police contact, it's just the Benefit where we'll need all the help we can get."

"Sure, sounds good. See you tomorrow then. See you Jenny. Oh, and thanks for dinner." The last bit was directed at Harlan.

Signboy laughed cheekily as he walked off into the dying light towards a Victoria Street that now hummed urgently with the kind of Friday night vibe that must have long ago inspired Harry Vanda and George Young to write the greatest Australian song of all time.

Harlan turned back to face Jenny just in time to maximise the impact of her open palm on his right cheek. He was rubbing his cheek in disbelief when Jenny followed up with a verbal that was just as stinging.

"Shut up and listen, Harlan," she said, not entirely necessarily. She clearly had his attention already. "That was dangerous what you made Signboy do today. You don't know how much of a thug that guy is, anything could have happened."

Harlan nodded. Jenny hadn't stipulated how long he should shut up for, but he figured it would be wiser to shut up for too long rather than speak too soon.

"This isn't a game. You can't joke your way through this without a care in the world, and hope everything will turn out okay. The odds are actually stacked against us, you know? Do you think we're the first ones to try to bring Mick Dawson down?"

Two questions in a row. Surely they couldn't both be rhetorical. Instinct suggested it would be more obvious when the ban was lifted than trying to judge how many questions in a row could be rhetorical. He remained silent.

"Look, I know this whole thing is because of me, because of my article. I'm grateful you guys are helping me, I am. But if something happened to either of you, well, it would be horrible."

Harlan realised Jenny was truly concerned, and suddenly everything she'd been saying sunk in. He reached across and placed his hand on hers reassuringly. They looked into each other's eyes, all four of them glistening in the clean white light of the Burgerman signage hanging overhead.

"Just be careful with him," said Jenny. "He's only a kid, and for some reason he's chosen you as his role model."

"Of course," said Harlan, choosing the perfect moment to break his silence. "I just didn't think about it like that. I've never had to before. I won't let him take any more risks like that."

"And you?"

"Oh, I can't promise that, Jenny. If the opportunity to do something heroic for you came up, I don't see how I could turn it down."

Jenny smiled.

"Good," she said. "I've always wanted a hero at my disposal."

Harlan didn't know what to say. Jenny laughed at his relapse into silence.

"No pressure Harlan, I can settle for someone who just buys me a burger."

"While I still can anyway. After telling Jonathan I'm in cahoots with the woman he hired me to follow, I'm not sure I'll see any money from him."

"You told him about me?"

"Well, it seemed the surest way to get him on board. You're the ace up our sleeve - the article is the one thing we can use against Mick Dawson he can't do anything about. And neither can Jonathan."

Jenny smiled again. Harlan realised he had firmly aligned himself with Jenny by risking his job for Jonathan. Not that there'd been any doubt in his mind, but now he could see there was no longer any in hers.

"Come on," she said.

She stood and started walking slowly down the hill, away from the busy Victoria Street. Harlan looked at the menu, did some more quick mental arithmetic and left enough to cover all three of their meals. He stood up, did the sums again quickly to be absolutely sure he'd left enough cash, then jogged as casually as he could to catch up with Jenny.

"Where are we going?"

"My place."

"But I thought ... "

"Shut up Harlan. Don't make me change my mind." She took his hand in hers and used it to pull his arm up over her head and around her shoulders. As they left the Friday night sounds behind them, Harlan doubted he'd ever been happier.

CHAPTER 23

"Harlan! Get up!"

Harlan didn't remember getting a novelty alarm clock. He looked around. It wasn't his bedroom. Mirrored wardrobes showed him probably naked between white sheets on a queen-sized bed. A nearly empty bottle of red wine and two nearly empty wine glasses sat on a bedside table next to the far side of the bed. A thick curtain failed to block out a window above him to his right, explaining how well-lit the room was.

"The bed's against the wall," he said. He'd have to roll to the far side of the bed to get up. It wasn't as daunting as the tone of his voice suggested. When he reached the other side, against no odds, he swung his legs off the bed and sat up.

"Carpet?" He looked to his right where the thick weave ended abruptly and floorboards carried on out of the room and down the long hallway. "No, rug."

He spotted his trousers on the floor and slowly got up to pull them on. As he finished buckling his belt, he heard dull footsteps approaching. He looked up to see Jenny come into the room. She was already dressed in black jeans, a white singlet and socks, and had her hair tied disarmingly into a pony tail.

"Jenny," he said, realising, without remembering, where he was.

"Here, throw this on," she said, handing him a white T-shirt. He pulled it over his head, she pulled it down and straightened it out around his waist as he worked his arms through the short sleeves. When she was happy with it, she rose onto her toes and gave him an all too brief kiss on the lips.

"Now, come on. We can talk over breakfast. Not much of a morning person are you?"

Harlan leant sideways to catch a quick glance of himself in the nearest mirror before following Jenny down the hallway. She was right. He looked half-dead. It only registered halfway through the house he was wearing an "I heart NY" T-shirt.

"No, not really," he said, trying to flatten his hair a little with both hands. He'd followed Jenny past two closed doors and into a room that might be described as a kitchen slash dining room, made up as it was of a kitchen along two walls with a small dining table set against a third. Jenny went to the stove where she was working on something. Harlan smelled something frying, maybe just butter. Something was definitely sizzling, until Jenny poured a bowl of something else into the frying pan. Scrambled eggs, thought Harlan. No bacon. It would have been cooking by now. He would have smelled it.

"So you love New York huh? The city or the state?"

"Very funny." Jenny motioned for him to sit at the table. He chose the yellow of the four different coloured Ikea folding chairs sitting under the long sides of the table.

"Some kind of ironic statement I guess?"

"Present from my Dad actually. He travels a lot, always brings me back a tacky T-shirt."

"Does he know you use it to dress strange men the morning after?"

"Ha! You're way off, Harlan. Just one strange man. But then, I haven't had it that long." She turned around long enough to hand him a plate of scrambled eggs, then returned to pottering about at the bench.

Harlan smiled at Jenny's back. He was just three things short of the perfect Saturday morning.

"Coffee?" asked Jenny. Make that two.

"Please."

He watched as she ground some coffee in an electric grinder and then made two double espressos with a small domestic espresso machine, stirring a teaspoon of sugar into each when she was done. She turned around to find Harlan staring at her.

"What? Did I do it wrong?"

"No, I was just watching." Jenny looked quizzical. "Still a bit dazed, sorry." It was better than 'I think I'm falling in love'. He'd only known her a few days.

She seemed to accept that and placed the coffees on the table, sitting down opposite him, on the white chair.

"This should wake you up."

"Smells great," said Harlan, closing his eyes to breathe in the exotic aroma. When he opened them to pilot the steaming cup to his lips, he spotted the Saturday newspaper still freshly folded at the end of the table. One to go.

"Ah-ah," said Jenny, pulling the paper away from him. "No time for that. We need to plan the day."

"Of course." Harlan put down his espresso and started on his eggs, which were deliciously light and fluffy, while he tried to resurrect the plan of action in his head. Jenny, with the advantage of an extra hour or so of brain function behind her, was a step ahead of him.

"First, you call your police contact. Get him to look up the file on the dead models for us and call you back."

"Why do you assume it's a 'him'?"

"You said it was a 'him' yesterday."

"Right."

"Second," said Jenny, unperturbed by Harlan's playful but annoying argumentativeness, "you text Biff, ask him for the revised itinerary."

"Assuming he hasn't sent it already."

"He hasn't, I checked your phone. Also Jonathan still hasn't called."

"He will." Harlan felt a slight trespass had occurred, but figured he still didn't have the moral high ground he needed to make an issue of it.

"Third," continued Jenny, "we head to the State Theatre, see if we can't latch onto Stephanie Clarkson there."

"Subject to the itinerary coming through and telling us where she should be."

"Of course."

"All right then, what are we waiting for?"

"You. Finish that, then take a shower. There's a clean towel in the bathroom for you."

"You're not going to join me?"

"I don't think that would get us anywhere, do you?" Harlan knew exactly where it would get them, but didn't say anything. "Besides, while you were dead to the world in there I've already been up, gone for a run, gone to the shops, taken a shower and, you might have noticed, made you breakfast."

"Impressive."

"Thank you, now hurry up. It's already nine, we've got to get moving."

Harlan made light work of the remaining eggs and coffee, stealing a glance at the front page headlines when he could. He always found reading sideways to be the most difficult angle. Upside down he could usually keep pace with a person looking at the same text the right way up. And the right way up was, of course, the easiest, having been the way he was taught as a child by his thoughtful parents. But sideways was unfamiliar, the cross-strokes weren't striking enough, bs and ds he had to learn all over again. In the minute it took him to finish breakfast, he'd only just located a brief story about Christian Dieter being mobbed at the airport ahead of the Hope Celebrities Care Benefit. There looked to be a photo disappearing around the fold, but Harlan couldn't make it out.

"Good, now shower. Second door on the left." Jenny took his dishes away and put them in the sink.

"Shouldn't I make the call first?" asked Harlan as he stood up.

"You can't call someone looking like that, now go." Jenny ended the discussion by playfully shoving him into the hallway.

"Okay, okay." Harlan complied, although he knew there was a *non sequitur* in there somewhere. As he closed the bathroom door on what was probably his favourite breakfast ever, one thought lingered. Some bacon would have been nice.

*

"Have you seen my smartphone?" called Harlan towards the kitchen, as he dressed in his clothes from the day before. Jenny had hung his shirt in the bathroom so it had freshened up a little from the two showers it had witnessed. With a sneaky turning inside-out of his boxers, Harlan actually felt rather clean. Not hearing an answer from Jenny, he called out again.

"I mean, apart from checking it this morning for the itinerary, of course. Have you seen it since then?" He pulled his trousers on for the second time that day, and again the action was followed by the sound of footsteps coming up the hall.

"Here's your *smart*phone, you left it in the kitchen last night. I just thought it would save time if I could check the itinerary while you were still sleeping."

"Of course, it's fine. Thanks." Harlan took his phone from Jenny and woke it up with a swipe. He hesitated before entering the code, realising Jenny must have done so to check for the itinerary.

"Oh," said Jenny, guessing at Harlan's realisation. "Signboy mentioned last night it was the year your favourite book was published. We spent a while trying to figure out which one it was."

Harlan smiled. So Signboy was interested after all. He just had a generational reputation to uphold.

"So, what did you come up with?"

"A pretty good shortlist. I'm pretty sure I know what it is."

"You can't turn this into a guessing game for me. You're the ones who are intrigued here, not me."

"Oh really? You don't want to know how you're perceived?"

Harlan realised he did, but didn't want to be perceived to. He decided to change the subject instead.

"Why don't I make this call? You'll tell me when you're ready."

"I'll tell you when you ask again," said Jenny, smiling as she sat on the bed. "Go on then, make the call."

Harlan sat as well and began scrolling through his contacts.

"You can press on the initial you know, you don't need to scroll through all your contacts."

"I know, I'm just trying to remember what I put him under."

"Not his name?"

"Possibly." Harlan hoped he'd find it before Jenny delved any further. This guy was in the Signboy category, which was even more embarrassing considering he'd known him for ten years or so.

"Well, why don't you check his name first? And why are you scrolling backwards through the alphabet?"

"It started at you, I figured it's more likely to be before 'R'. Here he is." Harlan pressed the entry titled "Cop Buddy".

"Cop Buddy?"

"Yeah, sometimes it helps me remember each contact easier."

"Clearly. So what's his name?"

Harlan ignored the question, indicating the phone was ringing by holding an index finger upright.

"Hello?"

"Hey buddy, it's me, Harlan."

"Harlan, it's been ages."

"I know. We should catch up over a nice meal sometime soon. But unfortunately I'm calling for a favour."

"Well, I'm sure I still owe you a few, what do you need?"

Harlan explained about the dead models and how he needed to see the police file for a case he was working on.

"Yep, shouldn't be a problem. When do you need it by? And don't say yesterday, only wankers say that."

"Well, then obviously that's not what I was about to say. But I do need it sometime today."

"Today? Jeez, I'll see what I can do. You're lucky, I only work every second Saturday, and this is one of 'em. Can you give me the exact date then?"

"The exact date?" Harlan didn't know it. He looked to Jenny, who was already googling it. "Um, just a second, I've got it written down in my case notes somewhere." Jenny held up her phone for Harlan to see. "Sunday, October twenty-three."

"Got it. All right mate, I'll call you when I've got it in front of me."

"Great, thanks buddy."

"Oh, and Harlan?"

"Yes?"

"It's Paul Wessel, write it down for christ's sake. We only used to bunk together."

"Paul Wessel! Of course, sorry. Thanks buddy. I owe you one."

"No you don't mate. Speak to you later."

Harlan looked at Jenny. He wasn't sure whether she heard the other side of the conversation, and was trying to estimate how much she would have picked up from his side alone.

"Who's Paul Wessel?"

So just his side then. But now she had asked, Harlan had to admit his secret. He'd promised he wouldn't lie to her again. He held his phone out so they could both see the screen, and edited the 'Cop Buddy' contact, changing the name to 'Paul Wessel'.

"You didn't know his name?"

"I couldn't remember it, there's a difference. It's my own fault, I used to sometimes use nicknames to put people in my phone, and then all I could remember was the nickname."

"Show me my contact."

"I don't do it anymore." Harlan saw a very insistent look on Jenny's face, so began scrolling back through his contacts to her entry. He scrolled fast, not wanting her to see in case Signboy's came on the screen. He should have done the alphabetical comparison in his head first. In the end, he was scrolling so fast he went straight past *Jenny Randall* and ended smack bang where he least wanted to.

"Wait, Signboy?"

Harlan cringed.

"Don't tell me you don't know Signboy's name?"

Harlan nodded, acutely embarrassed.

"Again, I've just always called him Signboy," he said. "After the first few times he did work for me, it would have been awkward to ask his name. And it's never come up since."

"That's very weird, Harlan. Even for you. I know his name, and I've known him for two days."

"You know his name?"

"Of course. I asked him when you weren't around. I didn't want to make a big deal about you not introducing us properly. Now I know why though. Don't look at me like that, I'm not telling you. It's in there somewhere, Harlan. I'm sure he'd appreciate it if you made the effort to remember it yourself."

Harlan stared at the Signboy entry in his phone, as if he could will it to change and reveal his name.

"Okay, not right now," said Jenny. "We've got to get going, seriously."

Harlan put on his socks and shoes, then followed Jenny out of her bedroom. He wondered if she'd ever invite him back.

CHAPTER 24

Despite the lack of parking in the city, they agreed Jenny should drive them to the State Theatre. They were expecting some stakeout time, and didn't want to rely on finding a taxi if they had to move in a hurry.

After texting Biff to ask for the revised itinerary, Harlan familiarised himself with the interior of Jenny's car. Despite seeing thousands of them on Sydney's roads, he'd never been in a Golf. It contained no surprises though, just a general assurance of utility, until he spotted a black satchel on the floor behind the driver's seat. It wasn't the bag Jenny usually carried, which was on the back seat proper.

"Is that Jonathan's bag?"

"Oh, yes. Sorry, I thought Signboy took it with him."

Harlan detected a slight emphasis on 'Signboy'.

"Shall we have a look inside it? He told me it contained things for the Benefit tonight."

"What's stopping you?"

"Well, it's Jonathan's bag. He told me what was in it, he didn't give me permission to rifle through it."

"I think, given the circumstances, we should definitely rifle through it. We still don't know anything about that

'Kisses' thing Mick Dawson was talking about. There might be something on that in there. And Jonathan still hasn't called you like he said he would."

Harlan realised she was right, as usual, and convinced himself the circumstances did warrant invading Jonathan's privacy. After all, Jonathan hadn't told him *not* to look in the bag.

He reached back and pulled the bag into his lap. It was made of some kind of plastic fibre and as Harlan pulled the flap open they heard the satisfying tear of velcro parting. This wasn't like the expensive leather satchel Mick Dawson had been carrying, but maybe it said something about Jonathan Foxe. Maybe the small decisions, the ones he was still allowed to make, he used to rebel against the wealthy symbolism he was usually surrounded by. Or maybe he was just a tightwad.

Harlan held the main compartment open, sensing Jenny looking out of the corner of her eye as she drove. Not sure what he was expecting, he was a little disappointed to see a solitary ring-binder, and a couple of stapled piles of A4 pages that with a quick flick across with his thumb looked like two printouts of the same Powerpoint presentation. He fished deeper in the compartment and pulled out a Celebrities Care branded thumb drive. A quick search of the smaller compartments revealed nothing else.

He pulled out the ring-binder and held it up for them both to see. Some professional looking graphics and logos surrounded well-laid out text that read "Celebrities Care presents Kisses - a hand-picked range of Celebrities Care branded products that let you share in our goodwill".

"Is that it?" asked Harlan.

"Open it up."

Harlan did. It was another Powerpoint presentation, probably the same one.

"What does it say?"

"Just a minute." Harlan figured he'd be better off skimming through and then summarising. Jenny patiently focussed on driving while Harlan flicked through the presentation, then closed the ring-binder and stared at the cover again.

"Well?"

"It's a marketing presentation, aimed at big companies, household names. Basically they pay a Celebrities Care celebrity to endorse their product, at a below market rate. They also get to use the 'Kisses' logo on their product, and donate an agreed amount of the purchase price to Celebrities Care. They're looking for a specific range of products, each matched to a suitable celebrity. Mp3 player for a singer, smartphone for a social butterfly, sneakers for a sports person, etc. The range of products will have a central marketing budget, supplied by all the participating companies, who are free to market their specific product separately as well."

"So Mick Dawson once again leverages off Celebrities Care to make money for his clients, his marketing buddies, himself, and Celebrities Care gets a small donation from each product sold." Jenny clearly wasn't impressed.

"That's the idea, yes," said Harlan. "And Celebrities Care sells its goodwill to a bunch of global companies who will use it to sell more of their products."

"If they launch this tonight," said Jenny, "it could be huge. A primetime U.S. audience, that's millions of people."

"Maybe that's what Mick Dawson's so excited about. His trough's about to get much, much bigger, and his web of corporate legitimacy much, much tighter."

"Not if I have anything to do with it." Her determination filled the car, spurring them on to the State Theatre, along with some aggressive pumps of the accelerator.

A minute later they turned into Market Street, approaching the State Theatre on the left. They both realised there was no parking other than a taxi zone across the street from the theatre. Jenny slowed the car as they got nearer the theatre. The red billboard over the front door advertised the Benefit. *Live at the State - 11 December - Hope Celebrities Care Benefit.* Unsurprisingly, with the Benefit more than nine hours away, there was no activity at the front door.

They rolled past the theatre and stopped at a laneway they both noticed for the first time between the theatre and the next building, with a couple of cars parked along most of its length. There was room for another, but Jenny and Harlan shared a look, agreeing it would be too conspicuous.

"It looks like the lane goes through, maybe we can come in from the other direction?" suggested Harlan.

"But if we get parked in, we're stuck," said Jenny. "I think we're better off parking nearby, and setting up in that coffee shop with a view of the laneway." Jenny pointed across the street at a café.

"Agreed. Do you have any go-to parking spaces around here?"

"Kent Street. Should be a few there on a Saturday."

"Good, that's just a couple of blocks."

Jenny drove on. It took a couple of minutes to get through the four sets of traffic lights between the theatre and Kent Street, but as they turned right onto Kent they realised it was a good move. Jenny parked the car in the first free space, just a couple down from Market Street.

Harlan went to the parking meter and swiped his credit card for the maximum time, checking as he did for any ambitious parking inspectors with a dogmatic view of the world. The transaction cleared remarkably quickly, and Harlan took the voucher back to the car, where Jenny placed it haphazardly on the dashboard. This irritated Harlan, who felt that whenever an opportunity came to line geometric shapes up, it should be taken. Secretly he wished it to slide off the dashboard somehow and for Jenny to get a parking ticket. He shook off the nasty thought, dismissing it as bitterness over his own recent ticket.

"Come on Harlan," said Jenny, already walking back towards the theatre with her backpack over one shoulder.

He started to follow when Hall & Oates struck up a tune in his pocket. He pulled out his phone, hoping it wasn't Biff. It was an unknown number. He looked ahead at Jenny, who had turned around when she heard the ringtone.

"Well, answer it," she said.

Of course, he thought sarcastically, and made the necessary gesture across the screen.

"Harlan Valeri, Indetective ... "

"Harlan, it's Jonathan." He was whispering.

"Jonathan, hi. I'm glad you called." Harlan whispered in return. Jenny walked back to where Harlan was standing to try to listen in.

"I don't have much time. What's the plan? And don't whisper, unless you're also in a toilet cubicle with Mick's people floating around outside."

"Biff?"

"He's one of them."

Harlan loved Biff's job more every time he heard something new about what it entailed. He looked around before talking, more cautious now he wasn't whispering.

"Okay, we figured tonight is the best opportunity to prove Celebrities Care can survive without Mick Dawson. We'll need Stephanie Clarkson's help, but basically the plan is to get to all the celebrities before the show and tell them about the article Jenny's writing, which will be published tomorrow."

"Tomorrow?" mouthed Jenny. Harlan waved his hand dismissively.

"And what will that achieve?" asked Jonathan.

"We ask the celebrities to perform anyway, to help us expose Mick Dawson. It will make the story bigger, they'll be on the right side of it, and they'll be doing the right thing."

"So the Benefit goes ahead as planned?"

"Yes, but there'll need to be a mention of the story up front, which gives the celebrities a reason to distance themselves from Mick Dawson. We were thinking when you and Stephanie Clarkson open the show."

"Sounds like this is pretty good publicity for her story."

"Jonathan, it's like we discussed. This story is your only weapon against Mick Dawson. You use it to get through the Benefit without him, and then you can fix up Celebrities Care, run it the way it was supposed to be run in the first place."

"What if he finds out? He's not going to stand by and watch you bring him down."

"There's no way he can find out until it's too late. He'll be in his seat getting ready to watch the show when it all happens."

"You'd better hope so. Just make sure you tell as few people as possible what you're planning. And don't mention my name. Mick would kill me if he knew I was going behind his back."

"Kill you?" Jenny's eyes widened at the words.

"Me, you, whoever's working against him."

"Kill me?" Now Harlan's eyes widened.

"Well, maybe not kill. But he's got a hell of a temper, and only one priority: success. I wouldn't want to be in the same room as him when he finds out someone's trying to take it all away from him."

"If all goes to plan you will be. You and a few thousand Hope Celebrities Care supporters. He'll only find out when you and Stephanie Clarkson preempt the story in your opening address."

"A crowd's probably the best protection against a man who cares so much about reputation. Let's just hope he doesn't lose it altogether. And how are you going to get Stephanie to help? Have you spoken to her?"

"No, um," Harlan realised this was a big weakness in the plan. "We're hoping to catch her some time today."

"Shit Harlan, do you know how busy she is today? What if you can't 'catch' her?"

"We will, don't worry. Just make sure if you get a chance to ... "

The line went dead. Harlan hoped it was nothing more sinister than Jonathan hearing Biff come in to check on him.

"What happened?" asked Jenny.

"He hung up."

"And?"

"And ... He liked the plan."

"And what about getting killed?"

"Oh, I think he's just getting a little scared as his betrayal of his long-time collaborator approaches. Anyway, we'll be safe and sound backstage when it happens. And there's not much Mick Dawson can do in a crowded auditorium filled with cameras."

"Good. Come on, let's go and get in position." She sounded like they were planning an ambush, with a mix of determination and excitement in her eyes to match. It made her look a little insane, which Harlan didn't mind. He was sure he had a similar look in his eyes. After all, an ambush is pretty much what they were attempting.

*

A couple of coffees each later, the mood had changed. The caffeine in their bloodstreams still gave them a slightly insane look in their eyes, which belied a deflated state of mind. Harlan's phone sat on the table between them, it's inanimateness a stark contrast to the fidgeting hands either side of it. Jenny's laptop sat on the seat next to her. She'd given up trying to make some headway into the article when she realised she was typing faster than she could think. Double espressos were never meant to be a chain drink.

"I have to pee again," said Jenny, standing and leaving the table. Harlan watched her disappear past the counter, his eyes darting back to the table to avoid making eye contact with the waitress standing behind it. If she came over again he might end up ordering another coffee, and even in his fragile state he knew that would be a mistake.

He returned his attention to the window, staring at the alley across the street. They'd seen a few people go in and out of the side door to the theatre, but nobody they recognised. They'd agreed there would be enough event planners and volunteers involved that Stephanie Clarkson wouldn't have to show up until the red carpet was rolled out. They'd tried to find a phone number for her, but none was listed on any website they could think of checking. They'd called the Hope Foundation head office, but all they got was a recorded message about the Benefit, with a 'Press 1 to donate now' tacked on the end. They'd also checked Twitter regularly but there was no update to *Now it's the Hope Celebrities Care Benefit. Sure do!* Basically, they'd exhausted all their options for contacting Stephanie Clarkson, a list Harlan now realised was embarrassingly short and optimistic. He doubted he'd ever sunk so far mentally within the space of sixty minutes.

Which was why he jumped out of his seat when his phone came to life. The screen lit up, the whole table vibrated, and the three other people in the café learned of Harlan's obsession for Hall & Oates, or at least they would have if any of them were more than vaguely familiar with the *Kiss On My List* keyboard hook.

He juggled the phone, a combination of nerves and caffeine jitters, before reading the message. Harlan recognised the same number that had called him earlier as the sender. The message consisted only of another mobile phone number. He was supremely confident Jonathan had found time to send him Stephanie Clarkson's number.

"Did someone call?" Jenny returned to the table to find Harlan grinning euphorically at his phone.

"No, better." He held the phone across the table towards her. To Jenny, the two mobile phone numbers carried no special significance.

"Phone numbers," she said, as if it were a psychological assessment and Harlan was showing her an inkblot.

"The top one's Jonathan's." Just say whatever comes into your head, he thought.

Jenny thought for a second. "The bottom one's Stephanie's?"

"Exactly." He returned the phone to a less obtrusive position on the table in front of him.

"So what are we waiting for? Let's call her."

"Wait a second. I think Jonathan's telling us more than just her phone number here."

Jenny reached across and tilted the phone back towards her in Harlan's hand, as if she might have missed part of the message.

"No, I don't think so Harlan. See, here," she pointed to the message, "where he starts with her phone number. And here," she pointed to the message again, "where he finishes with her phone number? I think that's all he's trying to tell us. Notice how there's nothing else in the message?" Jenny's impatience after a fruitless morning manifested itself in her being patronising.

"Yes, thank you. That's very ... insightful. And helpfully explained." Harlan wasn't above a little patronisation himself. "But it's the method I was thinking of. He sent us a text message. Suppose they're in a meeting right now. Suppose it's dragging on, Jonathan knows we don't have much time. Biff leaves the room, to get a beer for Mick Dawson probably, Jonathan takes a chance and fires off a message."

"That's a lot of supposition. Aren't detectives supposed to avoid that?"

Harlan let a second pass. He hadn't fully explained to Jenny how averse he was to being called a detective.

"Indetective," he said coolly.

"Sorry, indetective." Now she knew.

"Even supposing that's true ... " Harlan paused, realising the web he was attempting to traverse, "which is itself mere supposition. When there is nothing else to go on, I think detectives and indetectives alike should do nothing less than embrace some well-reasoned, statistically probable supposition. Anyway, what's the point of being the only indetective in the world if I can't make my own rules up?"

Jenny let this last, petulant comment slide.

"Okay," she said, "so they're all in a meeting. What does that mean for us?"

"We do as Jonathan did. We send her a text message. She can read it at the table, even respond to it, without raising Mick Dawson's suspicions."

"How is that different from a call? Surely she could take a call without Mick Dawson suspecting she's about to be offered a role in what's effectively a coup against him."

"Yes, but why would she take the call? That's the other lesson from Jonathan's message. People read messages, whether from an unknown number or not. But do people interrupt important meetings to answer phone calls from unknown numbers?"

"Good point," said Jenny. "Okay, so what message do you send her?"

"Something short and sweet. How about: *Important information about Celebrities Care, must see you before the Benefit.*"

"Hmm. It's to the point. But will it get her to call us?"

"Why wouldn't it? If you got a message the other night from an unknown number that said *Important information about Harlan Valeri, must see you before you sleep with him*, what would you have done?"

"I probably would have asked you what the hell was going on. What if Stephanie Clarkson reacts the same way? Mick Dawson will just bullshit his way out of it like he always does."

"Okay, so we implicate Jonathan somehow, let her know he's in on it but that she can't say anything in front of Mick Dawson about it. Something like: *Can't trust Dawson. Must have Benefit without him. Foxe is in. Call us as soon as possible.*"

Jenny looked at Harlan.

"'As soon as possible?'" she said.

"What's wrong?"

"How about ASAP?"

"Doesn't impart the same urgency."

"Surely someone who has the time to write out words in full instead of a universally known acronym can't be discussing anything that urgent."

"But 'urgent' isn't just about being time-critical, it's also about importance," said Harlan. "You can't have an urgent need to meet for a drink with someone you haven't seen in a while, but you might say 'let's catch up ASAP' in an email, for instance."

"Or you might say 'let's catch up as soon as possible', if you had the time to type it out."

"I think the acronym has been overused though, it softens the meaning."

"And I think it's interchangeable with the phrase, funnily enough."

"So what word would you suggest to convey the urgency of the situation?"

As the words were leaving his lips, they both realised the ridiculousness of the argument. Harlan tapped at his phone until the unabbreviated phrase had been shortened to nothing, and began typing. When he finished, the message read:

Can't trust Dawson. Must have Benefit without him. Foxe is in. Call us urgently.

"Here," said Jenny, taking Harlan's phone. She moved the cursor back to after the word 'Dawson', and added something to the first sentence.

Can't trust Dawson, he will tarnish Hope.

"Perfect," said Harlan, reading it as Jenny passed back his phone.

"Well, you have to look at what motivates people if you want them to respond."

Harlan thought he detected a hint of flirtatiousness in Jenny's voice, and more than a hint in the way she ran her finger seductively across the low neckline of her singlet.

"Well, I can't argue with that," he said, as he felt himself responding.

"Ha, see? You're such a pushover," Jenny said, noticing Harlan shift a little in his seat. "Now send the message."

CHAPTER 25

The minute it took Stephanie Clarkson to reply didn't go quickly for Harlan and Jenny. Nor for the other patrons in the café, who had to listen to their feverish tapping of fingers and feet while they pictured the supposed meeting they were trying to covertly interrupt.

For Harlan, Stephanie Clarkson played it cool. Her blackberry already on the boardroom table in front of her, when it flashed subtly she simply had to lift her eyes from whatever papers they were poring over, adjust her glasses for the movement, and press her index finger onto the scroll wheel to read the incoming message. Mick Dawson didn't even stop talking as she made eye-contact with Jonathan, who nodded almost imperceptibly to confirm his allegiance. Biff re-entered the room with a fresh Crown Lager on a service tray for his master, providing a distraction while Stephanie Clarkson quickly checked her schedule and typed out a reply. Jonathan was the only person in the room who even noticed she'd received a message.

Jenny's mind played it out a little differently. Mick Dawson noticed the flashing blackberry first, interrupting Stephanie Clarkson to point it out. She checked the message and froze, causing Jonathan to do the same. Mick Dawson looked back and forth between them, muttered a 'what the hell's going on here', and was about to reach forward and take the device from Stephanie Clarkson when Biff came into the room with a can of VB. While Mick snatched the beer from Biff, demanded some potato chips to accompany it and started sculling it down regardless, Stephanie Clarkson was able to resume her composure, exchange a knowing glance with Jonathan, and draft a reply which she sent off just as Mick Dawson crushed the empty can of VB against his forehead and threw it at Biff, who was fumbling in the corner with a packet of chips.

To both minds, the message that accompanied the phone's multi-sensorial attention grab was a disappointing end to the scene.

Who is this?

"That makes sense," said Harlan.

"What do we say?"

"There's no point making an introduction by text message. She's almost certainly never heard of us. We just need to entice her to meet us. Today."

"We've got her attention at least," said Jenny. "I think we've probably only got one shot at it though. Remember, her main interest is protecting the reputation of the Hope Foundation."

"What are you suggesting - we summarise the story, tell her it's all coming out? I think you're missing the limitations of the medium here."

"At least give it a try Harlan. Quickly."

"Okay, how about this?" He typed something on the screen, then turned it around for Jenny to see.

We are journalist and indetective. Have proof MD blackmailing JF to exploit CC, using HF to legitimise and leverage into global scam. Must meet today to thwart.

"Harlan, take it out," said Jenny, quite correctly using her 'no time to make jokes' voice.

He was tempted to try his first 'that's what she said' gag on the fly, but agreed with Jenny's tone. He deleted the reference to indetective and pluralised 'journalist'.

"Not the first time we've pretended to be two journalists," said Jenny, approving the change.

"Don't be so hard on yourself," joked Harlan, as he pressed send.

They continued their separate imaginings as they waited for another reply, this time without the tapping. Their nerves had settled a little having made first contact. Not so much, though, that they didn't jump a little when another reply came through.

Hope your info is better than your timing. Swissotel Room 1711, midday. Wait for my signal for all clear.

"Excellent," said Jenny, beaming.

Harlan agreed, nodding and smiling back at her. "Exactly what we were after. That gives us another hour or so. The Swissotel is right next door, it makes sense she would be close to the venue tonight." He put his phone facedown on the table, and looked at Jenny seriously. "Now, about your article. I don't know what arrangement you have with the newspaper, but I think you've got a front page story on your hands for the next couple of days, plus the feature in the magazine next weekend."

"Shit." Jenny looked him in the eyes. It was obvious she hadn't appreciated the full scale of the story. "You think so? I haven't arranged anything other than the feature, and I've only told them I'm fifty-fifty for being ready to go to print next weekend."

"Well, I think you should call them. Let them know you've probably got a scoop for tomorrow's paper."

"Tomorrow's Sunday though. A scoop for a Sunday paper is a stage-managed photo-shoot and interview with a minor celebrity about how she's taking to motherhood. I can pitch it, but I doubt they'll want anything but photos for the social pages tomorrow. Monday's when everyone gets their news from the weekend."

"Okay, Monday then."

"The problem is, so far I've only spoken to the *Weekend*. It's run completely separately to the newspaper."

"Hmm. If only you knew someone high up at the newspaper who was familiar with the story. Someone who's going to be there tonight anyway to see it all go down. Someone you might even run into when you meet her at six-thirty outside the theatre. Someone ... "

"I get it, Harlan. Good call, I should've thought of that. I'll call Diane now." Jenny produced her phone from beneath the table and prepared it to make the call.

"Wait. Actually, don't you think we should speak to Stephanie Clarkson first? What if she doesn't go for it? I don't want you to give Diane a bad impression by promising a story and not coming through. If it's for Monday's paper, we're not in that much of a rush."

Jenny nodded. "You're right. It wouldn't be a good look if I have to call her in another couple of hours and tell her I was wrong, there is no story." She smiled at Harlan. He had recognised the importance to her career of building a connection with Diane Adams. He'd also wasted her time, but what was that compared to a moment of incremental trust-building in a fledgling relationship?

The waitress returned to the table, apparently determined to get some more items on the bill.

"Another couple of coffees? Anything to eat?"

Harlan stirred his spoon in one of the empty espresso cups left on the table from the last round of coffees. Unfortunately the scratching of metal on porcelain only served to emphasise the emptiness of the cup, rather than fool the waitress into thinking he wasn't finished, which was his intention. To drive the point home, the waitress picked up the empty cups and accompanying spoons, and stood with her spare hand on her hip demanding some kind of order to be placed.

"Can we see the menu please?" asked Harlan, stalling further.

The waitress grunted, then regained her limited professionalism and fetched two menus from the counter.

"Thank you so much," said Jenny in mock bubbliness. The waitress matched her with a sarcastic grin and walked off to find some real customers.

"We should probably order something," said Harlan. He perused the menu earnestly, hoping to find something he wanted to eat that wouldn't just seem a token gesture.

"What, because of her? Don't worry about it, it's not like the place is full or anything. We're not stopping any better customers from sitting down."

She had a point, the place had about a dozen booths and the same number of smaller tables, and only a few other customers had been through all morning. Harlan put the menu down. It was impressive only in its complete lack of imagination, which might have explained the low level of business they were doing.

They were back to waiting, although at least now they had something specific to wait for. Harlan decided to use the time to enter Jonathan's and Stephanie's numbers into his contacts while he still knew which was which. Having worked through some of the caffeine in her system, Jenny set up her laptop and resumed work on the feature.

Before Harlan had finished setting up Jonathan's contact, he got another message. The window that popped up preventing him saving the contact told him it was from Paul Wessel. The name was familiar, but Harlan couldn't place it until he read the message.

Harlan, looked into the dead models, call me when you get a chance. Paul.

"It's from Paul," Harlan said as if he'd known his name all along. "He's got something for us on the dead models." Jenny pushed her laptop to the side, preparing to listen in on the phone call Harlan was making.

"That was quick," answered Paul.

"Paul, I was going to say the same thing. Thanks for getting back to me."

"Sounds strange when you say my name to be honest, I'll have to get used to it. Feel free to drop a 'buddy' in every now and then to make me feel more comfortable."

"Sure thing, buddy."

"There you go. Anyway, these dead models - I've got the file in front of me. What did you want to know?"

"Well, what happened to them? Was it ever a murder investigation?"

"A murder investigation? Not according to the file. Pretty much a straight forward case of drug overdose. No witnesses or anything, one person of interest questioned ... Jonathan Foxe. It was one of his parties, but he didn't know the girls. Toxicology reports pretty identical, an overdose of gamma hydroxy-butyrate, high levels of alcohol and heroin contributing."

"Gamma hydroxy-what?"

"GHB. A cheap party drug, easy to OD on because it's cheap, liquid, hard to measure out and you don't build up a tolerance to it."

"So nothing suspicious then?" Harlan was surprised at his own reaction, which was surprise. On some level he'd apparently expected the police file to contradict Jonathan's version of events.

"No, nothing in here. Everything pointed to accidental overdose. It's probably the most vanilla write-up of an OD I've ever seen, and I've never even seen a double OD before."

"Interesting. Okay, thanks Paul."

"Let me know if you need anything else."

"Will do, speak to you soon."

Harlan ended the call.

"According to the file, Jonathan was telling the truth. He was never under suspicion, the girls overdosed on a party drug."

"According to the file?"

"Weren't we suspicious Dawson used his contacts to stifle the investigation? If that's the case, surely the file was cleaned up as well. Paul said it was the cleanest he'd seen on an OD."

"So it doesn't tell us anything."

"I'm not so sure. Remember, Dawson was using the police attention to pressure Jonathan out of the Executive Club. If he had the file sanitised, he wouldn't have told Jonathan."

"So Jonathan *is* telling the truth."

"Must be. Remember, he volunteered the information about the girls. I didn't have to ask him."

"So if Mick Dawson did pull some strings, he wasn't pulling them for Jonathan."

"No. Probably for his mates selling the drugs."

"Good," said Jenny. "I mean, not good, but, you know."

"I know. It's nice to know we're not helping out a murderer."

"Exactly."

*

About ninety minutes later, a little later than the midday she'd indicated, Harlan got the 'all clear' message they were waiting for from Stephanie Clarkson, telling them to come to the room now. Jenny took a few seconds to make sure all the evidence was easily accessible on her desktop, then they went next door to the hotel.

The reception was surprisingly small, basically a counter, a small waiting area and access to the lifts. They walked straight past the counter and into the elevator bay. Jenny pressed the 'up' button, and one of the elevators opened immediately.

"Level 17, I assume," said Harlan, based cleverly on the room number. They got in the elevator and Harlan pressed the button with '17' on it. The ride up was accentuated by a nervous silence. Harlan distracted himself by reading the poster on the wall. It was 'Silly Season' at the hotel's bar, Crossroads. Two-for-one cocktails between four and six. Harlan checked his watch reflexively. He doubted he'd get to take advantage of the deal, which didn't bother him in the slightest.

They stepped out of the lift and followed the signs to room 1711. Harlan looked at Jenny, exchanging a nod before reaching forward to knock on the door. Jenny stopped his arm short.

"Wait," she whispered. "How do we know it's her on the other side of the door?"

Harlan paused. All they were going on was Jonathan's message. It could have been anyone's phone number he sent them. It could even have been Biff or Mick Dawson who sent it. Harlan realised they could be walking right into a trap.

"Who else would it be?" he asked. He didn't want Jenny to think he had his doubts.

"I don't know. It's just ... So far it's been falling into place so easily, I feel like we're not being careful enough."

"Easily? This has been the toughest week of my life. I've been kidnapped. I've kidnapped somebody. I've had staff walk out on me. I've had other staff threaten industrial action. My petty cash box was broken into. This is our only chance to bring it all together. Either Stephanie Clarkson's behind that door, and we can persuade her to go along with our plan, or ... "

"Or she's not," said Jenny.

"Right. Either way, we have to find out."

"I know."

A few seconds passed as they both prepared themselves for the worst. Again, Harlan looked at Jenny, exchanged a nod, and this time succeeded in knocking on the door. Jenny grabbed his arm tightly as they waited for a response.

CHAPTER 26

They heard someone turn the handle from the inside. The door opened into the room. Jenny's grip on Harlan's arm tightened to painful levels when she didn't recognise the man who opened the door. He was dressed immaculately in shoes whose outlandish pointiness was matched only by their shininess, grey pinstripe trousers and a fitted powder pink shirt. Harlan barely noticed the pain from Jenny's grip. He was focused on making the logical leaps necessary to accept the reality that Darren, Marisa Foxe's assistant, was standing in front of him.

"Mr Valeri, a pleasure to see you again."

"Darren, I thought I might find you here."

Jenny snapped her attention back to Harlan. She suspected for a moment he'd kept something from her again, but by now she recognised the look on his face when he was bluffing. Looking at Harlan, she missed the shudder of joy that rippled through Darren as Harlan remembered his name.

"And this must be Ms. Randall," Darren offered his hand to Jenny, who shook it in a daze. Harlan was impressed how much Darren knew, and used the information to help conjecture how he came to be there.

"Please, follow me." Darren led them through a small entrance area into a sitting room, where Stephanie Clarkson and Marisa Foxe sat together on a sofa. They were similarly dressed for working on the weekend. Flat casual shoes, jeans, comfortable T-shirt. Marisa's hair was down, Stephanie Clarkson's was up. Neither bothered with contacts, they'd be in at the Benefit tonight no doubt. Designer glasses were given a rare opportunity to justify their price tag.

The floor to ceiling drapes were drawn behind them, Harlan assumed to remove any glare so they could use the laptop sitting on the coffee table in front of them. Still, the little natural light coming in at the edges was doing a lot more bouncing around than the dim, yellow, overhead lighting in the ageing hotel room. Two armchairs faced the sofa from across the coffee table, and Darren gestured for Harlan and Jenny to sit in them. Before they could, both Stephanie Clarkson and Marisa stood up to greet them.

"Harlan, fancy seeing you here," said Marisa, disingenuously.

"Hi Marisa, good to see you again," said Harlan, also disingenuously as he was still trying to decide whether he welcomed this turn of events.

"And you must be the reporter who's been following my husband around."

"Jenny, Jenny Randall." Jenny shook Marisa's hand confidently. Harlan was pleased to see she'd recovered from the shock at the door and was back to being the assertive woman he knew. He wasn't so pleased to find Marisa knew about Jenny's investigation.

"Ms Clarkson," said Harlan, "I'm Harlan Valeri and this is Jenny Randall."

"Pleased to meet you both, I think," said Stephanie Clarkson, shaking their hands in turn. "You two have met before?" Stephanie looked from Harlan to Marisa and back.

"Yes," said Marisa, smiling cryptically at Harlan. "Harlan's done some work for my husband in the past."

It wasn't just the smile that was cryptic. Either Marisa was being clever making a deliberate reference to the nature of the work he was doing for her or she was being devious and letting Harlan know she knew he was also working for Jonathan.

"Please, sit." Marisa was assuming the role of convenor. All four of them sat down. "Can I get either of you a drink? Darren makes a great cappuccino."

"No," said Jenny and Harlan in unison, still a bit caffeine-shy after their morning overload.

"Okay," said Marisa, a little bemused by the emphatic response. She quickly shook it off and dismissed Darren with a curt nod. He disappeared through sliding frosted glass doors into the bedroom, closing the doors behind him. It was a strange place to wait. But it was either that or the corridor.

"Now," continued Marisa, "why don't we get started. I'm sure you appreciate Stephanie is extremely busy today."

"Thanks Marisa," said Stephanie Clarkson. "Jenny, Harlan. I have to say your messages have me worried. Of course I've got my own ideas of the kind of businessman Mick Dawson is, but why don't you assume I know nothing. I want you to explain everything behind the messages you sent me today. Then I'll explain why Marisa's here, and we can go from there."

"No need, Ms Clarkson," said Harlan.

"Stephanie, please." Jenny and Marisa exchanged a look. They'd had the same problem when they first met Harlan.

"Stephanie. As I was saying, it's perfectly clear why Marisa is here. Jonathan couldn't be here without Mick Dawson, so Marisa is here to represent him. Whether Jonathan had you contact her, or the other way round, doesn't really matter. If I had to guess, I'd say he did both just to be certain but, like I said, it's not important."

"No, I suppose not," said Stephanie. "In that case, it's only you two who have the explaining to do."

"Indeed," said Harlan. He looked at Jenny, who pulled her laptop out of her backpack and opened it up on the table.

"I think," she said, "this is the best place to start." She pressed something on the keyboard and the speakers on the laptop came to life with a click and then background noise. The first intelligible sound was Jonathan Foxe's voice.

"Look, Mick ... "

They were silent as they listened to the recording of Mick Dawson and Jonathan Foxe discussing Mick's plans for Celebrities Care. Harlan first watched Marisa's reaction. She'd had the recording since he saw her yesterday. A look of recognition as Jonathan first spoke told Harlan she'd listened to it. That explained why she was there then. To help her husband.

He turned his attention to Stephanie. He was pleased to see her squirm uncomfortably and tut scornfully as Mick Dawson discussed his preference for English speaking orphans and drooled over the moneymaking potential of the Benefit. The Bugboy 300 was one of the best investments Harlan had ever made.

As the recording neared its end, it was Harlan's turn to squirm as the conversation turned to him. He felt Jenny's sideways glance like a flick in the ear, reminding him of his deceit.

The recording ended abruptly. Jenny waited a few seconds, letting Marisa and Stephanie reflect on what they'd just heard.

"Stephanie," she said. "You can't let this bloodsucker sink his fangs into the Hope Foundation. Based on his moral standing alone you shouldn't let him be seen within a hundred metres of any Hope wreath, let alone waving victoriously behind one at your biggest event of the year."

"I can't disagree with that," said Stephanie. "I already had my concerns, but it was Jonathan who persuaded me to go ahead with the partnership. When he showed me the numbers they could deliver for the Benefit, well, how could I turn that down? Do you know how far a million dollars goes in front-line charity work?"

Jenny and Harlan shook their heads, eyebrows raised expectantly.

"A long way. Just five-hundred dollars can supply clean water to two-hundred families. So a million dollars can do the same for ... "

"Four-hundred-thousand families," said Harlan.

"Yes. Thank you." Harlan heard some annoyance in her voice. He should have known the Hope Foundation CEO would have more than a passing familiarity with the numbers her charity works with. "Even knowing what I know now," she continued, "how can I turn that down?"

"Well, that's why we're here," said Jenny. "If our plan works, you won't have to."

"Your plan?"

Jenny explained the plan, from the hijacking of the celebrities and the exposure of Mick Dawson in the media to the subsequent cleanup of Celebrities Care.

"And if we can get the celebrities to go along with it tonight," she wrapped up, "you'll still get the donations you were hoping for. Even more over the next few weeks with the publicity generated."

Stephanie sat still, her hand supporting her chin, thinking it over. Marisa sat forward, eyeing Jenny suspiciously.

"And what about my husband? Won't all this bad publicity affect him?"

"Trust me, Marisa," said Harlan. "Your husband wants to distance himself from Mick Dawson more than anyone else. This is his opportunity to do it, and then be free to turn Celebrities Care into the charity he dreamed of." He was practically admitting his connection and allegiance to Jonathan.

"Well, if you know my husband better than I do, which seems more likely to be the case every time I see you, then I guess I'll have to take your word for it."

"Marisa," said Jenny. "Even if Harlan's wrong, which, believe me, is a distinct possibility, I'm afraid Jonathan's only real choice is to go along with it."

Marisa's eyes widened. She clearly wasn't used to being spoken to like this. Harlan guessed the fact it was a younger woman made it even more galling.

"I'm exposing Mick Dawson no matter what happens tonight. Either Jonathan plays the victim, and uses tonight to take Celebrities Care in a new, Mick Dawson-less direction, or he stands beside Mick Dawson and takes what's coming to him. He's not innocent in all this, but he can do the right thing now and hope his supporters give him a second chance."

Harlan admired Jenny's courage. She was addressing two of the more powerful women in the city having only just met them. One of them she was threatening with an ultimatum for her husband. He checked her extremities for any signs of nerves but found none. Her conviction amazed him.

"Jenny," said Stephanie, eyes wide too but more with admiration than umbrage. "I'm sure Jonathan will do the right thing. I've found him to be a gentleman in all my dealings with him, genuinely caring, a good person. Clearly a different kind to Mick Dawson altogether."

Marisa turned to Stephanie, maintaining her glare. Even sharpening it a little, thought Harlan. Jenny was just an upstart who didn't know her place. Stephanie was a rival. And, Harlan remembered, Mick Dawson was an old friend. The ramifications of this hadn't hit him until now. Maybe it wasn't so clear why she was there.

"Jonathan has already decided to do the right thing," said Harlan. "He proved that by sending us your number, Stephanie."

"Yes, that's right," said Stephanie. She regarded Harlan and Jenny in turn. Again Harlan saw admiration in her eyes when she looked at Jenny. He couldn't blame her. "In that case I think you've got what you came here for. I'm in. I'm not going to sit by and let that man sully the Hope Foundation. If we can save Celebrities Care at the same time, so much the better."

"Excellent," said Jenny. "You won't regret this."

"Let's say I would regret it more if I woke up tomorrow morning and the Hope Foundation was just another publicity weapon in Mick Dawson's arsenal, and I hadn't done anything to stop him."

"Agreed," said Harlan. "Well, no doubt you've got other things to be getting on with Stephanie. You can call us later this afternoon to arrange the logistics."

"I certainly do. You've no idea how much planning goes into one of these things. I'm having my last meeting with the event manager at four. I'll organise your passes then, and call you afterwards to discuss the details."

"Perfect," said Harlan. "Needless to say, the less people who know about this beforehand the better. We don't want Mick Dawson finding out what's going on until it's too late."

"Of course," said Stephanie.

Harlan looked around the room. Jenny was grinning at Stephanie. Marisa had composed herself, a cold stare all she offered anyone. Stephanie, like Harlan, was looking around the room as well. It was that awkward moment where a meeting has ended but nobody knows what to do next. Harlan made a mental note. If he ever put together a meeting agenda, the item after 'any other business' would be 'everyone make their farewells and leave'.

As if on cue, the sliding doors reopened and Darren emerged. He was extremely well trained.

"Mr. Valeri, Ms. Randall," he said. "Thanks so much for your time. Let me show you to the door."

*

They returned to the car, the short walk completed in silence with both of them too busy thinking to talk. Jenny obviously hadn't made any headway on the informational sudoku that had just confronted them. As soon as they were sitting in the car, she burst.

"What the hell was that all about?"

"That," said Harlan, "was unexpected."

"No shit. What was she doing there?"

"I don't know. My best guess is our worst fear."

"What do you mean?"

"I hope she was there as Jonathan's eyes and ears. But I can't realistically imagine a scenario where he would have arranged for her to be there. It wouldn't make sense."

"Why not?"

"Jonathan had all night to tell Marisa what was going on if he wanted to. And if he did, things would have happened differently today. Marisa isn't the type to sit around and wait for something to happen. He must not have told her."

"So he told Stephanie to call her, maybe he thought she could help."

"No," said Harlan, flatly. "It wouldn't make sense to keep her in the dark up to now and then suddenly get her involved through Stephanie."

"So Stephanie called Marisa of her own accord?" Jenny was clutching at straws.

"There are two possibilities I can conjure up that make sense. The most favourable for us is Marisa put off looking at the thumb drive until this morning, when Jonathan had already left for the day. After reading everything on it and listening to the recording, she had a similar idea to us and sought out Stephanie to try to help Jonathan somehow."

"I like that one. What's the other one?"

"The other possibility is she was there because of Mick Dawson." Jenny nodded solemnly. Mick Dawson having a spy in that meeting was a devastating prospect.

Harlan prepared to outline his theory. In his experience saying a theory out loud was often the best way to test its cogency and a good way to appreciate the gravity of its implications, which in this case was enormous. He wanted to get it right.

"Marisa looked at the contents of the thumb drive," he began, "but it wasn't enough to make her risk her comfortable life by supporting her husband's wishes to change. Remember, we're talking about a woman who hired me to keep her husband's infidelities a secret, so we know she's not above a moral compromise."

"How could I forget?" said Jenny. Harlan carried on.

"As for Mick Dawson, he can keep Jonathan under watch, but he has no control over Stephanie. So he calls his old friend Marisa. He tells her he's worried Stephanie might not be able to pull off the Benefit. If it doesn't go smoothly Celebrities Care will take a hit, Jonathan will lose face. 'Why don't you give her a call, offer to help out, say Jonathan suggested it.' So she did."

"And Stephanie thinks Jonathan put her up to it," said Jenny. "She thinks it's connected to our messages somehow, so she brings her along."

"Correct. And now Marisa holds the key. Either she's on our side, and Mick Dawson is none the wiser. Or she reports back to him, and he finds out exactly what we're going to do."

"So which is it?"

"I'm afraid we have to assume the worst," said Harlan, "and hope we're wrong."

"I'd rather assume the best, and hope we're right."

"Me too. But if Mick Dawson knows what we're up to, he'll go to great lengths to stop us. We need to be prepared."

CHAPTER 27

They agreed to head to Jenny's place for the afternoon. If Mick Dawson was on to them, they needed to lie low until the last minute. From there, Jenny could contact Diane Adams. Whatever happened now, it would definitely be newsworthy. Meanwhile Harlan would prepare a speech for the celebrities. He couldn't imagine getting more than a few minutes with them all together before the show, so whatever they were going to say had to be perfect.

Before Jenny started the car though, Harlan's phone again performed ominously to herald the arrival of a text message. Harlan swiped his finger irritatedly. Maybe he should find a less insistent grab for his incoming message tone. One that wasn't designed to startle you into dancing involuntarily.

"What is it?" asked Jenny, seeing the concern on Harlan's face as he read the message.

"Signboy - says to meet him at the office as soon as possible."

Jenny glanced at Harlan's phone, quickly reading the message sideways as easily as if it was just a matter of rotating the whole text ninety degrees in her mind.

"He obviously knows your feelings about acronyms. What do you think he wants?"

"I think he wants me to meet him at the office as soon as possible."

"Very funny."

Harlan scrolled to the top of his conversation with Signboy and pressed 'Call'. It rang out with no answer.

"He must have flicked it on to silent accidentally or something. Stupid smartphones."

"Try calling the office," said Jenny.

"There's no phone in the office."

"Oh. Very twenty-first century."

"Thank you. Look, I better just go over there. Why don't you drop me at Town Hall, I'll get the train to Newtown and see what he wants. Then we can bring my car over to your place. Two birds with one stone."

"Your car's already near my place after last night, remember? You left it in Darlinghurst."

"Perfect. Three birds then."

"Three birds? Don't you mean one?"

"The car's already where we want it. That's worth two in the bush. Plus bringing Signboy back into the fold. Three."

"Sure, three then."

"Thank you." Harlan was gracious enough to appreciate Jenny's concession to his clearly flawed logic. "Anyway, we'll just get a taxi back."

"Okay, but be careful. If Marisa does go to Mick Dawson with our plan, he's sure to get someone to watch your office."

With a couple of jabs Harlan brought up the Inner West Line timetable on his phone.

"If he does, he'll have to be quick. Come on, next train leaves Town Hall in four minutes."

"Four minutes? We won't make it driving. Just cut through the QVB."

Harlan knew she was right. These days you had to factor in at least a couple of minutes per block in the city.

And they had to circle the block they were on to get back to Town Hall, which was effectively three blocks just to be facing the right way.

"Okay, see you soon." He patted her leg as some kind of farewell gesture, then jumped out of the car and broke into a run back up towards Market Street.

"Good luck!" he heard Jenny call after him.

Harlan turned left onto Market Street and sprinted up the hill towards the Queen Victoria Building. The Monorail glided past overhead as he used a break in the traffic to cross the street. If only it went somewhere useful, he thought. At York Street he had to dart between two buses, prompting another absurd analogy with wildebeests and a prolonged press of the horn by the driver of the second bus. Harlan turned his head long enough to read his lips through the windscreen. Despite the driver's negative opinion of his mental health, Harlan nodded gratefully as he ran past.

When he reached the arcade entry into the QVB he glanced at his phone. Still four minutes. He was making good time. Unfortunately he had to slow down to negotiate the throng of shoppers ambling through the shopping centre. Half way through the centre he ducked down the side staircase to be on the same level as the underground station entrance. He chanced another glance at his phone. Two minutes.

"That was never two minutes," he grumbled to the confused amusement of the nearest shoppers. He increased his vigour, picturing Jenny cheering him on. The underground passage veered left and Harlan saw the turnstiles ahead. He fumbled in his pocket for his wallet while scanning the overhead signs on the concourse for which platform he needed to go to. He slowed to a walk as he approached the turnstiles, sliding his weekly ticket out of his wallet in perfect time to feed it into the reader. One minute.

"You've got to be joking," he said breathlessly.

More amused passersby watched him dance in a half circle on the concourse trying to spot the right staircase or escalator down to the Inner West Line platform. The last sign on his visual circuit directed him down some stairs to his immediate left to Platform 1. He swung around the banister and sprinted down the stairs to a platform flanked on neither side by a train.

He looked up at the nearest plasma screen. Two minutes. He looked at his phone. Due out. Harlan added the mobile timetable to his mental list of imperfect things. He thought twice. Not really the timetable's fault the train was late. He crossed it out and added CityRail instead. He thought again. No sense in an accurate timetable if the trains run whenever they want. He added the mobile timetable as well.

Harlan strolled down the platform, catching his breath. He did his best to look like he hadn't run unnecessarily. It was more socially respectable to stride onto a platform and nonchalantly miss a train than to run to catch one when you didn't need to. It was even better to run and just miss one. At least then everyone who saw it was on the train and out of sight within seconds. Now Harlan had to endure the superior looks of the other people on the platform. He walked to the opposite end to get away from them. There he was just another casual commuter who had arrived comfortably in time for the train, which duly arrived when the plasma screen had promised.

The trip was only four stops. Ten minutes. At Central the train emerged from underground and Harlan tried again to call Signboy. Still no answer. Harlan wondered whether he should be worried, but there was no point until he got off the train. He decided to wait.

As the train pulled up at Newtown station, Harlan was first out the door. He was at the right end of the platform. He thanked his insecurity as he sprinted the short distance to the long staircase up to King Street. Three steps at a time proved the easiest stride to manage after attempting four nearly proved disastrous. After negotiating the ticket barrier, he reached the footpath, rounding a couple of homeless people and their belongings as he hooked left and hit the home stretch to the office. Now he was worried.

He slowed to a quick walk when he reached Whitehorse Street. It had been nearly twenty minutes since Signboy messaged him. A few seconds to check the street for suspicious cars couldn't hurt. He scanned the cars on both sides of the street as he crossed. They all seemed perfectly at home. He reached number 24 and hurried inside.

The chiropractor was open on Saturdays. Harlan tried not to appear too frantic and avoided looking in as he walked past the open door. He wasn't in the mood for Shannon to offer him a soothing cup of herbal tea and a free stress assessment.

He reached the stairs and looked up. The door was closed. Signboy usually left it open so he could hear anyone coming. Worry graduated towards alarm with each step. Something didn't feel right. Harlan went through his senses. Nothing wrong there. No other sight, smell or sound out of place. This was either instinct or paranoia.

At the top of the stairs he tried to squint through the frosted glass. Without a light on inside it was pointless. He turned the handle. It was unlocked. Maybe Signboy had just stepped out while he waited for Harlan.

Pulling the door open slowly, Harlan peered around its edge into his reception area. Empty. No offence to the fern. He walked in, leaving the door open behind him. The door to the back office was closed. Harlan performed another slow-open-and-peer-around with it. Empty.

Alarm subsided, giving way to confusion. Why had Signboy called him here? Again he pulled out his phone and called Signboy. As it started to ring, Harlan heard a call for all the single ladies coming from downstairs. Interesting choice of ringtone. Signboy must be watching TV. He was about to hang up when something caught his eye on the counter. The fern. Not the fern, something about the fern. The cigarette butts bent into the soil. Had he cleaned it up after last time? There was only one before anyway. Now there were two. *All the single ladies*. The steps coming up the stairs were too heavy to be Signboy's. Why had Signboy called him here? Why did someone else have Signboy's phone? He looked at his phone. It was definitely Signboy he had called.

"Shit." Harlan remembered adding a new entry for Signboy very recently. Signboy New. It seemed clever at the time. Clever, though, would have been changing the old entry. Then he would have known he'd been called to the office by the SIM card they'd put in the Bugboy 300. "Shit."

He turned to face the music. A hand holding the ringing phone emerged first. *If you liked it then you shoulda put a ring on it*. Biff followed it into the room. *Wah-oh-ohh, oh-oh-oh-ho-ho*. Biff mouthed the empowering refrain. His lips curved sharply around the syllables, an evil grin bending sadistically to form the ohs. His eyebrows were raised to avoid being singed by the insane look in his eyes. Harlan nearly threw up. Beyonce probably would have, hearing her voice and seeing that face. Harlan put an end to it by jabbing at his phone.

There was no explaining this away, even to someone as thick as Biff. Harlan prepared himself for a long afternoon.

"Biff, thanks for dropping by."

"*In*detective. Good to see you. You've got some explaining to do." Quite unnecessarily Biff produced the Bugboy 300 from his pocket. He held it in the air for a second, then threw it at Harlan, who caught it against his gut, nearly knocking the fern over as he backed up against the counter to do so. "I believe this belongs to someone you know?"

Maybe he was thick enough for an explanation.

"What is it?"

"The Bugboy 300. Can't you read?"

Harlan turned it around in his hand. 'Bugboy 300' was printed on one side.

"Bugboy 300?"

"It's a bug. A listening device."

"I know what a bug is."

"The SIM card inside had your number in the contacts. The SIM card you've been trying to call for the last half hour."

"Well, obviously I know nothing about the bug then. Otherwise why would I be calling it?"

Biff thought for a moment. It was a good point.

"I don't know. But you need to explain why your number was on it in the first place."

"I imagine whosever SIM card it is knows me, and has my number in their contacts. Or is it the technical aspects you need explaining? Because it's quite common for people to save their contacts onto their SIM card."

"Nice try. You know whose SIM card it is. Otherwise why would you be calling it?"

It was Harlan's turn to concede a point.

"I received a strange message from that number. I thought I'd come into the office to check it out, and tried the number a couple of times to see who it was."

Biff stood silently, glaring at Harlan. He obviously wasn't expecting to have to think his way through this encounter. When he broke his silence, it was clear he'd had enough of trying to.

"Don't explain it to *me*, *In*detective. I don't care. You need to explain it to Mister Dawson."

Harlan looked over Biff's shoulder, half expecting to see Mick Dawson enter the room. He wasn't disappointed when he didn't. He knew Mick Dawson wouldn't really want an explanation. He'd want blood. Now it was real for Harlan too, he understood Jonathan's fear.

"Well, Biff, I'm pretty busy today actually. Can it wait?"

Biff walked to the open office door and looked in. Apparently satisfied with the empty room, he turned back to Harlan and pulled his jacket open with his right hand.

As Jenny had pointed out the day before, Biff carried a gun.

"You need to come with me, now. Mister Dawson wants to see you."

Harlan wondered why he hadn't opened with that. It was very convincing. He was about to say so when he heard considerably lighter steps coming up the stairs. Biff had heard them too, and dropped his jacket closed. A threatening glance told Harlan not to try anything. He marvelled at how easily 'no funny business' translated to facial expression alone.

A professional-looking woman appeared at the top of the stairs. She looked first at Biff, then Harlan. Harlan and Biff looked at each other, both shrugging their shoulders. They looked back at the woman. She was thin like children used to be, average height. Reddish hair just about tidy. A straight grey dress started near her chin and finished below her knees. A thin black belt tried to insinuate a curve at her waist. She looked at them through nervous eyes and unremarkable glasses. Harlan thought he should say something before Biff. A rough word might break her.

"Hi, can I help you?"

"Sorry," she said. The voice suited, unsure of where it should go in the room. Like her, it seemed rooted to the top of the stairs. "I'm here about the position?"

She held up one of the signs Signboy had posted earlier in the week. Harlan noticed she carried a soft plastic folder. Almost certainly her resumé.

"Sorry, I shouldn't have come on a Saturday, but I work in the city all week."

"Not at all," said Harlan. He felt Biff heating up across the room. "But now isn't the best time. Can you leave a copy of your resumé, and I'll get back to you?"

"Well, I've only got one. Saving paper. But I can leave it if you promise not to throw it out?"

"Sure, perfect. We're a paperless office here, so you're off to a good start. I'm Harlan by the way, Harlan Valeri."

She looked behind her, confirming his name was the one she could read backwards through the frosted glass on the open door.

"Hi, Mr Valeri." She stepped into the room with all the certainty of climate change theory in the eighties and extended her hand.

"Harlan, please," he said, meeting her more than halfway to shake it, shifting the Bugboy 300 to his left hand to do so.

"Harlan. I'm Shauna Kinneally."

Biff cleared his throat.

"Sorry, Shauna," he said. "We're on a tight deadline."

"That's fine, really. I understand." She started to look in his direction but changed her mind. She gave Harlan her resumé. "I'll come back for it next Saturday?"

"Yes, perfect," said Harlan. "See you then."

She glanced quickly at Biff's feet, then nodded at Harlan and walked back out the door. They waited for her steps to fade out of the building. Harlan turned and put her resumé on the counter, then slid the Bugboy 300 underneath it. If he could get away with it, he'd get to keep it and still charge Jonathan for the expense.

"That wasn't very nice," said Biff.

"What do you mean?"

"Taking her resumé like that, telling her to come back next week." He flashed his weapon again. "If I were in your position, I wouldn't be making any plans at all. You know, in case you're not around to stick to them."

Biff walked over to Harlan and started patting him down.

"There's no need for this Biff. I don't carry a gun."

"Why not? The amount of enemies you must make ... " he trailed off as he sank to his haunches to pat up and down Harlan's legs. Harlan didn't bother to explain. Biff stood up and gestured for him to lead the way outside.

"All right then, *In*detective. Let's go."

CHAPTER 28

Harlan walked out of the room and down the stairs, aware of Biff following close behind. He saw Shannon standing at the door of his waiting room. Not exactly the infantry he needed right now. To Harlan's complete surprise though, it was Biff he was waiting for.

"Matthew? My one o'clock just cancelled, if you wanted to have a consultation now?"

Harlan walked straight past him, bracing himself for a violent reaction from Biff. Whatever Biff had told him must have been a cover while he was waiting for Harlan to show up.

"Thanks mate. But Harlan's turned up now, I'm taking him out for a bite so we can catch up. Can I come back during the week?" Harlan couldn't believe his ears. He kept walking, looking over his shoulder slightly to see if Biff had stopped to talk. Maybe he could make a run for it. He felt an arm on his other shoulder just as he began to seriously entertain the notion. "I'll call you on Monday, Shannon," said Biff, steering Harlan out the front door.

"Nice guy that Shannon," he said to Harlan as they walked down the front stairs. "Let me wait in his waiting room till you came. Gave me a cup of tea. Beats standing in your reception."

"I'll bet it's no smoking though."

"Yeah, that's true. It is good of you to let me smoke up there. Go right."

Harlan did as he was told, turning right out of the gate and heading along the footpath, away from the station. He looked around for the Mercedes-Benz, guessing they were going to see Mick Dawson in the city somewhere. That would give him some time to think on the way.

"Here we are."

They stopped alongside a silver Toyota Prius.

"You drive a hybrid?"

"Yep," said Biff, opening the passenger door for Harlan. Harlan shook his head and got in. Biff closed the door on him and walked around to the driver's side.

"What kind of hired goon goes to a chiropractor, and drives a hybrid?" he asked himself before Biff had opened the door.

Biff got in and turned the car on with the press of a button. He turned to Harlan as he clicked his seatbelt in.

"Now, this gun," he flashed it again, "is loaded. And I will use it if you try to get away. So just sit still and keep your mouth shut till we get there."

Harlan was glad he didn't carry a gun for protection. Biff would have two guns now, something he didn't want to contemplate. It didn't matter how many kilometres Biff got to the litre, or how few greenhouse gasses he and his car emitted in the process. The man was a thug.

He let Biff drive in silence. When they stopped at the lights, so did the noise from the hybrid engine as it switched to electric power. Surely the same engineers could get the stereo volume to move in line with the engine noise. They turned onto King Street and headed towards the city as Harlan expected. He took the opportunity to assess his options. They weren't many.

He ruled out trying to make a run for it. Being shot at had never been in any of his plans, and would completely negate his reasoning behind not carrying a gun in the first place. Besides, as long as Biff was occupied with Harlan, maybe Jenny and Signboy could carry off the coup without him.

He also wanted to see Mick Dawson. It might be valuable knowing how much the bastard knew. There was still plenty of time before the Benefit to try to escape after meeting him, if that's what it came to.

It occurred to Harlan he should try to let Jenny know what was going on. More importantly, that she should proceed without him if she had to. He doubted his life was actually in peril. He didn't want her to come looking for him if it meant not going ahead with the plan.

With that selfless thought, Harlan realised he was actually invested emotionally in something that didn't directly concern him. He wanted to stop Mick Dawson. He wasn't just going along with whatever came his way. He wasn't just trying to make Jenny happy. He wasn't even just trying to do the right thing. He wanted the right outcome. He went to pinch himself to make sure he wasn't dreaming, and found he was still holding his phone in his right hand. He slowly brought it into his hip where Biff was least likely to see what he did next.

Keeping the face turned where he could see it but Biff couldn't, he brought it to life, being sure to move only his thumb under cover of the phone itself. After a couple of surreptitious prods and swipes, he was starting a text message to Jenny.

Biff ...

They stopped at some lights, the engine noise disappearing. Harlan froze.

"That's the way," said Biff. "Is this the longest you've ever been quiet?"

"It's only been a minute."

"Must be up there, still."

The light went green and they moved forward again. Because he was being so careful, it was taking a long time to type out the message. It took a few more sets of lights before he'd finished.

Biff has me don't worry call sb

He pressed send, realising just in time the phone would make a noise when the message went. He was just able to scrape the side of the phone on his thigh and flick it to silent before it did. For a second he wondered if Jenny would make the same mistake he had and call Signboy's old number, but realised she'd only met Signboy after he got his new phone.

Thinking ahead to when Biff inevitably confiscated his phone, he took a couple of seconds to delete his messages. His caution extended to deleting Stephanie and Marisa from his contacts. As an indetective, these kinds of precautions were automatic. Occasionally belated, sure, but automatic nonetheless. When he was done, he returned to his homescreen and to a more comfortable position with his right hand, still holding his phone, sitting in his lap.

They were now in the city proper. A left turn off George Street suggested to Harlan they were going to the same place he had picked Jonathan up the night before. Sure enough, Biff next turned right into Clarence Street.

The familiar scene reminded Harlan that Biff had recognised Signboy from when he planted the bug in Mick Dawson's bag. He pieced together how much Mick Dawson definitely knew. Whoever planted the bug knew Harlan. The same person had created the diversion when Jonathan disappeared. When they'd messaged Harlan, he dropped whatever he was doing and was at the office within twenty minutes, calling them three times along the way. It was safe to assume Mick Dawson put Signboy as working for Harlan. But what about Jonathan? And had Marisa now told him about Jenny and Stephanie Clarkson's involvement as well?

The approaching meeting could answer his questions, but it depended on how much Harlan was willing to exchange. He expected a kind of information negotiation. Each party would begin claiming they knew nothing, then gradually tease information out of the other. Harlan's only hope was if he knew more to begin with.

Biff pulled off Clarence Street and into an underground parking garage. They parked in front of a small sign that read "Reserved for Matthew Loman".

"Not Biff?" asked Harlan, pointing his head towards the sign.

"You're the only one who calls me that."

Harlan knew it wasn't true, but it was revealing. Obviously he didn't like Mick Dawson calling him Biff either.

They took a lift up to level six, where Biff walked him down a corridor and through an unmarked door, flashing a security card across a reader to unlock it first. One completely empty room and another security door later, they came to a room Harlan realised he might be in for a while.

"Sit down."

It had no windows and only the one door they'd come through. It looked like it had been an office that had been vacated in a hurry. There was only one chair and no other furniture. Cables still came out of the wall, no longer attached to any equipment. A telephone sat on the floor in the corner. The cheap commercial carpet needed a vacuum. The only thing that was clean was the whiteboard mounted on one of the walls. Someone with a passing familiarity with Australian political history had made sure there was no trace of whatever had been written on it last.

The chair was an ergonomic armchair not entirely dissimilar to Harlan's own. He sat down, reflexively reaching down with both arms to find the lever to release the back. Luckily the lever was on the left side, because he was holding his phone in his right hand. He realised he still hadn't let go of it since seeing Biff. It must have been subconscious. A security blanket for the digital age.

"That's right, make yourself comfortable. You'll be here all night."

Biff was leaning by the door, which had closed and locked automatically.

"Aren't you going to tie me up?"

"Do you have a security pass?"

"No."

"Then there's no need, is there? It's not like you could overpower me."

Harlan considered how hard he could throw his phone. Considering the rubber case was designed to soften any impact, he doubted he could throw it hard enough to knock Biff out. Not without sacrificing whatever accuracy he might have to begin with.

"Oh, one more thing." Biff walked towards him and grabbed his right wrist with one hand while he took Harlan's phone with the other. "No telling what you might get up to with this." Harlan wondered why Biff had waited so long.

Biff pocketed the phone and pulled out his own to make a call.

"Mister Dawson ... He's here ... Sorry, I forgot to change the SIM cards back ... Okay."

He muttered something under his breath Harlan didn't catch, but again he had cause to think maybe Biff wasn't the lapdog he had initially taken him for.

They waited in silence for a few minutes. Biff leaned against the wall by the door, fidgeting with his phone most of the time. To pass the time Harlan pretended he still had his. He was going through the motions of sending Jenny an update text while holding the phone down by his side. He doubted it was possible without looking at the screen.

Both real and imaginary phone-play came to a stop when they heard the outside security door open. Biff shoved his phone in his pocket and almost stood to attention, side on to the door so he could still see his prisoner. Harlan spun around in the chair and offered the door his back. When he heard the beep of the second security door, he counted a second then slowly spun around to face it, hoping somehow to give Mick Dawson the impression he had been summoned to meet Harlan and not the other way around.

The door burst open. Mick Dawson stormed in, his eyes found Harlan's immediately. If the slow rotation put him off he didn't show it, not hesitating at all as he marched forwards. Harlan, on the other hand, brought his hands up to grip the arms of the chair and began kicking himself back towards the wall behind him the instant he saw the whites of the charging man's eyes.

Momentum was on Mick Dawson's side. He reached Harlan before he ran out of room and stopped the chair by grabbing Harlan's shoulder with his left hand. If Harlan could have torn his eyes away from Mick Dawson's, he might have seen the balled fist careening towards his gut. As it was, the first he knew of it was when all the air in his lungs exploded up through his throat, leaving only agony behind. Mick Dawson let go of Harlan as he landed the blow, sending him flying backwards. The back of the chair hit the wall flush with a sickening smack, then bounced off, pitching forward as the wheels hit Harlan's feet still going in the other direction, causing him to lurch out of the chair and crumple face-first into the carpet, the chair crashing off to one side.

He held both arms tight across his body, trying to smother the pain. Violent, involuntary gasps contorted his torso as his body struggled to re-establish its oxygen supply. The inhuman heaving sounds filled the room. He rolled onto his side, the view up at Mick Dawson standing over him clouded by the crushing pain. He closed his eyes to block him out completely.

Harlan remembered some schoolyard advice to bring his knees to his chest to help get the air back in his lungs. Still gasping loudly, he rolled onto his back and sat up. Gingerly he pulled his knees to his body, rocking slightly back and forth with the lingering pain. Slowly his lungs began to accept air again, the guttural moans receding. Finally, after nearly a minute, normal breathing resumed.

He felt arms hook under his from behind and lift him to his feet. Opening his eyes, he saw Mick Dawson still standing in front him. It must be Biff dragging him back to the chair and dropping him down into it. As best he could, he sat up straight, at the same time bracing himself for another attack and acting as if he hadn't just been writhing on the carpet incapable of basic pulmonary function. The pain in his gut, at least, sharpened his sense of self-preservation. Maybe his life *was* in danger.

"Right," said Mick Dawson, brushing his hands against each other as if he could wipe the violence off them. He stood a couple of metres in front of Harlan. Like Marisa and Stephanie, he was dressed for a Saturday in the office. Brown boat shoes, chinos, blue polo. No cravat. So it *was* just an image thing. The short sleeves showed Harlan what his gut already knew. In between all the partying and fine dining, the man found time for the gym. "Now you've got your breath back, you can start explaining what the bloody hell it is you're up to."

"Like I told your henchman here, I don't know anything about that bug."

"I don't believe you." He held one arm out towards Biff, but kept his eyes on Harlan. "Give me his phone."

Biff handed Mick Dawson the phone.

"What's the code?" he asked.

"Why would I tell you?"

Mick Dawson took a step towards him.

"One-nine-three-nine."

He entered the code, then smiled. Harlan wondered what he was looking for, but didn't have to for long.

"Recent calls - three to a 'Signboy'. What kind of a fuckin' name is 'Signboy'?"

"It's a nickname."

"Whose nickname?"

Something stirred briefly in Harlan's mind, but it was gone before he could even glimpse what it was. He realised though there would be occasions, like this one, where it might be beneficial not to know somebody's name.

"I don't know his real name."

"Then why did you rush to meet him when you got his message?"

"He does some jobs for me from time to time."

Mick Dawson reached behind his neck and stroked his ponytail with his left hand. With his right, he continued exploring the phone.

"And you didn't know he'd put a bug in my briefcase?"

Harlan had to stop himself from saying 'satchel'. Instead, he shook his head. "No," he added, when Mick Dawson looked up from the phone.

"Then who's Signboy New? Signboy's Vietnamese half-brother?"

"Sorry?"

"You will be, don't you fuckin' worry." He turned slightly, still working the phone and his ponytail in a bizarre display of coordination. The new angle revealed to Harlan a dark patch of sweat under his arm. It wasn't much consolation, but at least he'd exerted some effort in reducing Harlan temporarily to a wheezing invalid. Either that or it was just the normal human state for one living in Sydney in early December.

"What were you up to yesterday, about quarter past five?"

"Working."

Another step forward.

"Look, Mick,"

"Mister Dawson to you, you prick."

"Sorry, Mister Dawson. Let's not pretend here. We both know I'm working for Jonathan Foxe. Yesterday evening I was doing just that, following the woman who was following him."

"Okay, fine. Let's not pretend. So how does working for Jonathan end up with your mate Signboy planting a bug in my briefcase?"

Harlan decided to try to lay a plausible theory on the table.

"Early on in the job I watched this woman take a keen interest in a lunch meeting between the two of you. I needed to discount the possibility she was working with you, setting up Jonathan somehow. So the next time I saw you together, I had Signboy plant the bug."

"Go on."

"Well, what we heard from the bug was inconclusive, but gave me other concerns for Jonathan. He's my client. I'm obliged to look after his interests, you understand." Mick Dawson nodded, still stroking his ponytail.

"Yesterday my concerns grew, as I noticed Biff here manhandling Jonathan into the backseat of his Mercedes-Benz."

"My Mercedes-Benz."

"Right. Anyway, I thought he was in real trouble, so I staged a rescue operation. While Signboy distracted this guy," Harlan jerked his thumb in Biff's direction, "I rescued Jonathan."

"Rescued?"

"That's what I thought at the time. But after chatting with Jonathan for a while, it turned out it was more kidnapping than rescuing. He wasn't in danger, I'd misread the whole thing."

"So," Mick Dawson stopped playing with his ponytail and began pacing back and forth. "Your story is this: You thought I was involved in having Jonathan followed, somehow setting him up. You planted a bug on me to check your theory, but came up empty-handed. You saw Biff pushing Jonathan into a car and thought he was in trouble, so you rescued him. Then you spoke to him and he told you he didn't need rescuing. And now?" He stopped to face Harlan.

"Now?"

"Yes, now? What are you planning to do, right now, to fuck my day up?"

"Nothing. If Jonathan's happy, it's none of my business."

Mick Dawson approached Harlan, looking him in the eye. His left hand went to his ponytail again, his right hand on his hip. Harlan could hold the stare as long as he needed to. Another fundamental skill in the repertoire of an indetective.

"Good then," said Mick Dawson, relaxing his corneas. "You won't mind being locked up in here the rest of the day. Biff - get him some food, maybe he'll feel more in the mood to talk on a full stomach. I'll drop back before the Benefit. I've got a lunch with that minx Andrea and her vampire fuckbuddy."

Harlan, for another uncharacteristic time too many that week, was speechless. The bastard was talking about sixteen-year-olds.

Mick Dawson turned away from him, walked to the door and scanned his security card. As he pulled the door open, he turned to face Harlan again.

"Oh, one more thing, Mister Valeri."

"Yes?"

"If a detective is a dick, and you're an *in*detective," he said, grinning, "what does that make you? Dickless? Or just a cunt?"

He threw Harlan's phone to Biff and left, laughing, letting the door drift closed in the anticlimactic way that only the science of pneumatics allows.

CHAPTER 29

Four hours passed before Mick Dawson returned just after six o'clock. Biff had fetched some fast food, which Harlan ate eagerly, not realising how hungry he was until he had it in front of him. Then Biff had left him alone. Harlan had immediately confirmed his suspicion that none of the cables belonged to the phone, then returned to the chair. The rest of the afternoon Harlan had sat still, quietly, waiting. Biff had checked in on him every fifteen minutes, but really there was no point. There was nowhere for Harlan to go.

When Mick Dawson returned, Biff led him into the room. He had changed into a tuxedo, with a golden cravat sadly emphasising both the greyness of his hair and the robustness of his ego.

"So, dickless," he said, wearing a familiar grin. Harlan wondered if he'd been grinning the whole time over his hilarious wordplay. "Still sticking to that bullshit story of yours?"

"It wasn't bullshit. I really don't know what you think I'm going to do, but you can't just keep a person prisoner like this."

"Don't worry, just a few more hours. Of course, if you told me the truth, I could probably let you go now. If you promised to stay away from the Benefit of course."

"Why would I go to the Benefit?"

"Because, *In*detective, I know your little secret. I know exactly what you're planning to do. You and your little reporter friend."

That was it. He knew everything, then. Marisa must have panicked and called him sometime during the afternoon. Once more Harlan deflated in front of Mick Dawson, although this time not from violent impact to his midriff. His eyes glazed over and his mouth went dry. For some reason his only thought for a few seconds was how difficult it was to swallow. That led to more depressing thoughts. If he couldn't even swallow, how could he get out of this mess and stop Jenny and Signboy from walking into a trap too. Or was he too late for that anyway? Was that what Mick Dawson had been doing since his lunch, overseeing other henchmen round up Jenny and Signboy?

"Nothing to say to that? No skin off my nose. What did you think, the Balmoral Brawler was just gonna stand by while a couple of bleeding heart fuckin' do-gooders hijacked one of the biggest nights of his career?"

Harlan said nothing. Aside from his personal rule of ignoring people who spoke in the third person, let alone using self-styled nicknames, he had nothing to say. His only hope now was to wait for Mick Dawson to leave and take his chances against Biff. It wasn't much of a hope.

"Biff, keep him here till midnight, then take him back to his office, make it look like he had an accident or something."

"You're going to kill me?" Harlan couldn't believe it.

"What? No, I meant to explain where you'd been all afternoon."

"How does that work when I'll still be around to say what really happened?"

Mick Dawson again went to his ponytail, where he kept all his answers.

"It doesn't, you're right. Okay Biff, if you think you can get away with it, go for it by all means. Your call. And if he doesn't," he turned to Harlan, pointing a stubby red finger in his face, "you better keep your mouth shut, and keep out of my way from now on. You and your friends. Next time I won't leave it up to Biff."

It worried Harlan how flippantly Mick Dawson contemplated his murder. He hoped Biff would better appreciate the gravity of taking a life. Again, he didn't think it was much of a hope.

Once more, Mick Dawson left the room with an unsatisfyingly slow close of the door. Harlan looked at Biff, judging the best way to attack him. When they heard the second door close, Biff turned to Harlan.

"Come on, you don't have much time." He pulled out Harlan's phone and handed it to him. Harlan was too shocked to close his fingers around it, dropping it into his lap.

"Mister Valeri, come on. You don't have time to freak out."

Harlan tried to explain that freaking out wasn't something you generally had control over, but all that came out was a few vague syllables.

Biff knelt down in front of Harlan, shaking him by the shoulders. He raised his hand. "This is for your own good."

"I'm okay! Don't hit me." Harlan held his hands up to cover his face. "Don't hit me," he repeated.

"Okay," said Biff, standing up and giving Harlan some room.

"What the hell's going on?" Harlan slowly dropped his hands to rest on the arms of the chair.

"I'm helping you."

"Why? Why now?"

"Because you're helping Mister Foxe. Because if I helped you any earlier, Mick Dawson would know I was helping you, and wouldn't be heading off to the Benefit thinking he only had to keep an eye out for Jenny."

"So he doesn't have her?"

"No. He figured he could take care of her himself, *if she's even got the bloody guts to show up without her knight in fuckin' shining armour.* He doesn't have much respect for women."

"Clearly. But why didn't you tell me? You had plenty of opportunities."

"Wasn't worth the risk of him guessing something was up."

"So how long have you been 'helping' me?"

"Since dropping Mister Foxe home last night. We stopped for a drink, he told me what happened. Said I should help you if it came down to it, but that Mick Dawson couldn't know anything before the Benefit."

"But now he knows everything. Have you spoken to Jonathan since?"

"He doesn't know I'm helping Mister Foxe. And no, I haven't. I'll text him on the way, let him know we'll make it."

"You're coming with me?"

"Mister Foxe said you'd need all the help you can get. Sorry, but you don't have time for any more questions. It's quarter past six now, it starts at seven. You have to call Jenny."

"You've spoken to her?"

"I used your phone to call her, let her know you're okay. She's waiting for you to call."

Harlan nodded. He picked up his phone and called Jenny. She answered on the first ring.

"Harlan?"

"Jenny." A wave of euphoria coursed through his body upon saying her name. "Jenny, I'm all right." He grinned like an idiot.

"Thank god. I wasn't sure I could trust Matt, but I didn't have much choice."

"Matt?"

Biff waved at Harlan.

"Oh, right, Matt. Anyway, what have I missed?"

Jenny explained how she'd met up with Stephanie and gotten passes for the Benefit. Now she was with Signboy, who she'd called after getting Harlan's message, and Paul Wessel, who she'd contacted as a precaution before she'd heard from Matt and had insisted on being there to help once his shift had finished.

"Meet us at six-forty-five, I'll tell you the rest then. Same coffee shop."

She ended the call in a hurry. Harlan remembered she was supposed to meet Diane Adams at six-thirty. It was six-twenty already.

"Does Mick Dawson know what Jenny or Signboy look like?"

Matt shook his head.

"He never saw the video of Jenny, and he would have only seen the back of Signboy the other day. It was me who chased him down and we were round the corner before I caught him."

"Good, so they're safe until they do anything. They've got a cop with them as well, a friend of mine."

"Won't that attract attention?"

"I doubt he's in uniform. He's just there because he owes me a favour. Anyway, how did Mick Dawson plan to stop her if he doesn't even know what she looks like?"

Matt shrugged. Something didn't make sense about it all to Harlan, and apparently not to Matt, but he didn't have time to analyse it further. He stood up from the chair, wincing from the sharp pain he felt in his ribs as he straightened his torso for the first time in hours.

"You probably cracked a rib," said Matt.

"I didn't do anything. That neanderthal did it. Do you have any painkillers?"

"There's a first-aid kit in the office, I'll go get it."

Harlan was left alone again. He ran through the names in his head, trying to account for everyone involved. He knew where he, Signboy and Jenny stood. Jonathan and Matt he was pretty sure of, but after the latest twist he wasn't taken anything for granted. Other than Jenny and Signboy.

Stephanie? She had seemed convinced, but Marisa had had all afternoon to work on her. Although, if she'd been successful, then what did Mick Dawson have to worry about? They couldn't get to the celebrities without her help. And she had given Jenny the passes. No, she was on side.

Marisa? He was near certain she had told Mick Dawson everything she knew. But why? To help Jonathan against his lesser judgment? To keep the house? Out of loyalty to an old friend? Why was more a question for Jonathan than Harlan.

The dark horse was Diane Adams. They'd told her a lot, and ever since they had, he hadn't been kept in the loop by Matt. It was possible she'd had a bigger role to play in dropping the Executive Club story than she let on. Maybe she'd been paid off? That might explain how quick she was to offer Jenny a ticket, so she could keep an eye on her. Jenny hadn't mentioned her on the phone. Harlan made a mental note to check when he saw Jenny what Diane's reaction had been to the full story.

His mind was racing, about to start on its second lap of suspicion when Matt returned. Along with some pills and a glass of water, he'd brought a black tuxedo on a hanger he held in his teeth and some very shiny black shoes dangling from a couple of fingers.

"Almost forgot this, sorry. Mister Foxe said you'd stick out if you didn't have one."

"Of course, I hadn't even thought about it." Harlan didn't attend many society functions. He quickly swallowed the pills, looking forward to the pain relief. "You know, I've never worn one of these." He decided there was no time for modesty, and began taking off his clothes.

"Really? No weddings? School formal?"

"No."

"Oh."

Harlan started dressing in the tuxedo. Matt looked on unselfconsciously.

"What about those university balls? You must have gone to university."

"For a while." Harlan tucked in the pleated shirt and fastened the trousers. "But I never really got into the social side of it."

"Oh."

Matt helped him with the cuffs, using some plain gold cufflinks he said Mick Dawson kept as spares. Then Harlan stood nervously while the bodyguard's big hands effortlessly tied a perfect bow around his neck and straightened his collar.

"A good bodyguard needs a few tricks like that," he said, handing Harlan the jacket. He slipped it on, again with Matt's help.

"What do you think?" Harlan held his hands out ready to catch a compliment.

"Shoes."

"Of course."

He put the shoes on and stood up, stepping back and forth to test the fit.

"How did you know my sizes?"

"A good bodyguard can tell."

"Amazing. So, what do you think?" Again he posed for appreciation.

"Very sharp, Mister Valeri."

"Harlan, please."

"Sure, Harlan."

Harlan looked at his watch. It was six-thirty-five.

"Shit, I better go. Thanks, Matt. For everything." He held his hand out to the good bodyguard.

"I'm coming with you, remember?" he said, ignoring Harlan's open palm and spraying some cologne first on Harlan's neck and then on his own. Harlan realised Matt had replaced his regular tie with a bow tie, transforming his well-dressed goon's uniform into a passable dinner suit.

He accepted, with a small amount of embarrassment, the trick wouldn't have worked on his own ageing threads.

"You can thank me later," said Matt, throwing Harlan's clothes and any other evidence they'd been there into a plastic bag. "There's every chance I'll have to save your bacon again."

*

They met at the same booth they'd spent the morning waiting in. When Jenny saw Harlan she stood to greet him. Harlan froze, stunned by her appearance in a black dress, the soft fabric hanging over her shoulders and flowing down to just above her knees. She wore her hair down, hanging loosely about her neck and shoulders. Black high-heels completed the red carpet look. She blushed slightly when she saw Harlan's reaction.

"You look amazing," he said.

"Thanks." She smiled and stepped towards him, hugging him tightly. "We were worried about you. I thought you were going to be more careful." Harlan had nothing to say, returning the hug for as long as he thought they could spare the time.

As they moved apart after a few seconds, Signboy stepped forward and clapped Harlan on the shoulder. Like Matt, he was wearing a nice looking suit that took only a sharp bow tie to become formal wear. A pair of trendy dress shoes gave him an extra inch of height. It was the first time Harlan had seen him in anything but sneakers or thongs, and he realised for the first time Signboy was just about as tall as him.

"Some more great detective work that," said Signboy, "figuring out Matt was on our side."

"*In*detective work," said Jenny, laughing.

It was Harlan's turn to blush, embarrassed both at how easily he had walked into the trap, and how apparent their relief at seeing him safe was.

"Thanks Si-," started Harlan, but he remembered Jenny's challenge to use his actual name. Unfortunately that was all he remembered. "Thanks Signboy. I think we'll have to come up with something new if you're going to be wearing suits now, it doesn't quite fit. Signboy, I mean, not the suit. Which looks great."

Signboy gave him a confused smile. Jenny decided now wasn't the time for Harlan to make significant strides in his relationship management skills, and pulled him towards the booth.

"Come on, let's go over the plan."

Harlan noticed two people still seated. One was Diane Adams, also wearing a black dress but with her hair up and a square fringe sitting above her glasses. A delicate orange shawl wrapped over her shoulders. The other was Paul Wessel, dressed in a tuxedo and bow-tie incredibly similar to Harlan's.

"Last minute hire?" asked Harlan, flicking a finger between the two suits.

"What, me or the suit?" Paul laughed, clearly happy to see his old friend.

"You didn't need to come you know."

"No, you're right, you were doing fine without me."

They shook hands eagerly, Harlan smiling and promising this wasn't the catch up he'd intended.

"And Diane, you look great too. Thanks again for helping us out." He still wasn't sure he could trust her, but he trusted Jenny's instincts. If Jenny brought her to this clandestine meeting, she must be pretty confident where her allegiances lay. In any case, once again it was a matter of having little choice but to accept it, with no time to waste.

"Thanks Harlan. I can't really compete with Jenny, but I think I do all right given the fifteen-year head-start."

"Oh, please, Diane, you look like my younger sister," said Jenny.

"All right, everyone," said Harlan. "It's great there's so much mutual affection here, but we haven't actually achieved anything yet. Jenny, do you want to take us through the plan?"

"Sure, do you want to do the introductions first?" she said, nodding her head at Matt who had stood quietly in the background while Harlan did the rounds.

"Oh, shit. Sorry Matt." Matt stepped forward for his presentation to the group. "Signboy you know, obviously this is Jenny." Nods and smiles. Signboy rubbed his nose subconsciously. "And this is Diane Adams, a journalist with the *Herald*. And last, but not least, Paul Wessel, the policeman I was telling you about." More nods, more smiles. "Jenny?"

"Right."

The six of them squeezed into the booth as much as they could, Matt and Signboy pulling across chairs from adjacent tables while Harlan, Jenny, Paul and Diane huddled on the bench seats. Jenny waved away the waitress who approached assuming they were now ready to order, and started laying out the plan.

Jenny and Diane would use the tickets Diane already had to go into the Benefit first. Just before seven, Paul would use his police badge to gain access for himself and Matt, posing as his partner. At the last minute possible Harlan and Signboy would use the two backstage passes Stephanie had given them, for the least chance of being seen by Mick Dawson's people.

Just after seven, when a pre-gala educational video was to be shown to the audience, Stephanie was going to lead Jenny and Diane backstage under the guise of giving a quick interview for the *Herald*. At five-past Stephanie would use the backstage paging system to gather the celebrities in the green room.

Meanwhile Paul would take up a position in the theatre to keep an eye on Mick Dawson. Matt would keep a low profile somewhere backstage and try to gauge what kind of presence Mick Dawson was maintaining there. He knew a few of his colleagues were working as bodyguards for the celebrities, which meant they'd be backstage, floating between the dressing rooms.

A couple of minutes after seven Harlan and Signboy would enter through the backstage entrance and take up a position in the green room ready for Stephanie to introduce them, along with Jenny and Diane, to the celebrities. After the introductions, Stephanie would then take the stage to deliver her welcome address with Jonathan. At this point, Jenny and Harlan would present to the celebrities a summary of the article that was being published, thanks to Diane, on the front page of Monday's *Herald*, with a feature to follow in the next *Weekend* magazine. Then it was a matter of persuading them to take the stage, knowing it would end their association with Mick Dawson.

Matt had brought along four pairs of wireless earpieces and lapel microphones which he, Paul, Signboy and Harlan would wear to stay in communication. They all agreed Jenny and Diane would look suspicious if they wore one. In any case, as Harlan pointed out, neither of them had lapels.

"What about Mick Dawson?" asked Harlan when Jenny and Matt were done.

"If he tries to go backstage, I'll stall him for as long as I can," said Paul. "Flashing a badge and asking a few questions usually buys a few minutes."

"That doesn't rule out him turning up in the green room at the wrong time," said Jenny.

"No," said Harlan. "But it might not be the worst thing in the world if he does turn up. If he's there while we explain to his celebrities what a bastard he is, I doubt he'll do himself any favours. He's a violent man, with a foul mouth and a short fuse."

"And some armed bodyguards who will definitely be there with the celebrities," added Matt.

"What are they going to do, shoot us in front of the celebrities?" said Harlan. A few nervous glances around the table suggested people weren't too sure they wouldn't.

"The only thing that matters is whether we can persuade the celebrities to take the stage knowing that Celebrities Care is ending its association with Mick Dawson based on the article coming out about him. If they don't, if they for some reason remain loyal to him, we hold our hands up, say we tried our best, and hope the article does enough damage on its own. If they do, Mick Dawson, and his bodyguards, will have just run completely out of friends."

"Which is when he'll be at his most desperate," said Matt. "You should all know, he's a dangerous man to cross. He's always kept me out of the dodgy stuff, but I've heard what some of his other guys have had to do over the years. These guys have dealt with bikies, drug dealers, you name it. If it doesn't go smoothly, just get out of the way. Let me and Paul handle his men if it comes down to it." Paul nodded in agreement. The table went silent as they contemplated the danger they might be getting themselves into.

"It's ten to," said Jenny. Everybody checked their watches to confirm. "We've got to go. I'm sorry we don't have a better plan, but that's the way it is. If anyone doesn't want to take part, please, you don't have to. I know it's risky, and I'll feel responsible if anyone does get hurt. But I'm definitely going ahead with it. I can't sit by and watch Mick Dawson treat the most disadvantaged people in the world like just another resource for him to plunder. I have to try to do something about it because I know those kids will never get the chance to."

Jenny's eyes were watering as she remembered the friends she hadn't heard from in so long. Harlan's chest swelled as he watched her. He couldn't imagine anyone backing out after hearing that. Looking around, he knew that wouldn't be a problem. Everybody's faces were set determinedly, inwardly geeing themselves up for the imminent coup.

After a couple of seconds a chorus of 'I'm in' and 'well said' went around the table. Jenny stood, smiling nervously.

"Thanks everyone. And good luck."

Signboy and Matt stood and returned their chairs, allowing Jenny and Diane to sidle out of the booth. Jenny looked to Harlan, who nodded to reassure her. She winked conspiratorially back at him, sending a surge of emotion through him. Then she and Diane waved goodbye and left.

Matt quickly handed out the earpieces and microphones, showing the others how to put them on and then conducting a quick test of each one.

"Don't worry," he said. "I know what frequency they'll be using, we'll have our own. And I can even switch over to theirs if I want to listen in for a bit." Harlan and Signboy looked at each other in confusion, then realised it was for Paul's benefit who was playing with a dial on his earpiece.

"All good, let's go then," Paul said to Matt. They exchanged handshakes and well-wishes with Harlan and Signboy, and then followed in the wake of Jenny and Diane.

"So it's just the two indetectives left," said Signboy, sitting back down in the booth. "Bit of Dutch courage?"

"That," said Harlan, "is a great idea."

They got the waitress' attention and ordered a shot of vodka each.

"You're not going to call me racist?" said Signboy when she'd left.

Harlan thought for a second.

"Should I?"

"Well, doesn't it imply that without alcohol, the Dutch had no courage."

"Not necessarily. I think it's just one of many anti-Dutch phrases that became commonplace when they were fierce economic and military rivals to the British."

"So it is racist."

"It was at the time, I guess."

"What's changed?"

"Probably just that the Dutch have slipped down the pecking order in terms of nationalities the British consider rivals. French, German, Spanish, Irish."

"So because the sentiment isn't there, the phrase is harmless?"

"Not at all. Discrimination depends on the victim, not the discriminator."

The waitress arrived back with the shots, and the bill. Apparently it wasn't a café that encouraged people to sit around having shots of vodka.

"Do you think the Dutch mind?"

"Would you mind?"

"Prob'ly. It's a cool phrase though, I reckon I'd be happy for people to use it, so long as they weren't making fun of me."

"Very generous of you Signboy. Of course, the British would say the Dutch wouldn't be so generous. So if you listen to them, you probably shouldn't use the saying."

"But the British are just being racist. I'm sure the Dutch are very generous. I think I'll just keep saying 'Dutch courage'."

"Because you think they'd be happy for you to use it?"

"There's that," said Signboy. "Plus it beats saying 'let's get slightly drunk to overcome our nerves'."

CHAPTER 30

About five minutes later Harlan and Signboy crossed Market Street to the State Theatre. Being slightly drunk did overcome their nerves and for a few seconds it felt like they were just out for a night on the town. They joined the trickle of late arrivals on the red carpet that led from the modest street front into the incredibly ornate gothic foyer. A few cameras snapped as they walked past, in case they turned out to be somebody, but generally they were recognised as the nobodies they were.

The red carpet cut a line through the intricate art deco tiled floor to the row of six polished copper and bronze doors that separated the foyer from the assembly hall. Above the shining barrier two life-sized stone statues guarded the theatre. Harlan recognised one as St. George by the shield resting against him, the reference driven home by the painting in between the statues of a knight on horseback fighting a dragon. He refrained from drawing any analogy out loud.

The two centre doors hung slightly open where an usher was admitting people to the Benefit. They reached the end of the red carpet and flashed their passes, eliciting a furrowed brow from the usher.

"Wow, you guys are running late," she said. "You have to go to the dressing room entrance, down the lane outside to the left."

Harlan glanced quickly at his pass, which clearly read "Musician - Stage entrance only". Stephanie had obviously grabbed whatever passes she could.

"Of course, our mistake," he said.

They walked back down the red carpet, increasing their pace since they were now cutting it pretty thin.

"If you see a pair of guys with French horns trying to talk their way in, don't let them see your pass," said Harlan as they rounded the corner into the lane.

Signboy's nervous laugh suggested the Dutch courage was already wearing off, the dark alley they walked down bringing the seriousness of what they were about to attempt into clear focus. They walked past a couple of closed double-doors heading directly into the theatre, took a half turn to the right and stopped outside a solid metal door leading roughly in the direction of where they guessed the backstage area was. There were no French hornists hanging around to reclaim their passes. No hornists of any nationality in fact.

"Is this it?" asked Signboy.

A low voice came from behind them.

"You after the dressing rooms?"

They turned to see a security guard standing in front of a couple of doors across the alley.

"State Theatre?" asked Harlan.

"Yeah, goes under the street, doesn't it? Gets everyone." He motioned them closer with a conspiratorial wave of his hand. Out of alternatives, they crossed the alley to him, hoping he wasn't one of Mick Dawson's men.

"You can come in here," he whispered to them, "or there's another entrance further round the corner. Being guarded by some private security guy though, a real jerk if you ask me. One of the celebrities' personal bodyguards. Told me to tell him if anyone was trying to sneak in. Like he's my boss or something. I've been working here fifteen years, you know? Never seen the like."

Harlan looked around, thinking. It was too sophisticated for Mick Dawson to lull them into a false sense of security like this. He had to be telling the truth. They flashed their passes again. His complete disinterest in their passes was a worrying indicator of the level of security the theatre had operated with for one and a half decades. Instead of checking them he simply jerked his thumb over his shoulder towards the door on the left.

Signboy stepped around the guard and opened the door. The not too distant drone of an excited audience flowed out. Harlan led Signboy through the open door and down the concrete stairs within. Sure enough the stairs doubled back under the alley towards the theatre. The crowd noise escalated as they descended a full two storeys. A workshop-like stench greeted them at the bottom of the stairs. A mixture of oil and WD40. An eighty-year-old heritage-listed working theatre must take a lot of maintenance.

They came to a short passage which crossed another before becoming carpeted and leading to an opening into the side of the auditorium. Through the doorway they could see rows of seated men in tuxedos and women in dresses. The houselights hadn't gone down yet. The crowd noise was overbearing at this distance.

Harlan saw Paul standing just before the threshold with his back to the wall. He waved, catching Paul's attention. Paul nodded in return, and tapped his ear before cupping his hand below his chin and speaking into it.

"What's he doing?" asked Harlan.

"Prob'ly wants you to turn your earpiece on."

"Shit, sorry," he said nowhere near loud enough for Paul to hear over the audience. He turned it on and immediately heard Paul's voice, impressively distinct through his microphone.

"I can see Mick Dawson from here, he's in the front row next to Jonathan Foxe. Next to him is his wife, can't remember her name, and then I presume that's Miss Clarkson next to her. I can't see Diane or Jenny."

A woman with a clipboard came out of the auditorium. Paul checked the pass hanging around her neck, and waved her on towards Harlan and Signboy.

"What are you doing?" asked Harlan.

Signboy reached up to Harlan's lapel and turned his microphone on.

"What are you doing?" repeated Harlan, this time to Signboy, although because Harlan's microphone was now switched on Paul could hear and responded.

"The floor manager said if I was standing here I may as well help her out by checking backstage passes. She was joking, but I figured it would give me a chance to stall Mick Dawson a little longer."

"Good thinking," said Harlan.

Matt's voice came through the earpiece.

"Harlan, Signboy, time for you to get in position."

Paul nodded. Harlan checked his watch and found it was two past seven.

"What's Stephanie doing?" he asked. "She should be bringing Jenny and Diane through by now." Paul shrugged at him.

"Waiting for the video to start," said Signboy, just to Harlan. "Come on." He turned Harlan's mic off. "It only needs to be on when you're talking, otherwise everyone's ears fill up with noise."

They exchanged nods with Paul again then turned right into the cross-passage and headed into the backstage area. Along the wall were piled rows of stage lights, meaning they had to walk in single file. As they went they heard the crowd go quiet as some touching music began. It was almost time.

The music crescendoed as they passed a door to their left labeled "Orchestra Pit". Harlan tried to pick whether they sounded a couple of musicians short, but conceded his ear wasn't up to it as Signboy hurried him along from behind.

They left the orchestra behind and followed the signs on the walls pointing to the dressing rooms. After just a few turns they were in a corridor somewhere behind the stage. Dark, commercial grade carpet replaced concrete underfoot. The piles of lights disappeared leaving room for two people to walk abreast. The music was dampened through the building but still clear enough to make out. Getting close to the dressing rooms they moved with caution, hoping to avoid being seen by any of Mick Dawson's men.

It was a long corridor ending in a T-intersection, another passage branching off to the right halfway down, a few doors on both sides. Most likely dressing rooms, which meant Mick Dawson's men wouldn't be far away. Luckily the first door on the right was labeled "Green Room" above the frame. Gratefully, they ducked into the open doorway.

The first thing they noticed about the green room was the black flooring and cream walls. Maybe it was an ironic nickname. It looked more like a commercial kitchen than the orgiastic party rooms Harlan had imagined over the years. A few people were milling about a table covered with snacks and drinks. They were all sipping on beer or wine, wearing passes around their necks to confirm they weren't celebrities. A mix of media and corporate partners, Harlan guessed. There was one team with a cameraman and a young woman with a microphone for backstage interviews. Their heads lifted for a moment when they saw Harlan and Signboy come into the room, then dropped in disappointment. The two nobodies huddled in a corner under a ventilation shaft, pretending they were deep in conversation.

"Stephanie's on the move, coming towards me," Paul's voice sounded in their ears. "Jonathan Foxe coming with her. Mick Dawson staying put, but he's watching them."

"From what I can hear," Matt's voice now, "Dawson's got two men moving between the dressing rooms and one on the back door."

"Okay, here's Jenny and Diane." Paul again. "Clarkson's introducing them to Foxe. Dawson still watching them. He's asking Mrs. Foxe something, they're pointing. She's nodding. Looks like she's picking someone out in a lineup."

"So he knows it's her now," said Harlan. "He's on to us."

Signboy again went to turn Harlan's mic on for him, but Harlan stopped him.

"This is just for you," said Harlan. Signboy nodded. "I don't want you in here when it kicks off."

"That's not fair ... " started Signboy, but an aggressive shake of the head from Harlan was enough to cut him short.

"It's not for your protection. Mick Dawson knows exactly what we're up to. Maybe he's got someone listening in to us. Maybe one of us is helping him out. Or maybe it's just all too obvious. We need to have something up our sleeve. You."

Signboy scowled. He wasn't convinced. He thought Harlan was just trying to coax his ego into getting him out of the way.

"I mean it Signboy. Head back out towards the auditorium. Find a good spot to hide where Jenny and the others have to walk past, then follow them. But don't let them see you."

Harlan relayed the rest of his plan to Signboy, who by the end of it was thoroughly convinced. His ego was more than a little coaxed. It was fully stoked.

As he watched Signboy leave the green room, Harlan flicked his mic on.

"Matt - how likely is Mick Dawson carrying a gun?"

"No chance. But the three bodyguards definitely."

"That's what I thought. Paul - what's the latest?"

"I just let them through - Jenny, Diane, Clarkson and Foxe."

"Do they know Mick Dawson was watching them?"

"I think so - Jenny and Diane both looked in that direction when they met Foxe. Then they only winked at me when I checked their passes. I guess they would have said something if they didn't think he was watching."

"Okay, good."

Harlan switched his mic off. He noticed the room was now empty, the people milling about must have gone to catch the start of the show, or in search of a celebrity. In the empty room he realised he could still hear the orchestra, which meant the video was still playing. He walked around the room, familiarising himself with the scene of the confrontation to come. There was an old TV mounted on the wall in one corner, showing what Harlan presumed to be the educational piece being played to the audience. The channel logo in the corner told him the Benefit was already being televised. He turned the volume up. It was the same music playing, but on a significant delay. He returned it to mute, wanting the room as quiet as possible for the confrontation.

He wondered if the images of starving children had any effect on Mick Dawson, if he ever felt guilty about what he'd turned Celebrities Care into. He found himself again wanting more than anything to bring Mick Dawson to justice. It would be perfect if millions of viewers were touched by these images, then found out the self-styled 'Balmoral Brawler' had usurped their goodwill towards the suffering for his own ends with Celebrities Care, and now had his eyes on the Hope Foundation. That would end him.

Harlan smiled at the thought he was playing a role in it. It was a far cry from giving a guy a solid alibi so he didn't have to tell his wife he'd been on a cocaine binge. He decided to clean up the indetective game when this was all over. Triple bottom line, code of conduct, ethical standards. Making the world a better place, one secret at a time. He'd have to work on the logic a bit.

"Dawson's on the move."

"What's taking them so long?" said Harlan to himself, but only because he'd forgotten to turn his microphone on. He moved to the doorway and looked into the corridor. There was nobody to his left, back towards the auditorium. To his right, he saw the back of two women in black dresses about twenty metres away, walking towards the T-intersection at the end of the corridor. Diane on the left, orange shawl. Jenny on the right, hair down. Harlan wondered whether they had walked past the green room and not seen him, or if they'd gone another way in order to use the paging system.

"Harlan." This time it was Signboy's voice in his earpiece. "They're going to the band room, not the green room, to avoid the reporters."

"Of course they are," said Harlan, to himself properly this time. He started following the two women. He didn't want to call out, not knowing the layout ahead and not wanting any of Dawson's men to hear him. In the corridor he could better hear the distant orchestra, but it still wouldn't cover his voice over any useful distance. It wasn't loud enough to cover the sound of his feet dragging slightly on the carpet in the unfamiliar dress shoes. He could even hear their high heels make the faintest scratching noise up ahead.

As the women turned right at the end of the corridor, a man in a grey suit came at them from the left. His immaculate grooming and musclebound stature gave him away as one of Dawson's men. Harlan saw he was holding a handgun and broke into a run, shouting Jenny's name.

The cry jerked the bodyguard into action. He cracked his gun expertly across the back of Jenny's head as she turned towards Harlan's voice, violent enough for Harlan to hear the sharp impact. Her body collapsed immediately to the carpet, lifeless. Harlan ran harder. Diane screamed. She started to drop to Jenny's aid but when she saw the gun she turned and ran to the right, disappearing out of Harlan's view. Dawson's man straightened his arm, pointing the gun after her. Harlan was too far away to stop him. All he could do was keep running.

Time seemed to slow, enough for Harlan to wonder why he was so adamant about not carrying a gun for protection. Right now, it seemed the gunman was the only safe person in the corridor. He looked completely secure as he calmly stared along the barrel of the gun at what Harlan assumed was a woman hopelessly running in a straight line away from him. The black metal shaft was perfectly still, even as Harlan could see the slow, deliberate movement of the man's finger squeezing the trigger. For some reason he noticed the man's cufflink, a silver bullet against a crisp white cuff, also pointing perfectly horizontally down the corridor. A man so precise wouldn't miss unless she changed direction at the perfect moment.

When it came, the gunshot wasn't as loud as Harlan expected. The man's arm recoiled only slightly. The cufflink barely moved. Harlan heard a sharp cry of pain from around the corner, followed by a loud thump. He pictured Diane hitting the floor, a gaping wound in the centre of her back. Instinctively he reached to his lapel and turned his microphone on.

"Paul, Matt, get down here now."

He was almost at the end of the corridor, but Dawson's man was already turning to point the gun his way. Harlan saw the barrel square up at him, again becoming perfectly still, pointed at his chest. He looked to the man's face. Deathly calm. It was target practice for him. Another gunshot sounded. Harlan stopped, expecting to feel a searing pain in his chest, to be knocked off his feet by the impact. Instead, he saw a small section of the bodyguard's right side explode in red. The man swayed slightly but kept his balance, turning to his right where the bullet had come from, ready to take aim at the new target.

"Biff?" he said, lowering his gun. "What are you doing?"

"The right thing," said Matt, coming into Harlan's view. Dawson's man looked back to Harlan, sheer incomprehension distorting his face. Matt relieved him of his weapon and with a steady arm across the man's chest encouraged him to drop gently to the floor. Matt then moved to the body lying prone alongside the bodyguard and checked its pulse.

"Is she okay?" asked Harlan, struggling to hear himself over his own pulse pounding in his ears. Paul was also saying something in his earpiece but he couldn't make it out, his attention firmly on the back of Jenny's head.

"I think so, you better check on Jenny."

"That is Jenny." Harlan choked on the words.

"No, it's Diane." Matt started to roll her over so Harlan could see for himself, but Harlan's heart had already stopped. He didn't need to see the face to know it wasn't Jenny. The panic rising in his chest told him it was true.

He screamed her name again, sprinting around the corner. She lay about ten metres down the corridor, her body twisted into an open doorway. Harlan digested the information as he ran. A lot of blood. Face down. Orange shawl. Hair up. They must have switched to put Mick Dawson off. Harlan despaired it might have gotten her killed.

He reached her still body, rolling her over gently, back fully into the corridor. She might have looked like she was sleeping if her face wasn't so white. He checked her pulse. It wasn't very insistent, but it was there, faster than he expected.

"Find the wound, Harlan!" yelled Matt.

There was hardly any blood on her front. He turned her over again and looked for the source on her back somewhere. It wasn't easy against a black dress, but a crimson pulse on the side of her left shoulder caught his eye. He held his hand to it, stemming the flow. Jenny winced with the fresh pain, not completely unconscious.

"She's been shot in the shoulder," he called over his to Matt, but Matt was already kneeling by his side.

"Must have hit her head on the way down." With Harlan's help Matt rolled her back onto her right side, the injured shoulder off the ground. He carefully ran his hands around her skull while he checked her breathing, putting his ear close to her nose. "She'll be fine. Here, let me." He replaced Harlan's hand with his. "An ambulance is on its way."

Harlan looked back down the corridor. Matt had tied Dawson's man with his own jacket to a pipe running low along the wall, leaving him just enough movement to keep pressure on his own gunshot wound. Diane lay neatly on her side nearby, still unconscious, her head resting on Matt's jacket. A phone was on the ground next to her.

Harlan heard Stephanie's voice. He looked into the room Jenny had been trying to run into. There was a TV on top of a bar fridge. Stephanie had started her speech. Under the table in the middle of the room he recognised Christian Dieter and Andrea Stacy huddled together, their wide eyes staring at Harlan. Harlan put his finger to his lips. They nodded.

"Where are the others?" asked Matt.

"Signboy's safe. Paul must be on his way." Harlan was looking at Jenny again.

"She'll be fine, trust me."

"That's a fuckin' joke, surely. Trust him?"

Harlan and Matt turned to see Mick Dawson coming towards them. The tuxedoed man in full stride, his face red with rage, cut a frightening figure. His silver hair had fought free of its permanent noose and swung wildly about his neck. The golden cravat had loosened only slightly, struggling to maintain a balance between the immaculate outfit below and the savage scene above.

Matt reached for his gun, which he'd returned to its holster, but stopped when a new voice came from the opposite direction.

"Don't do it, Biff." Another of Dawson's men stood five metres down the corridor, his gun trained on Matt who froze for a second, then nodded, his errant hand joining the other on Jenny's wound.

As Harlan returned his focus to the approaching Mick Dawson, he heard Paul in his ear. He was on his way after taking care of one of Dawson's men. That meant the one with the gun pointed at Matt was the last.

"Give us a minute," Harlan said to Mick Dawson, indicating the wounded Jenny with his arms, but hoping Paul would get the idea and not rush into the corridor. He needed the odds to appear in Mick Dawson's favour for his plan to work.

"No chance." Mick Dawson reached him, pulling him by his collar to his feet and throwing him against the wall. "I don't know how you got Biff to go along with your game, but it's over now." He pulled Harlan's collar tight around his neck, using his fists to push Harlan up by the chin until his shoes barely touched the carpet. Insistent knuckles dug painfully into his throat. The vicious red face closed in. Harlan could feel the hot breath on the side of his face as he looked over Mick Dawson's shoulder, looking down at Jenny. The bleeding looked to have stopped under the pressure Matt was applying. Her head was moving, a slight cough sounded. She looked like she'd be okay. Harlan couldn't be so sure about himself.

"Look at me!" Harlan felt spit fly against his face. He slowly turned his head and raised his eyes. "That's it." Now Mick Dawson had Harlan's attention, the rage passed from his face. His eyes bore into Harlan's. His voice became cold and malicious, giving Harlan fresh cause to fear for his life when he spoke. "Now listen closely. I want you to understand a few things, dickless.

"You're not fucking this up for me. You think those idiots out there really care where their money ends up? You think those spoilt brat celebrities give a shit? Did you really think telling a few teenage pop stars about Celebrities Care just being a fertile source of cheap call centre workers for me would change anything? They're not here to save the world. They're here to promote their movies and their albums. The mindless retards out there know it, and they can't get enough. Everyone just wants the fuckin' show to go on. Except you."

Harlan tried to say something, but couldn't open his mouth against Mick Dawson's fists. His grunting was enough to get his assailant's attention though.

"What? What could you possibly have to say that would interest me?" He loosened his fists enough to find out.

"Why abduct me?" Harlan had to catch his breath after every couple of words. "Why have your men attack journalists, shooting one? If we can't stop the great Mick Dawson from expanding his immoral empire, why have you done everything in your power to stop us?"

Mick Dawson considered Harlan with a confused look for a second, as if he was a different species that somehow spoke the same language. His face then smoothed out again, the hateful, belligerent stare returning.

"Because I like fucking with people. Why do you think I had both the Foxes hire you at the same time? It's all just a game to me." So it wasn't a coincidence. Harlan went to say something, but Mick Dawson again increased the pressure on his jaw. "No, don't get me wrong. It's a serious game. It's the only game, really. And you thought you could play with the big boys. You thought you could bring down the Balmoral Brawler. You fucking loser." He thrust his fists against Harlan's throat, twisting them around to draw the collar even tighter. Harlan couldn't breathe. His arms flailed pathetically. His face was now the redder of the two.

"Noooh!" A woman's cry came from around the corner towards the auditorium. They all turned to see Marisa running into the corridor, Paul holding her back by one arm. The distraction caused Mick Dawson to relax his grip just long enough for Harlan to squeeze a breath through. "Mikey, stop talking! They've got you bugged or something."

The affectionate nickname struck Harlan. He knew they were old friends, but Marisa had played their friendship down when he'd asked her about it. He watched her struggling to get free of Paul. Her face was twisted in anguish, her eyes empty of humanity, wild with fury. It wasn't the reaction of an innocent bystander seeing a friend in trouble. It was that of someone deeply involved, complicit in the mind and heart. Someone on the precipice.

Paul got a better hold on her arm, stopping her progress a few metres down the corridor. Realising the futility of her struggle, she simply bent forward, supported by Paul holding her arm at full stretch behind her, and wailed in despair.

Mick Dawson looked around the corridor like prey sensing danger too late. Up at the ceiling, along the walls, over his shoulder. Anywhere he could point his eyes without further loosening Harlan's collar.

"The microphone," cried Marisa, as Paul bent her arm behind her and pushed her to the floor, using his knee in the small of her back to hold her down as gently as he could. Having disabled her, he pointed his handgun at the remaining bodyguard. The bodyguard kept his gun pointed at Matt, but a distinct tremor now challenged its authority.

Mick Dawson finally relaxed his grip, looking down at the microphone on Harlan's lapel. Harlan breathed in deeply, painfully at first, then his breathing settled as Mick Dawson just stared at the mic. The growing silence in the corridor let the sound of the TV in the dressing room be heard. Mick Dawson's voice on delay. *You thought you could bring down the Balmoral Brawler.* Harlan saw realisation creep slowly across Mick Dawson's face. The big man dropped Harlan to his feet and followed where his own voice was coming from, stepping over Jenny and into the dressing room, ignoring Marisa's deranged pleas for him to end Harlan's life, to end all their lives, to do *something*.

"More police are on their way Mister Dawson," called Paul. That was enough for the last bodyguard, who holstered his gun and backed away. When he reached the end of the corridor, he turned and ran out of sight.

Paul took the chance to put handcuffs on Marisa, fixing her to the same pipe Matt had used earlier for the wounded bodyguard. She had stopped calling for blood and sat against the wall drained, defeated. Paul left her and advanced slowly towards the dressing room, his gun held in front of him.

"Mister Dawson?" It was a girl's voice from inside the room.

"Andrea, I-"

"I give a shit, you bastard."

A Sharapova shriek preceded a loud thud, followed in turn by a deep, anguished cry. Mick Dawson stumbled back into the corridor, bent double, clutching his groin. He tripped over Jenny's legs, falling to the floor at her feet. Rolling to his side, he looked up at Harlan. His eyes were beginning to water. The arrogance was gone. A pathetic attempt at vulnerability had replaced it. Harlan smiled back at him, bent down and ripped the cravat away from his neck, causing him to struggle for breath until the delicate fabric tore completely away.

"These things are ridiculous." He scrunched it into a ball and threw it at the Balmoral Brawler's face.

"Nice touch." Harlan looked to Jenny, who had come to and was looking past her feet to where the vanquished man lay. She tried to look up at Harlan, but winced as she turned, forcing her to settle back on her side. He smiled and moved towards her as Paul subdued Mick Dawson. Harlan squatted next to Matt and reached out with one hand, stroking Jenny's hair back behind her ear. He was about to lean forward and whisper something foolish into it when the unmistakable sound of Dawson having his testicles non-surgically transplanted deep into his abdomen drifted out of the dressing room. Harlan lifted his lapel to his chin.

"I take it you got all that, Signboy?"

CHAPTER 31

Harlan rode with Jenny to St. Vincent's Hospital, which was about as close to the geographic centre of Darlinghurst as you could get. The paramedics sedated her in the ambulance for the pain. She fell asleep holding Harlan's hand, asking after Diane and Signboy despite already being told they were both okay. The paramedics assured Harlan she'd be okay too. She hadn't lost too much blood and it looked to them like the bullet had passed clean through the flesh on the side of her shoulder.

Once out of the ambulance they took Jenny straight into surgery, leaving Harlan in the waiting room to watch the Benefit on a small wall-mounted TV. He sat surrounded by an off-putting array of drunken assault victims, drunken accident victims and junkies whose friends had overdosed. A hospital waiting room on a Saturday night would be a good place to visit if you were drafting a comprehensive social policy.

Over the next twenty minutes first Paul arrived with Diane, who was taken through to be treated for concussion, then Signboy arrived on his own. Matt had been taken to the police station to explain the shootings, leaving just the three of them to keep vigil. They sat alongside each other in a row of plastic chairs, still in tuxedoes, watching Christian Dieter and Andrea Stacy perform a conceptually confusing but surprisingly moving duet version of Michael Jackson's *Man In The Mirror*.

"Told you they could sing," said Signboy.

"True," said Harlan. "Apparently they can care as well."

"I was more surprised to see you could."

"Hilarious."

"All right guys," said Paul, not familiar with their natural banter. "I really have to get down to the station and help sort this all out."

"I don't envy you," said Harlan. "This could keep you busy for a while."

"Well, it's only the shootings I have to worry about. And Mick Dawson's assault on you. Maybe conspiracy to kidnap, but that means getting Matt involved more than he already is."

"What about all the Celebrities Care stuff?" asked Signboy.

"White collar crime, none of my business. Always messy. No doubt there'll be fraud, misleading and deceptive conduct. State and federal charges I imagine. I'm sure the Tax Office will take a look as well, at Celebrities Care and Mick Dawson, Jonathan too."

"What a mess," said Harlan.

"They love it, don't worry about that. Anyway, I better go, we want to take Matt's, Dawson's and Mrs. Foxe's statements tonight. The guy who shot Jenny's in intensive care, but should be all right to make a statement tomorrow. Jenny's and Diane's when they're well enough, probably tomorrow too. Harlan, you can come in Monday can't you? First thing?"

Harlan cut Signboy off.

"How does nine-thirty sound?" he said.

"Perfect. See you then. See you round, Signboy."

"See ya Paul."

They watched over their shoulders as he walked out, the tuxedo drawing a fresh round of stares as he went.

When he was through the sliding doors leading outside, they turned back to the TV. Harlan was surprised to hear Paul's voice in his ear.

"You can probably take that off now, mate." He did.

The duet had finished. Applause for the young stars died down slowly. They were trying to say something.

"Thank you," said Andrea Stacy, wearing an uncharacteristically demure pink sequinned dress for the occasion. "Now we'd like to remind everyone watching to give generously to the Hope Foundation and Celebrities Care tonight. I'm happy to announce that Christian and I are donating half of our royalties from our upcoming movie *Camp Vamp*." Ecstatic applause.

"Thank you," said Christian Dieter. "Before the show continues, we'd like to invite our great friend on stage, the CEO of Celebrities Care, the man who brought us here, Jonathan Foxe!" More applause. Jonathan bounded on from the side of the stage, waving deliriously at the crowd and the cameras.

"First," said Andrea, "can I just say that tonight Jonathan has, at great personal risk, exposed my former manager Mick Dawson as a manipulating, immoral, corporate pirate who was abusing his influence with Celebrities Care to further his own business interests." Slightly subdued applause.

"And," said Christian, "Jonathan has given us personal assurances he will be travelling to every Celebrities Care centre, at his own expense, to eradicate all traces of Mick Dawson's influence and make sure your generous donations get to the people who need it the most, so we can all make a difference."

While the three people on television exchanged hugs and accepted the applause of the live audience, Harlan and Signboy exchanged glances and accepted the reality they just didn't have the star power to receive due credit for their roles in Mick Dawson's downfall.

"I'm surprised Mick Dawson's not in here, he was still clutching his nuts when they led him away," said Signboy.

"I guess they figured the injury was superficial too."

"Is that a dig at the 'Balmoral Brawler' or Andrea Stacy?"

"Ha," laughed Harlan, looking at Signboy fondly. "Both, I guess."

"But she's donating half her royalties, that's pretty generous."

"That depends on her royalties, doesn't it? She wasn't donating half of her lump sum fee."

"No, she wasn't. Anyway, how did you know Jenny's plan wasn't going to work?"

"It wasn't just Jenny's plan, we all came up with it, remember? There was just something about how cocky Mick Dawson was, even more than usual, just being satisfied getting me out of the picture when he must have known Jenny was the driving force behind everything."

"So you knew Marisa was in on it all along?"

"Not until Marisa came screaming around the corner. Up to then I just thought she'd gone to him after our meeting with her and Stephanie. Out of loyalty to an old friend, and not believing her husband was on our side. Or believing her husband stood to lose as much as Mick Dawson, if not more, and was doing the wrong thing by helping Jenny out. But there was also the possibility it was Diane, or her boss, after Jenny went to Diane this afternoon with the full story. Or even Matt, maybe Mick Dawson was trying the old triple-cross through him. That's why I only told you, any of those three could have been the one who compromised us, deliberately or inadvertently. That would have been enough for Mick Dawson to know what we were planning, have enough men there to deal with it, and keep the celebrities in lock-down until you and Jenny were out of the way. If we didn't have Paul and Matt there on our side, he'd have pulled it off, too."

"You mean if you didn't have such an able junior indetective on staff, capable of using the paging system to broadcast the sound from his headset over the house speakers."

"And if he didn't have such a massive ego. Mick Dawson, not you. Yours almost got in the way. But then, without his ego, not yours, none of this would have happened in the first place. It was a fairly safe thing to bet on in the end."

"Well, if you can call two people getting shot, another knocked out cold and yourself almost strangled to death 'safe', then yes, it was."

With that their thoughts returned to Jenny, their eyes to the TV screen, where Jonathan was talking about the new Kisses line of products. Apparently not all of Mick Dawson's corporate-charity win-win partnership ideas were so unpalatable.

"Speaking of egos," said Harlan. "He seemed pretty happy to take all the credit for tonight."

"An indetective needs to keep a low profile anyway, I guess," said Signboy.

"I was talking about the Benefit, but that's a good one actually," said Harlan, making a note on his phone.

"What are you doing?"

"Our next project - a handbook for the ethical indetective."

"You thinking of bringing more rookies on?"

"Not at all. I just think it wouldn't hurt for us both to be working from the same book, so to speak."

"You mean, my one week trial was a success?"

"I'd say so. Assuming Jonathan pays his bill, this was by far our best week ever. Of course, I can only hire you on a casual basis, and I don't want it to interfere with your studies."

"Yeah, yeah, nobody wants anything to interfere with my studies. You sound like my Mum. I'm twenty-one years old you know." Signboy stood up, glanced at the TV where Andrea Stacy had peeled off the lower portion of her dress to do a racier number they didn't recognise. "Wanna Coke or something?"

"Only if it's in a can, or a glass bottle. Please."

He watched Signboy walk out. A younger boy watched him too, Harlan noticed. Maybe eighteen. He didn't look well. Pale in the face and skinny as a rake. He reminded Harlan of Signboy at that age, taking him back to when he'd first caught him trying to pick his pocket while on a job in the backstreets of Kings Cross. *Collecting money for street kids*, he'd said, the cheeky smile bringing his pale face to life. Harlan asked his name, fully intending to march him down to the police station. But he refused to tell him. He said the police would be more interested in what a man was doing in a back alley outside an illegal gambling den than another street kid getting caught picking pockets. It was a good point. Harlan decided to take him to lunch instead, find out exactly how encyclopaedic was his knowledge of the seedy side of the Cross. It turned out to be very encyclopaedic, so Harlan offered him work. Told him to come to the office the next day. That's when he next asked his name. *What kind of work have you got for me*, he asked. The receptionist had just quit, so Harlan told him he had some signs that needed posting up. *So call me Signboy*, he said. *Nobody's ever bothered to remember my real name anyway*. And that was the last time Harlan had asked.

Signboy returned with a couple of cans of Coke, handing Harlan one.

"Signboy," said Harlan. Signboy stopped with the ring-pull half up.

"Yes?"

"You never did tell me your real name you know."

"Ha, right." Signboy blushed a little. "Well, when we met it wasn't something I had much pride in. And then after I'd worked with you for a while, well, it would have been pretty weird to come out and tell you my name. I prefer Signboy anyway, I tell everyone to call me that when we're introduced."

"Still, when the day comes, I can hardly engrave 'Signboy' on my door, can I?"

"That's not engraved, it's stickers on glass."

"Nevertheless."

"No, I guess that would look a bit unprofessional."

"And we'll have to get you some cards made up, now you're a junior indetective."

"Right."

"So?"

"Sal McCarthy."

"Sal McCarthy?"

"That's the one."

"Is Sal short for anything?"

"Nup. It's a reference to Salman Rushdie. I was born the day they issued a fatwa on him. My Dad thought he was a hero. He wanted to call me Salman, but Mum thought it was taking the homage to dangerous extremes."

"Your Dad must have been a real character." Harlan knew Signboy had never known his father, but they'd never spoken about why.

"That's what Mum tells me. I think she romanticises a bit though. I mean, she is Irish."

They lapsed into silence again, sipping on their cans of drink. Harlan was happy for Signboy to decide if and when he wanted to tell Harlan any more about his family. After all, it wasn't very indetective-like to pry.

"I found out something today, too," said Signboy after almost a minute's comfortable silence between them.

"What are you talking about?"

"I spoke to Paul. He told me about his prank, how he sabotaged all the pistols at the firing range."

"Oh." Harlan had never told anyone the full story. He didn't think it reflected well on Paul. And he didn't want to give anyone ideas for pranks.

"No wonder he was so keen to help you - he still can't believe you took the blame knowing you were going to get kicked out for it."

"Well, I was never going to enjoy being a cop. I knew that on day one when they gave me a uniform."

"Still, it's another indication that you're actually an all right guy, once you get to know you, if you know what I mean. That's way too many yous, sorry."

Harlan laughed and punched Signboy lightly on the knee. "I still can't believe they swallowed it," he said. "As if I would waste gum in the chamber of a gun. One saves lives, the other gets you killed."

"Oh, that's the other thing that makes sense now. Paul said you were a chain-smoker back then."

"Oh." That was another story Harlan had never told anyone. He didn't think it reflected well on him.

"Then you went through a period where you were chewing nicotine gum as though your life depended on it." Signboy laughed.

"I hope he didn't try to claim that joke as his own."

"Is it one of yours?"

"No, it's not. I'm sure I've read it somewhere."

Again they settled into a comfortable silence, turning their attention back to the TV. Judging by the number of celebrities and performers now on stage, the Benefit was nearly over. The two charities had raised over five-million dollars, according to the tally at the bottom of the screen. Harlan figured, as much as possible when you're spending most of it in the waiting room at the emergency ward, it was a pretty successful night.

*

It was close to daybreak when they were finally allowed to see Jenny. They had each nodded off at times through the night, but nothing you would describe as sleep. When Harlan had realised it was getting light, he chased down a nurse and asked what was going on. Jenny had been up for a couple of hours apparently. Someone had called Harlan's name. *Would you like to come through now? Yes, of course.* When they finally did they were both surprised to see Diane already seated by her bed.

"Hi guys," said Jenny, wearily but with a shining smile. Most of the colour had returned to her face. Her shoulder was bandaged up, her arm in a sling, and she was on a drip. Harlan took her hand and stood by the bed, opposite

Diane, who wasn't even sporting a bandage for her crack on the skull. Signboy took a position at the end of the bed. The three visitors exchanged nods.

"How's the shoulder?"

"Stitches, some minor muscle damage. Bullet passed through neatly, grazing my deltoid. No nerves, no bones, missed the artery. Very lucky apparently. Those guys tend to use bullets that don't cause too much damage. They want to knock someone down, not have complications that could see them done for murder. At least, that's what the doctor tells me. I think he had a bit of a fetish for gunshot wounds, very creepy. He loved mine."

"That's great news. About the shoulder, I mean."

"I hear the coup was a complete success - apart from me getting shot of course."

"I think so. The Benefit seemed to go well. Mick Dawson and Marisa Foxe were last seen in handcuffs on their way to the police station."

"Sounds like you guys should let Diane fill you in. She was on the phone cobbling together a story for the Sunday paper when she should have been getting a CAT scan."

"No problems with the editor this time?" asked Harlan. "Not covering up for Mick Dawson?"

"Not after his man attacked us," said Diane. "Even Vincent has an ethical bone somewhere in his body. We're running with a short story today, then the full report on Monday from our new investigative reporter," said Diane, smiling proudly at Jenny.

"Wow, congratulations," said Harlan, repeating the gesture.

"Well, wait till you hear the full story," said Jenny. "You might not be so thrilled." Harlan paused, considering whether she was talking about her article or her new job.

"Still," he said, deciding it couldn't change his sentiment, "a new job, that's deserving of congratulations on its own."

"Well, we had no choice really," said Diane. "Jenny's put together the story of the summer. Body on the line, committed investigative journalism. We need more of it."

"Tell them about Marisa Foxe - Harlan, you won't believe this."

"Late last night I tracked down a certain PA for some information about Marisa and Mick Dawson. Apparently they've been having an affair for years. They must have both been using Jonathan, setting him up as a fall guy if they ever needed one."

Harlan smiled. It must have shattered Darren to hear Marisa was involved. So much that he betrayed the woman he so admired when she was at her most vulnerable. He made a note to pay Darren a visit some time, take him out for a coffee. He was a nice guy.

"I just hope it started after their kids were born," said Jenny. "Surely she wasn't setting him up at the same time as having his children."

"What's Jonathan going to do?" asked Harlan.

"The first thing he's doing is giving us an exclusive interview tomorrow," said Diane. "The second thing, assuming he can cut a deal with the authorities in exchange for giving evidence against Mick Dawson, which I think is a fait accompli having spoken to a couple of contacts, is take his kids and tour all the Celebrities Care centres. See what needs doing exactly to make it a viable charity network again, and give us exclusive access to him as he goes."

"And what does he get out of all that?"

"Nothing, apart from some desperately needed publicity as he tries to consolidate his reputation, and the charity's. He just insisted we offer Jenny the role of traipsing around the world for the next six months on his tail."

"Wow, Jenny, six months, great, around the world." Harlan thought he was doing a good job at absorbing the bombshell, but it looked to any observer like he was giving his best impression of a gibbering fool.

"Maybe you should give us a minute," said Jenny to the others.

Diane and Signboy left them alone, Signboy after giving Harlan's arm a token shake to get him to close his mouth, unsuccessfully. Jenny had more success by squeezing his hand as tight as she could, and pulling him down towards her.

"Harlan," she said, pleading. "You know I can't say no to this. Making sure Celebrities Care cleans its act up, filing reports from around the world, getting a salary for doing what I'm passionate about."

Harlan nodded. Against his most fervent wishes, tears had started to well up in his eyes. He wanted desperately for Jenny to ask him to go with her.

"Maybe you can come visit me along the way, it doesn't need to be a full six months without seeing each other."

Maybe. Doesn't need to be. Harlan felt his defences stirring. They were about to make a bid for control. He looked at her face. Studied her green eyes. They were tearing up as well. That was enough to keep his defences at bay, for now.

"That would be great," he said.

"Promise?" she asked, her voice breaking. He saw now she had defences of her own. Maybe? Doesn't need to be? She wasn't pushing him away after all. She was softening the blow if he said no. He answered her with a kiss.

"Now," he said, after forcing himself to break the kiss and stand up straight. "Sal and I better leave you alone, you've got a big day ahead."

"He prefers Signboy, you know," she said, grinning.

Harlan nodded, his point made.

"Call me if you need anything," he said. "Like someone to pick you up, take you home, nurse you back to full health."

"You can count on it."

CHAPTER 32

The clock radio switched on with the alarm, Harlan waking abruptly with the last of the tones indicating it was eight in the morning. It took him a few seconds to realise it was Monday. He looked around his room. The lack of another body in the bed reminded him painfully that Jenny hadn't needed him in the end to pick her up and take her home and nurse her back to full health. She'd been too busy with the article and then the paper wanted her to prepare with Diane for a big day of radio and television interviews. Making the most of their new signing with the big scoop. He heard Mick Dawson's name in the radio news headlines. *More on that shortly.*

He pulled himself out of bed, turning the radio up so he could hear it as he moved through the house to the kitchen to make breakfast. Another week, another start on bran flakes. He saw a cheque on the bench from Jonathan Foxe. Memory triggered. Sometime during Harlan's hazy Sunday he'd come around to thank Harlan for all his help and apologise for the danger he'd been in with Mick Dawson. And the danger he'd thought he'd been in with Matt. And for his girlfriend getting shot. And for getting her sent overseas for six months in her new job. Did five thousand dollars cover five days' work and four apologies? It was about what he'd expected.

'Shortly' had passed, and sure enough the news reader returned to the big scandal of the weekend.

On Saturday night three people were arrested and one held for questioning over a backstage shooting at the Hope Celebrities Care Benefit at Sydney's State Theatre. Celebrity agent and concert promoter Mick Dawson was among those arrested after one of his bodyguards allegedly shot a journalist in the dressing rooms at the annual fundraiser. According to the Sydney Morning Herald the gunman was then shot by another of Dawson's bodyguards after he turned his gun on an innocent bystander.

The journalist, Jennifer Randall of the Herald, suffered only minor injuries. She was apparently working on a story exposing Dawson's blackmail of another Sydney identity, Jonathan Foxe, into misusing and misappropriating for Dawson's benefit the resources of the Celebrities Care Foundation, of which Foxe is the CEO.

The well-known philanthropist's wife, Marisa Foxe, herself well known on Sydney's culinary scene, was also arrested backstage along with the wounded bodyguard. And it's being reported today that she and Dawson have been having an affair over a period of many years, although it's not clear what her role was in either the shootings or the blackmail.

As for Mick Dawson, the self-styled 'Balmoral Brawler' as much as admitted his role in the blackmail of Mr Foxe and the misappropriation of the charity's resources on live television during a prolonged outburst, which was caught by backstage microphones and broadcast into the auditorium.

And later on we'll be replaying an interview with the journalist at the centre of it all, Jennifer Randall, whose story ran on the front page of the Herald today. Hopefully she can help us make sense of what was going on behind the scenes, if you will. Just another night at the theatre, really ...

Harlan laughed. Innocent bystander. Neither of the words fit. On the bright side, it looked like Jenny was going to do pretty well out of all this.

He called Paul and confirmed he was good to make his statement at nine-thirty. His would largely be corroborating Matt's and Paul's statements, but he would also have to address what Mick Dawson's and Marisa's statements said about his being hired by the Foxes. Particularly after Mick Dawson had bragged about orchestrating it on live television. No such thing as bad publicity. It wasn't a saying consistent with the philosophy of an indetective. Hopefully it would just be buried somewhere in the police file.

The thought of Mick Dawson having both Foxes hiring him reminded him of something he had to do. He pulled out his phone and made a quick note. *No commission to Mum for M Foxe business.*

He sat down to his bowl of bran flakes with skim milk and planned the day ahead. Pick up the car from Darlinghurst. Go to police station in Kings Cross, give statement. Collect Signboy, go to office. Hire that office manager. Get back to work. Back to life before the Foxes. Before side-swapping henchmen. Before Mick Dawson. Before Jenny. He dwelled on the last point, and the last bran flake, for a couple of minutes. Pushing the flake under the surface of the skim milk, he confirmed two things. At shallow depths, skim milk shared a lot of physical properties with tap water. And it was a lot harder to sink his thoughts of Jenny to the bottom of his mind than it was to drown a bran flake. Neither conclusion came as a surprise. He decided to call her.

Before he could, Hall & Oates interrupted him. Bells and guitar, not keyboards. It was Signboy calling.

"Sal," said Harlan, injecting his voice with as much enthusiasm as his melancholy would allow.

"Signboy, please."

"Signboy. Of course."

"Put the TV on, quickly. News channel."

Harlan kept the call open while he found his remote and switched on the TV. It was already on the news channel. A standard airport media crush was on the screen.

Jonathan Foxe, two kids in tow. Matt was there as well, wheeling three suitcases at once. Another skill of a good bodyguard, no doubt. *Jonathan Foxe departs to clean up Celebrities Care from the ground up*, read the caption. He didn't stop to speak to the press, but answered a few questions as he walked.

Harlan didn't hear any of the questions or answers, focused as he was on the part of the screen showing Jenny walking in the background with her left arm in a sling and her right wheeling a suitcase.

"Have you spoken to her?" asked Signboy.

"Not since yesterday. I was about to call her."

"Well, go on. I'll see you later. Still picking me up?"

"Yes, yes. See you then." Harlan pressed end, still studying Jenny on screen. She was out of focus, hard to read. From what he could make out she had the exact expression you might expect from someone about to check-in for a long haul flight. It reflected an internal mixture of summoning patience for dealing with the ground staff, summoning strength for the ordeal ahead, and wondering what movies will be on. He looked away just long enough to initiate the phone call. When he looked back Jonathan had stopped to hold a mini press conference. He watched nervously as Jenny walked right to the end of the screen before stopping and looking at her phone. She smiled. It might have been his imagination, but he was sure he could hear *Kiss On My List* drifting through the TV, stopping when Jenny prodded her phone to answer his call.

"Harlan, I was going to call you when I sat down. You wouldn't believe the day I've had."

"I'd believe whatever you told me. Unless you tried to tell me you weren't at the airport about to leave the country of course."

She looked around at the cameras, over Jonathan's shoulder, from about five metres in the background.

"That's what I was going to call you about. Can you see me?"

"I can - you look beautiful, much better than I last saw you. A little more out of focus though." She smiled again, winking at the camera.

"I hate this sling already. Anyway, I'm only going for a couple of weeks now, I just have to get the full Jonathan Foxe interview, file a couple of stories from the ground, and I'm doing some pieces to camera along the way for your favourite news channel. Then Jonathan's got to come back to assist with the Mick Dawson mess."

"Pieces to camera?"

"Yeah, well I did all the channels this morning and I guess they liked what they saw."

"Who can blame them?"

"You're biased." Harlan saw she was grinning. "Anyway, I've got to go check-in, I'll miss you-"

Harlan could see her still talking but couldn't hear anything. After a few seconds she looked at her phone, then pointed to it for Harlan's benefit. No battery, she mouthed. Then she winked again, blew a kiss, and disappeared out of shot. Harlan stood with his fingers to his lips. Grabbing another remote, he fired up his stereo and selected track 5 on the disc he knew was *Voices*. As the keyboards struck up excitedly, Harlan realised how much better the song sounded when he knew whose kiss it was on his list. "Of the best things in liiife," he sang as he danced around the dining table. When the music had faded out he pressed stop and replayed the conversation they'd just had in his head. Jenny would be back in just a couple of weeks. He hoped they weren't anything like the last one.

THE END

The PAPERLESS INDETECTIVE
TRISTAN DURIE

Enjoy *The Paperless Indetective?* Let other readers know by reviewing it online.

To review this book go to your preferred site(s) and search for **The Paperless Indetective**.

amazon.com   www.amazon.com

Google books   play.google.com

kobo   www.kobobooks.com

Download on the iBookstore   or in the iBooks store on your Apple device

Remember, the e-book also makes a great little gift!

Want to read more by Tristan Durie? Check out his blog, short stories or take the Paperless Indetective reality tour by visiting **paperlessindetective.com**

@TrizDurie | @TheIndetective | @TheRealSignboy